EVENTIDE

PETER J ALDIN

For Neen

ACKNOWLEDGEMENTS AND AN
AUTHOR NOTE

So you know, dear reader, you will find a GUIDE TO HUMAN-SETTLED SPACE immediately after the story to help keep track of 22nd Century references.

The original version of Eventide was 'completed' in 2008! It took another 12 years to polish, polish, polish …

And it's so long since that initial version, I'm hopeful I won't forget everyone who enabled me to finish it.

Police-persons Jeff and Rose lent accuracy to my portrayal of life as a cop. "Doctor Kate" assisted with many of the medical details. Aussie writer Cat Sparks gave passing advice that helped shave 35000 words(!) from the first version without sacrificing story. My son Jack insisted upon the "dropping kids at the pool" reference (he was 12 at the time, but even now I know he'd still insist upon it). My son Xander let me use his computer to format the final copy. Writing coach Sarah Lovett helped me polish and take this project seriously. Jonathan Pippenger lent a critical eye to the initial draft (back when we were Dad Bloggers together!).

And Janine helped iron out lumps and bumps from the final draft. I owe Janine more thanks than just *that*: as my life partner she has not only always encouraged me to write, but puts up with my writerly tantrums and an author husband who spends a lot of time and money on his writing biz. This book, hopefully, is proof that it was all worth it, hon.

Kudos to Alexandre Rito for the magnificent cover art.

PART I

FOURDAY

'Even after all these years there comes the dream
Of lovelier life than this in some new earth...'
- John Masefield, *Sonnets*

1

____

'Mankind should not remain enamored with its inventions;
Humans existed before technology
and they will exist long after it is gone.'

- Article 50: *The Articles of Life*
published by The Society of Andros, 2101

HEAVY BLAST DOORS parted with a hiss, admitting John Romaine to the transport ship's docking lounge. The steel and plastic room was fifteen meters long and empty except for the row of plastic chairs lining one wall. And the medical robot in the middle of the room.

Romaine hesitated in the white-lit passageway, shifting his kitbag from hand to hand. Beyond a docking lounge viewport, the black of space was broken only by the faint twinkle of stars. No planet in view. Forty-four hours of travel and the ship had - in its own words - "reached orbit".

But orbit around where?

Forty-*five* hours ago, Romaine had been halfway through a drinking marathon on Drop-in-the-Ocean station.

What the hell is forty-four hours from Drop-in-the-Ocean? he wondered for the twentieth time.

They couldn't have sent him to the orbital colonies around Theseus, could they? His stomach dropped at the thought.

No way. Not even Dreyfuss is that cruel.

Besides, from Drop-in-the-Ocean, Theseus would have been thirty-eight hours away at most.

'Okay. So not Theseus then.' He stepped inside the lounge.

As the blast doors sealed, the medical bot accelerated toward him, speaking in the same oily baritone that the ship had used during the journey. 'Commander Romaine. Medical examination, sir.'

'Yep,' he replied, dropping his bag and standing stock-still as it lined up in front of him. In a blur of movement, six retractable arms shot out and went to work on the human body in front of it.

Romaine frowned: an impromptu exam like this was unusual, weird. The last time he'd experienced one was in '33 when they'd been concerned about Dog Flu getting offworld from Pollux. *The last of the Superflus.* Perhaps he was about to be taken onto an orbital cleanroom or a hospital ship, orbiting some starless godforsaken rock in the middle of the void. He counted twelve seconds. In that time, the machine took blood and breath samples, retinal scans and skin scrapings. It measured heart rate and blood pressure and body temperature. To conclude, a final wormlike appendage slid out of his ear and snapped back into its socket in the robot's own 'head'.

'Commander, there is no need for quarantine. You are in good health.'

'Yep.'

Quarantine? Maybe there was something to that rumor about a new virus. He hoped to hell it *was* just a rumor. His breakfast of smuggled-aboard malt burned in his gut and tried to make its way back up his esophagus.

As if responding to the reflux, the robot said, 'There are traces of alcohol in your system, along with signs of pronounced stress.'

He blinked at it. 'And your point is?'

Without further comment, the robot scooped up his kitbag and wheeled off toward the ferry doors at the far end of the lounge. 'Follow me, sir.'

'Yep.'

———

THE FERRY CABIN WAS HALF THE LENGTH OF THE LOUNGE, WITH SEATING for thirty people. Romaine had it to himself. Made sense. No one on the transport ship; no one on the ferry.

This was how they rewarded him for stopping a serial killer: shoving him aboard a ship headed who-knew-where, with no one to talk to and no way of getting a head start on whatever-the-hell case he was assigned to. Forty-five hours ago, all he'd wanted was a week-long bender. He could have requested mnemonic therapy, but booze was more fun and he was old-fashioned that way.

Where the hell have they taken me?

He took a seat near the front with a good view of the forward windows. Like most ferries, there was no pilot to obscure the view. Not that Romaine expected to see more than the outside of a cookie-cutter-standard space station anyway. And so far, there was *nothing* to see out there but bright dots on a black velvet background.

The robot deposited his luggage in overhead storage and departed without another word. Seconds after the door sealed, the ferry began moving.

A hand-sized holo appeared in midair before him, projected from a reversed pedestal in the ceiling, the same smarmy steward he'd been seeing for the past two days. He ignored the projection, pulling his SCRoLL from his shirt pocket and watching the transport ship's hull slide past the window.

You will wait for me, darlin', won't you? This hopefully won't take long.

'Commander Romaine,' the holo said. 'Welcome to Eventide. If you have any questions, I can provide answers on a broad range of topics. I'll be your host for the journey planetside.'

'*Planetside?*' He sat straighter in his chair, alarmed. What the hell was going on here?

The Office always honored the unwritten agreement he had with them. No planets. No colonies. Definitely no Earth. They'd always given those cases to other Investigators. With colonization only a generation old, Romaine had stayed in space his entire career. It was safer, more predictable, more manageable, cleaner, wealthier. Standardized temperature patterns and gravity. All the perks. Asteroids were the most annoying part of Romaine's job with their varying gravity and their cold patches where insulation struggled to keep the void's freezing cold from seeping in.

But a planet...

He forced himself to take a slow deep breath. Perhaps there was an enclosed artificial settlement or research station down there. That would be tolerable as long as the gravity was close to standard.

Even so, this was not funky. Not funky, at all. It was statistically safer to live in space than on a planet and a helluva lot more comfortable. Besides, a cop's job was easier in artificial environments. Most of his past twenty years he'd spent solving fraud cases, catching water thieves, and – as practical jokes were illegal in CUSET space – sorting out who'd punked who. Things were spiced up a couple of times a year by drunken asteroid miners offing some poor bastard in a brawl. More challenging cases appeared occasionally: murders perpetrated by miffed lovers aboard gas harvesters skimming gas giants; researchers stealing tech for the Chinese; Naval personnel going ape after suffering from space-psychoses. Once in a while some moron jazzed up on Bliss or Harpydust took a laser to a lift full of innocent people before someone subdued them. Sure, there were crime syndicates and drug traffickers and pedophiles. But it was pretty hard to dispose of a body or other evidence without a camera or sensor picking it up, so professional crims were less prevalent and better behaved than their colonized world counterparts.

Yeah, space-life had planet-life beat, hands down.

'Yes, I said planetside –' the AI started.

'So this is an artificial environment I'm going to?'

'No. Eventide is perfectly habitable for humans.'

Damn it!

The AI continued without waiting for a further response. 'Commander, your purposes would best be suited if you confined your inquiries to matters pertaining to the planet and your current mission directives.'

Jeez, make your sentences longer, why don't ya. 'I *was* asking you about the planet.'

'Yes of course, but I'm to prep you for your mission post-haste. It would be better if we–'

'You're gonna brief me on my mission post-haste?'

'Yessir, I –'

'More like waiting until the last minute.'

'Yessir. This planet is still highly classified –'

'Why is that? *Eventide.* I never even heard of it. Sounds like a resort.'

'No sir. Not a resort, but a resource.' The AI affected a brief look of satisfaction at its wordplay.

You rehearsed that, didn't you, ya coded little bastard?

'Eventide is an Earth-type planet,' the steward continued, 'sixty-seven percent of which is covered by water. The planet would have much to offer as a new colony. Eventide is rich in mineral resources, precious and heavy metals, as well as fossil fuels. This makes it an excellent site for colonization for – as you know – should a future event or events sever the ties between colonized worlds, the existence of such resources during the subsequent isolation period would enable the population to return to an industrial society for centuries if necessary.'

'That certainly explains why it should be classified.'

'No, it doesn't,' the holo continued, not registering the sarcasm, 'but the reasons for secrecy are themselves on a need to know basis.'

'Whatever. Is there anything to eat around here?' he asked, hoping food would settle his gut, balance out the whisky he'd chugged earlier.

'It's a short trip, sir. We do have an extensive list of beverages aboard. Chai, coffee. Juices include guava, jitta-jitti and orange.'

Romaine's mouth puckered. The orange juice aboard the transport had been more brown than orange. And sour as hell.

'Coffee. Coffee will be fine. White, three sugars.'

A panel opened on his armrest.

'Straws are in the pocket on the seatback ahead of you,' the holo said helpfully.

Romaine reached through his electronic guide's chest and removed a sachet from the pocket, tearing it open to reveal a long straw. He waited until his armrest chimed, then stabbed the straw into the aperture there and took a long gulp of lukewarm coffee. It was creamy though, not bitter, exactly what the doctor ordered.

'Returning to the mission directive,' the holo started.

'Someone was murdered. I was told that much.'

'A Marine private named Emmanuel Gutierrez. You may want to take notes.'

Romaine waved his old model SCRoLL in the air. 'I'm recording.'

'Very well. Gutierrez was on sentry duty three nights ago when he was killed. A Private Lim discovered the body at 2319 local time, shortly after Gutierrez spoke with the Watch Commander via commlink.'

'Cause of death?'

'Tearing of the left jugular artery and subsequent damage to the trachea.'

'Murder weapon been found?'

'It was embedded in the dead man's neck.'

'And it was?'

'A wooden arrow, forty-seven centimeters long and tipped...'

The holo paused because Romaine had choked on his coffee and was now coughing and trying to say, '*An arrow*?!'

'Yessir. An arrow is a long piece of wood tipped with bone or steel which is launched–'

'I know what an arrow is. I just didn't know the Marines were using them.' He coughed again, hard. Who the hell used arrows? Was Admiral Dreyfuss playing some sort of expensive prank on him?

Pranks are illegal in CUSET space.

Just then the tip of the planet peeked above the forward windows like a silver-blue sunrise and reality gave his gut another twist. He was going there. He was going down there.

'Oh, it's not a Marine weapon, sir. The arrow was undoubtedly of Jarinyi manufacture.'

'Jaree – what? Who?' The corporation's name was unfamiliar to him.

'Jarinyi are the indigenous people of this planet.'

Romaine was silent for some seconds, blinking rapidly while the holo awaited his response. 'You're talking about aliens,' he said, feeling foolish as he said it.

The holo affected mild reproach. 'That is the culturally incorrect term, sir, but you are essentially correct. Intelligent, organized but pre-industrial.'

'We've discovered another sentient species?'

The little hologram of a man nodded sagely and folded his arms. 'In terms of having a society and some degree of technology, that is correct. However, the Jarinyi are far easier to communicate with than are the Anachromites. They are also bipedal and humanoid, unlike the Anachromites.'

Romaine sucked in another deep breath as if that would help him absorb this information more easily. 'You're saying that Gutierrez was killed by one of these Jar – Jara...'

'Jarinyi. I am not saying that at all, sir. I am conveying facts not conjecture.'

'Facts, my bony backside.' Though on one level, this was the most intriguing thing he'd ever heard, Romaine found himself feeling even more irritated than he had before. 'Why the hell drag a Military Investigator all the way out here to investigate a murder when the simple explanation is that one of the locals doesn't like this incursion into his homeland? It's a typical frontier situation historically. Hell, why don't the Marines just get out of there for a while until things cool down? Let the xenologists and diplomats smooth things over.'

Throughout all of this, the holo stared blankly, as if Romaine were speaking a language it didn't know.

'And why,' he continued after another sip of coffee, 'are we persisting with a military presence if the world is already occupied? That's not good PR. The pedecasters will lap this up when they get hold of it. Guess that's why it's still a secret, huh? How long have we been on this planet anyway?'

'We?' The holo responded to what he perceived as a direct question. 'You mean human personnel?'

'Who else?' *AI*, he thought. *Artificial idiot*.

'The discovery was made six months ago. The initial survey expedition arrived four months ago and the current administration under the command of Colonel Bob Glass is eleven days old.'

Romaine pulled the straw and dropped it into the waste chute. The drinks aperture self-sealed, armrest humming beneath his elbow as the interior was flushed and sterilized.

He could see the planet better now, as the ferry changed orientation, a jewel set in black. The emerald green of forests, the rich blue of oceans, a splash of dun for a desert on the western horizon. The small northern icecap took shape, reflecting sunlight like a beacon. No pollution stained the air or the waters. No satellites littered high orbit. No moon danced about its mass, not one that he could see anyway. Next to Earth, it may well have been the most beautiful planet yet discovered – and certainly a reminder of Earth's better days. Moving closer, mountain ranges and grasslands took shape on its surface. A belt of white cumulus straddled the coast of a great pangaean continent like frosting on pastry.

It was pretty. But that didn't make it any more enticing. Romaine shifted uncomfortably in his seat and turned away from the view. It had been a long time since he had walked in the open air.

He tried to focus on the case again.

'A week into the "current administration", young Gutierrez gets an arrow through the throat. What's so special about this planet that it has a military administration instead of a civilian or diplomatic one? And why haven't I heard of it before?'

The holo looked stricken. 'Twelve minutes until planetfall, sir.' It vanished.

'I'll be purged.' Romaine rolled up his notebook. 'A crazy AI.'

T~HE~ ~FERRY~ ~SLOWED~ ~NOTICEABLY~. R~OMAINE~ ~SHIFTED~ ~SEATS~ ~FOR~ ~A~ ~BETTER~ view through the side window. Beyond the low-lying clouds, he could see onto a vast grassy veldt. Small pockets of grey and brown trees and the odd river broke up the green. He passed a herd of animals twice the size of an elephant and sporting a three-fingered trunk. With these appendages the behemoths wrenched huge tufts of grass from the plain and threw them into their gaping mouths. He barely had time to say 'What is that?' before they were past.

The plains gave way to foothills and these became a low mountain range. The holo appeared long enough to say 'Two minutes to landing', but vanished before Romaine could quiz it further.

The ferry passed over dense forest on the other side of the mountains, continuing to decelerate as it did. Trees stretched as far as he could see in all directions. A broad river valley appeared, scarred by a ragged and circular clearing, the sure sign that human beings were present. Even from the air, the clearing seemed the proverbial hive of activity.

The ferry finally slowed to a stop before descending vertically onto a landing pad.

John Romaine was on Eventide.

2

'CUSET is technically the name of a legal document, the *Corporate Union Space Exploration Treaty*. It has also become the default name for the space-based civilization spawned by the various corporations comprising the Corporate Union (see Corporate Union), as well as for its Earth-based manufacturing and head offices and the many non-terrestrial colonies it has planted.

Within those colonies (planted under the CUSET agreement) there exist parties who are increasingly opposed to both this nominal association and to their continued direct governance by the Corporate Union...'

- from *Werber's Encyclopedia of Human Endeavor, January* 2141

CORPORAL FISHER ADJUSTED her web belt and inhaled deeply as she waited. It didn't smell like rain today, which was just as well. The humidity was bad enough as it was. Sweat pooled in all the places where her uniform pressed against her skin – her armpits, between belt and belly, her shoes.

The blackcaps had specially produced boots, perforated for aeration.

Me? she thought grimly. *I gotta wear the standard type. I guess that's what I get for joining the MPs, instead of the recons.*

She tracked the whine of the approaching ferry engines from where she could see Mount Methuselah's summit above the tree tops to the north-east. The noise resolved itself as a small blocky craft and she turned to face it as it came in low over the rain forest.

Behind her Private Lim sniffed wetly. Another cold. CO wouldn't like that. She thought about offering Lim a handkerchief but knew he'd be offended. *The Twenty-second Century and these guys still live by this macho garbage.*

The ferry was closer now, well into its landing cycle, extending legs, firing retro jets in short bursts. Fisher rearranged her web belt one more time, hoping more sweat would dry before she met the newcomer.

Almost as soon as the ferry ramp touched dirt, the lone passenger was striding down it, walking with a strange rhythm, obviously not used to the gravity. He wore the sky blue of Military Investigation in contrast to the camouflage or basic khaki sported by all planetside military. She felt sorry for him; the uniform would make him stick out like a boil. As she moved forward to meet him, he paused at the bottom of the ramp, staring pensively at the sky.

She snapped off a salute and adopted an *at-ease* stance. 'Corporal Fisher, sir. Welcome to Eventide. I'll be your assistant while you're here.'

The officer returned the salute lazily and his face softened into a tired smile. 'Romaine.' His gaze returned to the sky for a moment, then ranged about the nearby buildings and the forest beyond the fence. Despite his evident unease, there was a leonine set to his eyes, that casual attentiveness common to police. She wondered momentarily whether her eyes looked like that when she was at work.

Since he had not ventured his rank, Fisher had to check his collar for insignia. *Commander.* He had started off as Space Navy then, not a

Marine. She caught snuffling Private Lim's eye and jerked her head toward the ferry. He jogged inside.

'Private will get your things and place them in your quarters, sir.' She indicated politely for him to follow and set off at a brisk pace across the camp.

WITH SO MUCH TO TAKE IN, ROMAINE'S HEAD SWIVELED CONTINUALLY, even when Fisher led him through the narrow alleys between accommodation huts. He sucked in air through his mouth, lungs striving against the humidity. The thick air and a tickle in his throat both scratched at his composure. All around was patchy mud, sharp edges and the migraine-inducing hues of an alien star. His nose began to itch, something he hadn't felt in a long long time. Pollen or dust or some other unknown biotic in the air.

Alien allergies. Fantastic.

Fisher led him out from between buildings and into a broad staging area. Twenty civilians fussed over unidentifiable detritus littering a rectangle of folding tables. Romaine stopped for a moment to watch others running computer models on a *PortaPed* until Fisher coughed politely to move him along. The image had looked like cellular growth.

'Busy place you have here,' he ventured.

'Yessir.'

'Where are we going, Corporal?'

'CO wants to see you asap, sir. He's right nearby.'

Romaine stopped again, arched his back. He was at least four days away from sleeping in his own bed, but the quicker he got started here ...

'Tell you what, Corporal. Let's go take a look at the crime scene first. I can press the flesh after that.'

Fisher's eyes widened a little but she covered it quickly.

Don't want to cross the boss, Fisher? This is a CO who likes to rule, huh?

'Sir, Colonel Glass wanted to meet you immediately upon your arrival.' She planted her feet and lifted her chin, patiently waiting for him to make the correct decision.

Romaine blinked first. Back near the *PortaPed*, two middle-aged civs studied bacteria on a flat-panel microscope's screen. The table was pressed between two domed huts with protruding airlocks and air-filtration units. Both huts sported biohazard symbols.

His nose itched again. 'Anything I should be worried about, Corporal?'

She followed the direction of his stare. 'No sir. CO runs a very clean planet. You showered and were exammed before flying down here?'

'Yes, both.'

'Very good, sir.'

Fisher waved a hand at a small table out in the open about thirty meters away. 'Colonel's right there. I'm sure it won't take long, sir.'

Romaine nodded for her to lead on.

Closer up, the small table resolved itself into a large pedestal displaying a geographic holo, a survey map. A Marine Colonel and Lieutenant studied it with their lips pursed. The latter man had tightly shaved red hair and a black beret tucked into his right epaulette. Romaine raised an eyebrow at the sight of the headwear.

'Blackcaps?' he murmured to Fisher.

'Yessir. We have one squad of recons here.'

Interesting. While hardly surprising in a frontier setting, their presence would certainly spice things up a bit.

While a group of civilians in nondescript work clothes stood nearby in bored conversation, one of them – presumably a team leader – consulted the Colonel about the map. The Lieutenant noticed Romaine approaching and whispered in the Colonel's ear.

The Colonel didn't glance around, but told the civilian team leader in a gravelly voice, 'Tomorrow it is. I'll leave the details to you and Todd here.'

The Lieutenant – who looked young enough to be the colonel's son – saluted smartly and steered the civs away from the newcomer.

Romaine turned his attention to the CO. The man wore a name plate above his breast pocket: *Bob Glass*. The exposed and deeply tanned skin of his head and neck and forearms was dappled with so many white spots, Romaine thought it might be sun-damaged. Glass fixed Romaine with an alpha-male smile.

'Our Military Investigation unit is all here. John Romaine, I believe.'

'Pleased to meet you, Colonel Glass.'

Romaine offered his hand. The Colonel made no move to shake it, but turned toward the survey map. Romaine dropped his arm to his side and cocked an eyebrow at Fisher, which she diplomatically ignored.

Glass sniffed. 'Forgive my apparent lack of manners, Commander. You've obviously not been to the Red Star settlements in the past month.'

Red Star? The virus? 'No, not much of a traveler. Especially not to Chinese colonies.'

'Mm. If you had, you would have seen the effects of the PBT virus firsthand. Then you too would find it difficult to casually touch another human being.' He turned back, his eyes cold and hard. 'Thirteen thousand colonists dead at Fu Xing.'

Romaine gasped involuntarily. 'I heard some rumors but I thought they were...How many survivors?'

'None.'

Fisher's stunned expression mirrored Romaine's. This was news to her too then.

'*None*?' Romaine asked.

'Zip. We spent two days trying to cure the few we found alive, but they all died.' Glass made a sign in the air and the pedestal shut down. 'For hundreds of years, we've been waiting for the plague to end all plagues. We had some false starts, some near misses. Unless we can do something about it fast, this one could be it.'

Romaine felt a moment of disorientation, of disbelief. If there hadn't been a single survivor at Fu Xing, then this 'PBT' could indeed be the Big One.

The Colonel stirred himself, all business again. 'Anyway, I'm sure Corporal Fisher already quizzed you on your personal hygiene. She's nothing if not thorough. Hell, the damn 'bot up there would have killed you before letting you down here carrying disease.' He gave a short bark of a laugh. Romaine couldn't see the humor. 'Fisher will give you all the assistance you need to wrap this matter up neatly and quickly. So, go find my boy's killer.'

Romaine knew a dismissal when he heard one. He raised a finger to signal that the conversation wasn't over, but the CO was already moving away. Determined not to be dismissed, Romaine fired off another question before Glass was out of earshot. 'Colonel! Any idea where we should start?'

'The Jarinyi, Commander. Where else?' Glass touched a finger to his eyebrow and vanished into a scrum of Marines around the jeep pool.

Romaine wanted to call after him again, ask him more about this virus. Glass had to be exaggerating – he hoped. If there was any truth in what he'd said, Romaine would find out once he got back to the office. And he would get back there faster if he got on with his job.

'Fisher. Do you speak Jarinyi?'

'We have a person liaising with us on that. He'll meet us there.'

'Good, because I was wondering how the hell I was gonna question them.' A small buzzing insect – *insect-analog*, Romaine reminded himself – zipped past his ear. He ducked, swatting at empty air.

Yep. Planets suck.

'And when are our alien suspects arriving?' he asked her.

'Sir?'

He gave her a little frown. It wasn't a difficult question.

'Oh,' she said. 'They're not coming here. We're going to them.'

'You're kidding me. Isn't that a little ...' He nodded at the signs on the dome huts. '... hazardous?'

Fisher inclined her head. 'Colonel Glass anticipated you would have that concern. He told me to tell you that you'll be perfectly safe with our liaison. He's someone who's been accepted by the tribe.'

'As far as he knows.'

'You'll also have myself and another Marine as escort. And the Colonel offered the use of his personal body armor if you'd like.'

Romaine slid a hand over his brow. It came away sweaty. In these conditions, wearing someone else's armor didn't sound attractive. 'So he suspects the Jarinyi of murdering a human, but thinks it's safe to send four of us into their village?'

Fisher shrugged, meeting his stare. Well, she certainly didn't seem nervous about it.

'Have you met the Jarinyi?' he asked her.

Her face softened a little. 'Sort of. I visited their camp with Lieutenant Todd and some others to offer gifts to them. I stayed by the jeep but they ... seemed nice, sir.'

'Nice?'

She shrugged again. In her eyes was the kind of light Romaine usually saw in people who'd had a very romantic evening or a beatific experience. The woman had seen aliens, real live aliens with culture and language and ...

Weapons.

She said, 'There were only a few of them and our liaison was translating. But they seemed friendly. Calm. Interested in us.'

Romaine sucked in a lungful of hot wet air. 'If you say so. Your neck's gonna be in their crosshairs as much as mine, you know.'

She seemed to take the word *neck* as a reference to Gutierrez. 'Yessir, but Gutierrez's death doesn't seem like a coordinated attack by an entire tribe. More like the work of a rogue element, someone acting alone. In any case, I'll be watchful, sir, and you can remain in the jeep if you like until you're sure it's safe. Would you like to collect the CO's armor now, sir?'

'No, no,' he said tiredly. 'Got a thing against wearing other people's clothing. I'm funny that way.' He swiped his forehead again. 'But I'll put off visiting them until I've run through all my interviews here at the Camp. It'll be at least a day.'

If I'm lucky, that might even eliminate the need to put myself in danger.

'Sorry, sir, the CO said you were to visit them immediately. And told me to tell you that, *quote*, a Jarinyi did it so you may as well start with them, *end quote*.'

Fisher's voice was so monotonic that Romaine wasn't sure if the *quote-unquote* thing was irony. Probably not: she seemed a fairly humorless individual.

He arched his back again, fighting to control his temper. 'I don't work for Glass.'

'I know that sir, but he is the CO here. He also said to tell you that doing things his way would get you out of here sooner.'

Romaine considered the mud on his shoes and the dive-bombing insect-analog still making noise somewhere nearby.

'Well,' he muttered. 'He makes a good case there. And who knows. Visiting aliens might be *fun*.'

A moment ago, Fisher had certainly thought so, if she even understood the concept of fun. He smiled at her and she just nodded back.

Yep. Humorless.

Hacking Marines.

'First things first,' he sighed, pulling back his sleeve to reveal his seiko. 'What's the local time?'

'1156, sir.'

'And how many hours in a daily cycle?'

'Twenty-five point one two four. We call it twenty-five, sir. We run an eight-day week – Oneday, Twoday, you catch the drift. Today's Fourday. On the eighth day, we add an extra hour in the evening to balance things out.'

'Always wanted more hours in the day.' He finished adjusting his seiko just as his stomach rumbled loudly. He felt himself blush.

'Would you like to see the crime scene before we head out, sir?'

He patted his belly. 'I should. I will. But it'll be no more churned up in twenty minutes than it is now and I'm so hungry I could eat my own leg.'

'Mess is open in thirty, sir. But I'm sure I could convince them to serve you early'.

'They serve orange juice?'

'Yes, sir. Would you like some?'

'No, Fisher. No orange juice.'

THE MESS WAS THE LARGEST BUILDING IN THE COMPOUND AFTER THE Medcentre, Fisher told him. The best thing about it, Romaine thought as he approached, was the air-conditioning unit protruding from the sidewall. Accustomed to artificial environments for the past twenty years, he had all but forgotten that they were artificial. Twenty-two degrees Celsius with low humidity was the daytime norm for nearly every place he had set foot in his career. At Camp Columbus, it was at least thirty degrees Celsius and he estimated ninety percent humidity – although he didn't know what he based that figure on. He was about to ask Fisher – she seemed like she'd have those facts at her fingertips – when they were stopped by a shout.

A disheveled man in his late forties or early fifties was jogging toward them. Romaine glanced ruefully at the Mess doors only a few paces away.

I hope he's heading the same way we are.

His stomach rumbled again as if to underline the point. It was weird, he reflected. He hadn't been hungry for several days, not after what had happened at Drop-in-the-Ocean. Right now, right in the opening moments of a new case, he was suddenly ravenous. Maybe his renewed hunger was his subconscious attempt at procrastination. Maybe it was being back on the job, a *new* job, and his body wanted to fuel up. In a perverse kind of way, another mission might be good for him, get him back on the horse and all that.

And maybe this is all a dream and I'll wake up home on Bona Vista, by the pool, with a scotch in hand.

'This is our liaison with the Jarinyi,' Fisher said, snapping him out of his reverie. She looked bemused and he wondered why, until he remembered that the liaison was meant to meet them at the Jarinyi camp.

The man slowed to a fast walk, breathing heavily but showing no signs of tiring. From the waft of body odor that assailed Romaine's nose, the man had either jogged some distance or handled the humidity worse that he did himself. On closer inspection, he decided it was the former. The man was dressed in hardy outdoor gear and his frame was athletic, his bare forearms hinting at muscular limbs. For his age, he possessed an evident fitness that gave Romaine a passing stab of envy. His hair was shoulder length and curly, fused together into thick locks by sweat or dirt or both, with a touch of blonde still visible amongst the grey. A heavy beard framed his sun-toasted face.

He stopped before them, hands on hips, chin jutting, eyes smoldering with indignation. When he spoke, it was rapid and confident – no pausing to find the right word. His accent was mild Northern English, but bore the mark of higher learning.

'You're Fisher, aren't you? The MP. The one who's supposed to "bring the Investigator to the Jarinyi". Fisher, I'm going to rip your stinking Colonel's head off if you don't shoot me first! Who does he think he is, ordering me to play tour guide to some glorified Sherlock Holmes?'

Fisher remained calm through this tirade with the ease of someone who regularly faced the drunk and the abusive. The moment the man paused for breath, she interjected. 'Doctor Carswell, this is the Military Investigator, Commander Romaine.'

The man's next words froze on his lips. He appeared mildly chagrined, caught insulting someone behind their back only to find they were right behind his.

He recovered no more than a second later to turn his spleen-venting upon Romaine himself. 'Right. I guess you're the man I'm supposed to kowtow to, hmm? Well, get this, pal: I hold a Professorship at six universities. Six. I hold degrees in Xenobiology, Sociology, Archeology – *doctorates* in Linguistics and Anthropology. I'm not military personnel, my CUSET contract is up at the end of the year and I'll be freelancing after that, trust me. I have no interest in holding your hand, being your interpreter, or mediating between you and the Jarinyi. I have important work to do and it's already being interrupted. I only came back here to tell you to hack off and leave these peaceful people alone.'

Romaine flinched as the college professor's breath drifted his way. He tried to interrupt but the man was off and racing again ...

"Who do you think you are coming to the Jarinyi planet with a view to accusing them of a crime by your laws, standards and customs? And how the bloody hell do you think you're going to prove it one way or the other, especially with Glass and his cronies pressuring you to point the finger of blame quickly? Don't think I don't know how their type works in these situations.'

When Carswell paused again, the Investigator gave him a thin smile and said loudly, 'I'm no anthropologist, but the custom where I'm from is to introduce yourself with a handshake then exchange pleasantries. Only after that can you feel free to launch into a torrent of abuse.' Romaine stepped to the Mess door and opened it, took a step inside, looked back. 'I'm about to have lunch, Doctor. Would you care to join me?'

ROMAINE TOOK A TABLE CLOSE TO THE DOOR, UNFURLED HIS SCRoLL and tapped at it with the stylus. Carswell slumped across from him, folded his hands and studied the table, lips moving silently. His wet dog smell hung in the air, an invisible noxious cloud. Fisher stood by the table and, if Carswell's reek was bothering her, she was doing an admirable job in hiding it. Romaine was ready to ask for a gasmask.

'May I get you anything, sirs?' she asked.

Rank continues to have its privileges, Romaine thought. 'Coffee, white, three sugars. And the biggest meal they have. Thanks.'

Carswell simply said, 'Orange juice.' When she left, he leaned over the table and spoke quietly and placatingly. 'Look, I'm sorry. Romaine is it? I apologize. I don't even know you and ... that was a little rude ... well, a lot actually. Out of line.' He tried to smile, revealing teeth that hadn't been brushed for days. Not a man out to impress the ladies.

Romaine waved the apology away. Like Fisher, he was used to people venting their emotions on him. And if the man was to be of any use, it was good policy to play Good Cop with him. 'Forget it, Doctor.'

Instead of relaxing as Romaine had hoped, Carswell became intense again. 'You have to understand. I've been four months in the forest with the Jarinyi. It's taken me most of that time just to crack their language. I'm only now just starting to really understand them. It's a crucial time – race relations depend on my establishing a significant level of dialogue between our cultures. Not to mention they could do with a friend on our side of the fence, if you know what I mean.' He lifted his eyebrows in a meaningful way.

'No, I don't know what you mean.' Romaine wanted Carswell to know from the start that he was not here to take sides.

The xenologist sniffed and looked away. 'They're not exactly being consulted on all the activity here. We're setting up shop, prospecting and not even asking them if they mind.'

'Presumably they're being compensated for any inconvenience.'

Carswell snorted. 'A lot you know! Just like the indigenous Americans – throw 'em a few trinkets, a few glittering little toys and they're expected to part with whichever piece of real estate the conquering heroes decide to exploit.'

Fisher placed their drinks on the table, gave no indication she'd heard any of it and turned back for Romaine's food.

'Thank you,' Romaine said.

'Yes, thanks,' Carswell blurted.

Romaine noticed that Carswell's juice was tinged with brown, getting old like the juice on the starship.

Same catering company.

Carswell gulped it down thirstily then sucked his mouth into a sphincter of disdain. 'Bloody Helen! Doesn't anyone know what real oranges taste like anymore? What the hack is that made from anyway? Shouldn't it be the color of its name?'

Though he agreed wholeheartedly, Romaine didn't touch this remark. He asked, 'What kinds of trinkets?'

'Mirrors, heaters, hammers, nails, a camera.'

'Things that might improve their quality of living.'

'They're *nomadic*, for crying out loud! What in the universe do they need with a collection of paraphernalia they can't carry when they break camp? They need land, not merchandise.'

Fisher returned with a large bowl for Romaine and one for herself. She placed his in front of him with cutlery then sat at an adjacent table. Romaine opened the sealed sachet, tipped the fork into his hand and shoveled food. The meal was some sort of pasta with fish and was surprisingly good.

Carswell was watching him. Was he waiting for a verdict?

Romaine swallowed his mouthful and said as mildly as he could, 'Doctor Carswell, I'm not here to enter into sociological debates or to discuss history ... or even to judge the morality of CUSET's colonial expansion. I don't know the purpose of all this activity here. While I appreciate the background you're giving me, I'm simply here to investigate a crime.'

Turning to a window, Carswell muttered, 'Sherlock.'

Romaine tried to exchange a glance with Fisher but the MP was discreetly watching the steam rise from her food as she ate. Playing Good Cop with Carswell was going to take way more patience and energy than he'd thought.

He stuffed pasta into his mouth and spoke around it. 'Approximately two days ago, a Private Gutierrez was shot through the throat with an arrow. It killed him. I'm sure you would agree this sounds like murder not suicide. Thus, I am here to find a murderer. Now, the arrow being an alien weapon—'

'Aha! You betray your preconceptions. Some unbiased investigator you are.' He gave a pompous smirk. 'A human may have used the arrow. And – Commander – the arrow is an *indigenous* weapon not *alien*. We're the aliens here.'

'The arrow being an indigenous weapon, rather than a Marine's weapon,' Romaine continued smoothly, 'the Colonel thinks the logical place to start looking for our murderer is among the indigenous population. Frankly, it's logical and it's an angle we must cover.'

And then what, Johnny? Collar an alien? What the hell do we do even if we can catch him-her-it?

Carswell stood and began pacing in a tight line between their tables. 'It's ludicrous! First, the Jarinyi don't act this way. It's just not their *modus operandi*. They're not ninjas and they don't assassinate people.'

Fisher swallowed her food and cleared her throat. 'You're saying they're non-violent? Why do they carry bows, spears, slingshots?'

'To hunt with,' he said slowly as if she were new to the language.

Romaine knew right then that Carswell would make a terrible lecturer and his Professorships were probably honorary. To her credit, Fisher didn't give him the satisfaction of blushing or looking away.

'And yes, they do fight.' The honorary Professor had resumed his pacing. 'Usually with the people from over the mountain, the Nguwuu – but that is warfare, not clandestine operations.'

Nguwuu? What kind of name is that? Romaine forked more pasta into his mouth. 'And secondly?'

'Secondly, when a Jarinyi kills another Jarinyi or a Nguwuu, they aim for the torso. I've discovered that much. Shooting someone with an arrow through the neck is only used for capital punishment.'

'For which crimes?'

'Only one. Murder.'

Romaine narrowed his eyes at that. *Oh, that is interesting.*

Fisher had pushed her meal aside. 'Maybe the Jarinyi aimed at the chest and missed. Shot too high.'

'You see? You've already made up your mind like the rest of your Marine buddies. It would never enter your head that maybe one of *you* appropriated a Jarinyi bow and settled some petty argument with Gutierrez in a way that would ensure that the "Natives" take the heat.'

'Strangely enough,' said Romaine around another mouthful of food, 'that had occurred to me.' He swallowed. 'But if that's the case, where did they get this bow and arrow?'

'Stole it! Or,' he added less forcefully, 'found discarded artefacts in the forest.'

'Assuming that's true, how did she or he use it with such accuracy?'

Carswell leaned a hip against a table and stared unhappily at the floor while Romaine ate.

'Why did you come back here, Dr Carswell?' Fisher asked. 'We were coming to you. It's a long way back here on foot.'

Carswell made a noise. 'Got sick of waiting for this *gentleman* to arrive. Started out before dawn this morning.'

'You made good time,' she said brightly.

Carswell just made the noise again in response.

Romaine put a last forkful of food into his mouth and stood, wiping his face on a sterile napkin, groaned in satisfaction. 'That filled the spot. Corporal Fisher, my compliments to the Chef. Now we should get to work.'

'Oh, great,' grumbled Carswell.

'Doctor, I'm sure you'd be happy to drive back to the Jarinyi settlement with us. It'll save you another long walk.' Carswell looked anything but keen. 'The quicker you can interpret for us, the quicker we can clear this matter up. Ok?'

'Oh absolutely. I've always wondered what the Jarinyi for "shove it" is.'

3

'Wherever he steps, whatever he touches, whatever he leaves, even unconsciously, will serve as a silent witness against him.

Not only his fingerprints or his footprints, but his hair, the fibers from his clothes, the glass he breaks, the tool mark he leaves, the paint he scratches, the blood or semen he deposits or collects...This is evidence that does not forget. Only human failure to find it, study and understand it can diminish its value.'

— Dr. Edmond Locard

ROMAINE WAS EXTREMELY happy when Carswell insisted on a shower and a fresh outfit before they left. It also gave him a chance to inspect the crime scene, without the Jarinyi advocate standing around distracting him.

Fisher led him to the spot where Gutierrez had died, then ran off to the Quartermaster to get him a sunhat. Standing alone in the open, the exposed skin of his face and hands tightened under Eventide's star. It had been a very long time since he'd felt real sunlight; Harshini had

often teased him that his skin was as pale as the underbelly of a dead
fish.

Cheeky minx. The thought was tinged with old and familiar sadness.

He lifted his SCRoLL to his mouth and murmured into it, recording
his impressions of the personnel he'd met so far, particularly Colonel
Bob Glass. Done with that and still waiting for Fisher's return, he
surveyed the area, soaking in detail while filtering out the distractions
of heat and open sky and hack-knew-what-bacteria floating
around him.

His first thought upon studying the crime scene was that a frontier
mentality prevailed here, one with no regard for forensics. The scene
was not roped off. It had been trampled by two days and nights of
routine activity. When he and Fisher had approached it, a weary-
looking sentry, eyes fixed on the trees outside the cable-fence, made a
bee-line straight through it. With all that activity, there was only one
tell-tale sign that anything unusual had happened there, but that did
make it easy to see exactly where Gutierrez had died. When Fisher
returned, he nodded at the man-shaped burn mark on the thin grey-
green grass.

'Crude.'

'A laser-cutter was all I could find to mark the spot. CO didn't want
to cordon it off. He said it would compromise morale, remind
personnel of what had happened there.'

'As if they'd forget.' He sighed, took the proffered cap and slipped it
on. Its mottled green and khaki clashed with the blue of his uniform.
But damn it felt good to place something between his scalp and the
sun. 'The cutter was a good idea, Corporal.'

She handed over her slim, already powered on. 'Images, sir.'

'Even better.'

According to the date/time stamp, she'd taken these photographs
ten minutes after Gutierrez's body was discovered. For a moment his
mind dislocated, flashing back to another dead body sprawled in a cool
room. Once it had been a teenage girl, but now it had been transformed
by knife and by insanity into something other, something –

'No holos, I'm afraid, sir.' Fisher's voiced snapped him back to reality, away from memories he'd been avoiding for three days now. 'I don't know how to set up the cameras and the civs wouldn't come out here to help until long after the body was taken away, so I thought it was pointless then, sir.'

'Not a perfect universe, Fisher.' He had to shake his head a little to clear away the disorientation. The abrupt movement gave him a mild headache in place of the unhappy memory. He thought, *Far from it.* 'He was found by that Private Lim with the runny nose?'

'That's correct, sir.'

'He's coming with us today? I'd like to interview him asap.'

'No, sir. The CO ordered him to clear some underbrush between the fence and the tree line.'

The good ol' CO again. Might be fun to charge him with obstructing justice.

Fisher pointed out through the deactivated Gate twenty meters back along the fence where a handful of Marines waved tools around and joshed, headed for the forest. One carried a chainsaw.

They're pushing the forest back, extending the killing ground, making it harder for Jarinyi to shoot from cover.

If he didn't get out there soon, his secondary crime scene might be completely eradicated. If it wasn't already.

'Still alive or dead?'

'Pardon, sir?'

'Gutierrez. When Lim found him.'

'Oh. Dead, sir.'

The images confirmed as much. Gutierrez would not have survived long. Possibly he hadn't known what hit him. Even if he had, he wouldn't have believed it. Fisher's images were crystal clear and while Romaine would have preferred holograms as well, she had done a good enough job to give him a feel for the scene as she found it. He continued thumbing through them until he found two that provided clear close-ups of Gutierrez's throat. Sure enough, it had been pierced by a narrow wooden shaft tipped by a bone point. Presumably the murder weapon was being kept with the body in the camp's Medcentre. The arrow was as long as his forearm, thinner than his pinky, with a head as broad as his thumb. It had hit Gutierrez at a shallow angle, fired from somewhere slightly above his position. The arrowhead was coated in gore, something that might have been cartilage drooping from one edge.

'There was a sweep of the forest out there?'

'Not immediately, no, sir. Exterior lighting was shut down for the night. Reapers were launched to look for attackers about ten minutes after the Private's death was discovered. They found nothing. No one,' she corrected herself. 'Patrols swept the area after dawn but still no sign of any perpetrators. Perimeter sensors have been requisitioned from CUSET to be placed around the tree line to prevent any future surprise attacks. We're still waiting for them.'

'You have *no* motion sensors?'

'Some. Apparently, upon embarkation we were meant to have sixteen boxes of four. We only had one. One set.' She pointed at an egg-shaped object half-buried in the dirt just outside the fence.

'Did they at least conduct a head count? Before dawn, I mean.'

Fisher looked embarrassed. 'No, sir.'

He shrugged with his eyebrows. 'Not your fault, Corporal. Nor your responsibility. Just makes my job harder.'

'The CO believed it was an attack from outside the camp. Indigenous persons.'

'Not your job to defend him either. And at this point we don't know the Jarinyi killed Gutierrez. Tell me: who else arrived in the couple of days before February 4? *Oneday*, as you call it.'

A small crease appeared between Fisher's eyebrows. 'No one, sir. This entire compliment of military and civilian personnel arrived together on January 28.' The crease deepened as she considered his question further. 'You suspect someone came looking for Gutierrez? With a grudge?'

Romaine pursed his lips. She could think like a real cop; that was good. 'Maybe. Checking for strangers is a good thread to pull on.'

Fisher touched the military bob in her hair thoughtfully. 'Well, you're the first person to arrive after the rest of us did. And we're pretty much all a bunch of strangers here, sir. Apart from the recon unit who were with Colonel Glass on Red Star, hardly anyone here knew each other before.'

Romaine's eyebrow twitched. 'Really? See, that's *very* interesting.'

She nodded. 'It is, sir. That's why it stuck in my mind. I know that the Quartermaster and Gutierrez had been in a garrison on Centauri before this. And there's a couple of Canadians who knew each other previously. But it's like CUSETMA made up the expedition by grabbing a couple of people from here and one from there, et cetera.'

'Now that's a weird way of doing business,' Romaine said.

'I wondered if they wanted to prevent short-staffing other operations.'

Romaine grunted, not finding that convincing. 'And you? You weren't with Glass before this?'

She shook her head. 'I was pulled from duties on Theseus.'

'Anyone else know our victim before this, apart from the Quartermaster?'

'Not sure, sir. I have the personnel files in there.' She pointed to her slim. 'Copied them this morning.'

'Good. Transfer me some copies.' He handed the device back and crouched by the outline of Emmanuel Gutierrez's head, his knees complaining. He ran a finger through the dirt beneath the grass. 'Who's your medic?'

'Captain Ranarith is the base surgeon. He performed an autopsy if that's what you're wondering. There'll be a report ready for you when we arrive back later today.'

'I can't have it now?' He looked up at her, shielding his eyes against the sun.

She glanced away, embarrassed. 'I asked him that before you arrived, sir. He said he would finish writing this afternoon.'

'Not exactly cooperative with law enforcement, this camp of yours.' He spread his fingers, inspecting the grass more closely. Some of the leaves were stained with what looked like blood; whether or not this Ranarith had actually performed an autopsy, Romaine wanted a sample of it. He pulled out a sampling instrument and small plastic baggies from another pouch on his belt. The instrument took pinches of grass and soil. Romaine emptied them into separate baggies. He stood and passed the baggies to Fisher as a chainsaw roared to life in the forest.

'They have a lot of men extending the clearing?'

She made a perplexed face. 'Just those you saw a moment ago. If it were me ... Well, everyone seems busy on other duties.'

'What *are* those duties? Why all the research teams and biohazard signs?'

That furrow between her eyebrows again. 'Sir, I just stop arguments and carry boxes and ... peel potatoes.'

'An MP on KP.'

One corner of her lip twitched in self-deprecation. Perhaps she had a sense of humor after all. 'Mm-hmm,' she said.

'So they cut a few trees down. What else have they done to boost security?'

'Reapers have gone up at random intervals during the night. And the CO equipped the sentries with tensar collars. They also keep further back inside the fence at night.'

Romaine swiped sweat from his brow and watched a brief flurry of breeze shift the branches around his estimated secondary crime scene. The shadowy spaces out there stared back at him, black eyes brimming with malevolence.

What an imagination, Johnny. Imagination is just procrastination with polish: didn't Dad tell you often enough?

Fisher took a breath and waited a moment before saying, 'Dr Carswell will be looking for us soon, sir. We should find him and head to the jeep bay.'

Romaine snatched back her slim. 'He can wait a bit longer.'

He held the notepad at an angle that correlated to one of her images, matching the corpse with its laser-outline on the ground. He compared the two for a moment then turned and studied the tree line outside the camp.

'The killer fired from near that flowering tree there.'

Fisher followed his gaze. 'You can tell that sir?'

'Educated guess, but I'm pretty sure.' He handed her the slim again.

'The attack came from his left and slightly above him. The terrain over there rises gradually. The impact of the arrow twisted his neck and head around to his right and down, spinning his torso slightly sideways as he fell. But his legs are positioned as if he toppled sideways without taking a step. Look at this image: there's no scuffing of the soil around his feet, no death-tremor, no kicking around struggling against the inevitable – maybe the impact snapped his neck. To my mind, that all places the shooter roughly thataways.'

The last thing he wanted to do right now was traipse about in an untamed wilderness. But he swallowed his angst and said brightly, 'Let's go take a look at our secondary crime scene. Maybe your fellow explorers haven't been over to stomp on all the evidence yet.'

REGARDING VIRGIN SCRUB, ROMAINE PAUSED, SUPPRESSING consternation. This was not the environment he was used to working in. He had come to think of the floor and walls of manmade structures as blank slates on which the perpetrators had unwittingly – and some-times *wittingly* – painted their signature. Scuff-marks, fibers, skin flakes, hairs, blood-spatters. Centuries of forensic science made it so easy to read crime scenes that perps may as well have left a business card.

But *this*. This was wild, unkempt, chaotic – natural! Looking for clues amongst the litter of a forest, almost three days after the event, seemed like a lost cause.

He felt Fisher regarding him from behind, realizing that hesitation might lose him the respect of the only ally he had here.

Suck it up, Johnny. Your law enforcement ancestors had no problem examining crime scenes like this. The place is different but Locard's exchange principle is the same: every contact leaves its trace.

From the edge of the tree line, Romaine moved with care, inspecting each spot before placing his feet there. Fisher stayed behind him, placing her feet in the depressions left by his. He nodded approvingly.

Under the canopy of leaves, Romaine found welcome relief from the sun, though the humidity still made breathing an effort. As did all the crap in the air. *What is that? Pollen?* The cloying smell of the flowers above and beside him reminded him of cloves.

Give me cool clean filtered air any day.

His distraction was so great that he nearly missed the bird.

At first, he stepped over it, disgusted but disinterested. Dead animals were to be expected in the wild, a minor nuisance. It was his inner voice – that feeling some called *gut* – that drew his eyes back to the carcass, inviting him to scrutinize it more closely. The beak open in a silent scream, its eyes had been picked out. Bugs crawled around a belly wound. He knelt beside it, unconcerned with the putrid stink rising from it. It was ironic how he'd become more comfortable with the smells of death than with those of life.

The bird – it was analogous to those terran creatures – must have stood a meter high when alive and probably didn't fly. Its plumage was a sickly variegated green. Miniature teeth lined the gaping beak. But it didn't look like a particularly dangerous critter and – especially with Fisher behind him – Romaine was unconcerned about family members showing up.

He waved a hand over the dead animal to dispel the bugs. The crawlers ignored his gesture. The fliers took to the air momentarily before settling back onto the creature's torso, but it was long enough for Romaine to clearly see the death wound. Though the bugs had devoured much of the surrounding matter, it was obvious. A neat hole punched by a pulse rifle.

He stood. 'Killed with an AR-90.'

'Private Gutierrez's weapon discharged a few minutes before his body was discovered. The watch commander commed him for an explanation. The Private told him he'd shot a woo-woo bird.'

Romaine pointed down. 'That's a woo-woo bird?'

'Yes, sir.'

'And it's called a woo-woo bird because...'

'It says *woo-woo*,' they both finished together.

'So, Gutierrez – assuming this is that bird – he fires at some wildlife.

Then moments later he gets hit in the throat with an arrow. You think it's a revenge killing?'

'Sir?'

'You know, Momma Woo-Woo gets stiffed, so Daddy Woo-Woo pulls out his bow and arrow.' Fisher just looked blank. 'It was a joke, Corporal. You're allowed to laugh.'

'Very good, sir,' she replied politely.

Romaine's CHAD was now in his hand, a reader he could program to scan for various substances. He adjusted it and slowly waved it around him. It purred against his hand, finding nothing. He grunted, disappointed. 'Fisher, help me work this out. Why would Gutierrez fire at a woo-woo bird? I'm sure target practice is a no-no at night time.

She shifted her feet. 'You know what an AIRTAR is, sir?'

'Automatic InfraRed-Tracking and Ranging device.'

'Okay, so I was thinking that the bird activated his AIRTAR and he fired instinctively.'

'I was thinking the same thing, so you're at least as clever as I am. So, his AIRTAR bleeps. That must happen a lot out here. I mean there's obviously a large population of life forms in these surrounds.' He nodded up at some things that looked like flying possums regarding him from high in the branches above. He really didn't like the looks they were giving him.

'What do you mean, sir?'

'What I mean is, why *fire*? That's my first question. Was Gutierrez in the habit of firing every time his AIRTAR locked on a life form? Was he a nervous individual? What caused him to fire?'

'Sir, I get your drift. I've occasionally heard weapons discharging at nighttime. I've been told it's always at animals venturing close to camp. I guess the sentries get edgy. It's dark. It's an unfamiliar place. They start thinking there may be large dangerous life forms smart enough to get across the wire. Who knows? Most of these boys don't have a high education, but they do have fertile imaginations.'

He nodded at her turn of phrase. 'And the dark is pretty good fertilizer for imagination. Okay, you answered my first question. My second is this: did his AIRTAR sense the bird or did it sense the killer? See, this is roughly where the arrow was fired from. And here's a slight break in the brush comfortable enough for someone my size to sit or crouch with an uninterrupted line-of-sight to the fence. So killer and woo-woo potentially shared the same hiding spot.

'That raises a third and a fourth question. To satisfy the third, check your slim and tell me how large a life-form AIRTARs are generally set to pick up.'

Fisher didn't need to consult her files, responding with confidence. 'Depends on the way you count it. It takes into account body temperature as well as mass and profile. Basically, their default setting is for anything the size, shape and metabolism of a small adult ... and up.'

'Not something as light as this bird. That's what I thought. So probably it was the killer that set off the sensor. Might mean he was extremely lucky here. Question four: how close do woo-woos usually let people get to them?'

'I'll have to check. But I'd say there's no wildlife bigger than bugs that gets too close to humans. I'm not sure about Jarinyi though, sir.'

'Yep. No animal at nighttime is going to be too happy about sharing its personal space with a potentially dangerous *other*. So either it was some Jarinyi's pet, or our killer is a very quiet hunter. Apart from the Jarinyi, who do you know that can move though forest quietly enough they don't disturb wildlife?'

She thought for a moment, that little crease reappearing in her brow. 'I guess some of the blackcaps would be able to.'

There followed an awkward pause, while both considered this.

'You look uncomfortable with your answer, Corporal. But it's valid.'

Romaine rolled his shoulders and allowed his consciousness to drift, breathe in the scene, the gestalt, the evidence so far. An image began to form, to move, and he drifted with it...

A killer, faceless but as solid as the tree beside which he knelt. They're bent on violence, settling one knee into the soft leaves and mud, running a hand along the shaft of the arrow to remove impurities that might disturb the arrow's flight...

The Marine sentry appears among the glare of camp lights behind the fence, a dark and blurry shadow now distinct and sharp-edged as he moves into a new patch of light.

The killer draws the bow, waiting for the moment, the perfect moment. The sentry's so far away – it's hard to see the flesh the killer's aiming for – he needs that perfect moment, when will it come? One shot, just one chance, here it is! Letting fly ...

'One hell of a shot,' he murmured, blinking away the visualization. The killer was a marksman, patient with both discomfort and waiting, self-controlled. And confident. To fire one shot and do it well – to know you would – required extremely high ego strength. Either that or a great deal of familiarity with sniping, or hunting.

He scowled at his CHAD. Two more sensor runs had picked up nothing.

'Sir, are you looking for something in particular?'

Good question.

Most crimes turned out to have a very simple solution. Though all investigators loved a challenge, rarely in Romaine's career had he come across something that was difficult to solve. Usually there were no unexpected twists, no cunning masterminds to frame other people, no 'butlers' who did it. *Proving* things occasionally thwarted him, but he was used to straightforward resolutions. Why not just accept the obvious conclusion: a Jarinyi killed this grunt?

He glanced again at the detritus around him. What lay beneath the surface, the visible, the obvious? Layers. Layers of muck, layers of dead things, whatever else lay beneath all of them. Layer after layer, traveling down down down in his imagination until he struck the core of this world.

It's my job to explore layers.

'Corporal, I'm trying to rule out human involvement. I've scanned for saliva, hair, blood, phlegm, sweat. So far, no readings. Let's try skin flakes.' He held the CHAD closer to the ground and scanned slowly, stooping while taking a few more steps into the vegetation. His scanner began to hum and flashed blue and orange symbols when he passed a point by the base of the tree and again when he pointed it at a spot on the trunk itself.

'What have we here?' He knelt and scanned again. Same results in several places. He chose one area of dried mud, kept the scanner pointed at it with his left hand and reached into a pouch on his belt with the other. Taking out his sampler, he tapped it on the ground to break the skin of dried mud and vacuumed a space five by five centimeters. Fisher held a fresh baggie while he emptied the results into it. 'One more scan.' He cycled through the other settings on his CHAD, keeping it leveled at the closest tree. This time he found two hairs snagged in the bark of the tree at waist height, and another caught up in the foliage. Again, he bagged them and gave them off to Fisher.

'Your medico's name is Ranarith?'

'Yessir.'

'Run these last two samples over to him and ask him to test the DNA.' No one got into CUSET space without leaving DNA samples on file. 'I'll want a finding by sundown. But the samples from the primary scene, keep them. I'll look at them myself sometime.'

'Yes, sir. The skin samples are mixed with a lot of dirt.'

'It won't matter.' He peered through the trees back at the compound, couldn't see Carswell anywhere. 'And round up the Professor and meet us by the jeeps. We may as well get this Jarinyi visit over and done with.'

She nodded, lingering while he took a last look around.

There seemed to be footprints just past the tree but he had nothing with which to take casts. On closer inspection, there were three prints and they appeared to be what he would expect from the sole of standard issue Marine boots. But the tracks appeared to belong to someone walking past the scene, not into it or away from it. He took images with his CHAD, transferred them to his SCRoLL as they started back. Once they neared the Gate, Fisher jogged ahead to carry out his orders.

Romaine knew that the owners of the skin, the hairs and the tracks could have come out here for variety of valid reasons. A patrol stomping around looking for the killer the morning after. A person a week earlier taking their morning walk, taking samples of the flora, or taking a leak. If it was the latter, then a recent rain shower had probably washed away the urine.

Stepping across the boundary that separated Columbus from the rest of Eventide, he found a boyish part of himself reasserting itself, suddenly anticipating the contact with the Jarinyi with a little thrill, not because they were a lead to be followed, but for that more visceral reason of encountering something novel and dangerous and weird.

Aliens, Johnny, he thought. *You're finally going to see aliens.*

4

'You never get a second chance to make a first impression'

- Unknown

A TALL and gangly Marine regular awaited them in the jeep bay, bobbing on the balls of his feet.

He's highly anxious, thought Romaine. *Must be our escort.*

The Corporal introduced himself as Yario, but without the salute or deference Fisher had shown Romaine upon their first meeting. He stooped to pick up a thick green and grey vest while an assault rifle swung wildly from a strap over his left shoulder. Straightening, he offered the vest to Romaine. 'From the CO.'

Romaine told him, 'We've been through this already. I don't want to give the Jarinyi the impression I don't trust them. It might elevate tensions.'

Carswell made approving noises at his back.

Romaine held it toward Fisher. So far, she was the only person who'd played nice. 'You want it?'

Carswell switched to disapproving noises.

Fisher shook her head. 'I agree with you about sending the wrong message.'

'I'll wear it,' said Yario.

Romaine inspected the vest closely, sniffed it. Clean, in keeping with Glass's apparent OCD about hygiene. He adopted what he imagined was a fatherly tone, and said, 'Fisher, I think I might just order you to wear this.'

'It's ok,' Yario said brightly. 'I'm happy to wear it. Put it to good use, eh?'

Ignoring him, Romaine waggled it at Fisher with a mock stern look. She consented and slid it on.

Carswell grumbled as he boarded the jeep.

So did Yario.

———

ROMAINE HAD NEVER RIDDEN IN A NON-WHEELED VEHICLE BEFORE. THE jeep was essentially a four-person repulsorcraft, armor-plated and open-roofed to allow swift ingress and egress. The driver could make use of pulse-cannons mounted on the sides and the chin of the chassis, firing dual streams of electromagnetic pulses at the rate of a hundred per minute. A rear passenger could climb quickly into a tail-gunner's chair and take charge of a chain gun with a similarly obscene rate-of-fire.

Fisher drove, climbing the easy gradient out of Columbus's shallow valley and into the rain forest. She seemed as unperturbed as Carswell, who lolled comfortably across the rear passenger seat. In back with the chain gun, Yario fidgeted and muttered. As the forest closed in, Romaine found himself the victim of a creeping paranoia, imagining crystal-eyed sharp-toothed beings taking aim with bows and blow-pipes. He glanced at the faint crosshairs on the driver's side of the windshield.

Carswell said, 'They aren't out there and they won't get you.'

That obvious, huh?

Fifteen minutes earlier, the idea of visiting strange aliens in an exotic setting had sounded like fun.

What in hell was I thinking?

He asked, 'Are we there yet?'

Fisher gave a polite nod. 'Very good, sir.'

Yario muttered something about lame jokes and Romaine turned to look at him. Yario avoided contact, studying the trees. He reminded Romaine of a character from his childhood nanobooks, a scarecrow with ill-fitting clothes and limbs too long for his body.

'It's only about fifteen kilometers as the crow flies, Commander,' Carswell piped up helpfully. 'The route a vehicle has to take adds another fifteen to that. Shouldn't take more than an hour at this pace.'

'An hour?' Romaine faced forwards. 'I don't suppose anyone wants to join me in a rendition of *Forty Thousand Bottles of Beer on the Wall*?'

THEY FOLLOWED AN OLD CREEK BED. THOUGH MUDDY FROM RECENT RAIN, the creek wasn't flowing. Because the vehicle used no wheels, such a surface was no problem and their ride remained smooth. At various points, it seemed like earlier teams had cleared fallen trees from the sides. Twice they had to detour where the creek banks narrowed together. This – along with the watercourse's many twists and turns – made the journey feel clumsy and slow, which only exacerbated Romaine's anxiety further.

The forest was vigorously *alive*. Animals and bugs flew-skittled-darted about. The air resounded with hoots and yelps, croaks and clacks – the conversations of a thousand species. Plants grew on fallen logs, creepers on trees, fungi on creepers. Some kind of creature bounded kangaroo-like into the path of the jeep, narrowly avoiding impact as Fisher veered around it. A simple 'Sheesh!' was her only commentary. Romaine's heart clanged against his ribs.

His SCRoLL and the files he'd copied to it remained in its pocket; the thick forest seemed to keep out the breeze, leaving it too hot to think, let alone read. But he could still talk.

'Doctor, we're going to a village, but you said these people were nomadic.'

'I think they have a chain of campsites they rotate between.' Carswell straightened, warming to the topic. 'Their year is twice as long as ours, but essentially their seasons are the same four we're accustomed to on Earth. I believe their travel patterns follow those seasons. We don't know much about the people over the great river to the east – they're Jarinyi too, another Tribe – or the Nguwuu on the savannah over the mountains. They're a branch species, I think. But this clan of Jarinyi travel between here, the coast and this side of the riverbank. There's some indication the two tribes winter together up in the foothills, though I'm not sure about that.'

'There's more Jarinyi over the river?' Romaine asked.

'Known simply as River Tribe. At least, that's my Tribe's name for them.'

My tribe'. Interesting. Romaine removed his cap and tucked it down beside the seat, finger-combed his short hair. 'Why move at all?'

'Why not? By moving, their diet is a varied one. Shell fish and ocean creatures along the coast, fresh water critters from the river, fruit and roots and nuts and red meat everywhere else. When you move around, you allow species to replenish so there is always plenty for next year. You don't spoil the environment; you co-exist with it.'

'And what's the sentiment about these human newcomers?'

Carswell grunted. 'The Jarinyi are a wonderful people.'

'That doesn't answer my question.'

'Some things are on a need to know basis.'

What a nutbag.

'Doctor, at lunch you said it's taken you months to crack the Jarinyi language, and that race relations depended on you gaining understanding of their culture. Surely you wouldn't be alone in wanting to work towards this. What about the rest of the team that came with you?'

'Them? A survey team. All gone. Disappeared when the Military arrived.'

'Disappeared?'

'Pulled out and sent elsewhere by their CUSET Lords and Masters. Left without a word to me. Not that I care. They were worse than useless.'

'How is it you stayed, then?'

Carswell chuckled, an unnatural staccato sound as if someone had taught a goat to mimic a human. 'Simple. I went bush when we got word that Glass and his buddies would be arriving. Hid out with the Jarinyi for a few days. When I surfaced, I convinced Glass that he needed my help with the *indigs*, as the Marines call them.'

Yario muttered something about *indigs* from the back.

'So if you're the only one working with the Jarinyi, what's everyone else doing here?'

'Need to know basis, Commander,' Carswell crooned pleasantly.

In Romaine's peripheral vision, the scientist was tapping the side of his nose. Romaine allowed himself one brief shake of his head.

THE STREAMBED FORKED. FISHER TURNED RIGHT, REMEMBERING THE WAY from the other time she'd come here.

The Commander stirred to life beside her. 'Where would that left turn have taken us?'

'How do you know it would have gone anywhere?' asked Carswell before she could reply.

She cleared her throat. 'Toward the Pumpkin Patch, I think.'

'What's the Pumpkin Patch?'

'To be honest, I'm not sure. It's not part of my job.' She'd often wondered about it though.

'That's okay, Corporal. Like you, I don't need to know.' Romaine said this with a backward glance at Carswell who had his eyes closed but smiled anyway. The doctor was obviously getting under the Commander's skin. It should take a lot more than Carswell's rudeness to ruffle a Military Investigator, but then again Romaine hadn't looked at ease since stepping off the ferry.

Maybe it was all the restrictions being placed on him from the moment he touched down. Cops weren't meant to be told what to do; they did that to other people. Or maybe he hadn't been planetside for years. She had heard of people who went their entire adult life enclosed in artificial environments – ships, asteroid mines, orbital colonies, outlying space stations. The joke was that 'Spacers' thought *fresh air* meant gas from a recently opened canister. She couldn't imagine living that way. If that were true of Romaine, he wouldn't need the CO urging him to finish this quickly. He would want to get back on a ship asap.

Well, he *should* be able to finish it quickly. Seriously. If the murder weapon was any indication, this was a pretty simple case.

So did the Jarinyi kill Private Gutierrez? If they did, then which one? And how will we figure that out? Fervently she hoped it wasn't them. *Even I can see how bad it'd be if they're responsible.*

If it wasn't the Jarinyi, that made it one of her colleagues. And that unhappy possibility *had* crossed her mind before Romaine arrived. She'd found herself staring suspiciously at other Marines – especially the blackcaps – as they'd gone about their daily routine. That was the problem with any crime in a small community: it undermined trust.

She slowed further to avoid a fallen branch. 'Another fifteen minutes, we'll be there, sir,' she said.

Carswell began humming *Bottles of Beer*.

'The Pumpkin Patch is sacred to the Jarinyi, you know.'

The words drifting from the back seat roused Romaine from another reverie. He'd been thinking about the dead girl again. It bothered him that he couldn't just file her away and forget, move forward. This time the memory left a bitter aftertaste in the back of his mouth. And nightmares. Two nights full of the damn things.

'Hmm?'

Carswell made an impatient noise at having to repeat himself. 'I overheard some of the camp staff talking shop. Just thought you should know that your military friends are considering the plunder of yet another disempowered people. No respect for their opinion or needs.'

Romaine twisted around and gestured for Carswell to continue.

'The aggressors here are the Marines and their research team.'

Yario had left his AR90 on the rear passenger well's floor. The barrel slid toward Carswell's knee as the jeep negotiated a turn. Romaine wondered if the safety was on. Carswell knocked it away with the back of his hand without looking.

Surely the safety's on.

He brought his face closer to Fisher and in a low voice asked her if Yario was fully competent.

The ghost of a smile touched her lips and she said, equally quietly, 'He's ex-Canadian Army. Those guys know what they're doing; he's just a little ... casual.'

No kidding, Romaine thought, watching out of the corner his eye as Yario slapped limply at some bug on the chaingun's trigger guard.

Fisher straightened in her seat. 'Actually,' she murmured, 'he was the Watch Commander the night of the incident.'

'Yario?' It was hard to imagine him commanding anything.

'What? Are you guys talking about me?'

Romaine raised his volume. 'I believe you and I will be having a chat later, Corporal. You'll have the honor of giving me my first witness statement.'

'Great,' said Yario after a beat.

'Ten minutes, Commander, and we should be at their village,' said Fisher.

'More like twelve,' said Carswell.

Well, if that safety wasn't on, thought Romaine, the bright side would be that it should kill Carswell.

THE JEEP SLOWED TO WALKING PACE AS THE STREAMBED PANNED OUT TO A large undulating clearing dotted with clumps of grass, logs and strange-looking lean-tos. Romaine regarded the campsite with a mixture of anxiety and awe: long structures of wood, hides and bark ran between some of the dwellings, devices that looked designed to catch and collect rain water. Someone had made those. People. Non-human people.

As a teenager, his parents had taken him to the Xenodochium in Tokyo, when the zoo for extra-terrestrial animals was new. *Homo sapiens* had colonized few worlds at that stage, and most of the creatures on display were docile sorts from Centauri, although a special exhibit of ferocious aquatic demireptiles from Castor made the experience more gripping. For him at least. A precocious Japanese preteen standing nearby had been muttering to himself in English that these animals were just like his toy *cybermals* at home. Romaine had felt like slugging the little rat turd. And threatened as much, sending the boy fleeing in tears to find his parents.

For fifteen-year-old John Romaine, seeing all those offworld animals had filled him with a sense of adventure and wonder, as if someone had finally let him in on a secret that there was more to life. This was proof that there was somewhere he could go, far away from the unpleasantness of his family. The universe contained virgin territory unlike the cluttered decay of Earth. He could become a galactic bigshot, carrying out important diplomatic duties with alien beings.

In the thirty years since, he'd never met a sentient alien being. Neither had anyone else, except the handful who worked with the larva-like Anachromites, creatures whose sentience was still hotly debated. Space had not lived up to a young boy's fantasies. In the void, he had discovered not a life of adventure, but a life that was routine, predictable, and increasingly bleak. As the jeep crawled into the Jarinyi campsite, he had the sense all that was changing. If only the fifteen-year-old John Romaine could have fast-forwarded from the Xenodochium to this time and place, skipping the years between ...

Romaine blew out a breath, hoping the reminiscing would go with it. There was never anything good to be gained by looking backwards.

At first there was no sign of the 'indigs'. Of course, the repulsor noise would have given the creatures enough warning to be a kilometer away by now. As Fisher killed the engines and the field generator died, Romaine heard nothing but the soft chirrup of some crawling creature.

Then a warbling like birdsong from the far end of the camp, answered in kind from the bushes closer to them. A scent hung upon the air, like exotic spices mingled with something metallic. It made a pleasant change from the rotting vegetable stink of the creek bed. Streamers of mid-afternoon sunlight pinpointed spots upon the ground like stage lights.

Romaine slipped to the ground beside the jeep, massaging his stiff back. 'Kind of creepy.'

'Kind of normal,' Carswell responded beside him. He marched over and into the closest dwelling, little more than a grass hummock. 'My house,' he called from within. He was out a moment later, clutching a small shoulder bag.

Romaine took a few steps away from the vehicle. There was more birdsong from the far end of the camp. No other signs of life. 'So where are our Jarinyi, Doctor? Have we scared them away? Are they out working?'

Still in the jeep, fingers taut on the chaingun, Yario added, 'Taking aim at us? Planning our deaths?'

Carswell sniffed. 'The women and children have retreated one hundred meters into the bush. When they appear, you'll recognize the women by their neck frills, one either side of their head behind their ears. The males are hidden around the perimeter watching us. I probably shouldn't tell you any of that. Explaining their security procedures to you is no doubt a betrayal of their trust. Follow me slowly into the middle of their camp and don't do anything until I tell you.'

Romaine tried to exchange an irritated look with Fisher, but she studiously avoided the indiscretion, watching the bush back toward the stream. He forced his feet to move after Carswell, concentrating on the ground before him to avoid mud and what looked suspiciously like animal droppings. When he looked up again Carswell had stopped moving and a dozen alien warriors surrounded them, all crouching.

Certain there'd been nothing but an empty campsite a few moments earlier, he was more astounded at the suddenness of the Jarinyi presence than their actual appearance. It was as if they had materialized out of thin air.

Back by the jeep, Fisher let out a startled gasp. Yario swore.

Romaine tried to speak but his mouth felt like it was full of gum. The Jarinyi stood erect, became totally immobile, like statues. None was close to ground cover, so it was difficult to grasp just how quickly and quietly they had moved into their current positions. Carswell beamed.

Purge me, this is incredible.

The Jarinyi – the males? – possessed human average height, but were slimmer, leaner. They were bipedal, bifocal, wore clothing of sorts and possessed hands that looked like his.

Here the similarities ended.

The Jarinyi head was a difficult shape for Romaine to process, roughly triangular – like a rounded inverted pyramid. The face was *odd* – eyes double the size of a human's with catlike slits for pupils. Romaine caught an occasional glimpse of an inner lid when the Jarinyi blinked. Their ears resembled those of Earth folklore goblins, with the ability to move to follow a sound. There was no protruding nose – breathing seemed handled by a series of slits running down each side of the face beneath the eyes, four per side. Their mouths remained closed, tiny compared with a human's. Their miniature jaws jutted proudly forward, the chins capped with a kind of frill. The Jarinyi skin was a mottled tan, reptilian in appearance. And they were completely hairless.

Even in these initial few seconds' examination, Romaine had no doubt that he was dealing with a highly intelligent species. It wasn't just the upright posture, the weaponry held casually in hand or slung over shoulders, nor the artefacts these beings had constructed. In their eyes burned the indisputable fire of *reason.*

Carswell cleared his throat and spoke gently, adopting an undulating pitch in his voice. 'Commander Romaine, allow me to introduce you to the Jarinyi.'

Romaine smiled and nodded stupidly. Carswell inclined his head to indicate that Romaine should step closer to him. He obliged. Carswell then turned and motioned toward the tallest warrior.

'This is their Elder, their chief.'

The warriors still had not moved. Romaine ended that by stepping forward and offering his hand, out of habit. The Elder shuffled back while every other Jarinyi took a step forward. Two of them insinuated themselves in front of their leader.

'You are an absolute idiot.' Carswell delivered the rebuke in that strange singsong voice, then whistled three high notes, repeated them and held one palm up to the two bodyguards. One of them leaned in and sniffed it, all eight nostril-flaps flaring, eyes still fixed on Romaine.

Romaine looked askance at Fisher who shrugged. She had wandered closer and her hand hovered by her holster.

I knew this was a bad idea, he thought.

Fisher nodded toward Carswell, intimating that Romaine's attention was desired.

Carswell still spoke in that same singsong voice. 'You're applying conventions formed by Western civilization on Earth a thousand years ago to a planet lightyears away without a trace of the same culture. Shaking hands had its origin in a time when men used their right hands to bear swords against each other. Offering your empty hand was a way of demonstrating you had no hostile intentions; you were leaving your weapon in its sheath. Here – between strangers at least – it's an aggressive act. They probably think you were *reaching for* his weapon – to take it away from him.'

Romaine wasn't sure whether to feel stupid, embarrassed or scared. 'I – I'm sorry. I didn't think.'

'No harm done – *if* you follow my lead the rest of the time we're here. Beginning with your palm.'

Romaine glanced down at his palm uncertain. Having someone sniff it like a dog was –

'Commander, the longer you delay, the more reason they have to distrust you. As you are about to request their cooperation in your investigation, I suggest–'

'Okay. I get the picture.' He held his hand up feeling absurdly like an Earth traffic cop. The same warrior as before repeated the procedure. Romaine cringed at the wash of hot moist breath, the wetness he saw in the flaring nostrils-gills near his palm. He remembered Colonel

Glass and his refusal of a handshake. The Jarinyi were just practicing a variation, he tried to tell himself, but it still felt ... unclean. 'Why do they do this?'

'Maybe they can detect the presence of pheromones indicating aggression. They never use this form of greeting within their own clans, only with members of foreign tribes. And humans.'

The warrior had stepped back. Romaine discerned a faded scar running from temple to cheek on the left side of the head. On the right, part of the earflap was missing, whether torn or bitten he couldn't tell. *Scarface.* The nickname came unbidden into Romaine's mind and stuck there.

The Elder stepped forward again and whistled – without opening his mouth. The plaintive notes seemed to emanate from his nostrils.

And the tableau exploded into activity. Most warriors turned away, abruptly disinterested in the newcomers, moving with a spring in their step. Some begin to call out and Romaine realized he hadn't heard birdsong earlier; it was these creatures communicating.

Carswell produced a device from his bag which he hung around his neck, dangling from a lanyard. It broadcast English words in rolling tones as the Elder 'spoke'.

'May I help, Seeker?'

'You are most kind to assist, Wise One.' As Carswell spoke, the device translated his English into warbles, whistles, snorts and clacks. The Elder and his two bodyguards listened with heads cocked, the Elder looking at the translator the whole time. But Scarface stared at Romaine, while the other bodyguard gave Fisher the same attention.

Two more warriors had remained, standing further back. One was much shorter than his companions and would have barely reached Romaine's shoulder. These two seemed less on edge, but their attention stayed with Yario back in the jeep.

'This tall one is new to your world,' Carswell was saying. 'One of the Men has been killed. He comes to find the killer.'

Men? Presumably the device's vocabulary would have been loaded by Carswell himself, and Romaine added *sexist* to his own vocabulary of words describing the scruffy scientist.

The Elder spoke again. 'Is he a watcher or a ... judge?' The last word came out of the translator belatedly; it had had to search for the closest definition.

'Judge.' Carswell said it with a grim expression. There was something he didn't like in this title. When the Elder dipped his head, Romaine understood why. The designation afforded him some kind of respect.

Romaine tapped the scientist's arm looking for an explanation. Carswell touched the translator, pausing the interpretation. 'They have a very strict law and only the most senior warriors may enforce that law. Hence you are an equal.'

While you *are tolerated*? Romaine would have loved to ask. He couldn't help a slight smirk.

The Elder made a hand sign at the taller warrior watching Yario which made him dart away toward a lean-to.

Romaine found himself fascinated by the texture of the Elder's skin, his gaze roaming up and down the Jarinyi's chest and throat. Until a fly-analog zipped into his face and tried to alight on his eye. He grunted and waved at it. The fly buzzed angrily and shot off toward the trees. The group of Jarinyi stared at him blankly.

Finally, the warrior returned with a thick stick, hardened by fire and slightly polished at both ends. The Elder snatched it away and held it toward Romaine who felt a pang of alarm.

Through the translator, the Elder told him that the stick was a gift, a *chweechee*, and they hoped the Judge would use it to *tut-tut-tut-tut-tut-tut*. Romaine presumed the staccato chime meant the translator was signaling a translation error. He felt he'd got the drift, though. He took the gift gingerly, aware he should feel honored, but all he felt was weird. He mumbled a thank you, handed it off to Fisher and added that she would take care of it for him.

'They seem to like me,' he taunted Carswell.

The doctor sniffed. 'Well, I'm only an observer, a student, while you are a judge. This tribe normally uses the services of the judge who lives with the River Tribe, though they rarely need him. I guess they'd give him a gift if he'd come all this way to help them; it's only fair they treat you just as courteously. They are a very generous people, as you can see.'

Behind them, Fisher carried the *chweechee* to the jeep and suggested firmly to Yario that he climb down and behave in a non-threatening way.

The Elder was talking again and Carswell lifted his hand from his device. 'The ... judge is welcome to our *tut-tut-tut*. I am in council. *Tut-tut* will remain to help you. Health, Men.'

The Elder and his guards turned on their heels and moved back into the camp without a backwards glance, leaving the short Jarinyi behind, the one whose name the translator had struggled with.

Romaine sucked in a lungful of air, realized he had been breathing shallowly. *That was...civilized*, he thought. There had been no aggression. Other than that which he brought on by his own ignorance, and that had been short lived.

The small Jarinyi – Romaine decided to call him *Tuttut* because that's what the translator had called him – made a hand sign to Carswell who returned it. He then gestured at Romaine and twittered.

'Why does the judge wear the color of the creator?' came the translation. 'Is he more at home in the sky than on the earth?'

Carswell replied, 'In fact, you are correct, friend. He will walk here for a short time soon return to the stars.'

'Then he must be special *tut-tut-tut-tut* favored by the creator.' The Jarinyi made the hand sign toward Romaine and said, 'I will use my hands to help your *tut-tut-tut*.'

Can't we get this translation any clearer? I thought he said he'd cracked the language!

'You are very kind,' he replied, hoping he hadn't made another faux pas. Carswell looked calm. The translator didn't *tut*. Good signs.

A long pause ensued, broken by Carswell's exasperated sigh and another thumbing of the pause button. 'You are the *judge*, Romaine. You take the lead. What do you want to *do*?'

Romaine took a few more steps into the center of the camp, studying the tree line, the dwellings, the people. The world tipped to the left as a sudden and severe wave of vertigo crashed over him and he fought to maintain his balance with effort. Fisher seemed the only one to notice, stepping closer and frowning with concern. He smiled reassuringly at her and breathed deeply, forced the world to straighten and his focus to return to the job at hand.

Damn planet.

'Doctor, how can I be sure I won't offend our host or come across as threatening?'

'Just keep your movement as languid as possible and keep your communication simple. Address individuals as *friend*. Also try to get a bit of a lilt into your voice; it makes you seem friendlier.'

Romaine nodded and gestured for the xenologist to turn on the translator. He faced the Jarinyi. 'Friend. I have questions to ask.' His attempted lilt made him feel foolish but Carswell nodded in approval.

Tuttut's response was a series of fluting notes and clicks ending abruptly in a loud snort like a horse. 'You seek a person-killer. This is sacred work. We must wonder-know why you seek a person-killer here.'

'The man was killed with a Jarinyi weapon.'

Tuttut triple-sniffed in surprise. 'Jarinyi did not kill your Man. This people have no taste for that.'

'Okay. Nevertheless ...'

Tut-tut-tut.

Keep it simple, Johnny. 'The Man was killed with an arrow. A Jarinyi arrow.'

The translation of his words this time seemed flawless, but the Jarinyi made a querying gesture toward Carswell.

Carswell mimed drawing back on a bow and releasing an arrow, then indicted his neck as the point of impact.

Tuttut jerked his head away, ears pressed back and blinking hard. 'This arrow. You can show us?' he asked.

Romaine turned to Fisher. 'You have those images with you?'

As she fished for her slim, Carswell said, 'Don't bother showing them images. Physically they can see it, but they can't interpret what they're seeing. Their brain doesn't recognize representation.' To Tuttut he said: 'I have seen and I promise you it was an arrow.'

'Could you show me one of these weapons?' Romaine asked.

Tuttut bounded away with a gesture to follow.

Before they could, Fisher protested, 'Sir, it's not advisable to invite them to draw weapons.'

Yario drifted closer and made a noise of agreement.

'I hear you, Fisher,' Romaine said. 'But where else can I start? I'm ready to accept we're safe here. We've been treated politely and we have Carswell's acceptance among them as proof that they don't indiscriminately murder humans. And they just gave me a gift. And, well, Tuttut here seems nice.'

'Tuttut...?' Carswell asked.

'The little guy,' Romaine said. To Fisher, he continued, 'Your reservations are noted – we *are* in an unfamiliar situation and I'm treading as carefully as I can.'

As he moved off after the small Jarinyi, Carswell thrust the translator into his hands and walked away without a word. Romaine slipped the lanyard around his own neck, wondering how he was going to direct conversation with these people anywhere useful. Tuttut walked to the other end of the clearing and Romaine had a chance to study the tribe again. More Jarinyi had emerged from the forest – women, children, males shorter than Tuttut. Only the youngest stared openly at him. The women avoided the procession of humans, some turning their backs completely. One pulled her child away with a hiss.

If only Gutierrez had been killed with a normal weapon, he thought ruefully, a modern weapon. Then he could consider normal possibilities, normal lines of thought. Perhaps a fight over a lover, a dispute over gambling debts, a drug debt. But none of them would use an antiquated weapon like a bow, particularly not an indigenous one. He watched the mother continue ushering away her child while the little one peered over its shoulder at him, fascinated.

Don't look at me like that, he thought and bent his mind to other things. The Jarinyi were still his prime suspect.

5

'While the mid-20th Century's space race was a contest between the
USSR and USA chasing such milestones as placing a man in Earth
orbit and landing the first humans on the Moon, the space race of the
21st and early 22nd Centuries became a contest between the People's
Republic of China (see PRC) and large global corporations (see
CUSET) to utilize space-borne resources and eventually to colonize
other star systems...

'This has only once resulted in bloodshed to date, on the world
that came to be known as Red Star. The Expansion Treaty of 2097
established legal precedent for claiming new territory and had served
well until then. It was an unfortunate coincidence that in July of 2140,
PRC and CUSET expeditions landed on Red Star at approximately the
same time. Although the truth may never be proven, each party claims
they were first to land. What is clear-cut is that the expeditions landed
on the same coastline of the continent that became known as Fu-Xing
(see Fu Xing) within days (perhaps hours) of each other. They
encountered each other soon after. This encounter took the form of
military action, tempers boiling over as each tried to drive the other
offworld. While moving large forces through space remains
problematic and expensive (see Space Travel, see Leapfrogging), the

Chinese first wave had managed to land nine hundred and thirty infantry troops and three hundred and forty-three colonists. In contrast, CUSET (perhaps stretched thin by other concerns) had fielded just twelve researchers and eighty-nine Marines.

'These Marines were predominantly inexperienced regulars with only one of the renowned "blackcaps" squads to guide them (see Elite Marine Recon Unit, see CUSET Military Arm). The ensuing conflict took place over one afternoon in the Shui Valley (see Battle of Shui Valley). Chinese losses are still uncertain but the CUSET Marines casualties numbered forty-nine dead, thirteen wounded. The living were held prisoner for six months during the fierce political conflagration on Earth, which came to be known as the China Missile Crisis (see China Missile Crisis). Eventually Red Star was recognized officially both as a Chinese protectorate and the first and only shared world outside of Earth. CUSET were permitted to colonize a continent more arid than Fu Xing.

'Since the crisis, both Chinese and CUSET administrations have agreed to carefully communicate their intentions in exploration with each other.'

- from Werber's Encyclopedia of Human Endeavor, January 2141

ROMAINE WONDERED at Tuttut's size as he followed him toward the other end of the settlement. While the other small males around the camp seemed to be the equivalent of adolescents, Tuttut's skin was weathered and his movement more assured. Maybe a childhood sickness had stunted his growth.

Romaine whistled to Fisher quietly and gestured for her to stay close. As she picked up her pace, the children following in her wake darted off to surround Carswell who began to pivot in a drunken-looking dance, presumably for their entertainment.

'Strange strange man,' Romaine muttered. He reached for his SCRoLL. The cigarette-sized computer unraveled at a precise flick of the wrist and snapped flat, the stylus protruding from its socket at the bottom. Romaine slipped it out and began writing as he walked.

'Don't see too many of those in CUSETMA, sir,' Fisher ventured, joining him.

Romaine favored her with a smile. 'I've never understood the military's fascination with the qwerty keyboard. It's like the *chair*: convenient, sexy … and completely unnatural in terms of the body's posture. Mankind seized on both ideas as the greatest things ever invented and resisted any other ways of achieving the same result. Look. When I hold the stylus, my hand is naturally aligned with my arm, not twisted around to fit a keypad.'

He scrawled a couple more comments about the encampment and replaced the stylus. Another flick and the SCRoLL became flaccid again. He rolled it up and dropped it back in a pocket as they arrived at another lean-to on the camp fringe. Tuttut ducked inside and brought out a bow and a quiver of arrows.

'These are mine,' he told them via the translator.

The arrows were made from wood and appeared identical, precisely shaped by some process Romaine couldn't begin to speculate on. Tuttut drew one from the quiver and held it out for Romaine to inspect.

'It is well made.' The words passed into the Jarinyi language fine, but Tuttut didn't react. Romaine tried again. 'You must be a … fine … craftsman.'

This time the translator *tuttut*ted several times. Romaine decided to give up on flattery and turned his attention to the arrow. Not only was it well-fashioned, it was strong. One of these had been fired at Gutierrez from quite a distance – a hundred and fifty, two hundred meters – and had retained enough kick to punch clean through the man's throat. He wondered just how much force would be required to do that.

He handed the arrow back and gestured for the bow itself, which Tuttut still carried. The diminutive alien hesitated, glancing around him as if trying to avoid the subject, but he eventually complied. Romaine tested the tension on the bowstring. It was taut; he could certainly budge it but he couldn't control it if he pulled it further.

'Geez Louise! They actually fire these things?' He ignored the *random error* sounds from the translator and called Carswell over.

The older man came reluctantly, face cloaked in a blank stare.

'How strong do these guys have to be to fire these things?' Romaine asked.

Carswell dipped his head. 'Pretty strong. I've seen my friend here fire this bow without difficulty.'

'Really? He doesn't look ... brawny enough. I can barely move this string.'

'Well, first, that's not string, it's gut.' Carswell took the bow from him, allowing Romaine to wipe his hands on his trousers. 'Second, he's a lot tougher than he looks. And third, I'm not surprised you can't shift it. You're weak.'

'Excuse me?'

'Don't get all precious. I'm just saying that spacers don't get much opportunity to develop their muscles. There's no need for it up there. The muscles required for firing a bow are not the ones you use for writing reports and waving scanners around, are they?'

'I work out.'

'Obviously.'

'Is one of your doctorates in *Derisive Smart-ass-ness*?'

'No, I only managed a Masters in that.'

Romaine sighed and returned to the subject. 'So could a human use this weapon – a man who's not a weak spacer like me?'

Carswell snatched it from him, stepped over to Tuttut and took the arrow. He whirled around, nocked the arrow and aimed it at the tree-line. Tuttut's nostril-flaps flared. Carswell drew back and released the arrow but it flew less than a dozen meters, skidding along the dusty soil.

Tuttut began to warble something. The translator managed to inter-pret the words *'Friend, you are'* before Carswell waved him into silence and made a hand sign at him. Tuttut huffed, turned and stomped away, shrugging his shoulders agitatedly.

Carswell said, 'I've been here months and that's about the best I can do. Then again, I'm not a tough, buffed and augmented blackcap, am I?

Nope, not even a grunt, me. But if I can fire it that far, then Todd or one of his bigger cronies could manage a lot farther.'

Romaine ignored that comment and asked 'Why did you send your friend away?'

Carswell glanced after Tuttut. 'I didn't. He got annoyed with me using his bow without permission and left.'

'Call him back. I want to ask him something.'

'It won't do any good. He won't come for a while.'

'Ok, Doctor, I'm going to accept that a human *could* fire this, but I'd say it's a helluva lot easier for the locals to do it. So how do I find out if one of their bows is missing?'

'We'll ask the Elder. If he'll listen to us.' Carswell led Romaine in that direction.

'Ok, but I do all the talking.'

'Why?'

'I don't want you coloring his answers or leading him.'

If he was offended by the remark, Carswell didn't show it. 'Why would I do that?'

'Are you kidding me? You're not exactly objective here.'

'Ah. Objective. That's a good thing, is it?'

'It is if you want to get to the truth.'

'Oh, I'd love to hear your philosophical perspective on truth sometime, Romaine. I'm sure it involves lots of other words like *objective*.'

'You don't want me to be objective?'

'I'd like you to be circumspect. Informed. But the main reason I brought you here was so you could see how ridiculous the Marines' accusation is. I mean, if the Jarinyi meant us harm, if they'd killed one of us, why would they be so friendly and cooperative now?'

'Oh, many theories would answer that, and this is just off the top of my head. One, you told them to be friendly; you coached them in how to behave to avert suspicion. Two, these Jarinyi aren't the ones who killed Gutierrez. There are different tribes after all. Three, as Fisher pointed out to me earlier, it may be the work of a single Jarinyi, a rogue element.' Carswell's eyes flashed over at Fisher keeping pace to their left. 'Four, as you pointed out, there's a galaxy of difference between these people and me, so I can't even begin to interpret their behavior today as guilty or innocent.'

'This is their world. This is their territory. We've intruded but they've been extremely polite toward us. I brought you here to see how accepting and open they are. And I'd like you to cut them some slack. Actually, I'd like you to help me protect them. They need your help.'

Romaine recognized that the time had come; Carswell needed to be brick-walled. It was the moment that came often in investigations where stakeholder emotions ran hot. It was that moment when one side or the other would ask him to see it their way, to sympathize with their point-of-view.

It was time for The Speech.

'Dr Carswell, I am a Military Investigator. I don't work for you and I don't work for the Jarinyi. I work for the victim. My job is to find out exactly who murdered him and to prove it beyond reasonable doubt. I will follow due process. I will consider all the evidence. I will maintain my integrity as an Investigator. Please don't try to bend my opinion to serve your agenda. Just let me do my job.'

Carswell was quiet for a moment, considering Romaine's words. 'The Jarinyi called you Judge. I didn't hear you turn that title down. In some cultures, Romaine, a judge is not a person who arrogantly makes decisions about guilt and innocence, but someone who protects a people from injustice and physical threat. A judge stands in the way of the destruction of a people.'

'But to do that, they'd need to make a *decision* that someone's *guilty* of wanting to do the destroying.'

'Semantics.'

'Distraction. Let's talk to the Elder, shall we?'

Carswell remained close as they approached the knot of warriors softly warbling and snorting among themselves. He gestured for Romaine to hand over his translator.

'Elder, the Judge wants to speak with you. Would you like to speak with him?'

The Elder did not immediately look their way, but continued his conversation with Scarface and another warrior. Romaine opened his mouth to interrupt, but desisted when Carswell's hand gripped his arm.

After a full minute, the Elder turned their way. The third warrior in the group walked away while Scarface remained close to his chieftain. The two Jarinyi regarded the humans with those strange eyes, silent.

'Judge, you may speak now,' said Carswell in his sing-song tone.

'Elder, thank you for your time.' He noticed Carswell's eyeroll at that and suppressed a sigh. 'Have you lost a bow?'

The Elder's ears twitched. Other than that, he did not respond.

Carswell cleared his throat and adapted Romaine's question. 'Is there a warrior who can't find his bow?'

The Elder blinked and said, 'No.'

Romaine pursed his lips. *What now, Johnny?* He tried to stay within the boundaries of a simple vocabulary. 'Elder, the dead Man was killed by a bow. I need to know where it came from.'

The Elder's catlike pupils flickered toward Carswell, then he squatted and began tracing what seemed like random shapes in the dirt. Romaine too looked at Carswell who nodded at the translator. Romaine paused it.

'Did I say something wrong?'

'Not this time. He's thinking.'

'What about?' Romaine tried to follow Carswell's example and kept his tone modulated and pleasant.

'I don't know. I'm xenologist, not a psychic. They all do this at times, but the shapes don't seem to have any particular meaning. I assume they're doodling.'

The Elder continued drawing for several minutes. Scarface remained fully focused on the humans. Anxiety was starting to mushroom within Romaine, and there was an unfamiliar pressure behind his eyes. The urge to get the hell out of here was rallying again. Lunch gurgled within his gut as the muscles knotted there.

He murmured out the side of his mouth. 'We don't have all day. Can't you get him talking again?'

Carswell half-smiled. 'You may not have all day. He does. All right, all right, I'll see what I can do.'

He too squatted and looked closely at the figures in the dirt. Romaine half-hoped it was some form of writing, that perhaps Carswell would suddenly spring up with a 'By Jove, I think I've got it!' Only silence ensued and Romaine wondered how exactly Carswell was seeing what he could do.

Eventually, Carswell picked up a stick and tried to imitate the shapes the Elder was drawing. The Elder stopped, looked sharply at Carswell and shot to his feet, his small mouth opening and shutting like a fish. Romaine glimpsed small sharp teeth.

The Elder's nostril-flaps flared and emitted a short sharp sound.

Despite the clear translation of the word by Carswell's device, he slowly stood and repeated, 'That's their sound for *no*.' He twitched his shoulders at the Elder and added, 'We thank you for your help.'

The Elder rolled his own shoulders twice in rapid succession and stalked off into the trees, bounding effortlessly over a decaying log. Scarface was quiet a moment then wheeled around and followed him.

This is cooperation? What was that about?

Carswell read Romaine's thoughts on his face, blew out his breath in a mixture of frustration and resignation. 'This line of enquiry is a dead end, Romaine. You put him in a tough position. My opinion is he didn't want to admit that no bow is missing. He probably understood the implications of that; that you'd then suspect one of his people. I don't think the Jarinyi know how to lie. Actually, I don't think they even know there is such a thing as lying,' he added thoughtfully. 'So he doodled on the ground to stall. The stalling didn't work. He admitted they hadn't lost a bow, or had one stolen. He lost face and went for a walk to cool off. *Capice*?'

Romaine squinted into the trees. 'Mm. How would he know they've lost no bows? Couldn't he ask around to make sure?'

'He knows. He's their Elder. He knows everything that happens in the Tribe.'

'Well, if that's the case, I could have benefited from asking him some more questions.'

'Yeah, and you screwed that up for yourself by putting him in a tough position.'

Romaine rubbed his forehead tiredly at that, but remained quiet, still looking toward the trees.

Fisher took a step closer, spoke into the silence. 'I don't see how the Commander did anything wrong, Doctor. We can't know the effect our questions will have on Jarinyi. Perhaps there's someone else the Commander can question. That is, if you want to, sir,' she said to Romaine.

'Sure, I do. After I figure out what I can ask.'

He began a slow stroll around the campsite, studying the warriors in their conversation circles, watching Jarinyi children at play as they got under the feet of the women. Strangely enough, and despite the difficulties in communication, the scene began losing its foreignness.

After a while it occurred to him what he needed to see before leaving, and he conveyed it to Carswell.

The xenologist looked unhappily around the camp. After a moment, he waved his hand at the clusters of warriors. 'Take your pick. They've nothing better to do, apparently.'

They approached one group. Via the translator Romaine asked if one of them would demonstrate the bow. The tallest one stepped forward and took Tuttut's bow, which Carswell had been carrying until now. Fisher also handed over the arrow Carswell had tried to shoot.

The warrior searched the trees until he spied something high up. He made a comment over his shoulder at the other males. They click-clicked and touched each other's shoulders.

Romaine wondered if they were laughing.

For a second, the warrior's hands blurred, moving almost too fast to see. One moment he held the bow and the arrow in each hand, the next the arrow was up amongst the high tree branches. Fisher grunted. Romaine took a step back.

That was fast, dammit.

A grey shape the size of a Labrador plummeted from the tree and made a dull plop as it hit the ground. The whole group wandered over to look, as did some of the youths and the children. What had been a furry living *thing* was now a furry dead *thing*, its head mangled by the arrow that had skewered it.

'Purge me!' Romaine exclaimed. 'That shot had to be forty or fifty meters!'

Carswell's only comment was a sigh.

The warrior handed the bow back to the xenologist, cocked his head then grabbed the animal's hind leg and dragged it away. The crowd broke up. Carswell himself walked away toward Tuttut's hummock returning the bow to its home, his face clouded.

———

FISHER STEPPED CLOSE TO ROMAINE AND WIPED SWEAT FROM HER BROW. She still felt an adrenaline rush from the speed and accuracy of the warrior's bowmanship.

'That was basically shooting from the hip,' she said. 'Pretty impressive, sir.'

'Impressive, yeah.' Romaine still stared at the dead animal the tall warrior was now gutting. He fumbled with the translator until it turned off, dropping his voice. 'It's obvious they could easily have made the shot that killed Gutierrez. None of their bows are missing; they admit it even though it weighs against them. But at the same time...' He slid a hand across his hair and pointed surreptitiously at the warrior who'd made the shot. 'Here's this guy showing off for us, doing his absolute best, right? If these guys can make a headshot at fifty meters, with minimal aiming, and the arrow has enough force on it to pass clean through both sides of the skull even at that distance and angle, then why did Gutierrez's arrow *lodge* in his neck when it was fired on a level trajectory? With that much force, it should have passed clean through.'

'Good point, sir. Maybe it was a more difficult shot at Columbus. Through the wire and all. And it was possibly four times the distance.' He made a *maybe* face at her, not convinced. She added, 'So you think it was someone else?'

It couldn't have been a human, could it?

'At this point, I just don't know. If I was taking interviews back at camp, I'd probably be a lot closer to an answer than I am now.' He scratched awkwardly at his back and made a straining sound. 'And I don't know if these guys are smart enough to double bluff, frame the humans. Carswell says Jarinyi don't lie. If that's true, then creatures incapable of deceit wouldn't pull their punches, so to speak, wouldn't shoot an arrow into Gutierrez at half-power to make it look like a human being did it. Then again...'

He looked thoughtfully across at the youths across the clearing who glared back.

Her pulse accelerated slightly, as something else occurred to her. 'Perhaps someone smaller, you mean?' she asked.

'Yeah, maybe. It's a thought.'

'What about him?' She pointed across the clearing. 'The Doctor's little friend. You called him Tuttut.'

Romaine took a deep breath and let it out slow, his eyes narrowing at her in a way that made her feel affirmed and uncomfortable at the same time. As if he were truly noticing her for the first time, he said, 'Fisher, you have a very good brain.'

CARSWELL LOOKED UP FROM THE HUMMOCK TO SEE FISHER POINTING across the camp at his friend, the smaller Jarinyi. Romaine signaled agreement.

He scowled. *This damn spacer.*

He'd thought Romaine's arrival might be an opportunity; he hoped it was still true. Was this idiot going to be a help or hindrance? How was he going to get him up into the hills? One thing was certain. If Carswell didn't act decisively and quickly, things were only going to get worse.

6

'The CUSET Military Arm (CUSETMA) comprises the Naval Corps manning operations and maintenance of all vessels and space stations, a Marine Corps who are deployable in both ground and ship-to-ship engagements and a Military Investigation Office (see Military Investigation) staffed exclusively by Naval personnel.

'At the time of editing, CUSETMA's forces are presided over by Admiral Toshiro Nagaya. This military force was established with two aims: primarily to maintain the ability to respond to acts of aggression by either Chinese or unknown alien aggressors; secondarily to maintain order in the Colonies, WayStats (see Waypoint Space Stations) and mining colonies...

'Until now, the major role of the Marine Corps has been in quelling several separatist movements chiefly on Centauri. The Centauri Uprising (see Centauri Uprising) was largely quelled by the Marine Corps' six elite reconnaissance and special ops units (see Elite Marine Recon Unit) with minor support from armored vehicles and regulars. CUSET Marines also engaged with PRC troops (see PRC) briefly in the Shui Valley (see Battle of Shui Valley). During these engagements, CUSETMA's reliance on technological superiority and short response times has resulted in CUSET needing only small numbers of armed forces actually on the ground.

- from *Werber's Encyclopedia of Human Endeavor, January 2141*

IT WAS high summer and the sun set late. Shadows were long on the ground when the jeep pulled into the clearing. Sentries were preparing to activate the Gate as the jeep passed through, Fisher expertly dodging the knot of civilians drinking coffee just inside it. As they cut right toward the jeep bays, Romaine heard the civs use words like 'watchful eye' and 'timeline'.

He rubbed his eyes with the heels of his hands. His inner clock told him it was only afternoon shiptime, but it had been an eventful day. And he still felt a little nauseous, as if motion sick. He was looking forward to bed, though in reality his workday wasn't over if he was going to take this case seriously.

There was still a great deal of activity around Columbus. Craning his neck, he watched a Reaper dip below the buildings near the ferry pad. Two jeeps idled in the vacant space behind the Command Centre, a dozen researchers milling around while two grunts offloaded sealed containers onto trolleys. One of the researchers yelled at a Marine private to hurry up and received a torrent of abuse in return.

'That looks interesting,' he thought out loud.

Carswell had been napping. Now he opened one eye and followed Romaine's gaze. His scowl said he thought Romaine was talking about the containers, not the conflict. 'I bet I know what's in them too.' A moment later, the scientist pulled himself upright and vaulted out of the moving jeep to set off at a jog toward the activity.

Romaine presumed Carswell was going to further inflame whatever the situation was, and he wondered again about the intensity of Carswell's grievance before he lost sight of him.

Fisher parked the jeep in the motor pool and turned her custodial smile on him. 'How about dinner, sir?'

'Sounds good, Fisher. I bet they serve a terrific *soup-de-jour*. After that, I have some more questions for my friend here ...'

Yario scowled and mumbled something about toilets before lurching away.

'See you find me by 1900, Corporal!' Romaine called after him.

The scarecrow lifted a hand in acknowledgment without looking back. Romaine wondered if Yario was that casual with Glass. He'd been less than helpful during some light questioning on the return journey. Full of useless speculation and devoid of constructive information – apart from the mention of a lunchtime poker game the day of Gutierrez's murder. Gutierrez and Yario had been players at the table, along with three civs. And young Gutierrez had cleaned up.

That at least gave Romaine a loose thread to pull on.

Fisher was beside the jeep now, awaiting his lead. Despite his mild nausea, food did sound good. Maybe it would help. Then he remembered the samples. Food would have to wait.

'First, I better see Captain Ranarith re the test results on that sample I sent him.' He slid out of the jeep, leaning heavily on the side as the world tilted slightly.

Friggin' gravity.

RANARITH'S NOOK LAY IN THE OFFICE SEGMENT OF THE MEDCENTRE. IT reminded Romaine of a foxhole, with screens and instruments in place of earthen walls. Notebooks – both paper and electronic – were strewn about him like displaced soil. The surgeon was a small man with mahogany skin and river-pebble eyes. It took Romaine all of his manipulative skills to dig him out of his little research bunker. Even then the doctor fussed about the room, only half-listening. Noticing Romaine rubbing his temples got Ranarith's attention, but prompted him to waste more time by giving Romaine a thorough examination. The doctor's ministrations moved at a snail's pace. He refused to be distracted by questions about Gutierrez. Eventually, he slapped the desk beside Romaine and stared at him accusingly.

'I can't find much wrong with you. You said your head began to hurt as soon as you arrived? Sometimes headaches accompany the body's adapting to gravitational fluctuations – muscles under a different kind of stress than they have adapted to. More likely it's due to your eyes adjusting to the light spectrum; it's a little whiter than Earth Standard.'

'Yep. Even under the trees.'

'Well,' the doctor replied, 'the light does get there too, you know.'

Romaine dipped his head sheepishly then wiggled his shirt back on. 'So, I'm ok?'

'You drink too much.' The doctor snatched up the slim he'd used to record Romaine's vitals and tossed it into his nook where it sent others clattering to the floor. The short man indicated for Romaine to follow him across the narrow aisle to the mess he'd made. He sat to one side of the cramped alcove and waited until Romaine settled opposite him before touching a desk-screen. Facts and figures scrolled across it. 'You can copy my post-mortem report from here when you're ready. Regarding the samples the policewoman brought me ... We have DNA matches for three people.'

'Three? The area I sampled was no larger than twenty-five square centimeters.'

'But it's not far from the gates and there have been *two* expeditions here over the past months. If the skin samples got caught up in mud...'

'Still seems like a lot of people hanging out beside that tree.'

Ranarith fidgeted irritably. 'I'm just telling you what I found.'

'Alright, Doc. Ok. *Tell* me what you found. I'll figure the rest out.'

The doctor stroked his thinning hair the way someone might soothe an anxious pet. 'As I said, there is DNA for three people. One of the researchers who came here in the first expedition, Rowland Devlin. Also a Marine, Private Cooper. And Professor Carswell ...'

'*Carswell!*'

'Yes, Carswell.' Ranarith's hair-smoothing picked up tempo. 'And there is also Jarinyi DNA skin cells in the sample.'

Ah, crap. That I didn't want to hear. 'I guess it's not unusual they'd be hanging around their own jungle. Maybe I should be taking samples from the Tribe?'

Ranarith wobbled his head again. 'That would be conclusive. If you found the correct alien.'

Alien. Already after just hours with Carswell, the word sounded impolite. Wrong.

'Captain would you do me another favor and keep this to yourself?'

Ranarith's hands flew away from his hair and waved about violently. 'I can't do that! I work for Colonel Glass not for you! I'm not doing anything of the sort!'

'Ok, ok, calm down. It was just a request. You can tell the Colonel. I just don't want a bunch of heavily armed grunts blaming the Jarinyi and taking potshots at them whenever they appear.'

'They already blame the Jarinyi.'

Romaine stared into space for a time, while Ranarith expended nervous energy by tidying the workspace around them both. The discovery of the Jarniyi DNA made him feel an uncomfortable sadness. Today he'd finally met with members of another intelligent species, and cordially; tomorrow he might be asking them to hand over one of their own for sentencing. And if they actually complied, what kind of sentence would Glass carry out? The sentence for murder under CUSET colonial law was imprisonment or indentured labor. He tried to picture the diminutive Tuttut wearing outsized coveralls and firing up a laserdrill in an asteroid mine.

After a full minute, Ranarith cleared his throat. 'Commander, I have work to do. If that will be all?'

Romaine nodded, thanked him and watched him leave the office. He turned to the workstation and synced his SCRoLL to copy the results and the post-mortem report, then found the personnel directory with DNA files and copied them for later reference. Between his SCRoLL and his CHAD, he could do his own testing if need be.

His head swam again, partly with fatigue and partly with the information bobbing around in there.

Four people had left their mark on a crime scene. A Jarinyi. A researcher who'd already left. Cooper. Carswell.

Carswell was there? Did I just spend the day with a murderer?
Wouldn't be the first time, Johnny.

It was time to eat, he decided. *After* he took a look at Gutierrez's corpse.

———

THREE RESEARCHERS SAT AT ONE OF THE MESS TABLES, FACES ROMAINE recognized from the group arguing at the Gate earlier. The two Marines who'd been arguing with them slouched at another. Whatever that argument had been, it seemed resolved now. All of them stopped talking when Romaine stepped inside. The Marines stared, the researchers studied their drinks. It felt to Romaine like a saloon scene in a Wild West vid.

'Guess the blue uniform kinda stands out.' Romaine smiled politely at the Marines and they resumed their conversation without returning it. 'Well done, Fisher. So far, you're the only friendly human I've met on the planet.'

Fisher did not reply. From the foods on offer, she chose a pallid-looking meat and three kinds of steamed vegetables with a cream sauce. Romaine looked over the selection for a long time before deciding on the same as her. Joining her at the table, he felt the pressure of the *chweechee* in his belt as he sat. He slid it onto the table – truth be told, he felt happy to leave the polished stick there for someone to discard later. He poked at his food with a fork before sampling the meat.

'Chicken?' he guessed, chewing.

'Woo-woo. Freshest meat we have.'

He shrugged his eyebrows and swallowed. 'Not too bad.'

'Better than the chicken, sir. Trust me.'

'Hope it wasn't the one we found earlier. So, it's almost 1900. And no Yario so far.'

'He might be looking for you, sir.'

'Better be,' he said around a mouthful of woo-woo. He ate a while, thinking hard about the results Ranarith had given him. 'Fisher, do you know a Marine named Cooper?'

Fisher swallowed her broccoli before replying, 'Private Cooper? Yessir. He was on sentry duty when we were inspecting the crime scene today.'

So close and yet so far. 'How about a researcher named Devlin?'

'His name's familiar.' She frowned at her food for a moment. 'Oh, yes! He was part of the original expedition. But I heard he went missing, presumed dead, about a month before we arrived.'

'Any speculation about how or why?'

'All I heard was he went for a walk and never came back.'

'Right. Sounds like an idiot. Or maybe working with Carswell drove him to suicide.' Romaine pulled a piece of gristle from his mouth and lay it on the side of his plate. 'And Cooper. Why would he be wandering around in the scrub at our secondary crime scene?'

Fisher's eyebrows raised in query. 'Sir? Are you saying he was *there*? Where the weapon was fired?'

'Would you mind answering the question, Corporal?'

'Perhaps he was part of the patrols the morning after,' she mused.

'Find out for me. I want to see him tonight. Along with Lim and anyone else who was early on the scene.'

'The Colonel?'

'If he's free. And Yario, if he surfaces. Do we have a room we can conduct interviews in?'

'I secured a meeting room in one of the admin huts.'

'Excellent. Hope you're a night person, Fisher; we'll be up a while.' Romaine forked rubbery vegies into his mouth and slipped his SCRoLL out to bring up the post mortem report. He regarded the data dubiously. Could Ranarith's results be completely trusted? *Doubt everyone* was one of the maxims he lived by, along with *question everything* and *don't get emotionally involved.* No one was entirely trustworthy; they all had an agenda. Within minutes of his arriving, his investigation had been interfered with – chiefly by Glass and Carswell. Why Glass felt the urge to pressure him along the one line of enquiry was something he intended to find out; it could be that the CO was simply passing on his own pressure to stick to a CUSET deadline. Or it might be arrogance,

Glass honestly believing he already knew the truth. *Or* it might be something more nefarious.

'Let's look at post mortem results. What's new in the world of the dead?'

He angled it sideways so they both could read it, though Fisher seemed disinclined to look.

'Toxicology,' he read out loud as he skimmed through. 'Toxins associated with cigarette smoking, that's all. Signs he'd only been smoking for a short while, possibly a month or so. No other marks on the body except for two fading bruises, one on each shoulder. Mild spinal scoliosis. No infections. Arrow lacerated the jugular vein and nicked the carotid. Blood loss was profuse and rapid. He died quickly, or at least lost consciousness quickly. Hope that means he didn't suffer,' he added and meant it.

There had once been a belief that the victims of beheading could retain consciousness for up to seven seconds after the blade fell, experiencing a painful and horrifying purgatory. Romaine knew this to be a bunch of crap. The slashed jugular would have quickly drained blood from the brain and with it the young man's awareness, so that even the sensation of pain may not have had time to register before he blacked out.

He put more food in his mouth and spoke around it. 'No mention of spinal or spinal cord damage. His trachea was torn, the hyoid bone nicked but not fractured.' He chewed and swallowed, looked up at her. 'No surprises that the cause of death was consistent with the injury from the arrow.'

His last few words got lost in the clamor of Mess doors slamming open and four Marines in forest camouflage racing toward the serving bays. Romaine twisted in his seat to watch. All four were Sergeants and had black berets folded beneath their left epaulettes. The only woman was tall with the square shape of a bodybuilder, and she won the race to the food by yanking a whipcord-thin man back behind her at the last moment. He bounced off one of the others and cursed her loudly. Grinning, she spoke to him in Mandarin or Cantonese and took her time piling up her plate, thereby holding up the other three.

'Get on with it, Chua!' the tallest of the three males shouted good-naturedly, with a hint of Italian accent. He slapped the thin man on the back and Romaine could clearly see murder in the smaller man's eyes. This was a man who in the right circumstances would seriously injure you for a slight like that.

Ah, napoleon complex, entitlement and anger management issues in one skinny package. Hello, Person of Interest.

The Italian, by comparison, seemed unconcerned. 'Make sure you leave some for us,' he told the woman. 'Not like last night.'

The woman – Chua – waved her fork at him threateningly.

'Try it,' he growled affably.

She smirked and looked down at the mountainous serving on her plate. 'I guess that's enough ... for now.'

'Then get out of the way,' the Italian pleaded waving his empty plate at the tables.

Chua popped a piece of carrot into her mouth and sauntered away. Napoleon Complex dived upon the food and shoveled it onto his plate as if he hadn't eaten for a week.

Chua headed for the back corner, nodding to Fisher as she passed. 'Can't let these males get the drop on us, Corporal.'

'No, ma'am,' Fisher replied.

Romaine turned right way round in his seat, read the long tattoo on the woman's thick forearm as she passed. It mirrored what she'd just said: *The best man for the job is a woman.*

Sometimes, he agreed, that was true.

***

FISHER ONLY HALF-REGISTERED WHAT SERGEANT CHUA HAD SAID TO HER, eyes on the thin Marine over by the food. *Maglic*, she thought his name was. That one was trouble, him and the man-mountain they called Turk. Thankfully, Turk wasn't here. The problem with blackcaps units was that they attracted all sorts, from the honorable idealist to the career professional to the downright sociopathic.

On the night she'd announced she was joining the Marines, her town pastor had told her, 'In CUSET's opinion, skills are all that matter. Not morals, not faith, not character.'

That certainly seemed true of the selection of these elite soldiers.

As Maglic turned from the serving bay toward the tables, the doors opened again and red-haired Lieutenant Todd entered the room. Both men saw Romaine at the same time and exchanged glances. With his back to them now, Romaine didn't see it. She tensed slightly, anticipating trouble, shifting toward the edge of her seat a little. Todd gave a slight shake of his head and Maglic skulked away to the seat furthest from the doors. The Italian – a polite man whose name she'd forgotten – joined him.

Todd grabbed an apple from the counter and sauntered toward Fisher and Romaine's table, attempting a pleasant smile. Fisher had been in yesterday's staff meeting with him when they'd all been told to afford every courtesy to Romaine. So far, she'd found Todd anything but courteous, to civs, to her, to the other grunts. Only the CO and the other blackcaps enjoyed his good side. Even his polite smile came across snide, mocking. This was the first time she'd been able to work up close with an Investigator and she wondered if it was always like this for them: under-resourced, underappreciated, harried by strong personalities with their own agendas.

'Fisher, good evening. And Commander Romaine, you must be tired after your eventful trip to our indigenous friends.' He placed his apple on the table across the aisle from them. The fourth recon squeezed into the booth behind him and moved the apple so he could put his two plates of food down.

Todd plunged his hands deep into his pockets, standing beside and over Romaine, forcing the Investigator to twist awkwardly to maintain polite conversation. 'So, how'd it go?' the Lieutenant asked, eyes glittering with challenge.

Here we *go*, thought Fisher.

It was fascinating how reticent the Marines were to saluting him here, Romaine thought. The exception being Fisher. Todd scrutinized him, expression laced with malicious arrogance. His eyes flickered to the *chweechee* for a split second but he didn't comment on it. Short of stature, Todd obviously enjoyed looking down on two seated people. He had hair the color of rust and the kind of skin that would develop blotches under stress or excitement; it was beginning to now. Though he was trying to affect a casual mood around his men, his body language was keyed up.

'This is Lt Todd, sir,' Fisher said helpfully.

Romaine nodded hello. 'It was an interesting visit, Lieutenant.' Refusing to play the game, he untwisted himself, turned back to his dinner. 'Have you tried the woo-woo?'

'Tastes like chicken, as they say. So, I'm sure it was very interesting, but how'd it *go*?'

Romaine suppressed a sigh, smiled apologetically at Fisher. 'Fisher, would you mind changing tables? Perhaps the Lieutenant would be more comfortable sitting across from me.'

Fisher obliged. Todd hesitated long enough to indicate his annoyance, fetched his fruit from the other table and took Fisher's seat. The lieutenant's expression was strained, as if he never smiled for this long and the muscles weren't used to it.

Romaine leaned back, not hurrying his words. 'How'd it go? Well ... we learned some things. It was only a small part of the investigation and I have a lot more to do before I sleep tonight.'

Todd's smile evaporated midway through Romaine's comment. 'Part of the investigation? What else is there to investigate?'

'Lieutenant –'

'Just call me Todd. It's quicker.'

Quicker. Uh-huh.

'Ok. Todd –'

'And I'll call you Romaine. If that's ok with you. One less syllable than *Commander*.' The Marine across the aisle snickered. Fisher had taken the booth behind Todd facing Romaine and she tensed.

'Fine with me, but why do I feel like I'm being debriefed by a junior officer? Is there some reason you're in a hurry to get me out of here? Beyond your natural concern that a fellow Marine's death gets avenged? A sentiment I fully appreciate, by the way.'

'Gutierrez wasn't one of my men. He was a grunt. His death was tragic, but Marines die in battle. He died in battle.'

'What battle?'

Todd adopted the expression of a janitor discovering an unidentifiable carpet-stain. 'The battle for colonization. Whatever. The point is we have a mission here, the private died carrying out that mission, his death was noble, etcetera etcetera. Everyone else around here knows who did it and why. You're having trouble seeing it, but maybe that's because you're an outsider. We shoulda had Fisher or Ranarith sign off on the corpse, deliver a finding. Then we coulda gotten on with the job.' He shook his head. 'The Jarinyi are *primitive*. If I were them, I'd be pretty pissed at some weird alien incursion on my land. They killed our guy, it makes sense. What's the big deal?'

'So not a murder, but an act of war? That's a big deal in my book. I'd need to be pretty damn sure of myself before I signed off on *that* finding. Let's do this carefully and let's do it right, Todd. How's that sound?'

'Like the crappy spin of a policeman who doesn't like to be told how to do his job.'

Romaine regarded him for a moment, feeling the pressure build up at the base of his skull. He took a mouthful of food, chewing it slowly. It had lost all taste. His pulse accelerated. But his face didn't warm. He was proud of that fact.

It was Todd's turn to lean back in the booth, throwing an arm out to rest along the back. He adopted a look of mock sympathy. 'I think I know what the trouble is.'

'You do?' Romaine said around his food.

'Your thinking's all clogged up, distracted. And that's understandable.'

Romaine's instinct was to change tack and go on the offensive. He should have gone with it; instead he found himself asking, 'Why am I distracted?'

'The events of the past week or so. Catching a killer just minutes too late to save that girl. Must've been … harrowing.'

Romaine narrowed his eyes, feeling his blood pressure rise, his traitorous face flushing now.

Todd twisted toward Fisher for a moment. 'Terrible thing, Fisher. The Commander here took his time, followed his procedures, did things thoroughly – and a teenage girl got killed. Procedures took about an hour too long.' He faced Romaine, face a parody of sympathy. 'I'd be distracted for a few weeks if I'd walked in on the same butchery you did. Especially if I couldn't help feeling a little responsible for it.'

Romaine seethed, wondered how Todd knew so much about him. And why. Wondered how the little smartass would look with a tray wrapped around his head. Wondered if they had anything to drink around here.

'Makes me wonder, Fisher,' Todd continued, 'if the Commander can keep his mind on the job. This is all so fresh. Must be cutting him up inside.'

Romaine took a deep steadying breath and eased himself from the booth. He knew he was running, felt emasculated by it. He consoled himself that running was the better part of valor in this situation, but he didn't believe it. It was he who stood over Todd now, the air between them charged with something like the hum of an electrical field. He spoke through gritted teeth while picking up his *chweechee*.

'If you have anything relevant to contribute to *this* case, Todd, I'll be glad to hear it.'

'I'll look after that alien artefact for you, Commander,' Todd said, in what Romaine assumed was the man's preferred voice, his command tone.

His laugh in response came out a tad too loud and abrasive to sound confident. He turned, began walking toward the doors.

'You can't leave here with it anyway.'

'We'll see about that, *Lieutenant*.'

Fisher cleared her throat and Romaine stopped, executed a measured half-pirouette, turned his glare on her.

'Actually, sir, he's right. It would raise questions. Somewhere along the line you might make reference to Eventide or the Jarinyi. Plus, there's the quarantine issue –'

'And Eventide's classified, isn't it?' Romaine said, taking a step back toward them. To Todd, he said, 'What's so special about this place?'

Let's turn this back on you, see how you handle a little pressure yourself.

Was Todd, he wondered, the type to crouch patiently in the dark of an alien forest among the animal-crap and nightcrawlers, waiting for the perfect moment to launch an arrow?

He added, 'Why all this *need-to-know* crap?'

Todd's smile was smug. 'Do you need to know?'

'I might. Everything is relevant to a murder investigation.'

Todd lowered his volume even while his tone grew more intense. 'There is nothing to "investigate". The Jarinyi killed that grunt. All you need to do, *sir*, is give us the green light to smoke them. Then we can all sleep safely in our beds.'

Romaine squinted at him in horror.

Smoke them!

Them?

'Did you actually see a Jarinyi murder Private Gutierrez?'

Todd growled and lost all pretense of decorum. 'This is a job a preschooler could pull off. What the hell game are you playing? It's so hackin' simple. They did it!'

The Jarinyi called me a Judge. 'I guess I'll be the judge of that.' He squared his shoulders, gestured to the other blackcaps. 'I'll be interviewing these members of your team in the office the CO designated for me. Say around 2200 hours. Then you can set up interviews for me with the rest of them starting at 0900 tomorrow.'

Todd waited him out, his watery blue eyes turning icy. 'We have things to do. You want to waste your own time, fine, but don't waste ours.'

'I'm a Military Investigator, Lieutenant. I investigate the military. It's why I'm here. And you will cooperate.'

'No. We won't. We'll carry out the duties we have planned.'

'Then plan to have these four up late tonight, talking to me.'

'They'll be in bed, getting the rest they need to carry out their actual duties tomorrow.'

'Where were you leading up to midnight on February 4?'

Todd pretended to consider this, while the thin man made angry noises from his seat and was shushed by the bodybuilder woman. 'Let's see. That'd be the night that poor grunt passed away. I seem to recall I was having a manicure.'

'Cooperation or obstruction of justice. That's your choice. The easy way or the hard way.'

Todd took a bite of his apple and chomped noisily a few times with his mouth open. 'Let's make it the hard way, then.'

FISHER WATCHED COMMANDER ROMAINE LEAVE THE MESS WITH A sinking feeling. She stood, back stiff. Every eye around the Mess hall was on her now – even Todd, turning in his seat.

Well, she was used to that.

Eyes were always on her, no matter where she went. At home on furlough, people stared at her uniform as she cleared the spaceport, muttered resentful curses in her wake, fixated on the colors she wore, colors symbolizing oppression to them. Back on duty among her own military, she would enter a room and eyes would flick to her blue and grey MP armbands and turn cold. She could wipe the smile off a face just by showing up. *Military. Police.* Two words that guaranteed she was always persona non grata – alien – no matter where she went. Romaine was the only one of her kind within light years and she'd further isolated him too, with just a few words.

Why did I do that?

She gathered the fork, the knife, the bowl onto the tray, taking her time but feeling an almost psychic pressure from the staring faces around and behind her. Remaining composed herself, she carried her tray to the counter, went to leave. As she placed her hand on the door, Lieutenant Todd spoke her name.

'Fisher. Be careful near Romaine. Young women have a habit of dying around him.'

Fisher turned back, kept her face a steel mask as her gaze swept the room, meeting every eye. Maglic's eyes were hungry as he returned her stare; Chua's scowled at Todd's back. Only when everyone but Maglic had looked away did she push the door open. In her own good time, she stepped out into the cooling evening air.

7

'The right to swing my fist ends where the other man's nose begins.'

- Oliver Wendell Holmes

AN HOUR AFTER SUNSET, the Eventide sky sparkled with vivid arrangements of stars, a diamond inlay set in blue-black velvet, only partially obscured by cloud and light pollution from the compound. Standing in the splash of shadow between the Mess and the amenities block, Romaine contemplated a patch of forest beyond the fence. Some leaves high in their trees appeared to be filled with tiny lanterns that mimicked the array of stars directly above. It was probably coincidence; Romaine found it creepy.

He discovered he was grinding teeth. Images of inflicting pain on Todd popped into his head like fireworks. He forced his jaw to rest, the images to stop. If he didn't get a grip here, he was going to screw something up.

I really need a vacation.

'A type of firefly, sir,' Fisher murmured from behind him.

He had heard her approach, had caught her cologne – that slightly masculine scent she wore. Weirdly, Harshini had liked that one too, though Romaine couldn't for the life of him remember its name.

Fisher pointed to the lights in the trees. 'Someone told me it's their mating season.'

Romaine could hear the note of apology in her voice and felt perversely satisfied by it. She had undermined him. In his world, cops stuck together. It was code. More often than not, all they had was each other. But he wasn't in his world at the moment. There were no friends here, only witnesses. And at least one murderer. He wedged the *chweechee* firmly into the back of his belt and stepped out of the shadows into the camp lights.

'Supply Hut?' he said.

She gestured and led the way. He could feel the consternation coming off her like radiant heat. At that moment, he had no interest in making her feel better. When she opened her mouth to speak again – this time he could tell it would be a full-blown apology – he interrupted, pointing out and over the buildings between them and the Gate, bringing them back to business.

'So, Cooper was patrolling out there? Where the shooter was.'

She skipped a beat before responding. 'It's not that unusual, sir. There were a lot of patrols out the morning after the death. Actually, we checked the area thoroughly when we first arrived and I think the Colonel makes them do regular sweeps through the forest. Just outside the perimeter. But they always do it in pairs. Was there another Marine's DNA there also?'

'No. Just Cooper's. I want that chat with him. Tonight. And with Lim, with Yario, and his three poker buddies. And anyone who was already at the scene when you arrived.'

'Yessir. Now, sir?'

'Right after I've been to Supply. We've lost enough time on this as is. And before you hit the sack tonight, see if you can find out if Cooper was out at the secondary scene on Glass' orders.'

'Yessir. I'll check with the Colonel. You want me to stay with you at Supply?'

'I'm a big boy, Fisher.'

Her continued uneasiness showed in the glare of a nearby light and he relented, took his temper down a notch. Yes, she'd undermined him in front of Todd. But it was poor timing, nothing more. She was young, anxious to abide by procedure. Besides, he needed her, at least until he could get out of this sewage pit.

He revised his tone, making it lighter. 'You said the Quartermaster knew the vic previously? What's his or her name?'

'Menabu, Tristan. Male, sir.'

Kinda figured that from the name. He caught the sarcasm before it could leak out of his mouth.

'Well, it'll be better if I go in alone and see *Menabu Tristan* about some gear. I can play the part of the off-duty newbie. We'll see how that works tonight – tomorrow we'll put the thumbscrews on him if we need to. You rouse up my interviewees, send them over to our makeshift interview room, then come pick me up at Supply again. Be quick.'

She pointed. 'That's Supply there, sir. Door's around the corner.'

He nodded. 'Go get me someone to interrogate.' His voice grew quiet. 'And Fisher, don't fret about what happened at the Mess. I'm pissed at Todd and ... and my boss. Not at you.'

She puffed out one cheek, looked awkward. 'And the *chweechee*, sir?'

'I'll hang on to it for the moment.'

As she turned to go, he could tell she had no idea why he'd want it. In truth, neither did he. Perhaps he was just tired of being told what to do.

———

Visiting the Quartermaster was partly for the reason of interviewing him and partly because Romaine didn't want to spend another day wearing a sky-blue uniform with non-matching green-brown hat. His Commander's bars would attach just as easily to Marine camouflage as they did to Navy blues.

He could hear raised voices before he reached the door – no, he amended: a single raised voice, the unmistakable sound of senior rank bawling out junior rank. It was no surprise that the bawler was Colonel Glass. The hapless Quartermaster – a Marine regular –was hanging his head with a stricken expression. Romaine cleared his throat as he climbed the three steps, turning his body to hide the *chweechee* from Glass.

Glass neatly switched gears, smiling warmly, now the gentleman host. 'Ah, Commander. Here to pick up some things? *Mi casa, su casa.* How'd it go today, by the way?'

Romaine was relieved to see that the man didn't really seem interested in an answer. He certainly didn't radiate Todd's intense curiosity. Menabu wore a hang-dog expression, clearly embarrassed the newcomer had walked in on a dressing-down.

'It was so so,' he told Glass. 'At least I got my money's worth on that trip. Fascinating species, fascinating people.'

Glass chuckled. 'Yeah, they make for an entertaining Freak Show, don't they?' He moved to the doorway, fished a cigar from his breast pocket, clamped it between his lips while searching other pockets for his lighter. Romaine moved out of his trajectory. 'Well, I'll leave you to it. We'll talk more tomorrow.' Finding an ancient-looking bic, he lit up and inhaled slowly in a reverse sigh. Blowing smoke, he told Menabu, 'Give the Commander whatever he needs. Just make sure you keep a record of it this time, son.'

Glass plunged out into the night, a speedboat launching suddenly, all focus and thrust. The hapless Quartermaster seemed to bob in his wake, caught in the emotional wash of his earlier humiliation. His gaze scoured the floor, as if he'd dropped a ten-dollar coin.

Romaine stepped past him to the counter, giving the poor bugger a moment to collect himself. He leaned both palms on the fake wooden bench and faced the rows of fixtures beyond. 'Looks like a great place to shop.'

The lanky Quartermaster wandered back around the counter and picked up a notepad without making eye contact. 'What do you need, sir?'

'Sergeant, I need whatever it takes to make me smell clean-yet-manly. And makes me feel like I haven't spent a day swimming through humidity, alien pollen and dirt. In fact, what do you have that can make me feel like I'm back up there in space?'

The man smiled experimentally. 'Unfortunately, we don't stock what I'd recommend, sir.'

Romaine chuckled at the joke, hoping it *was* a joke and he wouldn't have to brig Menabu for drug possession. 'Actually, a good cold beer wouldn't go astray right now. Seems like you could use one too, huh?'

'Would not say no, sir.'

Romaine nodded toward the empty doorway, dropped his voice. 'What's his problem? Does he give everyone a hard time like that?'

'Wouldn't know. This deployment is the first time I've met him.'

'Come on, Sergeant. You meet a CO, you work with him for a week, you know the man. He's a mean bastard, right?'

'No, he was right. I screwed up.' Abruptly, he became a human windmill, all arms and hands. 'I don't know how the hell I did it! I've never lost anything before!' He turned full circle, swearing, a vein bulging in his temple.

Romaine asked him about it, keeping his tone neighborly.

'Mon, you'll probably lock me up if I tell you.'

'Buddy, I'm not investigating you. And it sounds like the CO is doing plenty enough on the punishment front.'

The Quartermaster nodded vigorously. 'He will if I don't find 'em. Oh, yeah. He'll take it outa my pay! I'll be workin' it off until I'm a hundred and twenty, mon!'

'Sergeant, I don't care what you did. My opinion? Glass is an asshole. You're obviously not stupid, let alone any of the other things I heard him calling you as I came in. It's not like you fired a weapon off in the Mess or crashed a Reaper. So you lost something: big deal.' The man now regarded him more openly, nodding slightly. 'Anyway. My name's Romaine.' He held out a hand, hoping it wouldn't be rebuffed a third time in one day.

To his relief the man shook it firmly. 'Menabu,' he said, relaxing as if a contract had just been settled. 'But call me Tristan, mon.'

'Then I'm John. So, Tristan, I need some stuff: soap, shampoo, a couple bottles of mineral water if you have them.'

'I'm on it, mon. I'll get you CUSET's finest goods. Easy-peasy.' Menabu made himself busy, moving unhesitatingly to the correct shelves. As he cheered up, he began to chatter. 'The showers here are pretty good for a frontier operation, mon. Best I ever had, actually, better than home. The boss, he's obsessed with hygiene. You usually work in space, mon? You must hate this place. It's like Mud City.'

'I work *completely* in space. I like space. The air's good, the pay's good, the food's good.'

'Mm. Maybe I should transfer to Navy.' Menabu dumped some items on the counter and turned serious. 'So, you're here to find Emmanuel's killer?'

Emmanuel? Gutierrez. Had they been friends before they got here? Or was Menabu on first name terms with everyone?

I wonder what Fisher's first name is?

He put on a bad Texan accent, recalling the Westerns he'd loved as a boy. 'Well, pardner, I'm like the US Marshall come to chase down the villain and make everyone feel safe again.' He touched the items on the counter. 'So what was Emmanuel like?'

He asked it lightly, eyes on a tube of toothpaste. Asking questions could destroy the rapport as quickly as he'd built it, polarizing them again.

'He was a good guy. Not the sharpest tool in the toolbox, but most grunts aren't. We wouldn't be working for the Marines if we were, huh? But he sure didn't deserve what happened. Was gettin' married next year, soon as his tenure was up. Lemme just get you that water.'

When Menabu returned, Romaine changed tack. 'Everything seems pretty spick and span here, bud. What went missing?'

Menabu scowled and slapped the counter. 'Rifles! AR90s. How could I lose AR90s?'

'Got any thoughts?'

Menabu chewed on the question for a moment. 'I think it's just an inventory discrepancy. Honestly. I think the supplier sent us an empty crate. Not that Colonel Glass agrees.' Suddenly concerned, Menabu rubbed sweat out of narrowing eyes. 'Sure you're not gonna get me in trouble for this, mon?'

Romaine laughed the suggestion off as if they were talking about the most trivial of matters. *Just a couple of guys shooting the breeze.* He twisted the lid off a mineral water, took a long swallow. 'Maybe I can help you figure it out though. AR90s come in boxes of three?'

'Indeed they do, mon. Three rifles, six charge-clips. Easy to carry, easy to pack.' He jerked a thumb over his head at something Romaine couldn't see. 'And that crate is empty.'

Romaine wondered whether he should offer to fingerprint it. It was risky, playing up his cop-status, but he was offering it to help Menabu. Unless Menabu had done something with the rifles. For the moment, he dropped the idea.

'Can people get in or out of here without you seeing them? Anyone else work with you? You leave the door open when you go take a leak?' Menabu was shaking his head to each question. 'You have cams?'

'No. No security. Just a hut with shelves. Very twenty-second century, huh?'

Actually, Romaine thought, *it is*. The modern human universe was a bizarre and contradictory mix of high tech, low tech and no tech. Along with abject stupidity. He was constantly amazed at where CUSET spent their money, and where they didn't.

'Why'd the CO come looking for extra rifles? Surely each Marine already has their own weapon.'

Menabu shrugged a shoulder. 'Not all of us. He started by saying he wanted some of us – like me, the cook, the pilots – to have one in their quarters in case there's more trouble. I don't want one, mon. I don't like shooting. That's why I work supplies.'

Romaine spun the toothpaste tube around, thinking.

Menabu lifted the crate and shook it. 'I mean, how could I lose them outa the container unless someone took 'em? And who'd want AR90s here when they've already got their own?'

'Well, not everyone has one. You just said that.'

The Quartermaster looked blank.

Romaine said, 'I'm certain it's an inventory mistake as you say. One stolen rifle I could understand, but not three. Where would someone hide them? Why would they need three?'

Menabu looked relieved to have an ally, to have corroboration. But Romaine had a niggling doubt. It could be a shipping error. It could be another one of the typical screw-ups that came from the twenty-three different corporations all trying to manage the same gargantuan inter-stellar project. It could be something as simple as that. But it smelled *wrong*. There was a thread here, one he was sure would cross another at some stage soon.

He filed the matter away mentally and clicked his fingers. 'Just remembered. I'd like a complete change of costume for tomorrow. Do you have some plain fatigues I can use?'

Menabu scratched his head. 'You'd be an XL? Only got forest camouflage in your size. The same as the rest of us regulars.'

Except Fisher. She wore plain green with her MP bands around each arm. 'As long as it fits.'

Menabu went looking and called back, 'Just one set? I can give you two?'

'One will be fine. I think I'll be done tomorrow. I want to nail Emmanuel's killer fast.' He sipped from his water. 'So. Had he pissed anyone off recently?'

'Manny? He was a teddy bear,' Menabu grumbled, returning to the counter with Romaine's new clothes. 'Mon, I can't think of a single person who'd want him dead. It was those indigs. Had to be. You went out there today? That stick thing you got there looks like something they'd use. Is that evidence?'

He touched the *chweechee* still poking out the back of his trousers. 'I have to cover all bases, Tristan, look at the crime from all angles. Did Emmanuel ever visit the Jarinyi as far as you know?'

'Beats me, mon. Most of the time he was here.' His eyes narrowed in memory. 'He did go out on a Reaper once.'

'Where to?'

'We aren't allowed to discuss specifics like that.' He looked thoughtful again. 'You know, I think he went out more than once. I remember a couple of nights before he died. He was sitting in the Mess looking sick, mon. Like he'd eaten bad shellfish, you know? Wouldn't tell me what was wrong. I thought maybe his fiancé called off the wedding. I asked him about that and he said, no it was cool. So, maybe something happened? Out there? You think maybe they got into a firefight with some indigs and he got killed as a revenge killing?'

'Beats me,' Romaine sighed, waving away the speculation. 'By the way, how does a guy get a drink around here? I was serious about that beer.'

Menabu looked sad. 'Dry camp, sir. No fun here.'

'Are you just saying that because I'm a cop and you don't wanna get in trouble? 'Cause I'm only asking as a guy. I could sure do with a cold one, Tristan.'

'Nothing to be had, mon.'

'C'mon. I'm sure a resourceful Quartermaster like yourself ...'

Menabu held up his hands and exaggerated his forlorn expression. Romaine sighed. The hipflask was all he'd brought with him. Almost nothing.

Have to ration it, Johnny, he told himself glumly.

He lifted his pile of supplies. 'Thanks for the goodies.'

'No worries, mon. Thanks for the pep talk.' Menabu threw him a friendly salute and reached for his keycard. 'Time for me to go chill.'

ROMAINE'S INTERVIEWS WERE WORSE THAN USELESS.

Cooper was hardly a suspicious character, though one shouldn't dismiss suspects on the strength of a colorless personality. A young man with little expression and a small vocabulary that included a lot of cussing.

Yario and the other poker players elicited no useful information: their staff files' financial records indicated their games were casual, with small stakes. One of them invited Romaine to tomorrow's game, smelling the owner of a bigger pay packet. He declined.

While waiting for Fisher to track down Lim, he went through Gutierrez's staff file. The tone of the elementary school writing in his outgoing personal messages was terse. Other than that, the man was as dull as the other grunts.

Lim arrived and gave a recount of discovering 'Manny's death body' that was full of poor standard English and heartfelt emotion. Romaine wasn't sure if the man's snuffling was from his cold or from sadness. Lim hadn't seen or heard anything outside the Camp. He'd swept his weapon about hoping for an AIRTAR contact, but it hadn't acquired.

At five minutes to midnight, Romaine tapped his SCRoLL to stop recording and released Lim. Fisher informed him that the CO would see him in the morning. He would talk over Romaine's needs then, she told him.

He leaned on the table in the small room and rubbed at weary eyes, then drained the last of his mineral water.

'Goodnight, Fisher,' he said simply. 'I'll see you at breakfast.'

She left, looking as tired as he felt.

He slouched in his chair for a few minutes, staring at a blank wall. The day was a total waste. Sure, he'd met aliens. That was kinda cool. T*he problem is*, he told that tiny boyish voice inside him, the one that wanted to be the aliens' friend, *if I don't find some proof to the contrary, the finger of blame is going to stop pointing at them and start pulling triggers.*

NEXT CAME A TRIP TO THE AMENITIES BLOCK. MENABU HAD BEEN RIGHT: the showers were fantastic. Although they were on a four-minute timer, the water pressure was better than he'd enjoyed in years, the hot water scouring both real and imaginary crap from his skin.

Maybe I shoulda joined the Marines.

When the timer ran out on the first shower, he took another.

HE TROD WEARILY BACK TO HIS ASSIGNED PREFAB HUT, *SANS* SHIRT, FRESH trousers pulled on over not quite dry legs. Though he knew it was still humid, the night air felt chilly after the heat of the shower, refreshing.

His room was one of three in the prefab. Fisher had told him hers was at the other end of the short corridor and he assumed the reggae music coming from the middle room belonged to Menabu — though it may have belonged to anyone, really. When he opened his door, he was sure they had assigned him a closet. It was actually smaller than the cabin on the transport ship orbiting above. He made a face and closed the door behind him.

I'm only using it for sleep anyway.

He slumped onto a bone-firm mattress and put his hands to his face. His cheeks were sandpaper. He considered pulling his Plazer pocket laser from his kit. *The only way to shave*, they advertised and he agreed, remembering his bloody experiences with the blade his father had given him. It was nearly twenty-five years since they'd parted company. He'd stuck with lasers ever since.

Shaving could wait until tomorrow.

He pushed his kitbag under the bed. Inside it, two vessels clacked together. The hipflask and a medicine bottle. Malt whisky and pills.

The booze was so cliché for cops that it was almost standard issue. The only cop he'd ever known who *hadn't* drank too much was Harshini. And a much younger John Romaine before Harshini got –

He snatched back control of his thoughts, focused on the unseen bottles. The pills he'd appropriated from the evidence locker on Drop-in-the-Ocean. They were contraband from the whacked-out *inchatters* who worked there, their bodies so unsettled by tampering with their own brains, they needed chemical assistance to regulate sleep, appetite, defecation. Those three pills represented three nights solid and dreamless sleep. He considered finding an incinerator chute, dropping them inside. That would be smart.

But dammit, if he couldn't get rid of the nightmares soon, he'd have to use one of them. And he only had three; not like it was enough to become dependent.

A couple of minutes on the hard bed made him wonder if sleep would be possible. That and the prospect of the dreams. He needed to sleep, but didn't want to. He thought about the pills, and put them off for one more night, was about to go digging for the hipflask but decided to prove to himself that he wasn't an alcoholic. He battled himself over it for a full five minutes, obsessing and hating the obsession.

He thumped at his bed with the flat of his hand.

I'm not a souse I don't need it just want it just need a good night's sleep –

He fidgeted with his SCRoLL, intending to review his notes and recordings, the personnel files. Nothing sank in. Nothing made sense. Nothing leapt out at him with the full force of epiphany or even the polite tap on the shoulder of the mildly interesting.

A faltering of his eyelids told him that he could finally attempt some shuteye.

He placed his notebook on the floor by the bed and turned onto his side. For a moment, he considered the *chweechee* lying by the door. Why give him that, of all things? Was it traditional to present gifts, a custom? Were they mimicking human attempts at trade? Were they trying to tell him something?

It was no good following that last line of enquiry. The only person who could help him figure out meaning was Carswell and he didn't trust him as far as he could throw a *chweechee*. Which probably wasn't far.

He turned his mind back to sleep.

'Lights down.'

The two thumb-sized globes remained alight.

He cleared his throat, tried it again. The lights obstinately refused to obey.

Must be an older system.

He clapped his hands.

No response.

Romaine groaned.

FISHER HAD FALLEN ASLEEP DURING HER EVENING PRAYERS. SHE WAS roused by a soft knock at her door. She lay still, wondering if she had dreamed the sound.

When it came again, a polite staccato out of time with Menabu's music next door, she called out, 'Who is it?'

Her diary slipped from the bed to thump onto the floor, spilling a few sheets of precious paper.

Romaine identified himself, sounding sheepish.

'Are you alright, Commander?' She didn't make a move toward the door. She could hear him perfectly well through it.

'My lights,' he said, and there was no mistaking the embarrassment in his voice now. 'How do I … ?'

She smiled to herself.

Spacer. 'There's a switch.'

'A switch?'

'Near the door.'

'How quaint. I'll see you in the morning. I set my alarm for 0600. Meet you in the Mess at 0630?'

'Yes, sir.'

'Good night, Corporal.'

'Good night sir.'

HE DREAMED AGAIN.

A girl – or was she already on the woman side of puberty? – walked ahead of him down a grey-walled corridor, then skipped, then somehow glided as if on skates. He ran behind her, shouting for her to stop. His words made no sound and his feet found no purchase on the carpeted floor. With long curls swirling about her, she stepped into the airlock and a dark figure appeared behind her like smoke, closing the door then vanishing into a wall.

Without memory of movement, Romaine was at the door. He clawed at it, shouting silently all the time. And abruptly it did open. And as his eyes panned down to the floor –

He awoke sweating, moisture in his eyes. He blinked them clear, rolled on to his side and tried to slow his heartbeat as he waited for sleep to return to him.

Eventually, he got up and rummaged through his kit for the whisky.

PART II

FIVEDAY

'Only two things are infinite.
The universe and human stupidity.
And I'm not sure about the former.'
- Albert Einstein

8

———————

'Technology is making gestures precise and brutal, and with them
men.'

\- Theodor Adorno

ROMAINE WAS WOKEN by a gentle rapping at his door. It took him a moment to orient himself. The room was washed in pale light from an opaque skylight above him. He was sweating, the air clammy.

More rapping and his voice came out like he was gargling gravel. 'Yeah?'

'It's 0636, sir,' came Fisher's muffled voice.

He sat up and coughed his throat clear. His mouth was so dry it was hard to swallow. The room swam.

Weird. Wasn't that much in the flask.

It took a few seconds to focus on his seiko and confirm the time. 'I'm sorry, Fisher. I didn't hear my alarm. Be with you in twenty.'

The floor bounced a little as Fisher's footsteps moved away.

Standing made his head spin. He slumped onto the bed. Maybe it was Eventide's oxygen levels. Maybe it was that difference in gravity. Maybe it was the week of sleep deprivation.

And maybe I don't want to face the day I give the Marines carte blanche to retaliate against the Jarinyi.

He simply didn't want to move. It took a few deep breaths to chase away his malaise.

Body, you are going to do what I tell you and not vice versa, he thought. *Forty push-ups should do it.*

He got to eight.

———

As he entered the amenities block for a morning shower, he passed Menabu coming out.

'Greetings and salutations, Commander. Fine morning, is it not?'

Romaine blinked at him. 'You certainly seem happier than last night.'

'Well, mon–' he leaned in close as if sharing a secret '–me mama used to say, "Boy, don't let yesterday's glum take the shine off today's fun.'

'Wise lady,' Romaine replied, wondering what kinds of fun Menabu could expect in a hellhole like this. 'Well, time for me to wash off some of yesterday's glum. Does it ever cool down around here?'

'Pretty much never, sir. Enjoy the shower. Oh, and Commander,' he added as Romaine began to step inside. 'Thank you for helpin' me get ma head straight last night. Mama woulda liked you.'

———

Breakfast looked more promising than dinner had been. Coffee, toast, an egg and real fruit. He was munching on a pear when he reached the table. Sitting across from Fisher, he tried to ignore the stares targeting him from around the crowded room.

'They can't do juice right but ... this is good fruit.'

'That's Centauran, I think, sir.'

'Nothing's too good for the heroes of the human empire.' This was from Carswell, seated across the aisle. Romaine found it hard to believe he hadn't noticed him. Maybe it was the fact that the xenologist had actually showered and trimmed back his beard.

Romaine tried to start the day off amiably. 'And how are you this morning, Doctor?'

Carswell just grunted and shoveled more oatmeal into his mouth.

Romaine sighed and turned back to his own food. He ate in silence for a while, savoring the pear before cracking open the boiled egg. It was disappointing after the fruit, the kind of mass-produced egg available out on space stations and mining colonies. He had once seen the 'chickens' that produced these eggs – if the grizzled lumps of flesh squeezed into life-support compartments and fed by drips could be called chickens. The sight had made his skin crawl and he had determined never again to ask where his food came from.

He broke his own rule all the time.

Carswell spoke twice more during the meal.

Once was to admonish Romaine for not sticking with his original blue uniform. Romaine replied, 'When in Rome.'

The second time was to mention he had something important to discuss privately. Romaine made a noncommittal noise. Carswell obviously hadn't listened to The Speech yesterday.

Meantime, Fisher sat patiently, studying her coffee mug. Occasionally she consulted her watch. Eventually she took the measured breath that Romaine had come to know meant she wasn't sure whether or not to speak her mind.

'Permission granted, Corporal.'

She blinked, then adopted a quizzical half-smile. He loved reading people's minds.

'Sir, I wanted to let you eat in peace. But Colonel Glass has asked you to join him in his office in five minutes' time. 0730,' she added unnecessarily as he consulted his seiko.

'No peace for the wicked. You'll have to show me the way.' He stuffed a final hunk of toast into his mouth, chewed, swallowed, rinsed his teeth with coffee. Standing, he clapped a hand on Carswell's shoulder. 'Would you mind waiting here, Doctor? I wanna talk to *you* about something. Back soon.'

'Soon? Don't bet on it.' The xenologist drew a second tray of food toward him.

'He may despise human civilization,' Romaine told Fisher as they left the building, 'but he sure likes the food.'

VIEWED FROM THE OUTSIDE, GLASS'S OFFICE APPEARED LITTLE MORE than a square box. The outer door whisked open to reveal an anteroom hardly bigger than Romaine's quarters. Fisher waited outside. Romaine was greeted by the Colonel's adjutant. The whippet-thin man nudged a pump-bottle of hand sanitizer toward him.

'If you wouldn't mind, sir.'

Romaine applied it and rubbed it in until the aide nodded approvingly and leaned over his intercom.

'Commander Romaine to see you, sir.'

'Well, let him in.'

Romaine next found himself in a slightly larger room entirely devoid of unnecessary detail or decoration. One desk, one chair, one coffee cup, one window and one Colonel.

Glass owned a SCRoLL too apparently. He pushed it aside to give Romaine his full attention. 'I like a man who's punctual, Commander. Early's even better. I'd offer you a seat but there aren't any.'

Romaine forced a chuckle. 'That's okay, Colonel.'

'How's the investigation coming?'

'...It's coming. I'm yet to interview the blackcaps, but I spoke with Lim and Cooper and –'

'What for?'

Romaine was wrong-footed by the interruption. He let his own words come out slowly and deliberately. 'Lim seems to be the Marine who most often teamed up with Gutierrez. I thought maybe he could give me some ideas of the victim's movements before the crime. And Cooper ...'

Glass shook his head, pointedly turning his chair to stare out his small window. 'You see that out there, Romaine? That's a new planet, a new world. Newer than Xerxes. We're not in Bonn or Tokyo. Not on Theseus. Not on some mining asteroid. Gutierrez's movements before the "crime" are irrelevant. He was hit by a Jarinyi arrow on the Jarinyi planet within spitting distance of a Jarinyi settlement. In my experience, things are usually what they are.' He looked sideways at Romaine as if he should be impressed by the incontestable wisdom of this last statement.

Romaine thought it sounded stupid.

He also knew what Glass was trying to do. *You're not pushing me into making the wrong conclusion.* 'The time spent with the Jarinyi gave me pause,' he said. 'I agree with you that this is not a run of the mill case. It requires a lot more delicate –'

Glass raised one hand and Romaine was annoyed with himself for stopping, for complying with such an arrogant gesture.

'Commander Romaine, we did the right thing in this situation. We called for an Investigator even though it would take two days to get one here. Even though it's an open-and-shut case. Our situation is made untenable by further delay. Even now, Ranarith has better things to do with his time than examining tissue samples for you. Fisher could be better used elsewhere even if it's lugging cases around. I expect you to wrap this up quickly and efficiently. So we can get on with our *work.*'

Romaine sighed. It was time for The Speech.

'Colonel Glass, I am a Military Investigator…'

Again, the CO raised his hand to shut him down. This time Romaine pressed on, only stopping when the color began rising in Glass's face. It wasn't a good idea to cross a guy like this on his own turf.

There followed a long uncomfortable silence. The CO's breath whistled faintly in his nose as he returned his gaze to the window. Romaine shifted his weight around on his feet, wishing Fisher had given him more notice of this appointment. Maybe he could have found a way to avoid it.

Glass jerked his chin at the activity outside the flexiplast window.

'Commander, you seem to feel you need to know more about the situation than I originally considered pertinent. I myself would have thought that a Jarinyi arrow fired through this Marine's neck was – as I said – open-and-shut. Nothing to it. But as you pointed out, you're the Military Investigator and I am just a lowly field commander.'

'Colonel, I never meant...'

'I'm guessing that – on top of circumstantial evidence – you Investigator types concern yourselves with *motive*.' He leaned forward and rested his hand above the intercom controls. 'I'll give you motive.' He touched the controls, said: 'Send Lieutenant Todd in.'

A moment later the recon officer stepped into the office.

When did he arrive?

'Good morning, sirs.' Todd was all politeness, without a hint of the previous night's animosity.

'Morning, Sean. You're off to the Pumpkin Patch now?'

Todd glanced at Romaine and replied uncertainly, 'Yessir.'

'Take the Commander with you. Time he understood our operation.'

'Sir, do you think that's wise?'

'*Lieutenant*,' Glass responded in a voice that would freeze lava. And Todd did indeed freeze. 'We need to fulfil all righteousness, as it were. The good Commander can't hand down a sensible verdict without understanding the Jarinyi's motives, the reasons for their animosity toward us. Without Commander Romaine's well-reasoned verdict, any forcible action we take to secure the Tigerclaw would not be credibly and legally defensible in the future. Have I not already pointed out to you that if word gets out – and it always does – that we took steps to use unnecessary force against an indigenous people, to acquire their resources without reasonable effort toward fair reimbursement, it would inflame tensions on colony worlds and hand the Separatists the ammunition they need to enlist more people to their cause?'

'Yessir.'

'You've fought on Centauri. What would those farm boy idiots do if they heard we just marched in here and harvested someone else's crops? Commander Romaine needs to understand the urgency of the situation as well as the lengths we've undergone to treat the Jarinyi with respect. He also needs to understand why the Jarinyi might be motivated to attack our personnel. Do you see the *wisdom* of my decision now?'

Todd remained rigid. 'Yes, sir. Sorry, sir.'

'I believe there's a work team out at the Patch now?'

'They're about to arrive by jeep, due there in ten minutes, sir.'

'And *your* team?'

'I have three men escorting the researchers – plus a couple of regulars as drivers. The rest of my men are ready to leave by Reaper now.'

'Very good. One of the Reapers will be returning to take two researchers and myself to an island off the coast for the day. To look for more Tigerclaw. That leaves you one bird down, so you'll have a delay when it's time to bug out, I'm afraid.'

'No problem, sir.'

'For now, I want you to take Commander Romaine and Fisher with you. Good luck.'

Todd saluted and both men turned to go. A cough from behind halted them. Though he was looking again at his device, it was obvious the CO had something more to add.

'I'm told you fellas exchanged words last night. That's both unnecessary and unprofessional. Romaine, you'll hand that damned stick over to the Quartermaster this evening.'

Time to grow up and behave yourself, Johnny.

'Sure.'

'Lieutenant Todd, you'll keep a civil tongue in your head and give the Commander the respect due his rank and his position. You'll co-operate fully with his requests for assistance. Is that clear?'

'Yessir.'

'Dismissed.'

ROMAINE MARCHED ACROSS THE CLEARING IN TODD'S WAKE, WITH FISHER in his. The female recon who'd spoken with Fisher in the Mess last night fell silently into step beside Todd. Her skin had tanned deeper under Eventide's sun and her black hair was crewcut. She was so powerfully built, she almost dwarfed her Lieutenant. Anything that made Todd seem diminished was just fine with Romaine. He liked the woman already, even before she tossed him a flirty wink.

Not my type, lady, but hey, appreciate the compliment.

'Lieutenant?' he called.

'What?' The shorter man didn't turn.

Romaine scowled and jogged a few steps to catch up. 'I guess you're going to explain all this mysterious Tigerclaw and Pumpkin Patch talk on the way.'

'No doubt.'

'And is it too much to hope that I'll get to talk to your team when we get there?'

'You have my full cooperation.'

'One more thing to ask.'

Todd stopped, put his hands on his hip, forcing politeness. 'What would that be, sir?'

'Carswell is coming with us.'

Romaine wasn't sure why he said it. Perhaps he didn't trust the xenologist to still be in the camp when he returned.

Todd looked disgusted, and the Sergeant spoke for him. 'Taking him along is bad juju. He'll try to get in our way. You didn't see the way he undermined us the whole time we were trading with the indigs, and he was supposed to be translating for us.'

'Juju?' Todd asked her, amused.

She shrugged without smiling. 'Little word I'm trying out.'

Todd swallowed his smile and refocused on Romaine, persisting with his parody of good manners. 'Sergeant Chua, this is *Commander* Romaine. You will show him full courtesy. Commander, this is Master Sergeant Nancy Chua. She's a very fine soldier and right now, she's making a lot of sense about Carswell. I'm not taking an obstructive, indig-loving, tree-hugging, self-righteousness freak into an already dicey situation.'

'We could argue about it for hours. But I believe the Colonel said full cooperation. I'm expecting nothing less.'

There followed a moment of stand-off. Both men stood facing each other, the blackcap officer with hands on his hips and a muscle ticcing in his cheek, Romaine with his hands firmly planted in his pockets, and a professionally blank expression.

Finally, Todd slumped. 'Where is the freak?'

Chua said, 'The Mess. Probably on his third tray of grub.'

With a look of resignation, he said, 'Go get him. We'll meet you at the Reaper.'

9

'Hide nothing,
for time, which sees all and hears all,
exposes all.'

- Sophocles

WHILE HE WAITED for Chua to return, Lieutenant Sean Todd considered the other members of his team standing lazily by the Reapers — and was distracted by a moment of professional pride. Three years since he'd joined them as unit commander to help quell the uprising on Theseus. Three years next month. They'd been excellent before he arrived; in his hands they'd become even better.

And he could read them like books. Romaine and the MP wouldn't be able to tell, but Todd's eye picked up the anticipatory edginess in their body language. If it came today, most would embrace action eagerly. He was almost eager for it himself: violence tended to resolve things one way or another.

Some members of the team ran diagnostic checks on their '90s:

'Chops' Vgrevski who always reminded Todd of a chimpanzee; brutally handsome 'Gally' Garlitos and ugly-as-sin Tom 'Fester' Festwell; Corporals Cathleen McGrath and Cristina Dumetriscu, enough alike to be twin sisters.

In counterpoint to the activity of the others, Zlatko Maglic slouched against the Reaper behind Fester, watching Fisher keenly. Maglic was a brooding ferret whom Todd couldn't stand personally, but he had the utmost respect for his skills. The ferret had bite. While other Marines bore epithets awarded them by comrades, Maglic had named himself: *Magic*.

Two more team members – Turk and Kwan – had gone to the Patch on the jeeps with the civilian team.

McGrath handed Todd his webbing, her face lit with a coy half-smile. 'Got all your goodies here, Looey.'

Todd buckled it on and ran a hand over his creative assortment of ordinance: a Spider mine, two chlorine grenades and a *Momma Bear*. The *Bear* was a defensive measure primarily designed to assist an outnumbered force to cover approaches they didn't have the manpower to guard. So-named because it attacked anyone who threatened its 'cubs'. Technically the *Bear* was a proximity mine, triggered by anything it deemed dense enough to constitute an enemy soldier coming within three meters of it. The victim would be subsequently cut to ribbons by shrapnel. Another feature Todd had always thought brilliant was its disbursement of shrapnel above a height of fifty centimeters, the height under which a recon unit kept while moving along the ground; any Marine inadvertently triggering it was therefore given a chance of survival. Three other members of the unit carried *Momma Bears*.

He finished adjusting his kit and fixed his team with his no-nonsense expression. 'This is Commander Romaine. You will afford him all respect. We are taking him and his … *team* … to the Patch.'

A few eyebrows shot up. Maglic dropped his cigarette and ground it beneath his heel. No one said a word.

'I'll take that as a *yessir*.'

A few muttered, 'Yessir.'

'Chua will be here shortly with the good Dr Carswell.' Someone groaned. Maglic spat again. 'Let's get aboard our birds and make ready to serve and protect.'

―――――――――

Romaine watched closely as the recon unit boarded the two fliers. They seemed lightly armed compared to the regular units he'd seen mobilizing aboard naval vessels. Either the blackcaps were so confident in their abilities they didn't need to carry much hardware, or they weren't expecting trouble. Or both. Each wore jungle camouflage fatigues made from a lightweight material that wicked away sweat and circulated air across the skin. Over these and on their torsos they wore Tensar body armor, the same armor Fisher had worn yesterday.

Romaine remained outside the aircraft with Fisher. He leaned toward her and subtly indicated the recons. 'Wanna be one of them, Fisher?'

'Right now, I'm enjoying my role with the Military Police, sir.'

That actually surprised him and he let it show. 'What makes it so enjoyable?'

'It gives me a chance to be a positive influence, to keep people safe because of bringing order. I can prevent people from harming each other. Things like that.'

'Sounds like a rehearsed answer.'

The flicker of a frown darkened her features – the shadow of a bird momentarily blocking the sun – before she pulled herself back to her professional impassivity. 'It's also an adventure, sir. I'm blessed to be seeing lots of different places and people, to not be stuck in one place. There are relatively few human beings who get to travel like I do.'

Sales Reps do, he thought. *And they don't get threatened as often.*

'Why don't you think about a career in forensics?'

'Sir?'

The words had come out of his mouth flippantly, but they'd struck some kind of chord with her. And, he considered, maybe it wasn't such a bad suggestion. She was definitely sharp. She could probably pursue a far better career than the MPs, being hated by pretty much everyone besides other MPs.

If you're going to be distrusted and despised, you may as well get paid well for it. So why not with us?

'You might be a solid Investigator, Fisher. So far, you've shown some natural aptitude for crime scene investigation, you have an orderly mind and you're sharp. The MIO could use you.'

'Sir, I don't think so. With respect. I'm not that "sharp", really.'

He scowled. 'I hate people putting themselves down almost as much as people big-noting themselves.' He paused. 'Look, I'm not telling you what to do with your life, but you're young enough to find a better career than hanging out with...' He dropped his voice further. '...Thugs like them.'

The heavy footsteps of Chua frogmarching a grumpy Carswell put an end to the conversation before she could reply. The xenologist forced his final chunk of toast into his mouth and avoided the eyes of the recons who watched him like caged carnivores from within the Reapers. He made a bitter remark to Romaine as he passed, but it was absorbed by the toast.

Todd steered Romaine and Fisher into a different flier than Carswell. When they were buckled in, Todd explained: 'I don't want the freak's presence complicating conversation.'

Romaine scraped sweat from his forehead. He hadn't thought it could get hotter, but here in the back of an aircraft with one door, no windows and lots of bodies pressed together, he began to ask himself what he'd done to deserve this. *Did I burn people at the stake in a former life?*

Fisher's cologne was strong in the tight space and thick air, cutting through the funk of Marine sweat. He glanced at her quickly; for that split second, that scent had conspired with his peripheral vision to make her Harshini.

With a lurch, the Reaper lifted away from the camp. His harness tightened automatically, constricting his breathing. Fisher bumped against him on one side and a female Marine with the nametag McGrath on the other. Something brushed his hair from above and he smacked it away with the back of his hand, knocking Fisher with his elbow and apologizing with a terse shrug. The buzzing in his head might have been resonance from the Reaper's repulsors. It felt like something was climbing into his brain through his left ear. There came a moment of detachment like falling. Romaine dropped both hands between his legs and clenched the bench seat, anchoring himself to something real. He remembered someone writing about the early days of deep space exploration, when people were out in ships for years on end then struggled to re-acclimatize upon their return. Somewhere in the article, the writer had coined the terms *space-legs* and *world-legs*.

I'm just getting my world-legs back, he thought, struggling to convince his brain that up was up, *and now they throw me in a flyer*.

He tried to shift his attention from his discomfort and tuned into the hum of murmured conversation between two blackcaps, Maglic responding with monosyllables to a steady stream of questions about his sex life from Chua. Todd stabbed an index finger at his slim as if squishing a nest of ants. Through the open door Romaine saw what looked like a carpet of broccoli, the immenseness of the wilderness made small by tricks of mind and distance. Then the Reaper tilted, changing direction. His stomach tilted with it, and he snapped his gaze away from the wall of green that rushed up at him. His eyes caught Maglic's at the far end of the cabin and – weirdly – the ill-will he saw there brought him back from the edge of panic.

Someone who hates me for no good reason. This I can deal with.

Perched across the narrow cabin from him, Todd suddenly tossed his notebook into the air to be snatched away by Chua. Without preamble he launched into an explanation.

'Our destination is three hectares of open space directly north of here. We call it the Pumpkin Patch because it's full of one plant – it's actually called Tigerclaw, but it grows fruit like miniature Halloween pumpkins. The fruit's okay. Tastes like salted banana skin, but it's highly nutritious, so the scientists say. The bark and the roots are good too. But the leaves are the goldmine.'

'Goldmine?' He found he could lift one hand from the seat without keeling over. As nonchalantly as possible he reached up to wipe his brow.

'Medically speaking. The eggheads call the plant Tigerclaw 'cause the leaf's shaped like a tiger's claw. Imaginative, huh?'

Romaine shrugged. *About as imaginative as calling the field the Pumpkin Patch.*

'But the name has a double meaning. They also call it that because it's about as brutal as a plant can get. It kills any domestic fungi or bacteria that try to attack it. Our researchers think there's only one kind of beetle that can ingest it – and it can only eat the fruit so it can spread the seeds, but not the leaves. Tigerclaw kills bad stuff like germs in the wild, and apparently it kills bad stuff in humans and Jarinyi, as well as boosting the immune system and cellular repair rates. The original survey team - the one that brought Carswell – told us of the indigs' use of the whole plant for medicine – leaves, fruit, roots. One of them witnessed an amazing recovery of a near death infant when he was given a tea made from the roots.'

Romaine made a *what's-this-got-to-do-with-me* face. Todd ignored it and went on talking. Romaine wiped sweaty palms on his trousers and tried to filter something relevant to his case from the details.

'The team only had a small sample which they tested here on Eventide, then sent the results and what was left of the plant back to CUSET. A few weeks later, they found some of the plant growing on a hill near the coast out in the open, not in the shade. Not much of it, but they dug it up and sent that back to CUSET too. Medicos have been running clinical trials on it ever since. I've read the files twice but I can't understand most of the scientific hoodoo in there, egghead stuff.'

Todd shifted and adjusted his webbing.

'When our own research team arrived eleven days ago,' Todd continued, 'they began looking for new sources of Tigerclaw while some of us tried to negotiate with the indigs for more of it. They refused. We explained we needed it to help our people survive; they played dumb. Then one of our teams located the Pumpkin Patch from a flyover in a Reaper and brought samples back. We'd probably flown over it twenty times and didn't realize what it was until someone landed and took a closer look.

'These leaves contain a bunch of chemicals that are incredibly ...' he searched for a word, then shrugged, '...*good*. Unique. Apparently – and this is with the small amount the eggheads had from the *original* survey team – they made significant inroads into treating a disease called chronic Hitchens disease. They treated one hundred patients who'd had the disease over ten years, completely cured ninety-four of them and slightly improved the symptoms of the other six. This was in six days. Apparently, if you know the disease, these results are amazing.'

Romaine got it now, mentally kicking himself for taking so long: Tigerclaw was a possible counter to the PBT virus. He'd put Glass's story about Red Star out of mind; maybe he hadn't really believed it, maybe he didn't want to. But Todd had his interest now. 'I've never heard of Hitchens disease, so I'll take your word for it.'

'Gets better. They also ran smaller trials with asthma and fibromyalgia sufferers. Significant improvements. Research says it's the biggest step forward we've made with medicine in a century. With the superflus of the last thirty years and the knack that other planets have for evolving things similar to viruses, CUSET are keen to investigate anything that might produce a revived chemical approach to fighting disease.'

Todd paused, presumably to let it all sink in. Romaine took advantage of the pause. 'How about cancer?'

He recalled the day his father had casually mentioned over dinner that The Big C had claimed his grandfather's life. Romaine's adolescent mind had chosen to believe that it wasn't cancer at all, that the old man had simply run out of reasons to get up in the morning, giving in to the futility of his own existence.

I always did think too much.

Todd nodded. 'The researchers used a small amount of Tigerclaw to treat a couple of cancer sufferers – big time shareholders who had weeks to live. They'd been using the original sample that had first been sent out. It arrested the spread of the cancer, but hadn't been able to defeat it completely. Then they got some of the second batch, the stuff they found out in the open air, not under the forest canopy like the first. Apparently, away from shade and harvested after the leaves had soaked in a day's direct sunlight, that batch of Tigerclaw was seventy per cent more potent and it did begin to kill the cancer cells. Instantly.'

Romaine nodded but stubbornly refused to look impressed by Todd's revelations. The cop part of his brain started generating questions again. If this was such good news, why was there so much anxiety surrounding this operation? Were the PRC in the area? Had Chinese spies picked up on what CUSET had found and sent their own mission? Could that be who killed Gutierrez? Some PRC infiltrator dressed in illegal and outlawed stealth-skin hiding in the jungle and firing stolen alien weapons. If so, the question was still *why*. 'You found some leaves. They're magical. What's the problem?'

'The problem is, when we started working the Pumpkin Patch, we found out it's a "sacred site" for these Jarinyi. They don't want us to touch it.' Todd's eyes tightened. 'We were sampling for a few hours until their warriors showed up and intimidated our researchers. So we backed off and we been wasting time ever since. And even if we could go back, we've had rain or cloud cover every day since. Until yesterday.' Fisher must have looked askance at him, because he added to her, 'Remember, it needs a day or more's direct sunlight to increase its potency.'

Romaine made a wry face. 'Well, it *is* their land.'

'We've tried everything to buy it. To compensate them. Like the Colonel said this morning, we don't want to steal it. We're not gonna take all of it and leave none for them. But we need a certain amount to begin treating PBT sufferers, to begin inoculations and to start growing it off-world.'

'Maybe they don't want to sell it. Once again, it's theirs.'

'But we *need* it!' Just then Todd's eyes lost focus and he touched his earpiece. 'Yeah, just check around to the west and tell the other bird to sweep north again,' he told someone. He refocused and explained, 'Both pilots have been running sensor sweeps of the nearby forest to see if the indigs are in the area. That's why the trip's taking so long.' The flier decelerated and banked, throwing Romaine against Fisher again.

He straightened up and wished they'd just hurry up and let him off. *Can't they do the sweeps after they dump us?* 'Look, Todd, I get that this Tigerclaw's important. If PBT is a threat to us, then fair enough. But if the Patch is the Jarinyi's only supply...'

Todd shook his head and scowled as if Romaine were a fool. For a moment, he resembled Carswell. 'It's not. I already told you the original survey team found some other small patches of it. Since we got here, we've also discovered some but the thing is, they're not as rich in the *good stuff*. They don't grow in direct sunlight. We've taken a lot of it and processed it, but it's just not as high-quality as the plants in the main patch. The Pumpkin Patch is *the* place to get Tigerclaw. And we need a lot of it, and quick!'

Romaine narrowed his eyes as he became aware of the nature of today's trip. 'So you're going in to take it, whatever the consequences?' Todd's lips pressed into a straight line and he held his gaze. 'I mean, the human race has finally met another similar race and this is how we act? Isn't the official Contact policy to treat sentient species with respect? To recognize their rights?'

Maglic actually snorted at this. Romaine realized that all eyes and ears were turned his way.

'Policy.' Todd sighed. 'Yes. Glass calls it the Golden Rule, whatever that means.'

'Do unto others as you'd have them do unto you,' Fisher chimed in. When they looked at her, she explained, 'That's the Golden Rule.'

Todd looked irritated by the interruption. 'Anyways, that's why we've tried negotiation up until now. Why we've had teams scouring the forest to harvest a leaf here and a leaf there while a tonne of the stuff sits in the Pumpkin Patch ready for the taking but helping nobody.'

'So now you *are* going in to take it? That's gonna look good to the Separatists if they get wind of it.'

'Separatists. The same idiots who'd use information like this to foment unrest will be the same idiots who'll plead us for Tigerclaw if PBT gets loose in their colony.'

Romaine wondered how the hell it would get loose in their community. It was a Red Star problem, and confined to one continent there. It wasn't a Centauran or Thesean problem ...

The cold finger of uncertainty traced a slow line down his spine. Had PBT gotten out of Fu Xing? Had it spread elsewhere? Romaine looked up as if seeing through the aircraft's roof and into space. There might be a big *big* problem out there.

Still, even if that was true, there was an immediate ethical problem to deal with right here. 'So you're ok with stealing from the Jarinyi? Taking *their* medicine?'

Maglic sniffed loudly and said, 'Whose side are you on, guy?'

Romaine shrugged. 'Asking questions is what I do.'

'Sure, the Jarinyi are sentient, but ...' Todd took a deep breath, leaned forward and turned his face to the open door of the Reaper. For a few seconds he watched the forest pass. When he turned back, his eyes were hard. 'Commander, unless you've seen PBT and the effects, its aftermath, you can live in a cocoon of blissful ignorance where you can be all noble about alien species and their rights and customs. But this virus is already on its way to bursting your bubble. Because you'll probably be facing the disease yourself one day.'

That cold finger played his spine again. 'Why do you say that?'

Todd glanced toward Chua who took over from him seamlessly.

'One month ago, January 12th, the Chinese colony Fu Xing on Red Star suddenly have people falling violently ill from an unknown virus. Within four days, the PRC lose contact with Fu Xing. No one's answering the phone. Our Red Star settlement can't raise them either. The Chinese ask our people to investigate. Colonel Glass is in command of the garrison there and he takes a team across the ocean with full hazmat gear on board their flyers.'

Todd interrupted, 'I guess the Proocs asked CUSET to go in because they didn't want to waste their own resources or people if something bad had happened, like an alien incursion or a radiation leak or something. And if we cocked up, they'd have something new to complain about to the United Nations.'

'The Colonel's team expect to get shot at,' Chua continued. 'But nothing happens. Then from the air, they see dead bodies everywhere. Blood everywhere. They put on their hazmat suits and go take a look. They discover about half the colony already dead, the other half wishing they were dead.'

'Actually, it was more like eighty percent already dead,' said Maglic.

'Eighty percent!' Romaine exclaimed.

'Go on, Sarge,' Todd encouraged.

Chua's flat tone belied the horror of the picture she was painting. 'Our medics try everything they can to help the sufferers but they all die anyway. All of 'em. One hundred per cent. We ain't never had a disease like this. Even ebola only has a ninety percent mortality rate at its worst.'

Romaine found his throat constricting, didn't want to believe that such a thing existed. Then snippets of history swam to the surface of his memory, from past reading, and he realized that this was entirely possible. Chua wasn't entirely accurate. During his studies, he'd read about a terrorist attack last century using a strain of smallpox that was also uniformly fatal. It had killed several hundred people in an Israeli suburb before containment. If what they were telling him were true, this outbreak of PBT far exceeded that atrocity and was no less horrific to contemplate.

He found his throat dry when he spoke again. 'There's more?'

Todd said, 'Everyone thought that'd be the end of it. But. On January 22nd, a small Chinese supply-carrier ship arrives at Golan Refueling Station. You know where that is?'

'I've been there. About halfway between Red Star and Chi, or the Edge-of-Nowhere mines, depending on which way you fly.' The Reaper banked again, pressing him into the wall.

'The fifteen people on board the supply ship are dead. PBT. Somehow they got off Red Star. Golan unseal the ship to take a look inside. Infect the entire station.'

'Why the hell did they unseal the ship?'

'The Proocs insisted we keep the virus quiet,' Todd replied. 'CUSET didn't object. Golan knew nothing about it, so they had no reason not to open the ship.'

Chua said, 'Three ships – two of ours, one of theirs – get out of Golan before the Station Manager seals it off. Our Navy rounds up the CUSET ships and quarantines them, tows them out into space where the poor bastards die in their own blood. But the Chinese one can't be found.'

'It's unaccounted for?' Despite the heat, that cold finger tickling his spine became a bucket of ice poured into his gut. He pictured a star map in his mind, with yellow lines spreading down the spacelanes from Golan to other human settlements.

'Can't be found,' Chua repeated. 'Everyone's hoping that its crew died and the ship got stuck and atomized in leapspace. So, we send a bigger team here to Eventide to find more Tigerclaw. There's a team looking on some islands on the far side of the planet where there's no indigs; no luck so far. And there's our operation here. Three days ago, around the same time that Gutierrez gets capped, we get a messagepacket telling us there's two more outbreaks: one at Chi and one at *Waypoint2*.'

'What? How can that happen?' Chi was a Chinese refueling station on the outskirts of the same system as the majestic Chinese colony-planet Yun Dao. *Waypoint2* was a naval Base on the spacelane between the planets Red Star and Oceana – in completely the opposite direc-tion. 'I can understand it getting to Chi – it was probably on that rogue Chinese ship from Golan. How'd it get to *Waypoint2*?'

'We have no idea,' said Todd. 'Possibly another Chinese ship got away from Red Star and thought they'd try for CUSET space where they might get a warmer reception than their own people would give 'em.'

Chua said, 'Gotta love the Proocs' approach to things. We sealed off our station. The Chinese did too after shooting down the ships trying to get off it.'

Romaine saw in his mind's eye the faces of people he knew vaguely on *Waypoint2*. Were they all dead now?

Todd's leg began bouncing agitatedly. It knocked against Romaine and he shifted his legs away. The lieutenant said, 'We got some Tigerclaw serum-pills-whatnot to *Waypoint2*. We heard in this morning's messagepack that it's helped save a few, but most were dead before it got there. And what we're worried about now is whether or not it's spread to Oceana itself. The human race has lost probably eighteen thousand to PBT so far and Oceana's population is about the same figure. That's eighteen thousand *humans*, Romaine! *And* we just lost contact with Oceana Orbital. We got that message this morning as well. If one infected person somehow got to Oceana itself, PBT'll be rushing through their population now. The first sufferers might be dead, others will be bleeding from pores in their skin and the sores in their throats.'

Romaine did not lean away when Todd put his face close to his and delivered words that obviously hurt the young lieutenant to say.

'My brother and his family are on Oceana, Romaine.'

Romaine placed a hand over his face. What he felt now was the overwhelming nausea of shock. This had to be a lie. It had to be a filthy ugly lie they were using to manipulate him. How come he hadn't heard about *Waypoint2* prior to leaving Drop-in-the-Ocean? Even en route here, how could he have not heard news of such devastation?

That's easy, Johnny. Information containment to avoid panic. Another magnificent CUSET policy.

Todd was talking again and Romaine heard the words as if through gauze pads over both his ears. 'The researchers here tell me that we can save that colony if we get twelve liters of a Tigerclaw serum there in the next four days. We've distilled less than one liter so far. One! I think the Jarinyi can spare a few more kilograms of their sacred plant to spare the lives of thousands of humans, don't you?' He tapped Romaine's leg with the butt of his AR90, pressing home his point. 'And think of Earth, the Dioscurin Moons, Centauri, Europa Space Port, Theseus, *Pride of Mao*, Yun Dao ... even the intersolar asteroid mines. What happens if PBT somehow gets a foothold on all of them? Our species will die, Romaine. We'll be history. The Jarinyi or some other race will be picking through our ruins centuries from now thinking "Poor little buggers. If only they'd gotten the right medicine in time".'

'Alright.' Romaine moved the rifle butt away. 'I see your point, Lieutenant.'

'I hope so, Romaine. 'Cause it's not just PBT that's the problem.' He touched Romaine's leg with the rifle again and despite his mounting nausea, Romaine felt like smacking it out the door. 'You mentioned Separatists before. We're aware of new insurgent cells already planning new uprisings on Centauri and now on Xerxes, of all places. There was a bombing on Castor last month and everyone's blaming the islamics -'

Romaine waved a hand. 'I do watch the news.'

Todd continued speaking, over the top of him. '–but we know it was a Xerxian group. Your "objective" findings on the Gutierrez case can stop riots, uprisings, even a war. Maybe prevent as many deaths in that regards as the virus has already caused on its own.'

Ah, crap. Romaine leaned his head back against the wall and stared at the roof as the flier decelerated. *I really didn't need this.*

10

'The first man who, having enclosed a piece of ground, bethought himself of saying "This is mine", and found people simple enough to believe him, was the real founder of civil society.

From how many crimes, wars and murders, from how many horrors and misfortunes might not any one have saved mankind, by pulling up the stakes, or filling up the ditch, and crying to his fellows, "Beware of listening to this impostor; you are undone if you once forget that the fruits of the earth belong to us all, and the earth itself to nobody."'

- Jean-Jacques Rousseau, *Discourse on the Origin of Inequality*

FROM THE AIR, the Pumpkin Patch was a broad nevus of green, darker than that of the surrounding forest and mottled with purple and gold and red. From a distance, the group of workers in one corner looked to Fisher like a clump of lackluster flowers waving in a breeze. A trio of jeeps sat against the forest edge on the opposite side to the workers.

She prayed a silent prayer to stave off her shock from Todd's revelations, and leaned towards the doorway as the aircraft banked one more

time on approach. As it neared the ground, she could see that the
clearing was entirely choked with a single type of plant, fruit like mini-
pumpkins hanging beneath three-pronged leaves that ended in claw-
like tips. What had been colored spots from the air were in fact concen-
trations of flowers. She found it bizarre the way the forest had stood
aside and allowed the plant to have an area all to itself; there were no
trees within its borders. Perhaps the soil was too shallow for the tall
trees to take root. Perhaps the Jarinyi had taken a step toward agricul-
ture, chopping down trees and cultivating their sacred plant. Or
perhaps this was a natural occurrence, and that was one reason why it
was a sacred site to the Jarinyi: a crop of a miracle plant growing under
the best possible conditions out here in the open.

Divine providence.

'Ladies first,' Chua said to her.

She checked the woman's expression expecting sarcasm, but Chua
seemed genuinely good-humored. She unbuckled her harness and
dropped out onto the spongy soil.

The Reaper hovered more than a meter above the ground, probably
to avoid crushing the valuable Tigerclaw. The staging area was a scrap
of earth just large enough for a dozen people to stand without touching, but it was already crowded with cases and water barrels. Fisher was
forced to step amongst the bushes to make room for those following
her. Some of the Tigerclaw had been cleared from the ground around
where the cases sat, presumably taken back to camp by an earlier work
crew.

A dozen paces away, more Marines spilled to the ground from the
second Reaper. Doctor Carswell made his own leap, finding his feet
easily until a Marine jostled him on the way past and he fell. He
bounced back up, indignant, brushing himself off and stomped closer
to Fisher. The way these recons seemed to feel about him, his trip must
have been very unpleasant.

She kept out of the way of the Marines who followed her out of her
Reaper and moved on to predetermined positions. The last one out was
Romaine. He lost his balance and toppled onto his backside. She

turned away, in part to give him his dignity as he clambered to his feet, in part to hide her face until she could repress her smile.

The Reapers lifted away and headed west. Most recons headed toward perimeter positions, supplementing the handful of Marines already present. Maglic, McGrath and Chua stayed with her and Romaine. Maglic immediately hopped onto one of the crates and began rummaging through his pockets, fished out a cigarette and his Plazer and lit up. Todd went to Romaine, murmured something to him she didn't catch and waded off through the Tigerclaw.

The Commander looked as shocked as she felt. She had been aware the expedition was performing medical research, but she'd been incurious about it. Now she realized this was one of the most important human expeditions ever made. She touched her dog tags where both hologram and audio messages from her family were stored. If the PBT stories were true, and if this mission was unsuccessful, her family could all die.

She pushed her worries aside, taking refuge in responsibility. Commander Romaine was still in alien territory with a job to do, surrounded by Marines hostile to him, as well as who-knew-what in the forest. He had moved to the edge of the staging area, leaning on a case, lost in thought. She edged closer so as to be ready if he needed her. He took his shirt between index finger and thumb, lifted it away from his chest and let it fall again. She wondered what was going through his mind. Was he thinking about the case or about PBT? And what was he going to do next? She wished he'd do something, tell *her* to do something. She wanted to be busy, too busy to have to think.

The three blackcaps near her affected a relaxed demeanor, but she could read the telltale signs of edginess. Had one of them used a Jarinyi bow to murder Gutierrez? Were they nervous about Romaine? Maglic sucked loudly on his cigarette. Carswell glared at him as he walked past, grimacing as Maglic blew grey smoke into his face. She braced to break up a quarrel, relaxed again when the xenologist made no comment and came to rest against the crate furthest from the smoker, watching the work crew like Romaine did.

Perhaps there wouldn't be an issue. Perhaps she wasn't even needed here.

WHY IS SHE STANDING SO GODDAMN CLOSE?

Romaine rubbed at the back of his neck and let his irritation at Fisher's watchfulness pass. Apart from that one untimely comment in the Mess, she had proved a useful ally and assistant so far. She played her hand across a clump of vividly iridescent flowers and released a tight puff of pollen. He suppressed a shudder and turned fully away, hoped the spores would stay over there with her, then wondered if they were poisonous. There was something unclean about touching the plants so casually, about touching anything on this world.

My kingdom for a washcloth.

Wistfully he summoned up mental images of his apartment on Bona Vista station. Thought about movie nights at the food court. Fantasized about lounging in his massage chair, watching news-streams wend their way across his picture wall while subversive satirists bobbed about on his *pedestal* making fun of well-known CUSET personalities. Imagined the warm embrace of a hot bath...

It had been so long since he'd been home. And this daydreaming wasn't going to help him get there. He forced his thoughts instead onto Todd's revelations.

If these things were true, then the worst-case scenario was a kind of viral Armageddon. Then again, if PBT killed a relatively small percentage of the human race and burned itself out quickly, the threat never quite registering on most of the colonial populace, then CUSET faced a different kind of difficulty. If the Separatists got even a whiff of CUSET abusing the Jarinyi, stealing sacred and precious resources from an indigenous and sentient alien people, that would accomplish exactly what Todd predicted: fuel that fire of revolt already simmering in many colonies.

And eventually the news would get out. It always did. If not from the civs working here, then via the regular Marines, who were usually only enlisted for the short-term and might easily blab about the things they'd seen.

Did Gutierrez see something he could blab about? he wondered fleetingly.

Now the script that Todd and Glass were reading from made sense, as did the true meaning of Admiral Dreyfuss' edict to him. The goal here was to make CUSET the good guys, the ones trying to save the human race while maintaining cordiality with the aliens. Have the Investigator with the spotless record make an official decision that the Jarinyi responded to fair treatment with irrational aggression, murdering one of our nice young soldiers. Show that the Jarinyi placed their interests over those of the human race when those interests were not at all mutually exclusive.

And anyone with half a brain would see it for the crock it was.

He sighed. Maybe the Jarinyi did it. Maybe they didn't. He hadn't had the chance to gather near enough information to start making theories and joining dots. In fact, there weren't many dots to join.

'So, you all know that PBT was geneered to kill ethnic Chinese, right?' Maglic said. He was speaking to Chua, but Romaine couldn't help but tune in.

'Not this again,' Chua groaned, scooping up a handful of soil and launching it at him. He turned his face away from it, let it impact against his lank hair and thin shoulders.

'What again?' asked McGrath.

'He was spouting his conspiracy theories last night in the Mess before we all left him talking to himself.'

'Seriously,' Maglic continued. A cigarette hung from the corner of his mouth, waggling about like a conductor's baton as he spoke. 'CUSET dropped PBT on Fu Xing 'cause the Chinks stole the continent from us. No offense about the *Chinks* thing, Nancy.'

'Right. How could I possibly find that offensive?'

'Well you're not PRC Chinese. You're just normal Chinese, ain't you?'

Oh, brother, Romaine thought.

'Normal Chinese? What the hell's that, you ignoramus? And why the hell would CUSET spread an anti-Chinese virus when a third of their population has Chinese genes, especially some of their biggest shareholders and upper management?'

McGrath twiddled her fingers, attracting Maglic's attention. 'How do you explain it spreading to Golan and killing all the *non*-Chinese there?'

'That's just a rumor.' He drew heavily on the cigarette.

'It's not a rumor, the CO told us himself.'

Maglic's words came out in a rush of smoke. 'Well, if PBT wasn't targeting Chinese, why would the Proocs in the UN be accusing CUSET of starting a biowar?'

'You ain't smart enough to talk politics, Magic,' McGrath said with a husky chuckle. 'It's simple. PBT started naturally. The Fu Xing settlers ate some kind of native animal they found in the forest and caught it from that.'

'Well, how convenient that we found Tigerclaw just before a major disease broke out,' Carswell piped up, turning heads. Romaine was unsurprised Dr Smartass couldn't keep his mouth shut. Carswell continued, 'PRC settlers catch a natural virus and lightyears away CUSET happen to discover the cure around the same time.'

'Exactly,' Maglic said. 'Convenient. *Too* convenient.'

Carswell hesitated, appearing astonished the wiry Marine would agree with him. A moment later, he used the support to gather steam, warming to the topic. 'I think CUSET discovered two things since they've been messing about out among the stars: a wonder drug and a killer virus. I don't think PBT is geneered for Chinese genomes, but I do think they tested it at Fu Xing. It's too coincidental that Glass and fifty people from his garrison had exactly the right gear to go in and investigate without being infected.' Romaine wondered how Carswell knew so much about it. Maybe he'd hacked someone's data.

'It's standard hazmat and decontamination equipment,' Chua scoffed.

'Still. The Chinese suffer immense losses at the hands of a new disease just as CUSET sources its own prevention and cure.'

McGrath swallowed water from her canteen and burped loudly,

causing Carswell to flinch. 'Yeah, and maybe weird shit just happens. Big universe means lots of coincidences.'

'Yes, but this coincidence would be more like the outbreak of the COVID virus in the early 21st, and a week after the first case, some backpacker coming home from Nepal, handing over the local variety of apples and saying "Folks, the Nepalese already had a cure for that virus, long before it first struck; here it is". No, CUSET have been sitting on PBT for a while and now they have something to cure it with, they're taking the Chinese out of the equation.'

Maglic hawked and spat, tried to take back control of the conversation he'd started. 'Yeah, like the egghead says. It's too convenient. I heard PBT started as a Chinese-only virus, then mutated.'

'Now it's mutated?' Chua looked across to Fisher and Romaine. 'You people buying this?'

Fisher shook her head seriously. Romaine just smiled.

Chua continued, 'Well, if it mutated and started killing the rest of us – oh, wait, the rest of *you*, non-Chinese people – then the eggheads who created it or discovered it must be pretty crappy scientists.'

'Or arrogant,' said Carswell. 'The human belief that we control nature is a complete delusion. I mean, we can't even control ourselves. That's what keeps Romaine employed.' He pretended to tip a hat at Romaine and Romaine's smile drooped.

Carswell put his hands out as if bracing himself against a lectern. 'You've never read stories where a zookeeper or circus performer gets mauled by the very animal they've happily worked with for years? We try to tame wild nature, but nature remains wild. We geneer things but they eventually mutate or break down. We design new nanotech to fix the faulty geneered tech, even though we lost control of the original nanotech last century. This time it doesn't kill people or destroy the internet and the economy, but it doesn't fix the geneered things properly either. I for one wouldn't be surprised if what Sergeant ...' He squinted at Maglic's name-patch but Maglic covered it with a hand. '... if what he says is true. Perhaps it was a biological attack that got away from CUSET and now threatens the lot of us.'

'Yeah. *Yeah*. The lot of us.' Maglic was smiling a mean smile now. He took out his cigarette and pointed it at Chua. 'I'm just glad we got you here, Sergeant Chua.'

'And why is that, Sergeant Tool?'

'Coz you're genetically Chinese. So you're more likely to catch it first. We see you go down, we run for it.'

He guffawed obscenely when McGrath added, 'You're our canary in the coalmine, girl.'

His laughing was punctuated by his smoker's cough. Romaine thought that he'd probably die a long time before Chua did.

'I gotta request a transfer,' she muttered, folding her thick arms.

'Don't leave us, Nancy,' Maglic coughed, still laughing. 'We need you.'

'Oh, I wasn't gonna transfer myself. I was gonna request they transfer you.' It was Chua's turn to laugh while Maglic's expression soured.

Carswell picked up the thread of the conspiracy conversation again, ignoring their banter. 'I've been reliably informed that there's other planets CUSET have under wraps. Places they're not colonizing. Places where they're experimenting, researching, developing all sorts of new tech ... *including* biotech. He told me he'd spent time on a rocky planet where they were geneering wildlife to use as battledrones. We can't trust them.'

'He who?' Maglic asked.

'Maybe your sources made it up,' said Chua at the same time, obviously bored with this. 'Maybe you are.'

Carswell cleared his throat with dignity. 'I'm just saying that our Lords and Masters might employ us but can't be trusted with our lives, our environments, our future...'

He had lost his audience, they'd dispersed – in spirit if not in body. He just hadn't realized it yet. Maglic flicked his cigarette into the bushes, reached for another. Chua found something out in the fields to catch her eye. Fisher seemed unsettled by his monologuing, following Chua's gaze. McGrath picked at specks of pollen on her tunic and webbing, blowing them from her fingers with mock delicacy. Carswell continued to lecture, regardless of their inattention, now bringing up the subject of indigenous rights.

Romaine turned his own attention toward whatever Fisher and Chua were looking at. A juggernaut – a recon unnaturally tall and broad – was striding toward them, indifferent to whether or not any plants got damaged along the way. While the other Marines present except Fisher wore Tensar helmets, this guy wore the famous black cap from which the recons got their nickname. Romaine was surprised they'd found one big enough to fit that melon of a head.

'Who do we have here?' he said brightly. As they turned to look, McGrath moaned melodramatically while Maglic let out an amused grunt.

Carswell, however, flinched. His self-important swagger deserted him, leaving him sagging like a sail when the wind has died. He swore under his breath.

'That's Turk, sir.' Chua waggled her eyebrows as if Romaine should have heard of him.

'Turk?'

'Sergeant Umit Bedirhan Attikula.' She grinned. '*Turk's* a lot easier to say, huh?'

Carswell spoke suddenly from right behind him. Sometime in the last few seconds he had retreated into Romaine's shadow. 'He doesn't like me very much.'

'Who *does*?' McGrath wise-cracked, drawing a cackle from Maglic.

Romaine could certainly understand Carswell being intimidated. Turk was built like farm machinery, fully two meters tall, a series of tiny shell-burst tattoos running right temple to right cheek, antiaircraft flak. He burst through the screen of bushes, swept off his cap to reveal an olive scalp shaved to a short Mohawk, pointed the cap at Carswell and started firing abuse in another language. He finished the tirade by throwing his hat on the ground and snarling, 'What are you doing here?'

'Shouldn't you be on the perimeter?' Chua asked mildly.

He didn't look at her. 'Shut up! Indigs won't show.' Carswell had shifted to keep Romaine between him and Turk. Attikula edged sideways to keep Carswell in view and snapped, 'Well?'

'I'm here at Commander Romaine's request,' Carswell replied, voice hoarse.

Turk now turned his glare upon Romaine.

Thanks a lot, Carswell.

'I don't want that puke here,' Turk growled.

Romaine lifted a hand placatingly. 'Sergeant, he won't be interfering, if that's what you're worried about. We're just–'

Turk's face darkened further. '*Worried*? I ain't some pantie-wearin' spacer like you.' He took two steps forward.

Fisher appeared from Romaine's left, placing herself between them. Like Romaine, she raised a hand and spoke firmly but calmly, the voice of the seasoned policeperson accustomed to defusing the temper of drunks and jarheads alike. 'Please step back, Sergeant.'

Turk actually did, but his face twisted in bewilderment. 'What? What did you say to me?' He threw down his assault rifle now and raised a beefy fist at her.

'Turk,' Chua began, taking him by the shoulder. He shrugged her off, a movement that might have dislocated the shoulder of a weaker individual.

Turk's focus remained on Fisher, his voice rising in pitch and intensity. 'You gonna tell me what to do, *girl*? You gonna make me step back? Huh?'

This was unnecessary, ridiculous. Romaine could defuse this with words. Fisher just needed to back down and he would fix it. When he reached for her arm to pull her back and she surprised him by raising it in a warning to him, moving out of his reach.

Romaine had the sinking feeling he was a helpless witness to a tragedy, as if it were preordained that this nice young woman would get seriously hurt and he would be unable to stop it. The feeling was depressingly familiar.

'Sergeant,' she said to Turk. 'No one wants any trouble. We just want Commander Romaine and Doctor Carswell left alone. And you can –'

But Turk was moving. Though it was incredibly fast, Romaine's sense of time slowed, his brain digesting every nuance of what happened next, every element of movement. Turk feinted as if he would deliver a straight kick, but shot out his left arm instead, fingers outstretched, aimed at Fisher's eyes. To Romaine's amazement, Fisher's response was faster still, moving her upper body out of the way of the strike, stepping to her right. Though Turk was off-balance and wide open for a counter strike along the left side of his body, she did not retaliate.

'Turk! Enough!' Chua shouted.

But he wouldn't have it. He whirled, calculating Fisher now, air hissing in and out of his nostrils. Romaine reached down for his sidearm, intending to fire a warning shot over Turk's head. Before the pistol cleared his holster, Turk was on her again. This time he launched a flurry of punches, each of which Fisher dodged easily. McGrath and Carswell both had to retreat amongst the Tigerclaw plants to escape being trampled. Then as Turk's mass drew close to Fisher's, he whipped an arm around to catch her across the neck. Shorter and more agile, she ducked backward beneath the blow, twirling herself around and catching his hand even as it passed over her.

By the time Romaine blinked, Fisher had Turk on his knees on the ground, the arm twisted unnaturally behind his back, hand curled and lifted high as it could go. Both of Fisher's hands gripped his, her thumbs pressed into the back of it, bending it to the point of breaking. Turk let loose a scream of pure rage. His free arm flailed at her in vain; the movement necessary to actually reach her would cost him the use of his hand, and possibly his elbow, for a long time to come.

McGrath and Chua exploded into cheers. Maglic slipped off the case and marched into the field, muttering in disgust. Romaine circled around to get a direct view of Turk's face and said 'Huh' when he saw that the big man's pupils were dilated even in the direct sunlight.

'You go girl!' Chua told Fisher. She put her face close to Turk's and said, 'About time someone put you in your place.' She dodged back as his free arm lashed at her.

Then the two female members of Todd's team twitched and bobbed their heads as if they'd been hit in the ear. Turk's eyes narrowed as he tried to listen to his earpiece, dislodged during the altercation.

Chua touched hers. 'Lieutenant, Turk's over with us. Thought he'd take on Fisher and lost.' She was quiet a moment. When she spoke again, she was all business. 'Yessir.'

She let go of the earpiece and put her face close to Turk's again, unafraid. 'Looey says if you don't get your fat ass back on that perimeter right now, he'll dock you a month's pay. Wait,' she added to Fisher who had begun to release him. 'There's more.'

11

'The insufferable arrogance of human beings to think that Nature was
made solely for their benefit, as if it was conceivable that the sun had
been set afire merely to ripen men's apples
and head their cabbages.'

- Cyrano De Bergerac

FISHER COULD JUST MAKE out what the big woman said as she leaned
close to Turk and whispered, 'Looey says that's strike two. You attack
anyone who's not a target *he's* designated again and you're off this team.'

Turk only huffed in response. The fight had gone out of him. Chua
straightened and nodded at Fisher to let him go. She did, stepping back
warily. But Turk just scooped up his '90 and his cap, and plunged into
the bushes.

Fisher's pulse hammered at her temples. She felt that strange
mixture of elation and regret she always experienced after conflict. She
took a gulping breath and rubbed her sweaty palms on her thighs. She

looked apologetically toward Romaine. 'Sorry, sir, that shouldn't have happened.'

His pistol hung limply from his hand as if he'd taken it out to shoot Turk. She felt a mild relief that he'd been ready to back her up, along with surprise when she saw admiration in his eyes.

'No need to apologize,' he said. 'He's an animal. You just did your job. And *good* job too.' He looked over at Carswell still standing waist-deep in the bushes outside the staging area. 'What d'ya say, Carswell? Good job, huh?'

'Yes. Thank you.' He said it stiffly, gathered himself, and walked forty or fifty paces out into the field to remonstrate with a worker there. The man raised his own voice in reply, appearing perplexed as to why Carswell was venting his spleen on him.

Fisher found herself turning in a restless circle, like a pup looking for a place to settle. People were staring at her again. She wished she could just disappear into the forest.

'Great style, gal!' Chua slapped her back as she passed. The contact stung. 'I been wanting to do that for months.' She walked out into the field to suggest loudly to Carswell that he desist bickering and let the man work.

Romaine stepped closer, bringing with him clashing smells of sweat and cologne. He took her arm, steering her away from McGrath's poker-faced stare. 'You going to file a report?'

'No, sir. I'll let it pass.'

But Romaine wasn't going to let it go. 'I know you're good people, Fisher, but don't let your personal niceness get in the way of your professional judgment. He should go on report.'

Niceness? The word brought Fisher a pang of offence. She was making a reasonable decision, a professional decision. Turk had been disciplined by his commanding officer and she saw no reason to add to that.

As if in sync with her thoughts, McGrath's harsh drawl cut through the thick air: 'Our Lieutenant's takin' care of it.'

Disapproval clouded Romaine's face, so she told him, 'Sometimes things are better off handled in-house, sir.'

Romaine made an *alright-alright* face but she could see he was still dissatisfied as he turned away. Whether that was with her professional judgement or with the outcome itself, she couldn't be sure. And try as she might to remain detached, it was beginning to irk her how quickly he could flip from approval to disapproval, from openness to withdrawal.

IT HAD TO BE FRUSTRATION CAUSING THE PINPRICKS OF LIGHT TO DANCE around the edges of Todd's vision. Not fully understanding the science at work, he wondered why the civs took so long to select and cut and store every single leaf. A week ago, he'd felt like he had the situation under control. Since last night's altercation with Romaine, control was slipping.

Everything. I've tried everything to get these hacking indigs out of way. Except blowing their 'village' to hell from the air. Yeah. That would have solved this 'ethical dilemma' pretty nicely.

In his mind, there was no dilemma. Humanity needed Tigerclaw. More than the Jarinyi did. And even if the expedition took it all, the plant would grow back in a couple of years at most.

Why couldn't we just shoot those little stone age turds the first time they hassled us?

He knew the reason of course. Glass – CUSET's surrogate manager here – had to play by the rules, the policies for Next Contact. And it must have been hard for the old warhorse to take off his military 'hat' and wear a diplomatic one, a business one.

It's a game. Gotta remember that. Just play the game, keep thinking outside the box, it'll be ok.

But he wondered if it would. If his brother was sick already, then things weren't ok. If PBT had gained a foothold on any colony world, things were not ok. If the Chinese caught a whiff of Eventide in this current political climate, if the Separatists continued to swell in numbers and resources ... if, if, if.

If only the idiots running this consortium could think militarily rather than financially. All these threats could be easily curtailed. CUSET had given birth to space-borne habitats, a navy, a Marine Corps and a dozen civilian colonies. But its management and shareholders still thought of those things as departments of a gargantuan sprawling economic empire. Todd was not the only one who could clearly see that in actual fact these elements were the raw material for a new civilization. Probably that raw material would not even begin to transform into anything near its potential until he and others of his generation finally had the chance to rise into positions of power themselves.

Positions of power. He contemplated that phrase angrily for some time, turning it over and over in his mind like a broken thing that wanted fixing. He was in a position of power, right here, right now. But that power was caged. If only Glass had trusted his judgement, allowed him to fire on the Jarinyi when they frustrated the first attempt to harvest the Pumpkin Patch. The reports would have said it was self-defense. Any bleeding hearts among the civs present wouldn't have dared contradict it.

He realized with a start that he'd been staring at one of those civs while lost in his thoughts. The field worker broke eye contact, grumbling expletives under his breath and turning his back. He'd probably assumed Todd's anger was meant for him.

Well, let him. If it makes him hurry up, then hoorah for the angry face.

Beyond the worker, at the other end of the patch, Turk paced like a caged animal along his strip of perimeter. Todd's stomach tightened. He didn't admit to being rattled by much, but Attikula was a real concern. In a quiet moment over drinks after quelling the uprising on Centauri, two of the girls had confided in Todd their suspicion that the previous Looey – who'd served only three days with them before being KIA – had actually been a victim of friendly fire. Not that Turk could be called friendly.

Todd had been watching his back ever since. And three years was a long time to do that. He'd considered dozens of ways to get rid of Turk. The only thing Turk actually feared was losing his income stream and though Todd despised that about him, it did present some leverage. That little tussle with Fisher had been perfect: that was Strike Two. Just one more documentable reason and they could ship him back to whatever Earth hovel he was born in.

He just hoped that whatever that slip was, it wouldn't cause too much mess. The man was a psychopath. It was lucky for Turk that none of Romaine's buddies knew what he'd done to that carload of Centauran civilians or he'd be serving hard labor for a very long time. Todd understood that CUSET had invested a lot of money in Turk's extra training and augments and all, but to keep him on after that, to keep a loose cannon rolling about on the ship, it was just asking for trouble.

Turk would eventually implode. Or maybe he'd just have an accident, maybe fall out of a Reaper from two hundred meters up.

Yeah. That might work.

THE FIRST HOUR TRICKLED PAST MIMICKING THE WAY BEADS OF SWEAT traversed Romaine's forehead, his back, his legs. He spent it watching workers carefully sampling the Tigerclaw plants, carefully testing, carefully harvesting the leaves, carefully storing them. Carswell had pestered many of them for a good fifteen minutes after the episode with Turk, but now even he had tired. Romaine had last seen him taking shelter from the sun just inside the forest, unconcerned about Jarinyi or wildlife. The realization finally dawned on Romaine that this would not be a quick trip. The Reaper had left for other business and would not return until Todd ordered it to. If he was here until they'd finished harvesting, this might take the entire day. They were benching him. The letter of Glass's order to Todd was to take the Investigator here. No mention of bringing him back, no compulsion to do more. He was stuck here until they decided it was time for him to move.

Normally he got to go about his business, commandeering whatever resources he needed. Local supervisors or officers bent over backwards for him. He wasn't as stupid as a number of other Investigators who took this cooperativeness as a mark of their importance. Romaine knew it was due to the heavy penalties CUSET could dish out for obstructing an investigation. They had a lot of leverage over their staff: their own laws and tribunals, private prisons, private armies, private police, financial consequences.

He meandered around the Patch, forcing himself to accept the scratchiness of the leaves. He refused to get panicked as he waved off the pseudo-flies attempting to eat the salt from his skin. Rather than gasping for breath in the thick air, he concentrated on keeping his breathing measured and even. Eventually he decided that he might as well get some work done while he waited for the Reaper's return. There had to be something he could find out even now. Any and every piece of information was a puzzle piece.

Behind his sternum he felt that little twinge again, that tussle between wanting to leave here quickly, and wanting to know who did it and why. 'The addiction of detection,' one of his forensics tutors had called it. That compulsive amalgam of having to know, having to solve, having to make it right. Even off the job, it lingered in the form of obsessively chasing down difficult crosswords and nonograms. Once or twice he and other cops had talked over beers about what came first, the job or the addictive personality. He still didn't know.

Tiring of being watched, he asked Fisher to wait for him by the cases in the staging area and picked his way toward one of the black-caps guarding the perimeter. Todd – who'd been biding his time between stalking the boundary like a nervous guard dog and looking over the shoulders of researchers and field workers – appeared at his elbow.

'Off to interview Sergeant Garlitos, Commander?'

'If that's his name. I assume it's ok if I do my job while you have me stuck out here in the wild.'

'Oh, for sure, sir. And I'm happy to replace Gally while you take him away from his watch. In case you were wondering.'

Romaine dipped his head. 'I was just about to ask if you could.'

'Oh, I know you were.'

'You're sure it's not inconveniencing you?'

'Not at all.'

'You're most kind, Lieutenant.'

'We aim to please, sir.' Todd picked up the pace and left Romaine wending his way more gingerly between leaves, twigs, prickles. Romaine watched him motion to Garlitos.

The noncom frowned then came forwards off his position. Romaine interviewed him standing there a dozen meters from the treeline. The morning sun was becoming hot. Although he would have loved to have sat down beneath the shade of the forest, he rationalized that sitting in amongst the creepycrawlies and the mud of an alien world was far less preferable than getting mild sunburn out in the open.

The conversation with 'Gally' led nowhere.

It was becoming a theme.

OTHER CONVERSATIONS WITH RECONS WERE NO MORE HELPFUL. ROMAINE avoided Turk, speaking only to the ones on the far side of the clearing from the brute. With the morning wearing on, he sat himself on bare earth in the shade of storage cases. Dirt or no dirt, he was sick of standing.

He pored over the files he'd earlier copied to his SCRoLL, immersing himself in the case, returning finally to the Gutierrez personnel file. He could find no connection to drug cartels, no gambling debts, nothing kinky. He hadn't yet ascertained whether or not the file had been sanitized, and now ran it through some customware provided him by an app-writer on Bona Vista.

Fisher had finally given up her stiff-backed bodyguard act, sitting on the ground nearby, cross-legged and looking hot.

Not hot *hot*, he corrected himself. *Overheated.*

There was room for her to sit in the shade beside him, but if he suggested it, she might take it as him making advances. And if she didn't take it that way, the other Marines would.

'Fisher.' She squinted at him in the sun. 'Drink some water.'

She nodded and reached for her flask. He mirrored the action, put his bottle on the ground when the SCRoLL chimed at him. He tilted it so the glare slid off the screen, but his eyes narrowed anyway.

What have we here?

The file *had* been sanitized, but the only thing affected was a text to the dead man's fiancé on Centauri, now deleted. It took the app about five seconds to reconstruct the message. Romaine tapped his stylus on his teeth as he went through it, frowning. There was nothing there. It was a run-of-the-mill message, half-pining half-whining, the lovey-dovey bits soppy as all get-out, the complaints terse and generic. Just a guy wanting to get the hell away from his latest deployment and be with his girl. A guy who didn't want to be where he was, but had no way out until his job was over.

I know that *feeling.*

Generic anxious frustrated whining. A guy who wanted out.

He made a *hmm* noise and turned to Lim's file, Cooper's, Yario's, a couple more grunts he hadn't met yet. Like Gutierrez, they'd sent a few personal texts out with the camp messagepacks without disclosing where they were or what they were doing. In this respect, their writing resembled Gutierrez's. But it differed in that none of their texts held that same trace of anxiety. They were just bored, matter-of-fact. He went through Emmanuel's message one more time. There was something there, an edge to the simplistic language and misspelling that hinted at something scaring him. Or bothering him. Or...

Or maybe you're seeing things that aren't there, Johnny.

He sighed, read the file a third time, trying to find something more concrete. Anything. But there was nothing. Emmanuel appeared to be a pretty simple guy. He'd barely passed Eighth Grade in Mexico City, leaving school for a bakery apprenticeship. He'd left the apprenticeship partway through to spend a few years bouncing in and out of unemployment before joining the Marines during the same recruitment window as Lim and Cooper.

The Mexican had proven himself a consistent under-performer ever since basic training and was planning to leave the service as soon as his first tour was up. Romaine lifted his canteen, sipped lukewarm water. So what the hell were *nuff-nuffs* like Gutierrez and Lim doing in a sensitive spot like Eventide?

By noon, when shade from the cases had deserted him, he was hot and cranky. And finally ready for conversation. He managed to get himself off the ground without groaning in front of the two Marines lounging nearby. Todd had sent over Lim and a bald recon named Fester to take a break, replacing them with rested Marines. Romaine stepped close to Fisher, drawing her with him out into the field.

'I've been reading the Columbus personnel files. As well as the star system's location.'

'Uh-huh?' Her face was flushed with heat but she seemed alert, more alert than he was feeling anyway.

'Interesting thing. We're further away from Earth than any other settlement. But every horticulturalist, every biotechnician, every regular was recruited from Earth – except for you. You're the only colonist in the regulars. Cooper's English, Lim is Taiwanese, Gutierrez was Mexican. There's Indians and Central Americans. Yario's Canadian. Ranarith's Cambodian. Glass is American. Almost all of the blackcaps were originally recruited from various Earth armed forces. Both your pilots might be Star Navy, but they were originally Australian police pilots. Aren't there CUSET staff born in the Colonies who are just as qualified for this place?'

'Gutierrez was about to acquire land on Centauri,' she said. 'We talked about it in the Mess one night. He showed me some holos of his fiancé who lives there.'

'But he wasn't Centauran. And I'll bet she'd moved there rather than being born there. This mission is filled with Earthers.'

Fisher's eyes were clouded; perhaps she was thinking about Gutierrez's fiancé or missing her own home on Centauri. 'I'm sure there's colonials here. Lieutenant Todd is a Castorian, isn't he?'

'Yeah. That's interesting too. You've got six biochemists here, all Castorian. And Todd and...' He paused, flicking through files. '...Dumetriscu are Castorian too. We all know Castor is the Colony most loyal to CUSET. *You're* the only non-Castorian among the colonials present.'

'That's interesting sir,' she said.

But she didn't sound interested. And that wouldn't do. As much as he hated to admit it, it helped to have someone to bounce off, to engage with. So he found a way to engage *her*.

'Let's take a good look at you, Corporal Jennifer Fisher,' he said, accessing her file. 'In December, you were offered your promotion to Corporal if you signed on for a third term. You were also asked to try out for the recons but declined. You have an exemplary record. In fact, I found notes on your file that indicate they see you as favorably "compliant".'

Though Fisher kept her features bland, he sensed new tension in her body language. She was offended by the word.

Now we're getting somewhere.

'Compliant, sir? What do they mean?'

'Judging by the other notes here, they mean that you do what you're told, don't ask questions and keep your mouth shut. Apparently you had something to do with quelling the riots in the Pan-Asteroid Communities three years ago?'

She looked even more troubled. 'The PAC. Yes, sir.'

'Not a happy memory?'

'Not really, sir. But I think I did my duty without causing any harm.' She raised her chin, stood her ground. He liked defiance in a fellow cop.

'Exactly. That's in there too. You weren't driven to excess in your handling of the rioters, unlike some other MPs and the rentacops local management brought in. And – this is noted in your file – you haven't talked to anyone about it since.'

She frowned. 'How do they know that?'

'What, you don't think they'd bug you?'

Her frown became more pronounced. 'But I had a four-week pass and went back home straight after that. I could have talked to people then.'

'But you didn't, did you?' She stared back for a time, then slowly shook her head. 'And they know that. So either your civilian clothes are bugged – or you were followed by plain clothes operatives. Either way, they know you've towed the line.'

She was quiet a long while, nostrils flaring, then simply said, 'Sheesh.'

'You have to forgive CUSET for spying on staff. Those events were a media nightmare. I don't know if you kept up with any Earth or Lunar pedecasts and blogs at the time, but there was a lot of talk that the way CUSET handled those riots lead directly to the first Centauran uprising. And you being a Centauran and all...' He let the implication hang in the air: CUSET trusted her less than other personnel simply because of where she was born.

Her lips were pressed tight, her jaw working. He certainly had her attention now.

He fanned his face with his SCRoLL. 'So we're part of a crew staffed almost entirely by non-colonials. Even me, Fisher. I'm a ...' He offered her a wry smile. 'I'm a *spacer*, to quote Carswell.'

SHE DROPPED INTO A CROUCH THEN, PRETENDING TO FIX HER BOOTLACE SO as to cover the angry flush in her cheeks. *They spied on me. How could they do that?*

Romaine was still talking, seemingly oblivious to her feelings. That was probably good. 'I get the feeling that all the personnel were picked to be unsympathetic to the locals.'

She straightened, shifting her weight from foot to foot, avoiding his gaze, feeling queasy. This was exactly the kind of talk that muddled her thoughts. Part of her wanted to go find whoever bugged her clothing and scream at them. Another part was chiding her to accept her place in the order of things.

It didn't feel right, all this talk about how bad CUSET might be. She heard her town pastor's voice – two sentences from a conversation long ago: *If we don't respect authority, we have no authority. Without authority, there's no civilization.* She'd remembered that because it seemed to fly in the face of the otherwise earthy and informal faith he normally preached. Her townspeople were all devout, but they'd built no chapel, held no regular services. Their spirituality was one that was removed from more institutional and hierarchical versions of Christianity. Their pastor didn't interfere in other people's lives, didn't ask for money, himself a corn farmer. And he claimed no authority over them. But on this subject – she thought the context may have been a sermon on respecting governments and employers – he seemed to be saying that making waves would eventually undermine society's order. He had also said, *It's God's job to bring down leaders if they're unjust, not ours.*

Well, regardless, she felt violated. She wanted to read her personnel file now, to see what other nonsense they'd written about her. And she knew she could, because she had a copy in her slim. If these people had been spying on her, surely they knew her faith was about keeping peace, not threatening it. *How can they think that I'd have anything to do with the Separatists?*

'You uncomfortable talking about this, Fisher?' Romaine asked, breaking into her thoughts.

She made a shrugging motion, ducking her head. 'I ... I guess I am. I know CUSET isn't perfect, but they're our employers when it comes down to it. We're employed to support them. We shouldn't be ... well, I don't know. I guess all this conspiracy talk feels wrong to me. I was raised not to gossip.'

He gave her a serious look. 'Maybe that's why they called you *compliant.*'

'Maybe it is,' she said quietly.

He studied her for a moment. 'You're ticked off about being called that, aren't you?'

She shrugged again. That ducking motion. Damn if she didn't look even more like Harshini when she did that. 'I guess that's not a word I'd have used to describe myself. It makes me sound ... like a doormat.'

'Well,' he chuckled. 'You're no doormat. Turk will testify to that.'

She flinched and he studied her more closely. 'Fisher, you also seem embarrassed you beat a recon in hand-to-hand combat. If that were me, I'd be pedecasting about it!'

She gave a half-hearted smile.

Romaine rubbed at his eyes, dragged his fingers down his face. The bright sunlight was giving him a headache and he was growing impatient with Fisher's inhibitions and awkwardness. 'Corporal. You did your job. You kept the peace, prevented a crime and you didn't even injure the man. Well, maybe his pride.'

She grimaced and gave him a frank look. 'Yes, sir, I'm concerned about that. Men like Sgt Attikula, pride is their problem. What he wanted to do to you, to me, to Dr Carswell: now that I've embarrassed him, that violence will come out some other way.'

'Not your responsibility.' He took a deep breath and blew it out slow. 'Now. I believe we were musing about the inanity and corruption of our superiors.'

'Sir, I'll be honest. I'm not just hesitant to criticize CUSET on principle. You mentioned surveillance before.'

'It's okay, Fisher. What do you think will happen if they do overhear us talking about them? They won't execute you. They won't imprison you. You're not breaking a law. And they might upgrade your file from *compliant* to *free thinker*. That's gotta be an improvement, huh?'

She refused to smile, just nodded politely.

'Okay, spit it out Fisher. I prefer it when you just speak your mind. Are you afraid of losing your job? Is that it?'

'Commander, I'm the biggest source of income for my family. They're not poor, you understand. We have amenities, good education, but our lifestyle back home is pretty basic. One day my folks will get old and they'll need district nurses to come out from the city. That kind of care isn't cheap.' She gathered her thoughts for a moment. 'There's no margin in our finances. There might be a flood or a fire, a drought, crops might fail. I do this job to put money aside for those things. I just don't want to jeopardize that. Sir.'

Romaine gathered his own thoughts, softening his tone. 'Listen. Our clothes and gear aren't bugged. I checked when we were in the jeep yesterday. I did it again before we left on the Reaper this morning.'

'Checked?'

'A guy I know – an appwriter – owed me a favor last year, put an anti-surveillance patch in my SCRoLL. Amongst other things. We can talk securely.'

She glanced at his old model notebook and visibly relaxed. 'Okay, sir. You were saying?'

'I was saying that we were all picked to be unsympathetic to the indigenous inhabitants of this planet and to Separatists. The Earthers among us were picked to be unsympathetic toward the PRC.'

'To the Chinese? Why would that even matter, sir?'

'Good question. I like questions. You were raised away from Earth, so this may take some explaining. Most Earth countries harbor some ill-feeling toward China mainly because of things they did last century. I mean they're the only ones who benefited when Western nations were nearly destroyed by the combination of first-generation nanotech, social upheaval, economic devastation, climate change and the viral evolution of Artificial Intelligence. Europe, Japan, Asia-Pacific, South and North America all paint the PRC as villains. And CUSET grew mainly out of those regions.' He looked closely at her. 'Well, I'll dispense with the history lecture. I find this stuff interesting, but your eyes are glazing over.'

She half-smiled again. 'Just don't really understand it, sir.'

He turned side-on to her, mainly to get the sun's glare off his face. 'Let's just say the PRC on Earth has lots of trade partners, lots of allies, but few real friends. Everyone continues to feel threatened by them. The corporations that make up CUSET included.'

A flock of *somethings* chased each other high above, appearing from behind him and wheeling southward. He tensed: their appearance resurrected a long-forgotten fear of getting hit with bird-poop. When nothing fell his way, he continued. 'Out here in the Great Wide Galaxy, the only people apart from the PRC with large financial investments are our employers. CUSET stakeholders hate and fear the Chinese, maybe even more than Earth nations and companies, because of our isolation. Out here, it's just Us and Them. We run-of-the-mill spacers who deal with the Chinese occasionally find them polite and helpful.

And you Colonials rarely deal with them at all, so you either have no feelings toward them in particular ... or from some conversations I've overheard, you sympathize with them, feel like they're treated as badly by CUSET as you are.'

The flock of somethings dipped below the trees half a kilometer away and reappeared, heading back his way. Maybe they'd pass across Todd or Carswell and empty full bladders and bowels upon them both. He could only hope.

'My point is this. I'd never heard of Eventide. You'd never heard of it. It's classified. That in itself is against new amendments to the Expansion Treaty. The Chinese aren't meant to be kept in the dark like this. But hardly anyone here would feel sorry for them.'

Fisher nodded, understanding.

The flying things banked right, aborting their return to his airspace, and fled south at high speed with a smaller flock of bigger somethings in hot pursuit. With the threat of aerial bombardment passing, he returned his attention fully to Fisher. 'There's a damn good reason why we don't hide planets. The PRC potentially could "discover" this place next week, send troops to take ownership of it, find us here and trigger another Shui Valley.'

She stroked a Tigerclaw leaf with the back of her hand. 'If it's so risky, why doesn't CUSET just disclose the planet? It's not like the Chinese would object or invade or something. Not once it was out in the open.'

'They won't do *nothing* either. Even if CUSET didn't disclose the things they've discovered here, once the Chinese had the name of the planet, their spies would know what to dig for. And they'd have a location to send their spy-probes. Eventually they'd find out about this.' He gestured at the field with both hands. 'I can easily imagine two superpowers fighting over who gets to exploit the Jarinyi and their wonder-drug.'

'Exploit?'

'Utilize.'

Fisher looked genuinely perplexed. 'But how would they utilize the Jarinyi?'

Shrugging, he said, 'I don't know. I'm only musing. Or maybe I'm catching some of Carswell's paranoia.' He hoped not. He had enough of his own.

For a while he turned ideas over in his mind, trying to surmise a link between CUSET's breach of the Expansion Treaty, the scarcity of Colonials among Glass's crew and the death of a Marine private originally from Mexico. Maybe there *was* no connection. Maybe CUSET's subterfuge was merely the habitual self-interest of powerful organizations down through the centuries, nothing more than a backdrop for Gutierrez' murder.

Then again, Romaine had a hard time believing context accounted for nothing.

Fisher had turned toward the forest to the west, watching Turk. The huge Marine was fifty meters away, strutting toward a new position on the perimeter. Presumably Todd moved his people around to keep them alert. Turk caught her looking and bared his teeth. He sighted along his shotgun at them. Fisher shook her head, turning her back on the gesture.

There's two kinds of violent men in this universe, Romaine thought. *Those with an agenda, and those with serious neurological defects.*

With a jolt, something cleared in his mind. There was no grand conspiracy – no agenda – behind this murder. It was simply his own lingering anger and guilt over Harshini's death that made him see another death born of CUSET subterfuge and betrayal.

Let it go, Johnny, let it go. It's been ten hacking years.

This murder was purely and simply about Gutierrez. In a murder case, the most likely suspects were first of all family, then acquaintances, then workmates; expanding circles of relationship. Turk qualified as both of the last two categories. And the man had a serious neurological defect from the look of him, made worse by the possible use of drugs.

He had already read Attikula's file but called it up again, skimmed it. There were no black marks on his record. No commendations either. It was thin, but the file hadn't been sanitized. If Romaine had been aboard a naval vessel, he could have run detailed background checks on Turk, made sure of what he was dealing with before he went after him. Out here he had nothing to go on but the man himself.

Waving a trio of the pseudo-flies away from Fisher's back he tapped her gently on the shoulder. He inclined his head toward Turk whose focus had shifted back onto the forest. 'I'm interested to see what might happen if we exerted a little pressure on Sergeant Frankenstein there.'

Her eyes widened. 'Why, sir? If I may ask?'

'I'm still at the musing stage of my investigation.' He mimed prizing something apart. 'Solving a crime is like solving any puzzle. You ask a question, try an idea, follow one path through a maze, pull on a thread. Turk is a thread. He's angry and arrogant enough to resort to sudden violence. Maybe he's also the type to premeditate it. He's strong enough to use a Jarinyi bow. A lot stronger than Carswell,' he chuckled. 'If Gutierrez did something to tick him off... While we're here, we may as well tug that thread and see what works loose.'

'Sir, a few minutes ago, you told me to just speak my mind, didn't you?'

'Yes, I did.'

She took a step away, clasped her fingers together and flexed them cracking her knuckles. 'So I'm just going to speak my mind then.'

'You do that.'

'Right. So. I think provoking Sgt Attikula is not an appropriate action for us to take.'

'In other words, it's stupid.'

She made a noncommittal face. 'Not stupid, sir...ill-advised.'

He chuckled again. She probably expected him to order her to go irritate Attikula, to pour fuel on his simmering rage. *No, not a good idea, that,* he agreed silently.

I need to get Attikula off his turf – the outdoors, with a gun in his hand – and onto mine – a small bare room, no weapons, just chairs and a table and a recording device. Make him sit for hours answering tedious question after question. Bore him into slipping up.

And if that didn't work, try the good cop routine, the best buddy act. Butter him up and hope he'd confide some valuable and incriminating piece of information.

And if that still didn't work, *then* provoke him with veiled insults about his intelligence or physical prowess until he loudly and violently asserted that he certainly did have the kahoneys to kill Gutierrez.

If none of that worked - and if he didn't get cooperation and progress by tomorrow night - he would return to Bona Vista and insist they send Columbus personnel to him *there*. Attikula could languish in an interview room on BV for a week, while Romaine went home at night to watch historical docos and other pedecasts, and drink perfectly chilled scotch and perfectly warm Guinness.

Yep. In his dreams.

They'd never agree to it. Once he left this place, the investigation would be over. He probably had a day or two more before it wasn't just Glass and Todd losing patience with him. Dreyfuss would be screaming for his best guess in a report. And somehow, he'd have to convince history not to blame the official Investigator if any Eventideans got killed over this.

He needed Fisher. He needed an ally here. He felt sure he had one in the Quartermaster Menabu, but couldn't see what good that did him. Fisher seemed to be a real cop, whether she even knew it or not; he'd seen it in her eyes when she took on Turk/Attikula/Frankenstein/whatever. And she seemed genuinely sympathetic to the Jarinyi, so she'd be reticent to cooperate with any conspiracy to falsely implicate them in this killing. He had to trust her, and draw her further over his side of the fence.

'Corporal, I'm not suggesting we go and kick him in the ass. When we get back to camp, I want to take away his weapons, put him in a meeting room and quiz him stupid until his teeny-weeny brain can't take it anymore and he lets something slip.'

'Oh,' was all she said in reply.

With a sigh, he fanned his face with the SCRoLL again and muttered, 'In a perfect universe, I'd pull him away from his environment and put him in mine. Here, the closest thing I've got to that is the storage cupboard you call an office.'

'Given his actions today, I'm just not sure that's safe, sir.'

Romaine made a dismissive noise. 'Welcome to the world of police work, Corporal. Look, he's been ordered to keep control of himself. And you've already beaten him once today. He's not likely to actually attack either of us.'

Fisher looked unconvinced and Romaine let it drop. Whether she liked it or not, he was going to do it the second they all got back to camp.

For the moment, perhaps he could maneuver Chua into disclosing some dirt on Turk. She didn't seem to like him much, after all. He excused himself and headed her way.

FISHER WATCHED HIM GO, FEELING AMBIVALENT. HER DUTY WAS TO STAY close, protect and assist him. But Romaine seemed to prefer working alone much of the time.

It was so hot, she honestly couldn't be bothered following him anymore. He would call her when he needed.

As they'd talked about Turk, they'd wandered closer to the edge of the Patch. She stayed there, looking longingly at the shade only a couple dozen meters away from her. It looked cooler in under the trees, but she knew that was wishful thinking. The humidity would be just as bad there as it was out here.

A glance at her seiko surprised her when she realized she'd been standing here staring for over ten minutes. She must have zoned out, dozed on her feet. Unbeknownst to her, two of the sentries had swapped positions, bringing Turk closer. A few dozen paces away, he scooped up a clod of soil and threw it at the forest, tracking its descent with his gun-barrel, then turned his malevolent glare on her.

She tried to find something other than Turk's mean mug to focus on, and her eyes fell upon a dying tree on the edge of the forest. The trunk was turning white, most of its branches denuded, clawing at the sky as if pleading for help. It made an eerily beautiful counterpoint to the greens and browns around it. Then she noticed what looked like Tigerclaw seedlings all around it. She took a step nearer. Yes, that's what they were. Some had embedded themselves in soil between the exposed roots of the tree. She remembered Lieutenant Todd saying the plant was 'hardy and aggressive'. It looked like the seedlings were either sucking the life from the soil around the tree, or were somehow poisoning it. That struck her as amazing: the small plant was stronger than the mighty tree.

Tigerclaw could possibly take over the forest! I wonder what keeps it at bay –

A flash of movement, out-of-place, made her snap her head around toward Turk. Two small Jarinyi – youths by the look of them – had taken advantage of the big recon's inattention, bolting past behind his back at a dead run. Another blackcap, Kwan, further around the perimeter, gave a shout. Fisher pointed. Turk whirled and gaped as the young aliens bounded through the Pumpkin Patch toward a trio of scientists. The three people had frozen, fear dawning on their faces. Kwan started their way, then stopped, recognizing his place was still at the perimeter. He raised his weapon and peered uncertainly into the trees, reached up to tap his earpiece.

Turk and Fisher launched into action simultaneously, and as the Jarinyi neared the scientists, other humans began converging on the spot. A nearby researcher flourished a pair of secateurs at them. Todd charged over from the staging area, Carswell from the far side of the field. Turk shouted obscenities as he ran.

The two Jarinyi stopped abruptly in front of the startled researchers, gesticulating and making sounds that reminded Fisher of outraged turkeys. The fourth researcher arrived next, taking hold of one of the scientists – presumably a sweetheart – and pushing her behind him. One of the others held up a pruning knife, swearing. Turk arrived, shouldering one of the youths aside and positioning himself in front of the other, shotgun held across his chest defensively, shouting at them to stand back. The Jarinyi he'd knocked aside fell heavily.

As Fisher neared, she noticed Turk's face was as red as it had been when she'd fought him earlier, his rage building. Dread trickled like ice water into her gut. 'They're just kids!' she shouted. She could hear Carswell shouting 'wait' over and over as he approached.

The young male who had fallen sprang to his feet, ducked behind

Turk and deftly snatched the secateurs from the researcher's hand. The researcher stumbled backward, knocking his sweetheart beneath the Tigerclaw fronds as he fell. Turk swiveled and thrust his shotgun butt into the Jarinyi's ribs, knocking him sideways again, away from the scientists. The second Jarinyi stepped forward just as Todd came up behind the scientists. Grabbing at Turk's weapon, the youth made a coughing noise, spitting mucus from its small mouth at the much larger human's face. Turk instinctively whipped his head away and caught the spittle on his cheek. He gave a cry of pure anger and twisted his weapon violently out the Jarinyi's grip. Fisher gasped in horror as the shotgun's muzzle turned toward the offending Jarinyi while his friend sprang forward to either restrain or assist him.

Turk fired.

The shot boomed so loud, it seemed to punctuate the moment, freezing time itself. For one eternal instant, all movement slowed to a stop – those people standing by staring silently, breath caught in their throats, those running closer now stumbling to a halt. The shotgun's report had sucked all other sound from Fisher's ears, enhancing the illusion of time standing still.

Then the two Jarinyi flew backward, limbs flailing in their wake, blood spray mottling Tigerclaw leaves a dark pink. People began reacting. Someone was crying, 'Oh no, oh no' over and over. Fisher realized it was her. The youths had fallen near her, one obviously dead, its torso a bloody mess, the other writhing soundlessly, left ribcage and arm shredded, pumping gore onto the soil, face-gills opening and closing like a landed fish.

She tore her eyes away from this horror, took in the reactions of the people around her. Carswell took a few wooden steps toward them. The scientists who'd been accosted turned away. The sweetheart released a sob into the protective embrace of the man who'd owned the secateurs. Todd pushed through them, peeling back a Tigerclaw frond and gaping in pale shock at the dead and dying Jarinyi. Marines not on perimeter duty were approaching now, their eyes fixed on Turk, expressions unreadable.

She forced her attention onto the Jarinyi again, could actually feel this moment etching itself into her memory. Commander Romaine had wanted to put pressure on Turk, hoping to provoke an error. What an error these poor Jarinyi had provoked.

Somehow Romaine was now at her side. Somehow he was echoing her thoughts, his voice in her ear sounding hollow as he murmured, 'God Almighty. I didn't mean this.'

A cough. A snort. The young Jarinyi made a clutching motion at the soil and died.

12

'If the tiger is lying down, do not say the tiger is showing respect.'

- Cambodian proverb

CHEST HEAVING, Todd stared down at bloody collateral damage, took in the crowd of witnesses, and turned his glare on Turk.

He hissed, 'What did you do?' then shouted, 'WHAT DID YOU DO?!'

'But...' Turk faltered.

'Shut up!'

'I thought... Aren't we -?'

'SHUT YOUR MOUTH!' Todd shouted again, lunging at him. Right now, he wanted to rip Turk's heart out.

Despite their size disparity, Turk took a step backward, frowning like an offended teenager. The shotgun dangled loosely from his right hand, pointed at the soil by his feet.

Through clenched teeth, Todd told him, 'If you don't start obeying orders, I'm going to shoot you myself!'

'Hey!' someone shouted. Cooper. He pointed at the trees where two more Jarinyi youths stood as still as stone. Then they exploded into flight, dashing back into the forest.

Kwan hurdled a log and gave chase. Turk broke away from the crowd to follow him, shotgun now held above his head as he ploughed through Tigerclaw.

'Cease and desist!' Todd barked into his commlink. 'Do not give chase, repeat, do not give chase.'

Turk kept on running.

Todd dropped his hand and shouted at him: 'Get back here, Turk! That's an order!' But Turk, nearing the treeline by this stage, plucked out his earpiece and tossed it aside before vaulting the same log Kwan had. Several other Recons shouted at him to stop, disbelieving expressions on their faces.

Moments passed, then Kwan jogged back into sight, heading for his assigned position, watching over his shoulder. Whether this was in hope of seeing Turk following him back, or out of concern about a Jarinyi attack of some kind, Todd couldn't tell.

He stroked his forehead with one hand. 'That puke! That sonofa*bitch*!'

Turk had lost control. Again.

Well, it would be the final time. A professional soldier losing control was an oxymoron in Todd's book. He cursed loudly as he turned to Gally. '*If* he comes back, he's finished.' Gally nodded in complete agreement. Todd touched his earpiece again. 'We're out of here, folks. But not without the Tigerclaw. Kwan, Maglic, move your positions forward to the treeline. Fester, Cristina, maintain your current positions. Chua, cover Turk's position. The rest of you, get these crates aboard the flier!'

As people rushed to attend to their jobs, he called the only available Reaper back, slapping Romaine on the shoulder as he did so and pointing to a pile of small containers the trio of scientists had been filling. Romaine took his meaning immediately and motioned for Fisher to help him lug the box back to the staging area. Todd felt a swell of satisfaction that the cop was following *his* orders.

When he'd finished speaking with Donaldson the pilot, he barked at nearby researchers caught staring in grim fascination at the dead bodies. 'Get some leaf into this crate and get moving!'

Lim was still standing by a couple of crates staring out into the trees, his '90 at the ready. 'Hey! Asshole!' he called. The Private took no notice. Todd could see by his rapid breathing he was close to a panic attack.

Never seen action, he thought with disgust. *Why the hell d'they send these green little grunts?*

He strode over, took hold of the man's rifle and pointed it forcefully at the ground. 'Private, you go waving that thing about like a hysterical girl and you're likely to kill one of my men. Or me. Flip the safety back on, bring a jeep over and load these two boxes on board. Then bring the jeep to the Reaper when it lands. Cooper, you go with him, stay on the gun,' he added, meaning the rear-mounted chain-gun.

'But sir,' Lim stammered, 'we bring the jeep, we'll crush the plants.'

'I'll live with it. *Move!*' He shoved the man away, looked up at a rich blue sky and let the turn of events and its implications sink in. 'Well,' he said to the sky. 'Let's hope it's a gift.'

A DOZEN METERS AWAY, LUGGING A LOAD THAT SEEMED TOO SMALL FOR two people but just too big for one, Fisher and Romaine passed Carswell. Romaine suddenly saw a different side to the man. He stood stock still, grinding his teeth, face wet with tears, eyes fixed on the spot where the two bodies lay – though from his vantage point he couldn't see them beneath all the foliage. His interest in the Jarinyi was not just professional; he *loved* them.

'I'm sorry, Doctor,' Romaine said.

Carswell did not respond, but moved woodenly toward the bodies.

EVEN PUSHING THEM HARD, TODD FOUND IT TOOK TWENTY MINUTES TO finish filling the crates with Tigerclaw leaves and loading them aboard the Reaper. That left little room for passengers, except the vacant seat up front by the pilot. Todd ordered two of the field workers into the back and another into the cockpit. All three hastily clambered aboard, avoiding angry and jealous looks from their unlucky cohorts. He gathered McGrath and Chua, told them to wait there with the remaining field workers who had flocked together near the staging area like chickens cowering in the corner of a henhouse, touching each other's arms anxiously and making noises that sounded exactly like clucking.

Disgusted, he told the women, 'I've called back Glass's Reaper. It's still forty minutes away. Be a squeeze, but you can all fit in.'

'Maybe Tiny here could sit up front,' McGrath deadpanned, gesturing to Chua. 'That'd give us half as much space again.'

Todd nodded. 'I'm sure she won't complain.'

'Damn straight,' said Chua with a sideways glance at McGrath.

Todd groaned quietly at the catty undertone. *Play nice, girls.* 'I'll get everyone else out via jeep. You ok if we leave now?'

McGrath shrugged. 'You're the boss.'

Chua said, 'You don't wanna wait for the fliers to come back for the rest of you?'

Todd was already shaking his head before she finished. 'If we leave the jeeps here, they might vandalize them. I'd rather keep 'em in one piece. Any warriors they have can't be too close; those indigs were just young punks acting on their own, probably without their parents knowing. If we hit that stream bed fast, they won't have a chance to hit *us* even if they are out there somewhere. And besides,' he tapped his helmet with the barrel of his rifle. 'What are they gonna do to us?'

Chua nodded, eyes flicking over Todd's shoulder. 'You don't want the sky-blue to come with?'

Sky-blue was Marine talk for navy cop. He said, 'There's no room. Scientists are higher priority. Romaine's with me.'

They saluted him and he saluted back, spun around to order people into jeeps. Romaine and Fisher were sent to the lead jeep with Cooper. Moving toward his own jeep, he heard Romaine call his name.

'What?'

Romaine pointed. 'What about him?'

Todd followed looked, saw Carswell now standing over where the dead Jarinyi lay. Todd blew out his breath in frustration. 'Pick him up if you want. What do I care?'

Cooper swung the jeep around and headed toward the lone man near the edge of the Pumpkin Patch.

THE CONVOY MOVED AS HASTILY AS POSSIBLE ALONG THE NARROW TRACK. Romaine and Fisher bounced around in the rear seat of the leading jeep. Occasionally Romaine caught the grim expression on the driver's face as he glanced in the mirror. His companion in the front seat – Carswell – had tossed Cooper's pulse rifle into Romaine's lap when Cooper offered it to him.

Fisher's head moved from side to side as they drove, her hand at her holster. Romaine leaned across Carswell to talk to her quietly. 'What are the chances of us being attacked?'

'Sir, Dr. Carswell would be the expert there.'

Romaine said his name, but Carswell just stared ahead impassively. He hadn't spoken since the Pumpkin Patch. Romaine grunted, his sympathy for the man already waning and turned his attention back to Fisher. 'Do *you* think there'll be trouble?'

'Sir, I don't know. I'm an MP. Sir, it might be best if you sat back in your...'

She never finished the sentence. The jeep swerved, slewing toward the trees. Romaine – angled sideways to talk with Fisher – slammed into the back of the driver's seat. The vehicle bounced and changed direction. Fisher's arm thumped him across the chest. Someone let out a cry of primitive alarm.

The jeep commenced a fast one-eighty-degree turn. Something warm and sticky sprayed across his forehead. His hand flew to his head as he was flung back into his seat again and came away marked with a red smear across his palm.

My blood or – ?

He had only an instant then to register the gestalt – the body of the driver leaning across into Carswell's lap with thick drops of blood flying from head and neck wounds - before the jeep hit a log on the north side of the track and became airborne.

He was momentarily weightless, trees and ground spinning around him. Fisher's scream stabbed at his left ear then got sucked away as he plunged through a net of branches which grabbed at his legs and chest before he slammed hard into dirt.

Romaine blacked out.

***

CURSES CHOKED IN TODD'S THROAT AS THE LEAD JEEP BEGAN ITS CRAZED dance. When it spun to face him, he registered the body of the driver and the blood, saw Carswell's vacant doll-like expression, glimpsed an assault rifle flung out and clattering along the stream bed. The passengers in the rear were thrown about like trees in a gale.

'*Keep going!*' he screamed at his own driver who was already sliding the jeep to a halt on the south side of the track. They had to get out of the kill zone. But the stupid bastard wasn't having it and the jeep nosed against a fallen tree, juddering to a halt. The driver was already bailing.

Ahead the forward jeep spun around again before hitting something and flipping into the jungle, coming to rest two meters in the air upside down amongst the roots of a fallen tree. Where the attack had come from was anybody's guess. With the troops in his jeep already following the driver and the rear jeep pulling up behind them uncertainly, Todd rolled over the frame of his vehicle and crouched behind it, shouting into his comm. 'South side of the track! Take cover!'

Men and women poured out of the rear vehicle, but not quickly enough for all of them. A volley of projectiles streaked out of the bushes opposite. Todd went to ground. Two Marines from his car fell nearby before scrambling for cover. One rose, a Jarinyi arrow hanging limply from the webbing of her Tensar vest. He jumped up and shoved at her. She stumbled toward bushes beside the path, throwing herself awkwardly into them.

The other Marine – a regular – struggled on the ground, one hand to his temple, blood pouring between his fingers. He had fallen from the back where he'd manned the tail-gun, completely exposed to their attackers. The idiot hadn't fastened his helmet and it had fallen off, lying nearby. Todd skidded to a halt, intending to go back for him, but a barrage of stones assailed the man, shattering bones in his legs, his arms and finally his skull when he could no longer protect it. He lay still. The attack had lasted no more than five or six seconds.

Todd pedaled backwards, numb. He'd never lost a man before, not even a grunt. He dived for cover himself, his earpiece erupting with shouts.

'*Man down!*'

'Leave him! He's gone –'

'Where are they? Where'd that fire come from?'

'I'm hit! My arm! *Shit!*'

'Get down! Get down!'

'*Quiet!*' Todd bellowed without bothering to use his comm. He crawled on his gut through bracken and slithered over a fallen tree still green with life. Dumetricsu lay there on her side, tugging at the arrow wedged in her webbing.

She smiled without humor. 'They should make a saint of whoever invented Tensar. Didn't feel a thing.'

He leaned over her and snapped the arrow off near the tip. 'Stay here,' he said and began snaking east where he might get a better vantage point. He thumbed his earpiece. 'Call in. Then retain comm silence.'

'Galitos, alive and well.'

'Fester, ready to kick some.'

'Kwan, A-okay.'

'Dumetricsu.'

'Maglic. They cut my *hackin'* arm.'

'Vgrevski. Twisted ankle but ready, sir.'

He waited half a second for Turk before remembering who'd gotten them into this mess. Taking a calming breath, he told them, 'Keep your heads down.'

Maglic added quietly, 'That other humptard grunt is climbing a tree back here.'

Todd twisted. The regular's green uniform was clearly visible a few dozen meters away. The guy had been in the rear seat of the tailing jeep. What was his name?

I'll just call him Idiot, he thought and kept crawling. *What part of* keep your head down *didn't he get?*

Another volley of rocks and arrows cut through the vegetation around him. Then everything fell silent again, including the nearby animal life. It was like entering a plastic bubble, a cocoon familiar from other firefights.

Carefully brushing aside a fern-frond, Todd found the other end of the fallen tree he'd slid over earlier. It was a meter thick at this end and the vantage point provided a clear view of the path. Lim already sheltered there, breathing in quick gasps. Todd rolled in next to him and gripped his arm, murmured in his ear, 'You're going to be okay, Private.'

Lim nodded and swallowed. 'I grabbed my '90,' he whispered. He clung to the rifle like a life preserver.

'You're a real pro. Keep your head down and don't talk unless I talk to you.'

He pulled his *thirdeye* from his breast pocket, a camera as long and thin as a drinking straw which fed wireless vision into Todd's nanoptic augments. The layer of video always felt like it appeared in the back of his mind, a transparent overlay *behind* actual physical vision, like watching both the road *and* a memory while driving. He slid the *thirdeye* above the top of the log and swiveling it, took a good long look around. There was no sign of the enemy. With his free hand he thumbed his send button. 'Fester, Gally, you got anything?'

'*Nada*'. Fester. 'I'm to the rear of the jeeps. All quiet here now.'

'Apart from a headache, nothing.' That was Galitos, who sounded like he was moving, the transmission breathless and scratchy.

'Gally, where are you?' Todd asked.

'Snoopin' and poopin'. Checkin' our six. I think we're alone back here but I'll keep lookin'.'

Good.

Fester asked, 'You want me to call in evac?'

'Where are they gonna land, Fester? And if they decide to provide cover fire from above the trees, without a line of sight there's the chance of us getting hit with friendly fire.'

Besides, it's been a while since some action; this'll keep us sharp. And we can send a message to these indigs, beat them at their own game on their home ground.

Fester made an unhappy noise in response.

'Anybody get a fix on that last volley?' Todd asked. Ambient noise – animal and wind – was beginning to register in his ears again, but it sounded afar off, the humid air like a woolen filter. He swept again with the *thirdeye* and withdrew it, shut it off, slipped it back inside his vest.

'I think I did.' Vgrevski.

'Put a couple of grenades down their throats. Let's make *them* nervous. Everybody else keep your rounds in your weapons until you can see what you're shooting at.'

'Have a little high explosive on us, assholes,' Vgrevski transmitted softly.

A deep *crump* came from across the track. Five seconds later, another followed. Wood chips and dust flew high into the air. As it settled, and the echoes from the explosions faded, they revealed no other movement or sound from across the path.

'Dumetriscu, over here with me. Follow my trail. Someone watch that space between the two vehicles.'

Maglic: 'The Magic's on the case.'

'Gally, don't deploy your *Bear*. We need a fire escape if things go rinky.'

'Gotcha.'

'Kwan, where are you?'

'Not far from Fester'.

'Grab his *Momma Bear* and get it out about twenty meters to his left.'

'Hey-okay.'

'Make sure you and the *Bear* cover that western flank between you. Cristina, where are you?'

Right then, her head peered out from among the ferns and she saw him, grinned.

He rolled his own *Momma Bear* over to her. 'Same orders as Kwan, only east. Tread gently.'

Dumetriscu slipped the mine into her hip-bag and winked. Todd watched as she disappeared into the scrub heading east. With all angles covered, it was only a matter of time until the Jarinyi made a move. And when they did, it would cost them.

TEN MINUTES DRAGGED BY. TODD PERFORMED ANOTHER SWEEP WITH HIS *thirdeye*. Still no movement. He wanted to handle this himself, but if this stalemate went on much longer, he would have to call in a flier to run a sensor sweep of the forest to determine if the Jarinyi were still there. He tapped his visor and the image of the path vanished. He found Lim up close and staring into his face.

'Private, get your weapon up on that log. And keep a low profile.'

Lim's adam's apple bobbed up and down. He carefully raised his head to peep over the log, brought his AR90 to rest on top. Todd rested his back against it.

A few more minutes and we'll see what happens. If nothing else, this is good training for Lim. Might make a man of him.

ROMAINE FIRST BECAME AWARE OF DARKNESS, TIMELESS AND ABSOLUTE. Next came the instinct to locate himself, to connect with something apart from darkness. He found thoughts and then light. As light returned, he squinted upward. Or was it sideways?

Nearby a woman spoke in a hushed tone, a gentle voice, but under-girded by steel.

'Harshini?' he croaked.

No that couldn't be. Harshini was gone. Then who...?

Fisher. Eventide.

He half-sat up, then as his head swam, he lay back down again. He remembered the jeep impacting but not how he got out here. The memory seemed as vaguely connected to his present reality as a dream does to the freshly woken dreamer. He lay face down in a cluster of velvety 'ferns'. They had broken his fall but even so, he hurt. At first the pain was a distant concern, but enough it felt as if someone was rhythmically jabbing him with a nail between the shoulder blades. His neck ached and the back of his head throbbed.

But I can feel my legs. I can feel my legs, thank God.

Lifting his head was like hauling up an anchor. The ferns surrounded him, some a meter high, some two, some three. The ground was alive with bugs, but he was beyond caring and the feeling seemed mutual. He pushed himself up on hands and knees, raised a finger to his forehead causing it to sting sharply, discovered it was bleeding.

'You're cut, but not bad.'

Carswell was several paces away, squatting before Fisher and gently inspecting her hand. 'I think she's come off worse than you, Commander. Two broken fingers, maybe three. We'll need a splint.'

'Not now,' she said, without a trace of pain in her voice. 'Two grenades went off a few minutes ago, sir. Since then, nothing.'

She was alert and on edge, her gaze darting about. Romaine's eyes moved gratingly, like bearings without lubricant. He felt sluggish and strange – until he remembered they'd been ambushed. The jolt of realization made his heart beat harder, cleared his thoughts. Steadying himself against a thick fern trunk with one hand, he drew his handgun with the other, then almost dropped it.

Carswell saw the weapon and sneered. 'Put that away. It's not going to help you.'

'Hack you.' He focused on Fisher, wiped blood out of his vision with his sleeve. 'You okay?'

'I feel better than you look, sir,' she replied. Her right hand injured, she held her own weapon awkwardly in her left.

Romaine couldn't be sure if the forest around them had gone silent or if he'd lost some of his hearing. Nothing felt right and the not-right feeling caused bile to rise in his throat.

Fisher's voice came to him as if through a tube. 'Any orders?'

'Let's get the hell out of here?' he suggested, dabbing at his eyes again.

Carswell pressed his face close and murmured, 'I'm only going to say this once. You have two choices. Stay here and die. Or follow me to safety. Make it a quick choice.'

They gaped at him.

'Come with you *where*?' asked Romaine.

The staccato thump of a detonating mine disturbed the silence – the sound incongruous in this edenic setting. All three froze as one.

Carswell cleared his throat. 'Somewhere not here.'

13

———

'Men have become the tools of their tools.'

- Henry David Thoreau

MORE TIME CRAWLED BY. Todd rested while listening, heard nothing. Perhaps it was time to call in that sensor sweep. He ran his right hand over his left sleeve, feeling for the long-distance communicator embedded there, but was distracted by a simultaneous curse from Lim and the whirr of the Private's AIRTAR. 'What is it, Lim?'

'Rifle's malfunctioning.'

Incompetent humptard. Todd raised himself on a knee. 'Show me.'

'Every time I sweep past that rock ... Watch.'

As Lim shifted his aim toward a mid-sized rock on the path, the tip of his barrel trembled and jiggled, as if it was searching for a target without being able to acquire. Todd frowned. On a whim he pointed his own rifle in the same direction. Same response. Lim gasped.

Todd swept his '90 through a wide arc now. It malfunctioned identically when aimed at a patch of fallen branches five meters across the path from him. 'This is not happening.'

He squeezed his trigger once, aiming at the fallen branches, but nothing happened except the drunken dance of the muzzle. Of course not: weapon wouldn't fire unless the AIRTAR decided it had fully acquired a target. He slumped on his backside, put his back to the tree, thinking hard. AIRTARs had never been known to malfunction like this. What could cause two tried-and-true assault rifles to break down in the same way at the same time?

'*Sir*?' asked Lim, starting to shake. The thought of being without a weapon in this environment was obviously not helping his composure.

Todd's blood had been running hot and fast in his veins since the initial attack, but a terse transmission from Fester was enough to chill him to the marrow: 'Weapon malfunction.'

Another...!

Then insight hit him like an electric charge. *Oh, dear Christ, no.*

'Turn your AIRTARs off!' he barked into his mike, and adjusted his own weapon.

Several voices instantly came back with the identical response: 'Say again?'

Lim whined beside him, 'But how do I aim?'

And then came the *whump* of a Momma Bear going off nearby.

DUMETRISCU HAD MADE LITTLE SOUND AS SHE MOVED EAST. Fernlike plants less than a meter tall and broad-leaved groundcovers carpeted the forest floor between the larger trees. Her passage through the plants would have gone unnoticed by anyone standing even a few paces away. The route with the widest gaps between plants was the one she favored, only pushing back foliage when she had no choice and even then only slightly. Stretching out her body along its left side, she kept left arm forward, right arm cradling her weapon, reaching forward with the leading hand to feel between the ferns before her and part them, her strong legs and left elbow driving her forward.

From above, she knew her movement would look like a doped-up version of a swimmer's sidestroke.

When she felt she'd traveled far enough, Dumetriscu lifted her head slowly between the fern fronds and looked around. To her left was a mold-covered stone or log. The sight of it made her freeze. When after a few seconds she accepted there was no enemy hiding behind it, she resumed a patient survey of the area, deciding that a denser patch of groundcover five meters in front would serve her purposes perfectly. She lifted the *Bear* from her hip pouch and primed it. For the sake of time, she pushed herself up on her elbow and flung it awkwardly. This turned out to be a mistake. The mine left her hand at an odd angle and landed less than three meters away.

Her old drill sergeant's voice screamed inside her head: *Shortcuts'll get you killed!*

Todd barked something over the commlink, which she ignored. She was in range of the mine and had maybe two seconds left before it armed. Swearing, she flipped over, ready to scurry away.

A Jarinyi warrior was diving for her.

What!

Dumetriscu barely had time to flatten out and raise her weapon as a shield.

The warrior held a sharpened stake. The point rushed toward her face but met the AR90's stock. Dumetriscu got her knee under her attacker and tossed him to the side before his full weight could settle on her. As fast as she was, the Jarinyi was faster: even as he flew away, his free hand locked onto her '90's barrel, compelling her to roll with him or lose hold of the weapon. The movement placed her on top. She made to press her weapon against his throat, but never got the chance. Somehow, her assailant's own leg was under her belly. He shoved with extraordinary force. She flew upright, flailing out of control, and her movement triggered the *Bear*.

At that range, even Tensar body armor was of little use.

Todd's heart skipped a beat at the sound.

'Cristina?' he said into his mike.

There was no reply.

Lim gave a little cry, frantically working the trigger of his rifle which wouldn't fire. He half stood and rasped, 'The rock. It moved!'

Crouching, Todd yanked Lim's head down by the chin strap and peered over their cover. 'Turn your AIRTAR *off*,' he spat. He aimed and fired at the rock, hitting it dead center.

Todd expected what happened next, but he still gasped. The rock came alive. Rocketing off the ground, changing shape and color, it leaped high, keening like a banshee. Queer pink spray issued from the pulse fissure.

Oh my–!

Two more trigger-squeezes and he'd hit the thing hard before it flopped onto the ground. Before he could ascertain if it was dead, a blur of movement snatched his attention to his left. A few steps away, what he'd earlier registered as a mound of dirt coalesced into a humanoid shape. It darted forward. The branch in its hand was actually a spear. Todd's weapon swung toward it; he managed one shot before the Jarinyi was on him. The round took a bite from the warrior's shoulder, not enough to stop it but throwing it off balance so that when the spear hit Todd's face, it was shaft and not tip. He saw stars, felt a foot and knee slip and roll over his vest, felt his rifle snag and tear from his grip. Lying on his back, he shook his head to clear away the spots in his vision, turned on his side. The Jarinyi had gathered and fallen on the rifle, an arm's length away.

As if through gauze, with time slowing, he watched his enemy gathering its bearings after the collision, Lim trying to aim and fire, the continuing failure of Lim's weapon to acquire, the Jarinyi focusing those big eyes on Lim.

'Turn your AIRTAR off!' he screamed, his words cottony in his own ears.

Lim's face was blank. And then the Jarinyi was active again, drawing a bone-knife from a sash and slashing at Lim's chest in one fluid movement. The Marine had no Tensar but his webbing protected him. The blade caught in it, but the blow flung him sideways and his rifle skittered away over the log.

Todd drew his sidearm. The Jarinyi bent low over Lim. Todd thumbed the safety. The Jarinyi slashed. Todd fired twice. A thin fountain of red spurted from Lim's throat. The Jarinyi spun and crashed into the undergrowth lying still. Lim writhed.

The slow-motion effect he'd experienced ended with a jolt. Todd lurched to his feet, not thinking now, acting purely on instinct. He gathered up his rifle by plunging his free hand through the shoulder strap and letting it slip down his arm onto his back, launching himself southward. Around him, the forest came alive with noise. Shouting, weapons discharging. He'd made it five meters, ten meters. Fifteen—

Three stray rounds smashed through the ferns near him. He stumbled and rolled into a shallow ditch, trousers soaking in water at the knees. He thumbed his comm.

'Chameleons! They're *chameleons*! Your weapons can't acquire! Fall back! Fall back!'

He hoped there was time for the message to save his men. But Todd himself got up and continued running.

FESTER HAD SPENT THE LAST SIXTY SECONDS SQUINTING AT A COLLECTION of stones out in the middle of the track and to his left, wondering why they gave him the heebie-jeebies. When he'd turned it toward them, the AR90 seemed to try and acquire a target but wouldn't lock-on.

'Weapon malfunction,' he said into his mike. *Gimme a good ol' huntin' rifle any day*, he thought. *Let me do the aiming.*

Todd's voice came back, ordering everyone to turn off their AIRTARS. Fester complied immediately: damn thing wasn't working anyway.

But Vgrevski – lying off to Fester's left – heard Todd's order, flashed Fester a *is-he-nuts?* look, and left his AIRTAR on.

Fester growled: in every military under every star, the one thing that held armies together was obeying orders. He was about to toss some dirt at him and signal him to comply, when from his right came the unmistakable sound of a *Bear* going off.

'What the hack?' he whispered while Vgrevski rolled onto his side to look that way.

Something made a scuttling noise on the path and Fester realized with a start that they'd both shifted attention away from the road. In unison, they whipped their heads around to find two Jarinyi with vaguely granite-colored skin sprinting at them. One fired a bow as he moved. The other hurled a thick, short stick. The two Marines fired, Vgrevski's AIRTAR locking on just fine now, punching holes through the hostiles' chests. Both Jarinyi pitched forwards, but the throwing stick hit Fester at the top of his left arm, below the edge of his armor. It hit *hard*, impact spinning him onto his face. Pain lanced up through his shoulder. The arm went instantly numb, and flopped like a stocking full of jelly when he tried to get it under him. He rolled himself over with his right. And gasped.

Vgrevski lay quivering on his back, an arrow embedded in his left eye.

Fester recoiled, put his buddy out of his mind, reflexively scanning for more enemy. *Where in hell'd they come from?* The rifle was difficult to balance with one arm so he shoved it away, drew his automatic, flicked off the safety. *C'mon, c'mon. Uncle Fester's got fourteen rounds just waiting for a new home.*

Other Marines were shouting now. No transmissions, just shouting. One scream. Some firing over by Todd's position and now from Kwan's. Then Maglic's. And now from above: was that the idiot who'd climbed the tree?

'Chameleons!' Todd's voice rasped in his earpiece.

Fester's breath stuck in his chest.

The stones! That's *how you got so close, you sneaky, snaky bastards. Well, Uncle Fester ain't giving you a second chance.*

Driving with his heels, he shoved himself backwards into the hollow at the base of a very wide tree, maintaining a light pressure on his trigger, sweeping the area. Nothing was going to get close to him without his seeing it and killing it first.

HIGH ABOVE THE MAN, WHAT LOOKED LIKE A LARGE FUNGAL GROWTH ON THE underside of a thick tree branch began to move. Scarface's camouflage faded, but he kept his movements slow and deliberate to avoid attention. Gripping the branch tightly with his legs, he lowered his upper body and aimed a loaded short-bow.

Scarface had studied the Men closely. Many wore a protective covering like a shell on their body and head. When he fired, he did so at the legs. He was already reaching for a second arrow when the first sliced cleanly through Man's left knee and pinned it to the ground.

FESTER HUFFED AND STARED AT THE LEG IN DISBELIEF. FOR A MOMENT there was no pain, but when it came, it did so with a vengeance. Long ago he'd learned there was no excuse for making noise and drawing more attention to yourself in battle, so the only vent he gave that pain was a low snarl through clenched teeth.

Another arrow appeared in his right thigh.

This time he threw his head back so hard, his helmet scarred the tree trunk. Now he did cry out, staring up at the trees through white-edged vision. There was movement above. He raised his handgun, emptied the clip. But his hand shook like a mad thing and not one bullet came near his target.

A noise beside him. Another indig leaned into the hollow. It raised a spear.

'Make it clean and make it quick, you inbred slime,' he snarled.

The warrior did just that.

TWO JARINYI BURST FROM AMONGST THE JEEPS, HURDLING MAGLIC AND racing toward the tree the grunt had climbed earlier. Maglic, looking the wrong way, only saw them as they bounded over him. He fired a wild burst in their direction, succeeding only in spraying intervening ferns and bush. He sprang up to give chase. Dodging fern-branches he saw one of the Jarinyi scaling the trunk beneath the grunt who couldn't see well enough to take aim. The other had vanished.

Jeez, they move fast!

He blasted away at the tree-hugging warrior, dropping him. The grunt fired a rapid burst at something else – *better not be targeting me!* – then Maglic was falling.

As he fell, he tucked himself into a ball, impacted lightly on a shoulder and rolled, ending up on his feet in a crouch on the other side of a shallow gully choked with new growth. He scrambled up the other side and leaned his back against a gnarled tree, panting.

Nothing had followed him. For the moment he was safe.

Safe. The irony of the word in the middle of a firefight set him to giggling. *Safe!*

The arm came out of nowhere, changing color as it moved, darting up under his helmet. He only noticed the bone knife until after it had slashed his throat.

Scarface danced through the undergrowth now, using trees for cover, crouching, springing, sliding, rolling – allowing no pause between his movements. His father had told him it was poor craft to allow an unseen enemy to settle their gaze upon you for longer than a heartbeat.

He had dispatched one of the Men himself. Now he had abandoned his hunting-craft caution so that he might quickly ascertain the remaining strength of his enemy, instincts telling him that the Men's ranks were already decimated. His tour of the scene confirmed this. Bodies littered the forest, mostly human, few Jarinyi.

His blood was hot with the exhilaration of success. When it cooled, however, he would mourn the loss of more friends and brothers. And for the stupid young ones.

Those young ones had raced ahead of their elders and prompted this crisis, thinking themselves invulnerable as was the way of the young, presuming they could protect the sacred-leaf without weapons. And without the fully formed ability to blend.

Noticing the Man in the tree, he distracted him with a loud hoot, allowing another warrior to load his bow and knock the Man from his perch. The Man fell with a cry into the bracken and was set upon by two warriors there.

The Men were poor in craft. They were slow in reflex and — like Nguwuu — they could not blend. They probably didn't even know it could be done. The ambush had been spontaneous; a split-second decision based on the quick report of the young ones' murders. He and his group of warriors had been en route to see whether the flying things of the Men had indeed been heading toward the sacred plant patch, the patch that must be protected at all costs. Somehow the young ones had pre-empted them, leaving and arriving there earlier. And according to the one who met them half-way, coming back, two of them had died there.

He had known this would happen eventually. The Men were just another kind of Nguwuu.

The ambush had been the perfect tactic and Scarface allowed himself the briefest moment of sentiment — humans would call it pride — before it dissolved in a jolt of realization: one body had been noticeably missing during his inspection. The Warrior-Leader, the one with the red fur beneath his head-shell, that one could bring more of the Men here with more weapons. And their flying things. A hurriedly planned ambush by warriors numbering only the fingers on three hands had succeeded here. He was under no delusion it would work again. Not now that the red-furred Warrior-Leader knew that they could blend...

He called to his warriors to find that Man. Quickly.

14

'Come, blunt your spear with us,
our pace is hot.'

- Hilda Doolittle

THE BACK of Romaine's skull throbbed and a low note hummed in his ears. Even the filtered light beneath the forest's dense ceiling of leaves seemed too bright for comfort. Though his muscles felt weak and lifeless, he pushed on after Carswell and Fisher. What choice did he have?

Carswell seemed to be leading them toward a dense thicket crowning a gently sloped hill ahead. Perhaps there'd be shelter there. Romaine hoped so. All he wanted to do was lie down and sleep. He could die out here and no one would ever find his bones. The thought kept him moving.

Fisher shot a concerned glance his way. No sign of her own pain appeared on her face. He envied her stoicism. And her fitness.

When a new swell of vertigo crashed over him, he wasn't sure whether it was because of the bang on the head or his *world-legs* problem. And then he wasn't sure it mattered. Caught in its grip, he put his hands on his knees, riding it out.

Fisher began to scurry back for him but he halted her with a hand-signal, took a long slow breath in, out. The vertigo was lifting. He gave a slight nod to show he was okay. She looked unconvinced then turned away. He resumed walking.

Todd had abandoned stealth for speed. His flight sent him crashing through bracken, bouncing off young trees, disturbing clouds of insects, lurching each time a foot splashed in a puddle, dropped into a rut. His breath sounded harsh and heavy in his ears. His heart hammered in his chest. He stumbled down a slight incline and collided with a scraggy tree. His sleeve caught and tore completely away as he fell down and rolled into a hollow. His arm throbbed from the jolt and blood welled from deep scratches along his tricep.

Hack it!

A noise to his right caused him to jerk his weapon up. A Jarinyi was rushing him. It took a rapid burst from the AR90 full in the chest as it hurdled a log. Flipping in midair, it landed on its head, already dead.

Todd was up and running again. It was automatic. His legs wouldn't stop.

After a few seconds he realized the sleeve he had left behind was the one with his long-range commlink sewn into it. His earpiece-transmitter only had a range of half a klick.

Thoughts hammered at him like blows in a street fight.

I can't call Columbus for evac.

I shoulda done that already!

Go back, get the commlink!

You're dead without support.

Sean Todd kept on running.

A few minutes later, the undulating terrain began levelling out. Even the vegetation began to thin.

His chest heaved, drawing ragged breaths. A new thought began to bubble up from the panicked clamor that had taken over his mind, one that warmed his cheeks with shame. *I left them. I ran.*

He had taken part in over a dozen hot missions. Each one had been successful, rated by the mission objectives. Retreat was a new experience. Defeat was a new experience. In fact, his unit had only ever experienced one casualty under his command, and that was a mere torn ligament. Now they were all gone.

No! Chua and McGrath – safe at Columbus.

Yeah, some consolation. I'm sure Christina's ghost will pat you on the back about that.

He forced himself to stop, threw his back against a tree, '90 clutched in a death grip. Should he go back? Surely they were all dead. Or running like him. No, they wouldn't run, they would fight to death. So why hadn't he?

I left them. I ran.

Somehow, here in this place, he had lost his nerve.

I left them. I ran.

First Lieutenant Sean Todd had never backed down from a challenge. He had graduated Officer's School with honors. He had not only survived special forces training on Castor, he'd graduated top of a class of thirty.

I left them. I ran.

Grief and self-loathing mingled with panic, spewing ugly thoughts like noxious gas from a volcanic vent. And then finally he felt his true self separate from the clamor, rising above the emotion. He told himself what his instructors had told him over and over again:

Let your overmind rule.

That voice – his voice, not the voice of the panicky child he'd been listening to for minutes now, but the voice of a warrior – began barking decisively within his mind:

Enough! You're a soldier! Act like a solider! Stop running blind! Start thinking!

Almost instantly the panic subsided. And though the stain of dishonor remained, he beat it down, stuffed it deep where it couldn't form words in his mind anymore.

There was no point going back. He had to keep moving away from the site of the ambush, keep distance between himself and the enemy who must be pursuing him, give himself time to think, to plan. He started running again, but this time he paced himself, taking stock of his energy, measuring it out carefully, and channeling it into necessary action. As neural augments kicked in, he regained control of his heartbeat and respiration. Occasional glances over his shoulder showed him that no one was close to catching him. As fast as they were, if he kept moving, he might keep enough of an edge to stay alive.

The battle is first won in the mind and with the mind, his inner commander barked. *Start reviewing, start planning the next move!*

Using a mental trigger-code, he recalled the map of the region he was in. He had been both trained and wet-wired to sustain the two simultaneous feeds of information: internal and external, virtual and actual. Just as he'd done with the *thirdeye*, a part of his mind maintained a steady awareness of his surrounds, while another poured over the 3D contour chart until he found something he could use.

There, he thought, jabbing a mental finger at the map. His nanoptics blinked off and he returned his full concentration to the actual world. He turned westward.

What he had seen would serve nicely when his pursuers caught up with him. And they would catch up. It was unavoidable. If he could not choose the time, he could certainly choose the place. He would be ready for them when they arrived.

Let's see how you enjoy a taste of your own medicine.

FOR TEN MINUTES NOW, THE TRIO HAD CREPT ALONG IN A HALF-CROUCH that caused Romaine's thigh and calf muscles to burn. They hadn't stopped at the thicket as he'd hoped, but skirted it to where the forest opened up again. Not a breath of wind stirred the vegetation around them. Perspiration ran in rivulets down Romaine's face and back.

How much further is this schmuck gonna drag us?

Carswell suddenly stopped and dropped to one knee, listening intently.

'Where are we going?' Romaine asked again but Carswell merely shushed him.

Romaine squinted into the bush around him, anxiety peaking. When nothing emerged to attack them, he felt a surge of anger toward the scientist, assuming he was playing up his role as bush guide, big-noting himself. The rush of blood made the pounding in his head worse.

Fisher moved beside him and touched his arm in solidarity. 'Doctor, we need to know your intentions.'

'I'm saving your lives.' His eyes narrowed toward a nearby sprawl of vines and he frog-hopped closer to them and held out a hand. 'Your gun, Romaine, quick!'

Without thinking, Romaine passed the pistol to him. Then found himself looking down the barrel.

'What – !' he choked off more words as the pounding spiked in his temples.

'Holster your weapon now, Fisher, or I take his head off.' Carswell's bearded lips curled into a snarl.

Fisher had no choice but to comply. For a moment Romaine was simply startled, unable to imagine what was motivating Carswell. And then some dots joined in his mind. His love for the Jarinyi, his anger over the human incursion, the harvesting of the Pumpkin Patch.

As she got the handgun back in its holster, Fisher put Romaine's thoughts into words: 'You knew, didn't you? About this ambush.'

Carswell lips curled further. 'It would be more accurate to say I guessed it might happen.' He nodded to their right. 'You remember my friend, don't you?'

Both turned and gasped involuntarily. Where before there had been a tangle of vegetation, now crouched a short Jarinyi.

'Tuttut!' Romaine hissed, backing away.

Carswell frowned then understood, pursed his lips and nodded. 'Not a bad name. Certainly easier to pronounce than ...' He somehow whistled and grunted simultaneously.

Despite Carswell's threat to use the handgun, Fisher began to drop her hand toward her own. She peered around her as if trying to divine whether other Jarinyi lurked beyond the nearest trees.

'You maniac, Carswell,' Romaine said. 'You allowed those Marines to drive into a trap. You nearly got *us* killed. You lied to us and led us right into their hands!'

Carswell bristled. 'You were already in their hands, you dolt. Think it through. If I meant you harm, why didn't I leave you there?'

The statement shocked Romaine because it made sense. He rubbed at his head distractedly and found Carswell pressing the pistol butt back into his other hand.

What?!

'Take it. I'm not your enemy and you're not mine. I just didn't want you to shoot ... *Tuttut* ... when he appeared.'

'Where did he come from?' Fisher wondered aloud. 'I should have heard him coming.'

Romaine was sure he must have been hiding amongst that tangle of vines. But ... where were the vines?

Carswell winked. 'There are more things in heaven and earth than you and I have dreamed of – and some of them have very interesting abilities.' He stood up straight, abandoning the pretense of stealth. 'Both of you will have a lot of questions. I'll answer them but not here, not now. If you'll stay with me, the Jarinyi will not mistake you for Marines and you'll be safe. They have no beef with you; I've vouched for you.'

'You've *vouched*.' Romaine shook his head carefully, swaying a little.

'Just shut up and listen. My friend here is both guide and guarantee of our safety. You'll note he is weaponless while both of you retain yours – a gesture of trust. But you're only safe while you are with us and *we* are not staying here.'

'So where are you taking us?' asked Fisher.

'I'm not *taking* you anywhere. You're free to go where you like. *I* am going away from that battle.' He stabbed a finger in the direction of the shouting and explosions they'd heard earlier. 'You're free to come with me if you want to live. If you want to die, go back.'

'What I don't get is why you seem to think the Marines are the losers in that "battle" back there,' Romaine growled.

Fisher picked up the thought: 'I'm concerned about that too. It was a good idea to move away from the general area and avoid friendly fire. From either side.' She nodded at Tuttut. 'But why can't we just wait to be located by Lieutenant's Todd's team? Or a flier?'

Carswell regarded them both with an expression of pity. It seemed to irritate her, the first time Romaine had seen her really becoming cross with someone.

This is what it takes to make you angry? Sheesh!

'The fact that we've heard no further fire for the last few minutes indicates that Todd's team are all dead,' Carswell said.

'Or the Jarinyi are,' Romaine continued to growl. 'They're black-caps, for Pete's sake! They're not that easy to kill. They might lose a couple of guys in an ambush but they're not gonna get taken out with bows and arrows and pointy sticks.'

'They have no idea what they're up against. Or rather they *had* no idea. And neither do you. And for the last time, if you stay with us, you'll be regarded by the Jarinyi as innocent by association. We'll get you to safety. But if you want to wander back there to the jeeps and be mistaken for a Marine – especially since you're dressed like one – be my guest.'

Fisher and Romaine stared at each other for a long moment, before the MP said, 'Your call, sir.'

'I don't want to issue an order that could get you killed, Corporal. What do you want to do?'

'As I see it, sir, all our choices are dangerous.'

'True.' He sighed, touched a fingertip to a bruise on his head, winced. 'While my body is telling me to lie down and fall into a nice peaceful coma, I think we better stick with Tarzan and his sidekick here. The worst I can see them doing is using us as bargaining chips.' This last comment he directed straight at Carswell, who smiled and nodded as if that was a marvelous idea.

'So you're coming,' the scientist said.

'Just tell me it's not too far.'

Todd broke out of the trees and found he was exactly where he wanted to be. Before him lay a shallow pond, insect-analogs darting down to its surface and away again. The pool was probably deeper during the wet season and the spring thaw. He estimated it was more than two hundred meters long and the flat outcrop of land that jutted into it from the other side was half as long again. From the air the pond would look like an elongated letter C.

His destination was that short spit of land on the other side, which contained no trees, only tall lean stalks like reeds. He had learned in a briefing that the next two months of the Eventide year would become increasingly dry – the pond would likely evaporate completely - until the area flooded in late Autumn then again briefly in Spring. While other vegetation might not cope with such dramatic pendulum swings in living conditions, the reeds obviously flourished in a situation where they were submerged for one part of the year and standing on dry ground for another. On the far side of the spit, the terrain rose into a sharp hill, cluttered with thick and thorny growth. His eye detected a single break in the thicket – a single back door in or out of the reed patch.

Perfect.

Before progressing, Todd whipped out his knife, jabbed his palm and left a firm print on the trunk of the nearest tree.

'Just so you don't miss me fellas,' he muttered and waded out into the pool.

Misery. Romaine was immersed in it.

Head throbbing, ears ringing, fear hammering against his sanity. The clutter of old growth and shadows suggested hiding places from which storybook monsters could launch vicious attacks upon him. Branches heavy with leaves and moisture hung above him like omens.

Misery.

One of his knees buckled and he stumbled into low-hanging branches, snatched at them to stay upright, concentrating on breathing. The others weren't slowing, bridging the rise ahead. Anger flared, providing a burst of strength. He straightened and followed, an automaton. A miserable hacking automaton.

One foot in front of the other. Like a machine. Just do it. One foot, then the other.

The ground – soft and loose beneath his boots – still felt wrong after years of treading artificial surfaces. Halfway up the rise he slipped in loose soil, took his full weight on his palms, swore lavishly.

Fisher told Carswell, 'Perhaps we should slow our pace. He isn't well.'

Carswell glanced back and clucked in disgust, kept walking. 'If he falls behind, that's his problem. If we want to be safe, we need to catch up with the rest of the Tribe.'

The rest *of the Tribe? What then?*

Romaine sucked in air. 'Not too many hills on starcruisers.' When Carswell's head disappeared over the hill, he raised his voice to carry. 'Don't feel sorry for me. I'll keep up.' But when he got to the top of the rise and saw it was just the beginning of another larger hill disappearing into thicker foliage ahead, he wondered if he would.

A few meters ahead, Fisher took Carswell by the shoulder and turned him round. 'Sir, please.'

He jerked away from her, glaring. 'We need to get away before the fliers arrive and start bombing the forest.'

'Bombing? That's a little unlikely.'

'When Glass discovers what's happened, he'll be looking for retribution. I plan to stay out of the way.'

'Why–' Romaine paused to suck air as he caught up. 'Why would they shoot at me?'

'They think we're all dead. They can't get a visual on you through *that.*' Carswell jerked a thumb up at the thick canopy above. 'All they'll see is a heat signature. They'll assume anything the shape and mass of a Jarinyi *is* a Jarinyi.'

Tuttut waited a dozen paces ahead, holding a branch back from the game trail they were following. Beyond that branch, the going looked even rougher than it had been, the route clogged with overgrowth. Fisher jogged up to the Jarinyi and peered into a dark tunnel of vegetation and muddy soil. She turned pitying eyes toward Romaine.

He felt like crap. He probably looked like crap. But if it was a choice between being julienned by shrapnel or pushing on, then there was only one thing to do. Romaine grit his teeth and pushed on.

15

'If you find yourself in a fair fight, you didn't plan your mission properly.'

- Colonel David Hackworth

MORE LIKE A PUDDLE THAN A POND, Todd thought, wading through ankle-deep water.

His smile bloomed from grim to exultant as he approached the grove of reeds. It was just what he'd hoped for. The average gap between the stalks was perfect to squeeze between if he didn't want to leave an obvious trail. Their color was a dirty white and – since his uniform was anything but white – this would have presented his greatest problem but for an unexpected bonus. The ground here was white clay, perhaps caused by plants' color leaching into it.

He tossed his rifle on the dry soil further from the pool and thrashed in the mud like a pig, scooping handfuls of it onto his face and hair. He lobbed his helmet far into the reeds, abandoning it. Now a blotchy white and brown figure, he picked up his rifle and launched himself between the thin stalks. Several broke. After a few steps, he looked back. Confident the Jarinyi would believe he had hit the plants panicked and desperate, he crawled deeper making no attempt to hide his path.

His plan was simple: draw them into an ambush in a place their camouflage-ability was useless. The reeds were too tall and too thin for Jarinyi to mimic. If they rolled in the mud like he had, he'd hear it. If they outflanked him, approaching from the rear, he'd hear that too. The reeds were dry as paper.

A rustling to his right and Todd dropped to one shoulder, weapon up. He flinched when a reptilian head appeared through the reeds. Golden eyes with pinprick pupils stared at him from a head not unlike an iguana's. The creature was easily as long as Todd but thinner.

They remained frozen for over almost a minute, eyes locked. A grey tongue flicking in and out of the animal's scaly mouth was the sole sign of life in the tableau. Then the creature blinked and crept away in a different direction. Todd's heart rate slowed as the crackling of its passage faded.

Purge it! Todd thought, realizing too late he should have killed it. If he deployed the spider mine in here, that creature might set it off rather than a Jarinyi. For a split second, he considered following and killing it. Not knowing how close behind him the Jarinyi were, he decided against it. There was no choice but to press on with his plan.

He changed tack now, doubling back a few meters before lying still and listening for a full minute. After he was sure nothing and no one was coming through the water, he veered off at a right angle from the trail he had made, now moving through the cover using the same technique Dumetriscu had done earlier, leaving no sign that he had passed this way. To the eyes of a tracker, his trail would vanish, and the lizard-creature's own trail would probably confuse them.

His enemy were such a long time coming that Todd began to wonder whether they were pursuing him at all.

Surely Columbus would be looking for the jeeps by now. Twice he'd thought he heard the soft drone of a Reaper but he saw nothing.

He brought his mind back to the here and now, relied on his *overmind* to heighten his senses. For over an hour now, he'd lain flat and still. To move would waste energy and risk detection. But the humidity and his exertions had drawn out so much perspiration that his throat was parched and he was beginning to feel sleepy. Reaching for his hip flask and drinking meant that his own body's noise – the rasps of clothing against skin, the gulping of water from the bottle – might mask the approaching sounds of an assailant. Nevertheless, he had to drink. The risk of dehydration was greater than the risk of assault.

He felt the water sloshing inside the flask as he lifted it, but heard nothing. The bottle itself was manufactured to dampen the sound. Quietly he unscrewed the lid and raised it to his lips. He savored the water before swallowing, held it in his mouth while he replaced the lid and then the flask to his belt, relishing the way his gums and tongue and throat swelled as they revived.

He peered out from his hide again and silently cursed as he swallowed.

Where are they?

———

Romaine dabbed with his palm at the fresh abrasion on his face, blood humming with fresh anger. It had taken almost an hour to claw their way through the patch of frustratingly thick jumble of trees. Taller than the others, he'd had to bob and duck and crouch. Stray twigs had added new scratches across his cheek and forearms. And while they'd been stuck in the tight corridor of vegetation, he'd distinctly heard the sound of Reapers more than once. No bombs. No missiles. They were looking for survivors. Sensing rescue was just beyond his reach had done nothing to improve his mood.

When he got back to the office, he was going to shoot the Admiral in the head for sending him on this one, court-martial or no court-martial. He might very well do it to Carswell before sunset. The last time he'd gone running around the woods, he'd been eight years old, and those woods had been a lot tamer.

I'm not trained for this crap.

While the vegetation had thinned, the gradient showed no sign of levelling off. They stayed close together in single file. Tuttut had taken up the position in front of Romaine, small ears flicking at sounds Romaine couldn't hear. Being last man in the line did nothing to help Romaine's nerves.

He leaned against a tree, and asked 'Where did you say we're going?' but his voice came out in a croak and no one heard him. Taking a deep breath, he stuck two fingers in his mouth, whistled shrilly.

Carswell whirled on him. 'Are you *crazy*?'

Romaine waved his objection away with a tired hand. He ran his tongue over his gums, attempting to make his saliva glands start working again.

'Why are you whistling at me?' Carswell hissed.

'Where are we *going*?' he asked again. 'Be *specific*.'

'The foothills.'

'Foothills!'

'We're at the edge of them now. Don't worry so much.'

'I thought you said we were just catching up with the Tribe,' Fisher interjected.

'And that's where the Tribe will be.'

'Can't we stop here, wait for evac?' she asked. 'Surely we're out of danger by now.'

Romaine exchanged a glance with her. She'd heard the Reapers too.

'My dear girl, we're not even close to being out of danger.'

'How far?' Romaine asked.

'Another three or four klicks and we can rest for a while. *If –*' he raised his voice to forestall Romaine's objection '–your whistling doesn't attract the attention of some predator or a stray Nguwuu.'

'Ngu-wuu?' asked Fisher.

'Is that like a woo-woo?' Romaine added.

'Nothing like it. There are fiercer things in these woods than Jarinyi hunters and blackcaps. Keep moving if you want to see tomorrow.'

He moved on.

Fisher slipped past Tuttut to examine Romaine, shook her head then pitched her voice to reach Carswell and no further. 'Doctor, a three-minute rest now will help us later.'

Carswell scowled then signaled Tuttut. The diminutive Jarinyi bounded away to scout around. The xenologist dropped to one knee.

Romaine sank to his haunches where water runoff had carved a niche in the hillside, gripping a nearby bush to anchor him. He waggled his eyebrows gratefully at Fisher. 'You're a *mensch*, Fisher. One o' the good guys.'

She nodded and traced a finger over the canteen at her hip, wished aloud that she hadn't already drained it.

Romaine had the same problem. 'I was trying not to think about how thirsty I am. I'd suck water off these leaves, but I'll probably end up poisoned. How's the hand?'

'Sore. I'm more concerned about your head, sir.'

'Aches like crazy and feels twice as heavy as it should.' He said this with a half-smile. 'But I can survive a mild concussion.'

I still remember the crash. Kind of. Should be a good sign.

Fisher wasn't buying it. 'Doctor Carswell, he needs medical attention.'

'And he'll get it,' Carswell said, meeting her gaze. 'The Jarinyi have some fine healers. They don't have photonic imaging and nanites, but he'll be okay when they get some of their medicine into him. When you feel its benefits, Romaine, you'll realize what CUSET is stealing from these people.'

'If I last that long.'

Carswell stomp-slid down the slope and seized Romaine's head in both his hands. He inspected the back of his head, the lacerations to his face and arms, his pupils. 'You're fine. Don't be such a baby.'

Romaine slapped Carswell's hands away and stood, tried to stretch his neck to one side. He felt like someone was inside him, twisting things that shouldn't be twisted. 'No offence to the indigenous medicos here, but what I'd really like is an osteopath, a hot bath and a handful of paracetamol.'

And a drink. How the hell did I get into this mess?

Maybe he was cursed. The last few weeks, his life had gone from bad to worse, and now it had slipped into *life-threateningly insane.*

Carswell reached past him, plucked a clump of grey moss from amid the clutter of the bush Romaine had held on to. He slipped it into Romaine's hand. 'Chew this. But don't swallow it,' he cautioned.

'What's this?'

'Paracetamol.'

Romaine eyed it dubiously. 'You've used this?'

Carswell growled in annoyance, tore another piece from a tree next to him and popped it into his mouth, began chewing.

Romaine stared at the moss, at the branch it grew on. He'd seen it more than once in the past hour. 'This stuff's everywhere. You had to wait until now to give me some?'

Carswell took a few steps up the hill. 'My mind was on other things, spacer. Start chewing and stop whining.'

'Enough. I've had enough. I'm not taking another step away from Columbus.'

Carswell spat out his moss. 'Do you really think I'm lying about the danger? Do you think Tuttut, as you call him, ran off to look around because he's bored? Get this through your thick head. This is not a holo-game. This is not a tame Centauran forest. There are ten things within ten meters of us that could harm us. Predators live in these woods. And if the Nguwuu happen to be around, they're the worst predators of all.'

He stared Romaine down until Romaine had to look away, admitting defeat. Carswell was the expert here. For the moment, he'd have to comply.

Carswell made a gesture as if patting someone on head. 'Now be a good boy and chew your moss. We head off in one minute.'

LATE IN THE AFTERNOON, THE THOUGHTS HE'D HELD AT BAY FINALLY overwhelmed Todd's defenses. Replaying those terrible moments following the ambush again and again, he tried to determine if there was anything he could have done. Anything.

What had gone wrong? How could he lose the entire squad?

He had to face the truth, as hard as it was to admit. Apart from lapses of discipline, it came down to a failure to implement a basic premise of warfare: know your enemy. There was so little known about the indigs. He – and Glass – had made assumptions, assumptions that dealt deadly consequences. Primitive did not equal pushover. Artificial technology had been countermanded by natural ability, pulse-rifles useless against a force of Stone Age nomads. Their AIRTARs had probably been confused over aspects of mass and shape and it was possible the Jarinyi could cool their body temperature, fooling the infrared sensors.

But how could anyone have foreseen that chameleon thing?

With a surge of fiery hatred, he realized someone had known. Carswell had withheld information that could have saved lives. Human lives. Carswell had betrayed his own kind with a sin of omission. It was small consolation that he'd probably died in the lead jeep's spectacular crash. He would have liked to put a round through Carswell's head himself.

There was another possible explanation however. For months now, he had been wondering if the Marine psyche hadn't lost its way somewhat, leaning on the edge that superior technology gave them at the cost of warrior basics like *instinct*. Despite the irony that he himself was a soldier who had taken that technology into his own body and brain, it was only instinct that had spared his life today.

So far.

He blinked away the thoughts and returned his focus to watching the trees across the pond. He just hoped they'd come before dark.

IT DIDN'T TAKE LONG FOR THE PAIN-RELIEVING AGENTS IN THE MOSS TO kick in, and Romaine was very glad he'd trusted the xenologist. This time.

Twenty minutes later, Carswell told him to spit it out, and not to pick any more. He pointed into a gully toward the sound of running water, and went that way with Tuttut at his heels. Romaine followed them to the small silver trickle, knelt down and scooped it to his lips. Beside him Fisher splashed her face and neck. Any hope for respite ended when Carswell and Tuttut started off up the hill on the other side once they'd finished drinking. Fisher offered Romaine a worried half-smile and suggested she take the rear.

Dragging himself up the new slope, Romaine muttered 'This will definitely not be good for my career.'

Here he was keeping company with a party who had aligned themselves against the CUSET military. But what were his choices? Back at the ambush site, he could hardly have hung around hoping the first person he saw was human. There'd been a very real skirmish going on there. And now he couldn't just turn around and start hiking back to Columbus ... wherever that was.

He wondered how Gutierrez had felt, even in those last microseconds of consciousness as his life bled out on an alien world. Was he as scared as Romaine?

Was he scared before it happened? Did he suspect someone meant him harm, or was he merely in the wrong place at the wrong time?

Turning his mind toward the investigation felt good, something familiar amidst the unfamiliar. Even out here in this hell of plants and animals and bugs and mud and God-knew-what-kinda-microbes, the case was unfinished business tugging on his consciousness like an ignored child.

Loose ends dangled like popped seams. Had Turk killed Gutierrez over some offence? Turk certainly seemed capable of murder, but in a fit of rage rather than planning it with the skill and patience this crime demanded. And why would he? There was nothing linking Attikula to the murder except his errant nature and combat abilities.

There was also the theory that the Jarinyi were being framed. Was it reasonable to suspect the Marines had gone to the trouble of killing one of their own men with a bow and arrow to implicate the locals? It was a stretch. The recon unit were tough, battle-hardened, maybe even CUSET true-believers. But no matter how desperate CUSET was for Tigerclaw, in the end they could just take it. Today they *had*. There was no need for the sanctioned killing of one of their own.

Things are usually what they are, Glass had said. Maybe this really was a case of offended locals making life hard for the intruders. In that case, he had to consider Carswell's claims that the locals were noble and principled. If that were true, then it didn't add up. If Jarinyi only killed out of vengeance, then why kill a Marine? Had the Marines slain some indigenous person before today and prompted an eye-for-eye killing? If the Jarinyi could be riled up enough to attack after the Pumpkin Patch episode then surely a murder of one of their own would have upset them too.

No, that theory didn't make sense either. If they were that ticked, why were they so civil when he visited their village?

Could it have been a rogue Jarinyi, acting without the tribe's knowledge or consent? And for crying out loud, what if it wasn't one of *these* Jarinyi, but a Jarinyi from the River Tribe?

How would Romaine know for sure? How could he prove any of it?

He growled with frustration. He could ask Carswell any of these questions but the man would withhold any information that might implicate Jarinyi. *And should I really be following him to God knows where?*

He allowed Fisher to catch up with him. 'I keep flipping between two opinions. One, Carswell's looking after us. Two, we'll end up some kinda human sacrifice. How 'bout you?'

She was quiet a moment. 'I hadn't thought of that last scenario, sir. Not sure I'm grateful you brought it up.'

'Oops. Sorry. Overactive imagination. Usually it comes in handy. Maybe not this time.' They moved into a dense array of vines that drooped like poorly laid cables between trees.

'Sir, I don't agree with all his statements and ideals, but he makes sense when he says he could have left us there. And this little guy here *is* unarmed.'

'Yeah, but – and here comes my overactive imagination again – for all we know he's got a spear hidden up ahead. Or he can spit acid. He could pick up a rock and use it as a weapon.'

She held a brace of creepers aside for him. 'Sir, I think the doctor wants someone to agree with him and take up his cause. He wants allies. The Jarinyi respected you, CUSET respect you and you're objective because of your role, so he sees you as his best chance of an advocate.'

'Very good, Fisher. I should've thought of that.' He touched the cut on his forehead, the bump on the back of his skull and gave his neck muscles another stretch. 'I'm coming up with more questions than answers, but what you said helps. Tell me this though: why'd *you* come?'

'To stay safe. Keep you safe. That's my job. And...' She was quiet a while, lost in thought.

Romaine flinched as an animal hooted and rattled undergrowth nearby. Was it fleeing or warning them to stay away? Fisher gave it no more than a cursory glance as she thought about her answer. Neither Tuttut nor Carswell appeared concerned, but Romaine couldn't help giving the area a wide berth.

Fisher said finally, 'I guess I just want to see where this all leads.' Her jaw worked uncertainly for a moment before she added, 'I know we might have lost personnel back there in that firefight, but worrying as it all is, it's still kind of ... interesting. Being out here with aliens, seeing how they live and how they work through this situation, I mean.'

She was *curious*? Romaine stared at her for a long moment before speaking. 'You definitely should be an investigator, Fisher.'

AND SUDDENLY, THEY WERE THERE.

Instinct, his soldier instinct, sensed their presence long before he saw anyone. Something was in the trees across the break and to his right, close by the spot where he'd emerged from the forest.

It took many minutes, but the warrior finally showed himself. He had been crouching in the nexus of two trees, undetectable. Todd's eyes must have swept across him many times without truly perceiving him. Though a good fifty meters away, the recon's enhanced eyesight was good enough to catch the shift in color. It was amazing to watch, a gradual and controlled morphing of shade and pattern until the warrior had resolved into its normal appearance. The Jarinyi remained inactive a few seconds more. Then he seemed to *flow* out from the trees armed only with a short sharp stick sticking out of the back of his loincloth. The warrior moved steadily across open ground and into the pool, hugging the surface on all fours like a cat, face above the water, head turning this way and that, ears pricking up at any and every sound. His movement barely disturbed the waters.

Todd gently shifted his AR90 that way, but resisted the urge to pick the indig off. Both instinct and reason told him there was more than one adversary out there. Giving away his position now might be lethally premature.

A few moments later he had another reason to be glad of his caution, gleaning a vital piece of information when something spooked the warrior. He watched as it stopped abruptly, curled its legs up beneath it, wrapped its arms around them before changing into the image of a thick clump of moss.

What the–? Why not start morphing while moving? Todd wondered. Then the answer came to him. *They can't.*

Eventually the warrior decamouflaged, and it continued through the water, arriving a full minute later at the reeds. It sniffed at the ground, eyes scouring the ground. With a flick of the head it disappeared from view. This wasn't cause for concern. Todd had covered his back and would hear him coming anyway if he got close.

He sensed another presence in the forest forward and to the right of his position – some telltale had impressed itself upon his augmented senses. There was another out there, probably circling the patch. That one would be heading for the 'back door'. If so, a nice surprise would be waiting for him: Todd had hurled his spider mine in that direction to land a pace or two inside the reeds at the bottom of the hill, a perfect toss.

Several minutes passed before he heard the whisper of someone's passage through the reeds. It was difficult to tell exactly how close they were: sibilant sounds carried a long way on a still day like this.

A dry twig snapped. And then all was quiet. That snap had been close. The warrior hadn't been fooled by his false path at all. Damn but they were good trackers. Todd imagined the warrior pausing, holding its breath, aware of its mistake. He moved onto his left side ready to face them.

Now it was happening, it was happening quickly. His instructors had taught him that in this business, you waited a long time to react fast. Far from feeling anxious, he felt a sense of relief: things were about to resolve one way or the other.

A full two minutes passed and the Jarinyi had still not moved.

C'mon c'mon. He mouthed the words.

Three minutes. The back of his left hand itched. An ant-analog was tickling its way toward the cuff of his sleeve. That's all he needed: a bug inside his clothes. He carefully twisted his hand over to wipe the ant off in the soil. It gave him a sharp bite but he blocked the pain, hoping the little bugger wasn't poisonous.

There was no sound from the direction of the Jarinyi.

FISHER CLENCHED HER TEETH AGAINST THE PAIN IN HER FINGERS. It would have been easy to catalog her discomforts, her blisters, her aches and pains, but she'd been raised to not complain. After all, what good did it do to dwell on things? Saint Francis of Assisi would have said: if you can change it, act; if you can't change it, accept it and move on.

Commander Romaine seemed safe with Tuttut bringing up the rear so she jogged forward to be with Carswell. 'I'm concerned about how we'll get back to Columbus, since we're heading away from it. I assume that you want to go back there at some stage.' Carswell didn't respond. 'Or at least for us to return there.'

Carswell kept quiet long enough that Fisher wondered if he was ignoring her. He could be an extremely rude man. Finally he said, 'Either the Jarinyi will help you get back or the Marines will show up in a Reaper, in which case you can signal for their help while the rest of us blend into the background. Hopefully if that happens, you'll be respectful enough not to direct fire at the Jarinyi. Or me.'

Tuttut appeared beside them, startling her. He touched Carswell's chest, hissing something like '*cssssssssssoool*'. He made a *stop* signal, listening intently to the bush back down the slope.

Romaine fingered his sidearm. Fisher watched him sway and brace himself against a rock poking through the topsoil. They listened for a while but no one seemed to hear anything.

Fisher gestured to her sidearm with a look that asked whether or not she should be wary. Carswell shrugged and a moment later, Tuttut signed something, then said '*Ngo*'.'

'We go,' Carswell translated.

Fisher wondered what Tuttut had heard that she hadn't.

THE SOFT DRONE RETURNED, CLEARER THIS TIME. A REAPER WAS definitely nearby. Todd tapped his earpiece and spoke softly but it must have been out of range.

With a deep *whoompf*, dirt and fire erupted ten meters to his right. The unexpected sound jerked his hand away from his ear. Warm air washed across him as he rolled onto his back. A cloud of cinders and grit drifted out over the water on the slight breeze. The warrior who'd been tracking him through the reeds had triggered the booby trap. Todd had pulled the pin on a grenade and left it balanced precariously on its strike lever beneath dirt and sticks.

One down, he thought grimly. *One or more to go.*

And hopefully, that Reaper might see the smoke and dust.

Slightly deafened by the concussion, he pressed his earpiece deeper into his left ear in order to hear better. Nothing. No signal. Twisting onto his stomach, he peered out across the water. Minutes passed. Where the hell was that Reaper? The sun was already brushing the western treetops.

The insect bite on his hand itched. He checked it, carefully rubbing away some of the mud he'd smeared himself with.

Doesn't look bad —

From the rear of his position came another *whoompf*, this one higher pitched and followed by the pattering of shrapnel slicing through dried vegetation. He recoiled, jerking against the reeds, snapping his head around toward the noise.

An arrow hit the back of his armor, harmless but startling. The rifle fell from his left hand. His reaction to the explosion had given away his position to a warrior hidden across the water. He twisted, returning fire blindly with the pistol, scurrying backwards into the thicket. Another arrow tore through reeds a hand's breadth from his calf. He flipped over, withdrew further, sliding on hands and knees, juking and jinking like a fighter pilot to throw off his assailant's aim. Three more arrows plunged through stalks nearby, but he was convinced the archer had lost track of him.

He had to move again. Making noise was not an issue now. The Jarinyi out there was making enough noise of his own. He'd left his AR90 behind in the mad scrabble to get out of sight. With the pistol clutched in both hands, he began towards the place he'd left his grenade. It was a relatively good place to wait; they might come for the body of their fallen comrade and then...

New plans formed in his mind. The soil was soft here. He could use his knife to dig a hole. Bury himself in or near the crater of the explosion where the ground was already disturbed. Poke his *thirdeye* through the soil to keep watch, cut a breathing tube from the reeds around him. And when they came near, he could erupt from the ground, take them by surprise, use knife and pistol.

His hand touched something wet and he recoiled. A loose slab of skin and flesh, bright pink with blood. Part of the warrior who'd discovered the booby trap. Ahead were more grisly remains. And a shallow crater, surrounded by dark and churned up earth.

Perfect.

Even if they set the patch on fire, he could possibly survive it under the soil, as long as he could breathe. And if no more Jarinyi came for him, he could wait it out a couple of days then head back to Columbus.

Splashing from his left. He swiveled onto his butt and lifted the .42 toward the sounds. Perhaps he wouldn't have to wait.

And then the deep thrum of the Reaper was suddenly near. He triggered his earpiece.

'This is Todd. Acknowledge.'

The pause felt like a week dragging by, and then the female pilot's Aussie accent responded. 'Good to hear your voice, Lieutenant. Where are you?'

'I'm inside a patch of white reeds. Can you see it?' The thrum grew louder as the Reaper turned toward him.

'Affirmative. We're close by your position and ... Lieutenant! You have one *indig* approaching your position through the water! Are you in danger?'

'Affirmative, I am under attack, repeat, under attack. We suffered heavy losses and indigs are now designated as enemy combatants. You have a go to fire.'

He was answered with the earsplitting sound of the Reaper's pulse-cannons opening up. Water hissed in the aftermath. 'Scratch one bogey,' said the pilot. She didn't sound happy about it.

The Reaper swung into view, ten meters up, its side door sliding open, McGrath appearing in the cavity. Todd stood to wave. McGrath cried out and pointed. Todd whirled. Only now did he hear the sound of breaking reeds above the noise of the Reaper.

The Jarinyi was on him fast, rocketing out of the pale stalks like a bird of prey. Todd registered the ragged mess that had once been an arm before the warrior's other arm struck him a fierce blow across cheek and nose, clubbing him to the ground. The warrior snatched up its torn-up companion's spear, lifted it high to strike. Vision greying, Todd wrestled with his body to respond –

Deadly and invisible pulses of energy punched through the Jarinyi's body, pile-driving it down into the soil, smashing head and chest and the remaining arm.

Todd blinked hard, sat up and stared. In one of those grotesque coincidences of battle, the warrior's remains had settled onto those of its companion. He turned his head, saw McGrath lowering the pulse rifle, released the breath he'd been holding, and waited for the remaining two members of his team to come down and get him.

16

'Fear not the sins of others; fear only the consequences of your own sin.
Another's sin may cause you harm, but it can never destroy your soul.
Your own sin can achieve both.'

- Article 22: *The Articles of Life*
Published by The Society of Andros, 2101

THE BENCH beneath him was hard, the wall he rested his head against even harder, but after the ordeal he'd been through, the inside of the flier felt as cozy to Todd as the inside of a womb. As soon as Chua and McGrath had hustled Todd inside, Donaldson the pilot had instantly taken off to prevent further attack. His jaw still throbbed where the Jarinyi had hit him but the pain was nothing. A reminder that he'd survived. It brought clarity, crystallizing his thoughts. As Donaldson performed a lazy turn to the east, Todd – his earpiece-commlink automatically patched into the flier's – pressed a finger against his ear.

'You're heading back to base?'

'Colonel's orders,' the pilot replied.

'CO wants to know what happened,' Chua added, eyes boring into Todd's. The subtext was easy to read: *I want to know what happened too.*

Todd felt a brief flutter of panic. If they found out that he'd abandoned –

'He can wait,' he replied to both of them, finger still pressed to his ear. 'We need to check out the crash site. The Jarinyi ambushed us and–'

'We know,' McGrath cut in, leaning across the flier and giving him a look so laced with concern it actually moved him. She had been worried about him. Few people in his life had ever worried about Sean Todd.

'Already been there,' Donaldson interjected. 'There's no one left, Lieutenant, I'm sorry. You're the only one we've had contact with. I've asked the other fliers to be on hand to retrieve the bodies.'

'Might be others out there,' he muttered.

'Maybe,' McGrath said. 'Maybe not.'

Todd slapped the seat beside him in only partly feigned despair – if anyone else had survived, they might know that he'd run. He rasped, 'Donaldson, turn us around. We're going to the Jarinyi campsite.'

'Lieutenant–'

'*Turn us around!* They're not getting away with this!'

Seconds passed. The flier continued on its course. His two team members – *two remaining*, he told himself before he could shut off the shock and shame once more – stared at him across the small space, Chua impassive, McGrath starting to allow the desire for payback to twinkle in her own eyes.

Todd began to wonder if he needed to shout at the pilot again. And then the craft was banking, accelerating, the forest flashing by beneath them. McGrath produced the flier's medkit and offered Todd painkillers. He took them gratefully, though the effort of chewing them made his jaw click in a funny way. She raised an antiseptic swab toward the cuts on his arm bleeding fresh through the dried mud, but he motioned her to put it away.

'Later,' he said.

'Sir.' Chua used the word to get Todd's attention. 'What happened?'

His eyes held hers for several seconds then moved to McGrath, a more sympathetic audience. 'We were ten or fifteen minutes into our trip, hightailing it. They hit the lead jeep. It crashed, overturned on the north side of the path. Probably killed them all: Romaine, Fisher, Carswell. My dumb driver pulled in, blocked the track so we all jumped out, tried to shelter on the south side of the track. The enemy fire had come from the other side, somewhere near where the jeep crashed.'

'Hope it landed square on top of 'em,' McGrath said angrily.

'Yeah.'

'What next?' Chua asked, her voice and face emotionless.

Todd breathed in deeply. 'One of the regulars got hit before he made cover. The rest of us went to ground. Gally took our six. We managed to get *Momma Bears* out on our flanks but it didn't matter. They were ... they were all around us.'

His words trailed off as he began to flash back.

Lim. 'My rifle's malfunctioning.'

The crump *of Christina's Bear detonating. Did it take her with it? Was it quick?*

A Jarinyi coming at him, swinging the spear around.

Blood squirting from Lim's throat.

The cries of battle around him.

The impulse to get away, grabbing hold of his will, his legs.

Running.

Trying his comms without any response from his team.

Running.

Running away...

'Sir.' McGrath's soft voice brought him back to the present. Her expression was a fusion of bewilderment and anger. '*How* did they overwhelm us? *How* did they kill the driver? We have assault rifles, we have Tensar.'

He shook his head making his face hurt even more, spoke through clenched teeth. 'Didn't help.'

The pilot's voice in their ears interrupted them. 'Coming up on the settlement, Lieutenant.'

'Scan the area for life signs.' He returned his attention to McGrath, still finding Chua's hard gaze unsettling. 'The Jarinyi are *fast*. They're strong. And they have this neat little trick that Carswell never told us about.' He paused for effect then said, 'They're chameleons.'

McGrath frowned, even more confused.

'What?' Chua asked.

'They can change color, even change the texture of their skin. They ... blend in with the environment. You think you're looking at a rock or big hunk of lichen growing on a tree, maybe the side of a large fern. You look away. You look back and that rock is swinging a club at you. The fern is loading up a bow.' He paused again. 'And they're accurate, they're almost clinically precise. Lim didn't have his armor fastened properly and got his throat cut. The one that got him came at my face with a spear and if I hadn't got a shot off, probably would have stabbed me in the eye.'

They both regarded him in silence for a long time until Donaldson spoke up from the cockpit. 'No life signs that indicate Jarinyi, Lieutenant. In the camp or in the nearby bush. What do you want to do?'

'I want you to turn their camp into mush.'

Chua blinked. McGrath didn't. After a beat, the pilot responded, 'You what?'

'You heard me. Strafe the campsite and fire a full spread of missiles into the surrounding forest. Level everything in and around the camp.'

Another pause. 'Lieutenant, I'll radio Colonel Glass for confirmation.'

'You won't,' he replied evenly. 'You'll do what I said. It's my responsibility. On the scene, I'm your commanding officer. So, pick a spot in the center of the camp and level everything within a hundred meters of it.'

'Lieutenant,' she said slowly, 'there's no one there. Just beasts and bugs.'

'Actually, we don't know that.'

'I did a full scan.'

'The Jarinyi have their own ... methods for concealment,' he replied in as reasonable a tone as he could manage. 'I've experienced it myself. There could be a hundred of them down there and we wouldn't know.'

McGrath leaned forward and said, 'But even if they can change color, they can't hide from sensors.'

'Yeah,' he replied simply. 'They can. They do. AIRTARs, infrared, it's all useless.' He tapped his communicator again. 'Pilot, we need a retaliatory strike and we need it now. Follow my orders or you'll be on report.'

Ignoring the throbbing pain in his face, Todd pulled himself out of his seat, shoved open the door and wedged himself against the frame, leaned out to watch.

Tersely Donaldson replied, 'It's your dollar, Lieutenant.'

The flier wheeled and rocked as Donaldson emptied its compliment of twenty-four missiles into the area immediately around the camp. Flame, debris and soil exploded into the air. Trees that had stood like Titans for centuries were torn from their bed of earth and tossed about, as if ripped out and scattered by the hand of a giant malicious child.

The pilot then turned her pulse cannons on the camp itself, firing through the burgeoning cloud of dust and smoke. By the time she'd finished, the landscape was disfigured, lacerated.

Todd nodded to himself and took his seat again. If that didn't get a message across, he didn't know what would.

'Payback?' McGrath said.

'Payback,' Todd replied with a tight smile, scratched dry mud from his trousers.

She squinted at him. 'They can really turn into rocks and stuff?'

'Appear to, yes. Yes, they can.'

'But they trigger AIRTARs?'

'Not when they're camouflaged. They must lower their body temperature or something. The AIRTARs either freak out when trained on them or don't register them at all.' He shook his head again. He was going to have to think hard about how to re-engineer the human technological advantage to *be* an advantage again.

'You think we got any just now?'

'I sure hope so.' As he felt the flier shift and turn sluggishly toward Columbus as if lost in its own thoughts. He commed Donaldson again. 'I want to visit our anti-Jarinyi friends across the mountains.'

McGrath looked alarmed and the pilot's response was instant: 'No way. Glass wants you back at Columbus for debrief and medical attention. He just called again, asking where you were.'

'What did you tell him?'

'The truth.'

Todd grunted. 'So you told him about our friends too?' She probably hadn't; the incident had been a week ago and Glass hadn't said anything about it.

'It hasn't come up. And you told me he was better off not knowing. Another thing you've "taken responsibility" for.'

Todd laughed and asked, 'I think you're just scared of our "friends". Is that why you don't wanna go?'

'Anyone with half their brain intact would be scared of those ... *things*.' She paused. 'C.O. wants you back. I'm taking you back.'

He put his head back and shut his eyes, allowing the adrenaline rush to fade.

A minute or two later, Chua who had barely moved or taken her eyes off Todd since his retrieval, spoke up again. 'So the indigs were all around you. What happened next?'

Todd's stomach knotted. Chua wasn't letting this go. A glance at McGrath told him she wasn't picking up on the other woman's suspicion.

'Sergeant, it wasn't like Xerxes or Centauri,' he said. 'We weren't calling the shots, we weren't setting the table. It was complete chaos. Weapons malfunctioning because AIRTARs wouldn't acquire, wouldn't fire. People were more focused on getting the AIRTARs to work than they were on their enemy. Jarinyi appearing out of thin air all around us. This bruise –' and he pointed to a spot full of splinters high on his left cheek that he knew would be a rich purple by now. '–this I got trying to save Lim. But he was already gone.'

He shifted on the bench, ran his finger over his jaw where that last Jarinyi had slammed him. He'd have to make this plausible. 'I ordered a withdrawal. I thought they were complying. Communications became confused, garbled. I'm yelling at them to turn off their AIRTARs but they wouldn't do it. I fought my way to Gally's position, trying to get the others to pull back with me. I don't know whether they just wouldn't listen, or they couldn't comply. The Jarinyi were so damned quick. The next thing I know, people are dead. No one's answering my calls. I've killed a couple of Jarinyi, but it was near impossible to tell where the next one would come from. My only choice was to get the hell out of there and find somewhere to regroup–' An unfortunate choice of words; he saw it in Chua's eyes. 'To ambush *them*.'

McGrath muttered something vengeful about the Jarinyi and settled back against the wall. Chua said nothing. She didn't have to. Though she had finally turned her gaze inwards, Todd could see she wasn't buying it.

When the flier began descending to the landing area at Columbus, Chua spoke up again. 'Why do you hate the Jarinyi so much, Lieutenant?'

He flushed. 'After today, you have to ask me that?'

'You hated them before that, sir.'

McGrath looked sideways at her with a *what-the-hell?* stare. Chua ignored it, keeping her features neutral.

Todd expelled air noisily. 'I don't hate them. They're in our way. If you're gonna suggest they have more right to that tiger*weed* than we do–'

'I'm not suggesting anything, sir.'

'–well, they don't. Not exclusive rights anyway. We need it more than them. It's our civilization that's dying out there, our species. We tried to buy it from them, you know that. We tried to treat them as equals but they didn't respond. Because they're animals! They don't understand trade or negotiation or sharing resources. We have to remove them as a factor in all this.'

'Animals, sir?'

'Animals. No moral code. No decency. No honor. And since they wanna behave like animals, the only way to deal with them is to show them that they're not top of the food chain.'

Chua closed her eyes and lay her head back against the wall.

Todd sighed. Although he knew Chua would never share her suspicions with anyone, their working relationship was effectively over.

Upon bugging out of Eventide, she would ask for a transfer to another unit. And Todd would grant it.

And that's another one I've lost.

STEPPING OVER A LARGE EXPOSED TREE ROOT, FISHER FELT A PRESENCE beside her and was shocked to see Scarface stride by, ignoring all three humans and stopping before Tuttut. She knew he was Scarface because Commander Romaine had pointed him out during their visit to the Jarinyi village and mentioned the nickname. She felt a little flush of chagrin that she hadn't heard the alien coming, before wondering if she should be feeling fear instead.

Watching as the two Jarinyi exchanged a short musical conversation, she frowned when she saw a flash of red pigmentation wend its way across Scarface's back and shoulders, reminding her of her own blush a moment ago.

That was weird.

Then Tuttut took off running forward. Scarface sent a half-glance at Carswell, turned away and took up Tuttut's position at the head of the party. Though he followed without comment, Carswell looked unsettled.

Romaine had caught up to him while the two Jarinyi were communicating and now murmured quietly, 'What's he doing here? Finished work early for the day?'

Fisher moved closer to listen in, and tried to keep an eye peeled for other things that might walk up behind them.

'What?' Carswell snapped, frowning.

'He's finished work,' Romaine repeated. 'You know, killing Marines.'

Carswell made an impatient noise and tried to put on some pace, to move away from Romaine. But Romaine caught his arm.

'Yesterday, I bought it,' the Investigator said. 'Hook, line, sinker. The Jarinyi are marvelous alien creatures, a kindred species, intelligent, principled, cultured, an evolutionary masterpiece. I thought they were dandy. Now, I'm thinking I never want to see another one as long as I live. And I'm none too happy about hiking around with them either. These guys may be in their own territory and have the right to stay true to themselves. But if staying true to themselves means acting savage and brutal, then we must be *nuts* following them. What makes you sure they won't kill us?'

'Because I'm one of them. I'm safe. And you're with me. It's as simple as that.' He stuck his face in Romaine's. 'And if they are brutal and savage, are we not ten times worse? Isn't our history full of brutality and savagery? I tell you Romaine, I am much safer with them than with Todd or any of his unit.'

'Maybe you are, but Fisher and I don't feel that way. Why can't you just get us back to Columbus?'

'You will get back there. Just trust me for a little while longer and you'll be happy you came with me.'

'Happy?' Romaine let out an almost hysterical laugh.

'At least be happy to be alive. And remember who it is that's keeping you that way.' Once again, he marched off, leaving Romaine staring after him.

'Is it just me, or does he look a little less happy at the change of escort?' Romaine said. 'I'm going to guess that ol' Scarface and Carswell don't get along so well

Fisher thought a moment then replied, 'Maybe as a linguist, he knows how to annoy people in lots of different languages.'

Romaine did a double take. 'Corporal Fisher! Did you just make a joke?'

She hid a small smile by rubbing the sweat from her face. 'Just a small one, sir.' Then she waved him ahead. 'I'll watch our six; you go ahead.'

At that moment, a soundtrack of destruction reached their ears. Fisher first noticed a noise like hissing or spitting cutting through the background noise of the forest. A ripping, crunching sound that could only have been explosions followed. There were a lot of them and then a slight pause. All animal noise ceased. Finally, barely audible, came something like rapid strokes played upon a kettle drum that seemed to go on forever.

Carswell pointed through tiny gaps in the canopy above and Fisher could just make out a plume of dust or smoke rising up to fill the space formerly occupied by sky. 'The bastards blew up their village. I knew it. I knew it.'

They were still staring back toward the explosions when another sound punctuated the silence - a strange staccato cry. Tuttut appeared from among ferns nearby and motioned them to duck down. Blanching, Carswell made a hushing gesture. The forest had grown deathly still.

The air split with a noise like lunatics laughing, increasing in volume, filling the forest around them. Fisher's blood ran cold and Romaine jumped visibly. As suddenly as it came, it stopped, leaving echoes diminishing like ripples in its wake.

Romaine had pulled his sidearm. 'What is that?'

Carswell shook his head frantically and motioned Romaine to be quiet again. The noise came again, from somewhere off to their left.

'Is that what he's spooked by? What the hell is it?'

The branches of a tree some way away shook violently and from that direction there came the thud of a heavy body dropping to the earth.

Carswell rushed over to him and shocked Fisher by clamping a hand over Romaine's mouth and one behind his head. Very quietly, in a voice slightly above whisper, he said, 'Shut. Up.'

A hush descended on the forest again. For a full minute, the absence of ambient noise made Romaine aware of the buzzing in his ears. Then came another sound. A cooing like roosting pigeons. An animal sound so innocuous that Romaine would not have noticed it had Carswell not startled and let go of him, whirling around.

'Gun,' he hissed holding his hand back.

Romaine looked sideways at him. 'Fool me once—'

Carswell leaned in, whispering. 'That cooing? *That's* the thing that's spooking him. The other things were birds.' He snatched the pistol from Romaine's grip, then pointed it out at the trees.

Romaine – weaponless – settled for crouching behind him, hoping that if Carswell were to spray gunfire in a circle around them, at least it would fly over his head not through it.

Scarface had disappeared and Tuttut shocked Romaine by crouching down and – turning into a rock! At least that's what it looked like.

He had no time to dwell on it. Something sleek and powerful plowed through the brambles between Carswell and the rock-that-was-Tuttut, landing gracefully and turning a face like something from a horror-story upon the three humans.

Romaine experienced fear as he had never known it before. Thoughts raced through his mind with phenomenal speed. He'd faced criminals intent on murdering him in their desperation to get away, Bliss-crazed junkies attacking him because the voices in their heads told them so. As a young man for a time he'd known the prospect of destitution and homelessness, betrayed and abandoned because of his father's greed. And the events of this day had continually put him in harm's way and in fear of his life. But looking into the eyes of a beast that actually wanted to *eat* him reduced him to a primal animal terror so stark he almost lost control of his bladder.

The creature was roughly the size and shape of a leopard, but rather than fur it was cloaked in a shell of what looked like randomly placed horns and scales. The predator parted cracked lips and emitted a quiet noise, almost hypnotic in its sweetness, the cooing he had heard earlier.

As one, Carswell and Fisher opened fire upon it. The creature tucked its head beneath the scales and spines on its back, weathering the hail of bullets for so long a moment, Romaine feared it would have no effect. And then the predator shrieked a sound very different to its earlier gentle cooing, rearing up on hind legs like a bear, before crashing clumsily away into the forest, yelping as it ran.

Romaine felt the adrenaline still racing in his system, the after-thrill of a near-death experience momentarily overcoming the stupor of a concussion. He whipped around to face his companions. Carswell rushed straight past him to Tuttut, dropping the handgun on the ground. Fisher ran a hand through her hair, sagging with relief.

'Oh, my friend, are you hurt?' Carswell was asking Tuttut. Romaine turned again to watch with disbelief as the rock transformed into the shape of a short Jarinyi uncurling from the fetal position.

'That was a close one, 'ey, lad? Ah, just a flesh wound, just a scratch,' Carswell said as he examined fresh lacerations in Tuttut's haunch. It didn't look like a scratch from where Romaine stood. Had the creature climbed over the little guy while fleeing?

'Wow,' Fisher said, locking the new clip in her weapon and racking the slide. 'That was bad.'

Romaine nodded heartily, headache returning. 'What the hell was that thing? And *what the hell did they just do?*' He pointed at Scarface who carefully lowered himself from a tree and contemplated the woods warily. He had somehow melded into the tree just as Tuttut had blended in with the ground.

'All in good time,' said Carswell, helping Tuttut to his feet and tapping the hide bag around the Jarinyi's waist. Tuttut dug his long fingers inside it, felt around and produced a hunk of what looked like Tigerclaw leaf. Carswell took it and began to chew it.

Romaine had finally had enough of Carswell's dismissiveness. High on adrenaline, he seized a fistful of the doctor's shirt at the shoulder and spun him around. 'No, not in good time. No more stalling!' Questions began to rack up in his mind like traffic on an offramp. 'What was that thing? How many more of them are out here with us? What did these guys just do? How did they do that?'

'Alright, alright,' Carswell said, evenly. He jerked his shirt free, spat the Tigerclaw into his hand and applied it to the wounds in Tuttut's hip and thigh. 'I'll explain. Just let me finish putting this on my friend here. There, how's that, lad?' Tuttut seemed to understand the question and placed a palm against Carswell's cheek in what looked like gratitude, before pressing it against his own hip to hold the makeshift poultice there.

Carswell turned to his human companions and grinned in excitement. 'Phew! Gave me a serious case of the *habdads*, that did. We haven't seen that bugger in weeks. Thought he'd left the area.'

'What *was* it?' Romaine repeated through gritted teeth.

'Don't have a name for it, unless you want to come up with one now. How about a spiky-leopard? No, that's cheap, I'll make one up later. Jarinyi just use their sounds for *danger* and *animal* when they've been talking about it. Tuttut here told me a while ago that a family of those things came into the area years ago, but the Tribe chased them out using fire. Lost a few warriors doing it though, and I can see why.' Carswell rubbed at his chest as if willing his heartrate to slow. 'I think it was this one that turned up last winter and took a child right out of the hands of its mother. They've tracked it here and there but haven't been able to get rid of it. Tuttut and I saw it a while ago, but it didn't see us, thank Christ. Now I know why the Jarinyi haven't been able to kill them. They're bloody fast and almost bloody indestructible. How many times did we hit it, Fisher?'

She made a musing face. 'Twenty, twenty-five.'

Romaine leaned closer. 'Now tell me what the hell your friends here just did and *how*.'

Carswell looked his friend over proudly. 'They're mimics. They have these little skin follicles like thick hairs they can use to change the surface shape and texture of their skin. The skin itself is actually translucent. My guess is underneath it are several cell layers like the melanophores Earth chameleons use to change their skin color. They probably shift pigment granules around at will, angle them so they can direct ambient light to specific pigments which then reflect the light back in different colors. Fantastic, eh?'

'And that's how they ambushed the jeeps?' Romaine let out a cry of frustration. 'You didn't think to tell CUSET about this, I suppose!'

Carswell scowled. 'And take away a Jarinyi advantage? No, for some strange reason, I didn't do that.'

'So you side against your own species...'

'Romaine, why can't you marvel at these people and their abilities instead of taking it personally?'

'This is insane. I can't trust these creatures. They're not marvelous, they're not noble. They're violent and treacherous.' He became aware again of the Plazer in his hand. As he put it away, he wondered if would help him against the Jarinyi if it came to a them-or-us situation. As he stooped for his handgun where Carswell had dropped it, he realized that if they could camouflage themselves, he wouldn't know what to shoot at.

'You're being melodramatic,' said Carswell.

'Well, I guess I hate being deceived. I'm weird that way. And while we're on that topic, you told me the Jarinyi can't deceive, can't lie. What would you call *that*? That trick of theirs?' He pointed at Scarface who just stared back and blinked slowly. 'That's a lie. It's basically a lie. They're just as capable as we are of deception. And you're the worst liar of the lot.'

'Oh, pssht.'

'You've lied to us over and over. You said we were going with the Jarinyi to stay safe. Well, they didn't exactly stand up for us just now. They left us to fend for ourselves.'

Carswell sniffed and watched as the two Jarinyi exchanged hand signals. 'That's different. The only thing they can use to fight that particular animal is fire and they don't happen to have any fire on them today.'

'So what are they protecting us from exactly?'

Carswell stepped away and peered into the trees. 'Other animals – they can take care of the rest of the local fauna, no problems. And Nguwuu.'

'I'm not buying this.'

'The other thing they – we – are protecting you and Fisher from is dying of hunger, thirst and exposure.'

Scarface and Tuttut started to walk away again, but seemed more anxious than they had been.

'Yeah, you're doing a fine job there. Have they fed you yet, Fisher? No? Me neither. And come to think of it, we've only come across one stream so far, so there's not much water either.'

Carswell bent over to pull up one of his socks, then turned to follow the Jarinyi. 'All the more reason to keep moving, spacer. If you want to get to food and water and shelter, you'll have to walk like the rest of us.'

The thing he was coming to hate the most about Carswell, Romaine reflected, was the times he was right.

17

'There is a way that seems right to a man, but its end is the way of
death'

- The Book of Proverbs 14:12

THE GRUNT NAMED Yario met them at the Reaper as it landed, wide-eyed
and jittery.

So the news of our debacle has preceded us, Todd thought. His next
conversation with Glass was going to be a doozy.

Despite the unaccustomed stiffness settling in his joints, he refused
Yario's offer of help as he climbed down from the flier. Maybe a visit to
Ranarith *would* be worthwhile, he decided.

Yario then said something that stopped Todd short. 'Sir, a data
packet came in. We got word from the Orbital Platform at Oceana.'

Eric.

He couldn't believe he hadn't thought about his brother at all since
leaving the Patch.

'CO wanted you to know there's no PBT reported on the station or the planet.'

Todd had to clear his throat to cover the foreign swelling of emotion that almost overcame him. *God, get a grip!*

'So why'd they lose communications?' he grated, hoping that the edge in his voice came across as weariness.

'Faulty signal buoy. They're now locked down, quarantined. Defense platforms programmed to shoot down anything entering orbit until the crisis is over.'

Crisis? Is that what they're calling this now?

'That's good news,' he mumbled and made to walk off again, but Yario stopped him.

'Uh, that's the only good news. The rest is bad. For starters, CUSET and the PRC haven't contained PBT as well as they thought.'

Donaldson and McGrath both swore loudly. Todd felt his heart rise toward his throat.

'Tell us,' he said simply.

'Well, Yun Dao for starters.'

'Who gives a rip about a Chinese world?' McGrath interrupted. She spat into the dirt, unaware of Chua's scowl.

Todd waved her quiet. 'The Chinese said they shot down the ships escaping Chi.'

'Obviously, they lied.' Yario dug his bony hands into his pockets, hunched his shoulders and continued unhappily: 'There's worse. Not just *Waypoint2* but Theseus Orbital.'

'How the hell is it getting from A to B?' Donaldson asked, but no one answered her because no one could even guess.

'We're gonna need a lot more Tigerclaw than we got today,' said Chua.

Todd nodded. 'Instead of hundreds of doses, they'll need hundreds of *thousands.*'

'CO's pretty pissed,' Yario continued, shrugging an apology. 'When he found out you'd ... left the Patch early, he hit the roof. Wants another team there right now, harvesting while there's still some daylight.'

Todd's gut tightened in anger. He turned his face to the summer sky.

There were probably a few hours of good light left out in the open. Nevertheless, returning to the Patch today was insane.

'He's been waiting to hear from you before he sends them out.'

Chua asked, 'He didn't find an alternate site today?'

Yario shook his head.

'He sends them back to the Patch today, they die,' Todd growled. 'Who knows what else the indigs have up their sleeves?'

'Hack this to hell,' McGrath muttered.

Todd said to Yario, 'Tell the CO I'll be in sickbay.' The Regular nodded and jogged off. Todd looked at the two women under his command in turn, unsettled again by the hardness in Chua's eyes. This was all that remained of his team. Clenching his teeth against a wave of conflicting emotions, he told them to go get some rest until he called for them. Then he headed toward the sickbay, walking stiffly, rehearsing in his head the script he wanted to follow when the CO came to burn his biscuits black.

Scarface's blood was beginning to cool after the encounter with the predator and the fast run he'd kept up to catch up with Warm Heart's band of Men. He had known from the sign along the way that Warm Heart was with them, his small footprints unmistakable. But he wasn't sure what he should do with the Furface, the Judge and the female.

At least he thought she was a female. Even after two seasons' contact, the outsiders confused him. He had wondered if it really was them who had killed River's Son. But the events of this morning had brought his deeper convictions back to the fore, renewing his hatred for them. They were nothing but murderers and plunderers. They were not like Jarinyi. They were more like Nguwuu.

He and the Elder had debated this very point for days. He had asked the Elder what good could come from the sky. The Elder had replied that Creator dwelled there and that rain fell from the sky and renewed the earth.

Yes, but rain also floods and destroys things, he had replied.

Then they truly are like us, said the Elder. For we care for the earth and for our people but then we also have been known to destroy and to bring evil.

Scarface had let the conversation cease at that point. It was right to honor so profound a point. Something so wise was not to be argued with immediately — even if he didn't agree with it.

After a full day had passed, he had mentioned to the Elder in passing that firerocks also fell from the sky at times, and that claw-kites swooped from on high to attack children.

This time the Elder had not replied, paying Scarface's contribution respect. And perhaps, recognizing that it was correct.

So. Autumn rain or firerocks? Which were they, these Men?

He rubbed at a twinge in his damaged ear. It often hurt when he felt confused. When he couldn't decide on something.

Pretending to watch the treetops for predators, he glanced back at the Furface. The rest of the tribe had their own name for him, but Scarface found that hairy visage distracting and bothersome. This one often acted as if he cared. He had learned their ways. He had shown them honor and even delighted the children with his foolish antics. He had fashioned what looked like a talking blade with which to communicate.

Did this all mean he was an ally? Perhaps he was like the Claw Wing, whose mother laid it in a nest of chicks of other species, who won the confidence of the chicks and their own mother over a full season, behaving as one of the brood, and who then ate the chicks after dark, one per night, until the unsuspecting siblings and their mother were all gone ...

The problem was he just could not see into their heart. While their bodies could not blend, their intentions and their character remained invisible to him. A Jarinyi, even a Nguwuu, signaled constantly, via shoulders, hands, ears, skin and gills. They signaled their intentions and their moods and meanings. They signaled their heart.

These Men — their signals made no sense, baffled him. And when the talking blade was silent, when they murmured to each other like a river running on rocks, he suspected evil in their voices. It was not the way of a Jarinyi to behave like a Claw Wing, but it was entirely possible that this was the way of the Men.

And when he remembered that the Warriors of the Men had murdered

*two of his young Tribe-brothers that very morning, he decided again that this
is exactly what they were.*

*And so he continued to lead the group to the hills, to honor the promise
Warm Heart had made them. But this time he would make it clear to the
Elder that they must not be allowed to leave.*

GRANITE-LIKE ROCK POKED MORE REGULARLY THROUGH THE TOPSOIL,
large half-submerged boulders with deep pores that retained rainwater.
As he lurched forward, Romaine tugged at the fabric covering his chest,
encouraging the air to dry his skin. He gazed down at the slightly-too-
large-shirt and just-right trousers. The clothes had become soil-stained
and were fast becoming ripe with his sweat. One sleeve was torn
slightly, probably from the crash.

At least I didn't pay for them.

Tomorrow – or the next day or whenever the hell he got picked up
by a Reaper – he could give the smelly rags back. Someone else could
have the pleasure of burning them.

He missed his blue uniform. It was blue. He liked blue. A uniform
meant he rarely had to think about what to wear. And it was essentially
free, paid for by his annual clothing allowance.

He'd once read that in the Twentieth Century, many 'third world'
countries had been forced to wear hand-me-downs if they wanted
western clothes, as if they were the younger siblings in a very large
family. A century later, an entire generation of westerners been forced
to do the same. The Twenty-first's economic depression had been more
like an economic collapse for the 'West'. His great-grandparents had
been born into that.

He'd only ever met one of his *grandparents*, and only the one time.
He'd been thirteen. The restaurant was small, cozy, intimate. The
young John liked the low light, the maudlin Nineties music, the
friendly waitress. He'd really liked the waitress. His father's presence
dominated the small venue, a sixty-watt light globe in a room of
candles. The adults were all smiles and pleasantries, but his Dad had

controlled the conversation, his mother unusually reserved and the old man, the stranger who shared his surname, even quieter.

That night his father had treated his grandfather with largess – the old man was wearing a suit of expensive clothes Romaine's dad had purchased for him for the occasion but the man looked anything but comfortable in them. He plucked at the seams the way Romaine kept tugging at his fatigues.

His grandfather was stolid, contained. At first John had been disturbed by the man's big hands, big head, big ears – the way they contrasted sharply with his narrow shoulders, thin chest and wiry limbs. The man couldn't have been more than sixty, but some invisible switchblade had carved up his face with worry-lines. A life lived mostly in poverty had sucked the marrow from the old man's soul.

Still he'd worn very nice clothes. Very nice indeed.

Romaine remembered where the money for those clothes came from and shuddered.

AHEAD AND AROUND THEM THE FOREST THINNED OUT. STUNTED strands of willow-like trees had begun to replace the taller types and thicker scrub. Romaine only noticed the others had stopped walking when he almost collided with Scarface. The Jarinyi was staring up at an escarpment, a grey bluff that marked the true edge of the mountains.

Romaine groaned. His head wasn't throbbing as much as it had, and though exhausted, he found his senses had become sharper, his thoughts clearer. But the last thing he wanted to do now was climb. He began forming the right words to vent his spleen at Carswell but gave up before they could spew from his mouth. There was no point wasting energy on futile arguments.

The rocks radiated the warmth of a full day spent in the sun. They were soothing when he lay his palms against them. He heard Goldilocks in his head: *This one's juuuuust right.*

The rest of the group began to climb, picking hand and footholds carefully. After procrastinating for a full minute, Romaine glanced back into the forest, remembered the leopard-thing and followed.

SCARFACE LED THEM ACROSS A LEDGE – ONE WITH A PRECARIOUS CAMBER – to where a thick runnel of water flowed down the rock face from above. The Warrior squatted to scoop water from the brook, then bounded up the rocks beside it.

'We follow this,' Carswell said simply.

Romaine craned his neck up. Water bounced off the rocks above and sprayed his face. It looked as if there were still many dozens of meters left before they reached the top of this escarpment. 'Dark in a few hours,' he said, longing to linger here, to rest.

'All the more reason to keep moving,' Carswell called down. He had already started up after Scarface, sending a slight shower of gravel skittering down upon Romaine. 'We'll stop at the top of this climb.'

Romaine sucked air and flexed his calves in turn. He dipped his hand in the icy flow and rubbed it across his brow. His palm came away muddy. Some inner compulsion overwhelmed him and he found himself frantically dashing water onto his face, rubbing his hands together, until his palms finally felt clean. He stared at the now white skin, felt the sparkles of fresh pain on his face after the furious scrubbing.

Fisher perched beside him, washing her hands with more measured movements. She drank, then splashed a little water on her own face. Circles darkened the skin beneath her green eyes. Her hair, a glossy red-brown at the start of the day, was matted with sweat and dirt. A diamond shaped leaf had adhered to the Marine-regulation bun. She stuck a finger in one of her boots and jiggled it, allowing a little air down under the heel.

'Blisters?' he asked.

She grunted. 'And so much sweat. If I could just stick my feet in this stream for a minute...If I take them off, I don't think I'll get them back on again, though.'

But Romaine was no longer listening, as a thought struck his addled mind. He forced himself to stand, thighs and calves burning, placed a steadying hand against the rocks on his left and shouted up at Carswell: 'Radio!'

'What?' The xenologist had paused ten meters up the slope, sitting watching them. Scarface was far beyond, almost at the top – at least it looked like the top. Tuttut was midway between the two climbers.

'You said Glass communicated with you at the Jarinyi camp,' Romaine shouted up. 'He didn't send a jeep for you. He must have radioed you.'

'He did. Wouldn't let me get a word in. Just told me an investigator was coming to "give a finding on the Jarinyi murder of Marine Private Gutierrez." His exact words. What's your point?'

'Where's the radio?'

Carswell shrugged. 'Left it in my sleep-shelter at the Jarinyi settlement you visited.'

Romaine sighed. 'Damn.'

Fisher gave him a sympathetic look and pushed herself to her feet. 'Be dark soon,' she said, repeating Carswell.

He glanced at his seiko, instantly forgot the time and had to look again. It was just past 1900 hours; being summer, they probably had an hour or two of daylight left.

Please don't let there be another two hours of climbing.

He felt a momentary temptation to just sit, to pout like a child, to throw a tantrum. The temptation both felt good and caused him shame in equal measure.

His hands lay against the rock wall, his feet braced behind him. The stone was still sunwarmed and pleasant. He turned and leaned his back into it, relishing the relief it brought his muscles. Fisher regarded him silently and sympathetically. Within seconds, the comforting warmth of the rock was undermined by its hardness and his back began hurting again.

'How the hell did we get into this Fisher?' he asked, turning then growling as he almost lost his balance. He let the surge of anger give him strength, found his first foothold. Centering himself, he developed a new strategy: uttering a different swearword each time he levered himself up the slope.

It seemed to help.

BOB GLASS MARCHED INTO THE SICKBAY ALREADY IN MID-TOPIC AS IF Todd had been reading his mind before he got there. 'It's like this virus has been sittin' round on its ass waitin' for a new host without immunity. Shazzam. We show up and all its Christmases come at once. The damn thing's taking every window of opportunity open to it, and rattling the locks on the ones that're closed.'

Todd had suffered the fussy ministrations of Captain Ranarith for a full ten minutes now and was almost glad for the distraction.

He saluted the CO from the gurney on which he sat.

Glass made a shooing motion at Ranarith and the doctor retreated to his office, pissing and moaning as he closed the door. Glass began to lightly beat a fist against the wall as he spoke. 'I want a team back at the Patch to acquire some complete plants.'

Todd sat straighter. 'It's not secure.'

'Well, what the hell are we going to do, Sean? The latest message-pack has senior Management screaming at us for more Tigerclaw. This is a disaster.' He began to chew at a hangnail. Todd had never seen him do that before. 'New ship's due in orbit 0500 tomorrow. Ferry'll be down an hour later to pick up as much Tigerclaw as we have. And we don't have nearly enough to make a dent in PBT.'

'I know, sir, I know. If you really want us to go back, then I guess–'

'You shouldn't have driven back, Sean.' Glass shook his head slowly, pacing about the room. 'You shouldn't have left the Patch. You should have kept working there. We coulda flown in more regulars.'

'Sir, we didn't know what the Jarinyi would do once we'd killed a couple of their kids. As it turned out, my gut was right. They did attack us. If we'd stayed there, they probably would have killed some scientists as well as our men. That's a lot of expertise to put at risk.'

'Your team had a lot of expertise in it too. You could have made two trips in the fliers and kept harvesting while you were waiting.'

'As I say, sir, I made a judgment call in a volatile situation, hoping to protect our personnel not endanger them.'

'But why insist on taking the jeeps instead of waiting in a secure area?'

'It was hardly secure, sir. Especially now with the benefit of hindsight, we know what the Jarinyi can do. That patch is so thick in places, the enemy could have crawled under cover and attacked at close quarters, even if we'd stayed in the middle of the LZ. If we'd moved out to the treeline to defend the open ground, it would have left us highly visible to a force moving in under cover of the forest. It was better to bump out fast.'

Glass seemed to accept this, but not graciously. 'Sean, it doesn't look good for a commander surviving an attack while every one of his people didn't.'

'You think I'm happy with that? Sir.' He maintained eye contact. He was already coming to terms with it. In the end, he'd done everything he could for his people. He'd honed them into a team who should've worked better together, he'd deployed them expertly under fire, he'd ordered them to turn off their AIRTARs, he'd warned them of the chameleon ability. In the final telling, he'd earned his survival and they had not.

I ran. I left them.

No, goddamnit. I survived.

Glass sniffed loudly, rubbed at his nose. 'You lost control of a situation you were sent to maintain.'

'Turk lost his cool. I'll let you decide whether or not I'm responsible for his choices, but he disobeyed my orders – not once but twice. If he was here now, I'd be court-martialing him. You've had no word of him?' The question was an afterthought.

'The last flier's returning now. No radio contact, no life signs. It's a big forest, but I think if he was still alive, we'd have found him. And any other personnel too. I'm assuming Romaine and Carswell died in the ambush?'

Todd nodded. 'Jeep crashed. Probably better that way.'

'*Better?!*' Glass slammed the fist against the wall.

Todd felt himself blush, sliding off the gurney. 'Sir, no one's denying this is a debacle. And I didn't exactly come out of this unscathed myself.' He touched his face, the deep scratches on his forearm. 'But if I could get my hands on Carswell, if he were still alive, I'd kill him. I'm sure he knew about this chameleon ability and never told us.'

'You were going somewhere with this? I'm not hearing how things are better.'

'I think we can use this situation to our advantage.'

Glass glared at him, fishing in his pockets for a cigar. With rock-steady hands, he lit up with a Plazer and puffed in Todd's direction. 'Our advantage. You're serious? Do you want me to list the delays we now face because of this? The complications? Thousands of people will die. And armed conflict with an indigenous people is going to make the Separatists' day when this hits the *pedenet*.'

'With Romaine and Carswell dead–'

'Missing.'

'–missing, but probably being made an example of by the aliens. Probably gutted with a stone knife. Or their dead bodies strung up in a tree as an offering to the gods or something. The point is, the only people left who could potentially cause trouble for us – Commander By-the-Book, Carswell the bleeding heart and Fisher the colonial – are gone. Our field workers and technicians, who saw what Turk did, aren't going to be terribly sympathetic to the Jarinyi, not once they know the full story of the virus we're up against. And they're not likely to go blabbing to the press when they signed non-disclosure agreements.'

Glass spoke around his cigar. 'And the pilot? Donaldson.'

'Donaldson's an Australian and an ex-cop: grew up in the most climate-affected place on Earth *then* had to keep the riff-raff in line. She's a team player. And she's interested in the survival of the species.'

Smoke curled around Glass in thick folds like scrim curtains. 'Ok. Continue.'

'For all the colonies or the pedecasters know, the indigs attacked unprovoked. It won't be hard to "document" how well they've been treated. Which is true, let's face it. Turk's mistake was an aberration. The rest of the time we've tried to increase their standard of living, trade with them fair and square. We could easily make the case that we had an agreement with them and they betrayed it.'

Glass growled low in his throat, pacing again, smoking. 'I don't mind secrecy, Sean. But I hate deceit. It becomes too hard to maintain, to cover all the asses involved.'

'If not that scenario, we could claim a misunderstanding. It's not far from the truth. No one knows of the Jarinyi's objections to us harvesting Tigerclaw, except my team and you. And a few eggheads on the payroll.'

'And Carswell.'

'I seriously – seriously – doubt we'll ever see anything of him again unless his remains turn up in a future archeological dig.' He took a step closer. 'Colonel. We could tell the field workers that the scuffle with the two indig youth was a complete surprise to us – which it was. That we had no idea how strongly they were opposed to the harvest – which is true. That we were attacked first – those youths did start the scuffle. And so on.'

Glass regarded him dubiously, but Todd could see he was getting through. 'And the rest of our personnel? They've known for days that harvesting's been delayed by issues with the indigs.'

'They don't really know what those issues are. Were. We drop hints that it was the indigs upping their fee, working on Stone Age time, generally being uncivilized. And if that doesn't work, then as I said, they've signed non-disclosure agreements, and they care more about protecting humanity against PBT than they do about few indigs who turned on us in our hour of need.'

Glass blew smoke between clenched teeth. 'I can't get past Carswell. He's been in the ear of people in my Camp. I still think bloggers and Separatists are gonna get hold of this story.' He stepped to the door and stared outside.

In the sudden quiet, Todd could hear Ranarith pacing around in his office-lab, talking to himself enthusiastically about whatever test he was running. *In the end,* he thought, *we all have jobs to do and just want to get on with them.*

'Carswell is a rogue scientist who lost his mind. I hear the things the civs say about him. They hate him. He's a nutbar, an attention-seeker. It's not hard to discredit the ramblings of someone who hides in an alien jungle when the rest of his crew move on. Someone who hid valuable military information from CUSET forces that could have saved our lives.'

'And if he's still alive and pops up on a newscast in two years' time, telling his story?'

'Ditto what I just said, sir. He won't be that difficult to discredit. And if he did survive and showed up here, he could always meet with an accident soon after. No one'd be surprised by him disappearing again.'

Glass turned and raised an eyebrow. 'Fairly severe measures, Sean.'

'The greater good, sir. To prevent insurrection and disorder that could cost thousands of lives, you'd not sacrifice one life? A pretty worthless life at that?'

'Of course I would. I just wouldn't like it. And I hope you wouldn't either.' He was quiet a long while, looking back over his shoulder at the gathering darkness outside. He took a long reflective pull on his cigar, savored it. 'Sean, I wonder if you're not better suited to a career in politics or Management. You've a devious mind. But I agree that we're here for the greater good. We have to stop this damn virus before it becomes pandemic.' He stepped onto the squeaky plastic molding of the doorway. 'But we're not gonna get any more Tigerclaw today, are we?'

'Probably not, sir. Bad light and possible boobytraps; not a good prospect.'

Glass jammed his cigar firmly between his teeth. 'Dammit. The ship'll just have to leave with what we've got, and we'll have to find some alternate sources before the next one arrives. Tonight's ship should have some more troops and enough personnel to set up a third site somewhere else on the continent, somewhere drier than this.' He turned his face to the sky. 'With rain rolling in, we're not getting any good leaf outa that Patch over the next couple of days anyway. I'll send the Reapers out to scout more alternate sites first thing in the morning.' He made a noise that was equal parts frustration and resignation. 'Dammit, I hope we get another recon team tonight. We could do with the firepower if those Jarinyi decide to bring the fight to us.'

Todd hoped his face didn't register the alarm he felt. All he needed was another blackcap Looey on his turf. 'Are we likely to get another Unit tonight?'

'That's what they promised us.' Glass shifted the cigar around his mouth. 'Get some rest. Tonight, forget about Tigerclaw and PBT and Jarinyis. Tomorrow you can start working out how we can harvest the rest of the Patch without further loss of life.' He paused, a hand on the doorframe. 'On either side.'

'Yessir,' Todd said to an empty doorway. 'Tomorrow.'

He already knew exactly what he would be doing tomorrow.

18

'Harmony comes from mutual love; when I seek your freedom at the expense of my own, I allow you to set me free also; when I pursue your rights, you are free to pursue mine; when I forgive you, you are released to forgive me; when I think about what is best for you, you can think about what is best for me. Thus we are all released from slavery to anxiety and self-preoccupation.'

- Article 18: *The Articles of Life*
Published by The Society of Andros, 2101

AT THE TOP of their climb they found an expansive area pocked with ledges, caves, puddles. Fisher was a little startled when two Jarinyi females materialized like holograms from one of the caves. Scarface immediately stepped up to one and they clasped hands, murmuring softly to each other in what sounded like gentle birdsong. She noted a subtle shifting of colors along the backs of their arms and necks, brief but unmistakable now that she knew of their camouflaging abilities.

For a moment, she forgot her fatigue, felt strangely touched by the show of affection between these indigenous folk.

That's his wife. No, his mate, she corrected herself. *They're not human. Probably don't have the same kinds of relationships we do.*

Still it was reassuring to find affection here. Despite the battle today, despite the Commander's words earlier about how savage and brutal they were, the Jarinyi were also lovers. Here was something she recognized on an alien world. Something that occasionally, in her prayers, she allowed herself to long for.

Romaine's surly voice snapped her out of her reverie.

'Oh, *fantastic*, Carswell! This is where we've been heading all day? What wonderful four-star accommodation! Point me to the spa!'

Over the last two hours of their arduous journey, the Commander seemed to have found a new reserve of strength, albeit drawn from a deep well of anger. That strength had carried him for the final part of the climb, but now it threatened to abandon him. She watched him sway unsteadily as he surveyed the area. Eventually, he sank onto his haunches then stretched out on the bare rock, pillowing his head carefully on his hands and staring up at the increasing cloud cover and darkening sky.

For the moment, I'll leave him be, she decided and wandered toward a spot where the thin stream pooled. She stared into water as clear as air, knelt and dipped her throbbing right hand into it. For a moment it felt as if the icy water was squeezing her injured finger and she hissed with pained surprise. Moments later, it brought the relief she sought.

One of the females appeared silently at her shoulder, touched her hair gently, flicked a leaf from the bun, then walked downstream. She squatted and held out her hand toward the human.

Fisher frowned. Did the woman –

I guess she's a woman.

– want her to come over? She decided to be polite. Manners usually stood her in good stead with people. She made the effort to comply, knees popping, thighs and calves complaining. The female blinked up at her then and put her hand in the water the way Fisher had.

'Oh, you want me to do it here? Why here? Is the water better?' She shrugged, knelt down again and gratefully returned her hand to the cold. Staring down at it, she lapsed into a flow of memories and thoughts.

After what might have been minutes or weeks, the female Jarinyi's hand closed lightly on Fisher's right wrist and lifted it from the stream. She studied it, pointed to the injured digit and trilled softly. From a belt pouch she produced a small cut of Tigerclaw leaf. She tore off a piece, no bigger than a human's fingernail, pushed it toward Fisher's mouth.

Alarmed, Fisher reared back and turned her head aside.

The female desisted, her head-frills ruffling, sat looking at Fisher with her head cocked. Fisher felt she'd offended her although there was no indication of any emotion in the other's eyes. As she looked into them, she noticed the irises for the first time, like grey marble flecked with gold.

'I'm sorry,' she said. 'I don't know what that is, what it will do to me.'

Carswell's voice answered her. He'd taken up station only a meter upstream. 'She's trying to help you. Let her splint that, and accept the leaf. Tomorrow you'll thank her for it, believe me.'

He stood, dipped his hand into his satchel and tossed a protein bar her way. It landed by her foot and she grabbed at it, suddenly ravenous. The Jarinyi made a wet snorting sound and she nodded at her, held out her Tigerclaw.

I'd rather eat the protein bar right now.

'Ok, I'll take it.'

The leaf felt like a snippet of rough cotton on her palm. She eyed it doubtfully then placed it between her teeth and bit down cautiously. The peppery taste surprised her, but she didn't find it unpleasant. It reminded her of wedding cake icing for some reason. The Jarinyi made a gesture, drew her attention, put a tiny sliver of the leaf in her own mouth then spat it out into her hand.

Fisher frowned, then brightened with comprehension. 'Oh, you want me to spit it out,' she said and let the pulp drop into her own palm.

The Jarinyi made a noise that sounded like *nyek* and pushed Fisher's hand with the mushed-up leaf back to her lips.

Fisher stared at her and sighed. 'This is going to take a while, isnt it?'

____

ROMAINE HEARD A DULL PLOP BESIDE HIM. HE OPENED HIS EYES TO FIND Carswell standing nearby and attempting a neighborly expression.

'Well done, Commander Romaine. You made it. I put a protein bar next to you there. I bet you're hungry.'

'You could say that,' Romaine mumbled as he turned onto his side and snatched the bar from the rock shelf's light layer of dirt. 'I could have used this earlier you know.'

'I know, but things like that predator would be attracted by the smell of the food.'

Romaine ripped the packaging from the snack bar and smelled it. He asked, 'What smell?' before tearing off half in one bite.

'Just because *you* can't smell it, doesn't mean it has no scent.' Carswell crouched down, still playing the part of the concerned friend. 'How are you feeling?'

'How do you think? I've walked – what – ten kilometers with a concussion. Through jungle.'

'More like twelve or thirteen.'

'And that makes me feel so much better.'

'Listen, the Jarinyi will probably make up some medicine for you later tonight. I've used it, it's perfectly safe. Like that moss. Trust what they give you. You'll feel a lot better in the morning.'

'If I live that long,' Romaine grumbled.

A light chuckle from Carswell, then: 'You will, my friend, you will.'

'You're a piece of work, you know that? Completely arrogant all day and now you're Mr Friendly.'

Carswell sniffed and glanced away, face souring.

Some distance away, Romaine could see Tuttut and one of the women breaking branches off the thin scraggly bushes that grew out of cracks in the rocks here and there. Scarface was squatting in the lee of a large rock, cracking rocks together to create a fire. 'The Marines will see the smoke and come to investigate.'

Carswell stood and pointed out over the lower lands beneath the mountain, his natural snarkiness emerging. 'You see that dust and smoke over there where they decimated the Jarinyi campsite? There's a *lot* of smoke about, Romaine. You see how dark the sky is getting? That's because it's about to become nighttime and you can't see smoke at nighttime, not when the planet has no moon.' He turned and gestured at Scarface. 'You see my friend there? He knows how to make fire that gives off very little smoke.'

Romaine swore at him under his breath and glared. 'Tomorrow I'm finding a way to make a signal fire. They'll find Fisher and me...'

Carswell's features softened again. 'Romaine, I wish you'd stop seeing me as the enemy. I'm honestly trying to help you.'

Romaine's head spun, not just with exhaustion but with Carswell's sudden switchback changes of tone and mood. 'Help me how?'

'Tomorrow you'll feel better. Let's leave conversation till then.'

'Fine by me. We'll have a fire-side chat. A signal fire side chat.'

Carswell smiled indulgently and wandered away. 'There's more food on its way, Romaine, try not to fall asleep just yet, pal.'

THE NEXT THING HE KNEW, THE SKY WAS CONSIDERABLY DARKER, THE cooling rock shelf he lay on was hurting his spine and Tuttut was chuffing and clacking at him excitedly. He'd fallen asleep.

He jumped to see an alien so close, so suddenly. During the walk he had gradually grown used to the sight of Jarinyi, the fluid way they moved, the music of their voices. This small shock made everything, including them, seem bizarre again.

'What? What?' he rasped, his mouth dry, flinching as Tuttut thrust a stick in his face. A moment later, it registered that the stick was not a weapon, but a utensil. With roast bugs skewered on it.

He held a hand in front of his mouth, bile rising in his throat. 'I can't eat that, Tuttut.'

Tuttut blinked rapidly, huffed and rolled his shoulders, stood and nipped at the bugs with his small mouth. A stink like old socks filled the air around them. Man and Jarinyi regarded each other for a few moments before the Jarinyi began to turn away.

'Wait,' Romaine said, forcing the word out.

If Carswell was right and Tuttut was an ally, maybe he didn't have to go through Carswell to work with him. Anything was worth a try.

'I need to get back,' he said slowly, accenting every syllable and pointing first to himself then toward where he suspected Columbus to be. Tuttut stared back. Romaine repeated the sentence, speaking even more slowly and miming walking motions with his fingers.

Tuttut breathed out wetly. Romaine held *his* breath, expecting a response. Tuttut stared back.

'Purge it,' Romaine said to himself, thinking. Thinking was hard. His head felt like it had been inflated with helium and was bobbing on the light breeze. And someone kept tapping on the back of it with a small hammer. He pointed to the fire and Tuttut eventually followed his gaze. Romaine made expansive gestures with his hands and what he hoped were flame noises with his mouth. 'Bigger. Make fire bigger?'

Tuttut rolled his shoulders twice and walked away.

Romaine swore despondently and dragged himself to his feet. Fisher appeared at his side and took his arm when he faltered.

'Ah, crap,' he said. 'I feel like an old man.'

She made a sympathetic noise.

'I'm *not* an old man, Fisher.'

'Yes, sir. But you need rest. And medical attention. I recommend letting the Jarinyi take a look at you.' She released his arm and held up her hand to his face. Two of her fingers were splinted with strips of hide and bone. 'I think they're good at it.'

Although it didn't seem to worry her to have pieces of dead animal wrapped around her fingers, Romaine recoiled from them. 'They ... don't know my physiology, Fisher. How often do you think they treat a human concussion caused by a jeep accident?' He instantly regretted the sarcasm in his tone and apologized.

'It's fine sir. I understand your reservations. But they knew what they were doing when they splinted my fingers. And the leaf they gave me to chew has made me feel a little better.'

'Better how?'

'Less pain in my hand and my feet. Not much, but enough to matter.' She shrugged. 'Calmer.'

Romaine thought that Fisher might be the calmest person he'd ever met. In fact, if she got any calmer, she might spontaneously turn into a leaf herself. No, that thought was wrong and weird, and a sign of how poorly he was forming thoughts.

My luck, I have brain damage …

He stared over at the fire. Four Jarinyi forms squatted around it along with a bearded human gobbling up the morsels they plucked from the fire for him.

'Carswell enjoys Jarinyi food?'

She glanced across. 'He seems to. I noticed you didn't eat the bugs?'

'Damn straight.'

'Wise choice, sir. I tried one while you were asleep and … well, I puked, sir. Lost the protein bar I'd eaten earlier.'

'Oh, crap,' he said again. 'That's bad, Fisher. We'll get you another one from Dr Tarzan there.'

'It's ok, sir. I can wait till tomorrow.'

'You need to eat.'

She gave a shy little smile. 'After chewing that thing, I honestly don't feel hungry.'

'Maybe later tonight. How do you feel otherwise? You can't really be feeling calm.' He hoped the leaf she'd used wasn't some new narcotic.

She considered his question for a moment. 'To be honest, I'm caught between complete fear, exhaustion and excitement, sir. Just have a little less fear since I chewed on the Tigerclaw.' She made as if to touch him then withdrew her hand. 'I know you're concerned that something's going to happen to us. I've been worried about that too. But I honestly think we're safe here.'

'Why?'

'It makes sense that they attacked the recons after the deaths of their young ones. The other one that got away obviously let them know what happened and the attack was a reprisal. I believe Dr Carswell when he says if we'd been caught up in the firefight, the Jarinyi would have just killed us too. But they've had time to calm down and to realize who you and I are. They called you a Judge, so they probably assume you're different to the rest of the Marines they've met. If they recognize me, it's as your assistant.'

Romaine made a skeptical noise, but didn't argue.

'*And* Dr Carswell has vouched for us, as he said. *And* they've allowed us to keep our weapons.'

Romaine scowled at that, unwilling to concede a point, watching the xenologist leave the fire and head toward some nearby caves. 'Except Carswell keeps taking mine. He won't be doing that again.' After a moment, he added, 'Safe or not, I don't want to be stuck out here and neither do you. Let's see if I can get us home sooner rather than later.' He headed off toward the knot of Jarinyi by the fire.

ROMAINE APPROACHED SCARFACE FROM BEHIND, SCUFFING HIS FEET ALONG the ground so as not to startle the warrior. Although he hadn't witnessed the battle between Jarinyi and Marines, he took it for granted these creatures were lethal. And he had never been a great fighter anyway: his slightly crooked nose was a testament to just how limited that skillset was.

Scarface had picked a small pile of nuts from the stubby bush beside him and was currently shelling them. The nuts looked far more appetizing than the bug-kebabs had, and were probably just as nutritious. How to ask for them politely, that was the question. Romaine chose to be direct, plucking a nut from the tree and showing it to Scarface.

Still squatting, Scarface glanced at it. Refusing to make eye contact with Romaine, he pushed half of the shelled nuts across the ground toward him with the back of his hand. The gesture was dismissive, apathetic.

Romaine grabbed the food without thanking him, not seeing the point of that, then went to the stream to wash them. Caution and hunger clashed within him for a moment as he studied the small kernels. Eventually he used his incisors to bite one in half, letting a piece sit whole on his tongue for a count of twenty. When there was no bitterness or stinging, he crunched down, releasing the nut's grassy flavor.

The taste instantly transported him back to a childhood memory. Romaine was ten or maybe eleven, lounging in a paddock outside the farmhouse his parents had owned in New Zealand for a year or two. It must have been spring or autumn because the sun was gentle on his face. Mimicking some sheep on the far side of a wire-fence, he chewed grass, spat it out before swallowing, then picked and chewed some more, spat it out ...

Blinking, he found himself back in the present, the memory fading like an afterimage. Any childhood recollection brought him a twinge of gloom rather than nostalgia, a grey melancholy worn thin by the years. His adult mind knew that the boy Romaine was not out in that field expressing his natural delight in the physical world, or his imagination. Rather he was escaping the cold and insecure reality of life inside the house. It hadn't been a snapshot of a boy at play, but rather one of a dysfunctional family taken from a certain angle.

Damned knock on the head was making him lose it. As was this hot and filthy place. As was being kidnapped by a deranged xenologist and his alien cohorts.

He bent to wash the rest of his haul.

Fisher approached Romaine as he squatted and rinsed the nuts in the stream. Acknowledging her with a nod, he dividing them into two groups: two for himself, seven for her. She opened her mouth to protest and he lifted a finger to show he'd brook no argument. For a time, they sat and slowly chewed their fare. Despite her earlier disinterest in food, Fisher wished for more once she'd finished them.

In the distance, thunderheads piled upon each other, rumbling ominously. Slightly to the north of those, the sun sank into a sheath of lighter clouds.

'Storm coming,' she commented.

'Should be fun. For you outdoors types.'

'Actually, this place is a little too humid for me.' Though she had to admit, it was cooler on the mountain here. They hadn't climbed far really, but even this elevation was enough to catch a breeze. She imagined she could detect the brine of the ocean fifty or more klicks away. Perhaps the storm front was kicking up the wind ahead of itself. In any case, the temperature had dropped somewhat and the air was moving – both of these facts were improvements on the past week's weather.

'What do we do for shelter?' Romaine asked.

She pointed back past where the Jarinyi were gathered. 'I saw small caves over there. I'm guessing they sleep in there.'

'Peachy.'

Better than sleeping in the open, she tried to convince herself.

He lapsed into a brooding silence. Fisher left him to seek out Carswell.

The xenologist was crouched by the fire. A wind gust carried his odor her way momentarily. She grimaced behind his back, and hoped she didn't smell that bad. Lifting the lapel of her tunic to her nose, she sniffed and decided she probably did.

'Dr Carswell. The Commander is exhausted. I think it would be prudent for the Jarinyi to look at his head and get him into shelter before dark.'

'Prudent, eh? That's a fancy word for a girl like you.'

The comment forced her to bite her lip.

He stood, wiping his hands against his dirty trousers. 'We could all do with the rest after today's excitements. I'll ask them.'

TEN MINUTES LATER, ROMAINE CONTEMPLATED THE JARINYI WOMAN fussing about inside the enclosed fissure, one of many that dotted the hillside around them. In the fading light, he could just make her out along with the dimensions of his 'accommodation'. It seemed to be about twice his body length deep, and not much more than a meter wide and high. The tart stench of wetness and rot issuing from inside wrinkled his nose, but as tired as he was, when the woman signaled him from within, he ducked his head and climbed inside without complaint.

The Jarinyi woman patted the bed of branches she had made for him from old and fresh branches snapped from the bushes that grew around this area. She warbled something in her language and made to leave. He tried to shrink back as she squeezed by, but there was no way to avoid her. He felt more than a little weird – unclean – at noticing the firmness of her musculature and the velvet texture of her skin against his arm and hand. And then she was gone and it was time for him to rest. The nest she'd made didn't look inviting. But when he turned over and lowered his backside onto the makeshift bed, he was surprised at its suppleness. He had expected to be scratched and stabbed by stray twigs – and while the plant matter was lumpy and uneven – that didn't happen. Using the light from his SCRoLL, he did a quick search for bugs which, reassuringly, exposed nothing. He unclipped his belt with its holster and sundry pouches, tossed it past his feet, lay back.

A noise at the cave entrance startled him. Tuttut blocked the faint light there. The Jarinyi gestured for him to come closer. Romaine wondered briefly if there was some taboo preventing two males sharing the space, or if Tuttut preferred to stay out of tight and smelly crawl-spaces. Groaning with the effort, he scooted over to crouch awkwardly within the entrance. From his pouch, Tuttut produced some of the Tigerclaw leaf and chewed it for a few moments before fitting it into a bandage made of animal hide. He lifted it towards Romaine's head.

Romaine pulled back. 'No way, buddy. *Your* spit on *my* head? I don't think so. Uh uh.'

'It's a compress for your bruising.'

For a split second in his tiredness, Romaine actually thought the Jarinyi was talking English. He felt foolish when he noticed Carswell.

Tuttut stood, dumped the compress in Carswell's hands and went over to the remains of the group's campfire. The little Jarinyi lifted what looked like a blackened bag made of hide from the coals. Presumably he had heated water in it earlier because he pulled something from his belt and put it into the hide, swishing the bag around in slow rhythmic movements. Romaine wondered what the hell he was doing.

Rough hands, human hands, began ministering to Romaine's head. Carswell said nothing as he affixed the skin bandage, maneuvering the wet compress to sit over the raised lump left there from the jeep crash. Romaine submitted reluctantly to his gruff care, losing the will to fight anything anymore. He felt more tired than he had ever felt in his life.

'There we are, almost finished,' Carswell said. 'Soon you'll be fast asleep. And tomorrow, before you know it, we'll be on our way to what I believe will be enlightenment.'

Romaine's face tried to frown, but give it up as too much effort. 'Enlightenment?'

'Truth, Romaine. Tomorrow you will finally arrive at a truth about this situation.'

'"A truth",' Romaine heard himself saying as if from far away. 'How many truths are there?'

Carswell made a musing sound. 'Many, many truths, of course. But in this case, I think there's a particular truth you will be introduced to which will make your job easier.'

Before he could respond, Fisher's voice came from the gloom. Had she been sitting by the whole time? 'The Tenth Article of the Androsite *Articles of Life* says, "Truth is boundless, but is only found along one path".'

Romaine thought Carswell might be smirking but neither man said anything in reply. Fisher too fell silent. Romaine could just make her out, seated on a crag higher than them, watching the darkness thicken and congeal. The phrase *Truth is boundless* bounced around the inside of his head as if there was nothing in there to absorb it. He had no idea what it meant. He'd never been a big fan of Buddhist kōans, Christian scriptures, cryptic crosswords or any other mystical statement that didn't simply bottom-line it for him.

Truth ... is only ever found along one path.

Whatever that damned path was, he sure hoped he was on it.

And that it would lead him home to Bona Vista.

Through heavy eyelids, he watched as Tuttut approached again. He was carrying that bag – Romaine saw now it *was* made from toughened hide. He leaned in to pour a bitter 'tea' between Romaine's lips.

Romaine gagged at first but managed to keep it down at Carswell's insistence. Tuttut gave what sounded like a satisfied snort and walked away to squeeze the excess on to the fire, then toss the hide kettle into a hole amongst the rocks

'That should help you sleep well, pal,' Carswell said.

'Hey, who's this Devlin guy?' Romaine said it in a yawn. 'Someone mentioned him back in camp. You knew him? Could he be the one running around out there with a bow and arrow, killing Marines?'

With a scornful laugh, Carswell blurted, 'More likely dead and rotting somewhere. But, you know, he was a reasonably smart man, resourceful. Anything's possible.'

'Did you two have an argument or something?'

Carswell heaved a wry sigh. 'You know me fairly well by now. I argue with everybody.' He patted Romaine's shoulder companionably and left him alone.

Romaine crawled back inside the cave, the funk not quite as noticeable now, and settled onto his bed of branches. Devlin was another loose thread. Turk was a loose thread. Scarface was a loose thread. And Romaine hated loose threads almost as much as he hated his predicament.

Free-associating now, his mind raised images from the jeep crash - the before-during-and-after of trauma appearing like a series of still photos in his mind.

'Second time in my life I've cheated death,' he whispered to no one in particular. *Why did I say that out loud?* He supposed he wanted the Universe to know it couldn't - it *wouldn't* - take him easily.

The whining of an insect distracted him from those thoughts and he wondered if the little bugger would keep him awake all night. He hated insects too. Or whatever these bugs were called, because they weren't true insects.

Three minutes later he was asleep.

IN THE EARLY HOURS OF THE MORNING, FISHER AWOKE ON HER OWN BED of branches. Her arm was cold from pressing against a rock wall. Immersed in absolute dark, she lay disoriented for a long while.

Where am I?

Eventually she heard the murmuring of voices, and a familiar soft hiss she couldn't place at first. Groggily, her mind caught on. The hissing noise was the sound of rain on rocks – it was raining heavily outside the cave. Jarinyi women were talking and doing something out there. From the noises they made, she eventually realized they were pushing dirt into a ridge across the entrance, 'sandbagging' it to stop water coming in, though some had already run through and wet one of her boots.

She murmured her thanks to them, said a prayer of gratitude and fell back into a peaceful slumber, confident she was being watched over by beings kind and capable.

PART III

SIXDAY

'Hear me, four quarters of the world - a relative I am! Give me the
strength to walk the soft earth, a relative to all that is! Give me the eyes
to see and the strength to understand, that I may be like you.
With your power only can I face the winds.'

– Oglala, Lakota holy man

19

'Everything is well when it comes fresh from the hands of the Maker;
everything degenerates in the hand of Man.'

- Rousseau

THE KILL-LORD *of the Plains Clan stood knee-deep in dewy plains grass and
sniffed at the morning air.*

Nothing.

The air promised nothing.

*He nibbled at another half-burnt grub from his platter without enthu-
siasm and gazed upon the nearby mountains. Long had that natural barrier
represented a spiritual barrier to his people. Tradition told that the original
Kill-lord had brought the Nguwuu here dozens of generations ago from a
great land across the ocean. Tradition told that they had prospered on this
continent to subdue it beneath their rule.*

*The traditions blatantly avoided mention of the Jarinyi across the moun-
tains as being an impediment to the Nguwuu's power. One could not rule over*

all of the grass and soil and rocks and forests and waters, without ruling over all of its denizens.

Jarinyi. He sucked air viciously at the thought of them and flared his gill slits in anger. The spur in the Nguwuu heel, their only rivals in all the world. Never had Nguwuu been able to conquer them, never had they dealt them significant casualties in skirmishes. Of course, the traditions said otherwise, but it was the right of the Kill-lord to dismiss the fabrications of the tradition-tellers and meditate instead on truth.

Truth.

There was probably, he reflected, little truth in the traditions. He speculated that his people had not come from across the sea — although they may have spread in that direction. It was his firm belief that Jarinyi and Nguwuu had once been one people.

There were major differences in their appearance of course. Jarinyi had several gill-flaps which made their language more difficult to understand. Nguwuu had only one pair of flaps. This limited their own ability to make sounds, forcing the use of hand signals, drawings and body language to communicate complex ideas. Nguwuu were larger and stronger than Jarinyi and had better hearing. But they were a little slower.

And Nguwuu could not blend.

However, the similarities were unmistakable also. The basic shape of the body was the same.

A scuffle had broken out amongst his junior-most warriors and he stuffed the rest of the grub into his mouth, stalked towards them ready to enact harsh discipline. For the moment, he pushed the problem of the Jarinyi aside.

THE WHINE OF THE REAPER climbed in pitch as it made ready to lift. Six field workers, plump in their coveralls, wandered by and watched with sallow eyes as the last living Eventide blackcaps boarded the flier.

Todd left the others to ride in back while he took his preferred position beside Donaldson in the cockpit. As the bird rose smoothly into the air, he looked down upon a camp already bustling just half an hour after sunrise. Some of that activity Todd didn't understand. Like what it was exactly that the eggheads did with the Tigerclaw to make it useful offworld. But a lot of it made perfect sense to him. Like Glass shouting at a pair of hapless civilians to load the cases *next to* the ferry pad instead of *on* the ferry pad.

The ferry would be arriving in the next half hour. If there was another blackcap team on board, Todd wanted some progress on his plans before some new Looey started interfering. Donaldson got the Reaper out of camp and headed toward the Pumpkin Patch before she asked, 'Orders?'

She looked a little nervous this morning. Todd suppressed a mean smile. She'd look even more so when she heard their eventual destination.

'First up, we're going hunting,' he told her. 'Let's see if we can find any indigs in the area around the Patch.'

And I'll tell you the rest after that.

ROMAINE WOKE WITH A START AND STOPPED A CENTIMETER SHORT OF cracking his skull against the roof. Dust motes spun on the column of morning light falling within the cavemouth. The motes reminded him of a holo he'd once seen: nanites at work in a water source on Earth, cleansing it from parasites and bacteria and guarding against further incursions. Now he remembered where he'd seen it; it had been a promo for another scheme of his father's: supply the rich with state-of-the-art water purification technology. And screw the people who couldn't afford it.

Water?

'Ah, purge it!' he growled and crab-walked his way out of the cave. It had leaked during the night. He wiped at the wet patch on the side of his trousers, then rubbed at the sore spot on the back of his head from the jeep crash, only to discover that it was no longer sore.

'What in the –?' He rubbed harder: the bruise had to be there. But the area had lost its tenderness. A few small hardened clots of blood clung to the back of his scalp, fusing some of the short hair there, but they were the only sign he'd even been injured.

He touched his face, the places where branches and the ground had scratched him during and after the crash. His fingertips found a number of small scabs, but they crumbled away beneath his touch, leaving smooth skin beneath, the wounds seeming to be days old rather than hours.

Tigerclaw?

'You are kidding me,' he said in quiet disbelief. He moved his head from side to side. The stiffness in his neck, all better. No dizziness.

His hip hurt though, just above the wet patch on his trouser leg.

But that's what ya get from sleeping on wet rocks.

He kneaded the joint with his knuckles, perversely pleased that he wasn't completely pain-free. Perhaps he didn't want to believe the Jarinyi medicine was completely miraculous.

'Just mildly miraculous,' he admitted to himself. He flexed his arms, breathed deeply, felt like he could fly. In fact, it had been a long time since he'd felt this good.

Except for this damn hip, he grumbled, pressing his fist against it.

He stepped from behind the boulders that obscured the cave mouth, noticed Fisher a dozen meters away at the edge of the drop-off. Something about her made him stop and stare. She stood gazing out over the lowlands below, rocking on the balls of her feet. Against one thigh she clasped a small and old-fashioned paper journal. A flat pencil protruded from between the pages. The way she let the wind blow through her hair, the way she now flicked at it distractedly. She appeared girlish, vulnerable. She appeared—

Very feminine. For the first time, though she was dressed in a stained and rumpled Marine uniform, Romaine noticed her as a woman. And just as quickly, dismissed the thought before it formed itself into words. There was no place for that here.

But damn, she even moved like Harshini.

This wasn't like him. He had never ever come over all amorous while on a case. More side effects of the Eventide wonderdrug? he wondered.

Yeah, Johnny, and that'll be enough of that, son. It's a brand new day. Let's get moving.

An hour's searching uncovered no Jarinyi. While it would have felt great to turn a few of them into grease-smears, what Todd really needed was for the damn Nguwuu – who knew the terrain *and* the Jarinyi better than he did – to do their damn job.

Finally, he ordered Donaldson to the far side of mountains. She sniffed but said nothing, turned that way. He sent the Camp comm-officer a short message lacking in precise details, letting Glass know he was out 'reconnoitering'. It was better if they didn't talk directly right now. While he admired Glass as an experienced warrior, the old man thought in straight lines. Todd was able to think fractally, creatively. To protect the human species, CUSET's slow but steady colonization of the galaxy, *and* to protect his brother, there was a creative way to remove the thorn in this mission's side. It was called warfare.

Fisher spent a long time allowing the morning wind to comb her hair before pulling it back into a bun and reapplying the hair tie. She'd woken to strange harmonics made by the wind on its way through and over the rocks, and scrambled out of the small hole in the mountain to find a world washed clean by the rain. Up here above the forest, it wasn't as clammy, the wind fresh and cool and, yes, smelling of the sea. The rain clouds were passing like a fading dream, blue skies returning.

Gosh, she felt *good* this morning. Despite the water that had seeped into her makeshift bed to soak the back of her pants. Despite the ordeal of yesterday. Despite everything.

Romaine's voice startled her.

'Beautiful day, huh?'

She turned to face him, surprised at both his words and the fact he obviously meant them. His voice, his facial expression – he almost seemed happy.

'Sir? I mean, good morning, sir.' She slipped the diary back into her shirt pocket; she hadn't been able to think of anything to write anyway.

He crossed the ground between them like a man navigating rock-pools on a beach. Where patches of soil filled in cracks in the rock, the rain had created mud. His finicky walk accentuated again his spacer personality, his fussiness. But. He was smiling as he did. The lines in his face had softened. This was not the surly, sarcastic Commander Romaine of yesterday.

She turned to look out across the forest again, reveling in the view and the breeze. As he joined her, she asked if he was as hungry as she was.

'Not hungry, Corporal. Ravenous. It'll be interesting to see what our hosts serve up for morning meal.' Noting the water stain on the back of her thighs and pointing to a sodden spot on his own leg, he added 'Rained last night. Gives new meaning to the term *water bed*.' Her expression must have registered her confusion at the remark, because he added, 'You never heard of a water bed?'

She shrugged a *no*.

'One of those quaint trends that seems to come around every fifty years or so. Mattress full of water. Simulates the womb, I guess. Tried one out a few years ago.'

'Did you like it?'

'Made me seasick.'

THEY LAPSED INTO A MEDITATIVE SILENCE, ROMAINE WONDERING WHERE Columbus was from here? The Pumpkin Patch? He could guess, but all he could really see were trees. Specks of color indicated movements of flying creatures, some in flocks, some alone, dipping and darting from the cover of trees to the open air and back again. As much as this world freaked him out, he had to admit it had some beauty. He just wished he was viewing it on a screen from a ship leaving orbit.

Thirsty, he was about to scoop water from the puddle at his feet when Fisher cleared her throat.

'Doctor Carswell said not to drink it. Something about the soil here.'

'So, the stream then? Would you care to accompany me? After we drink our fill of untreated mountain runoff, we can see if there's any bugs left for breakfast.'

'I'd prefer a protein bar.'

'How unadventurous.'

She looked at him quizzically. 'You seem ... happier today, sir. Is your head better?'

'Funny you should ask. It doesn't hurt a bit. I can't believe it.'

She peered at him closely, almost touched his face appearing to think the better of it. 'The scratches on your face, they've healed up too.'

'Yep. I have to admit ... Hey, how's your *hand*?'

Her face was transformed by a little girl's grin and she held her hand up for him to see. The splint was gone. She flexed slowly and carefully.

'I thought Carswell said your fingers were broken.'

'I think one was. Two more were sprained, at least. They haven't healed completely yet, but ...' She curled them some more. 'No inflammation, no bruise, it's incredible.'

'I think we both know why CUSET is so eager to get their hands on Tigerclaw now. There's a lot of money to be made from something this good.'

Her smile faded.

He looked down at the stream as they reached it and hoped it wasn't parasite-ridden. His father's water-purifying nanites weren't in plentiful supply in these parts. He stood, shook his hands dry and turned his attention to the Jarinyi. Three more warriors had joined them during the night. The growing numbers jolted him.

For a time, he watched them going about their simple routines, trying to read human mood into their alien body language. They seemed content, untroubled. The destruction of their village would probably have little emotional impact on nomads who could make their home anywhere, he guessed. What must it be like to exist this simply, living by the rhythms of the weather and seasons, unencumbered by possessions and the demands of a job? To hunt, to eat, to sleep, to get up and do that again? To not do crazy things like traveling between stars sorting out who stole what from whom and how, or who'd killed whom and why?

To be a part of a Tribe.

At a familiar sound, he squinted east. There it was, the small dot of a flier skimming the trees before disappearing behind the stretch of the mountains, heading northeast. The sight rebooted his hope and determination; Columbus were looking for him.

For us, he reminded himself, although Fisher didn't seem to have seen or heard the Reaper.

He stretched sideways, pulling at the stiffness in his hip, felt a small pop and some relief. Time for action. Time to find Carswell.

———

ALL OF SCARFACE'S ERECTORS — THE TINY MUSCLES THAT ALLOWED HIM TO blend — tingled with irritation as the Judge passed him.

Scarface's life-mate released a pheromone of amusement as she went off to the fire, chortling softly through her upper gills. That she found his anger amusing only made the situation worse. Like the others, she accepted these outsiders with good grace, though they were part of the same tribe that had killed her nephew only this morning. That was two nephews dead within a few sunsets. Killed by the weapons of the Men. He found it offensive that the Judge and his companion should benefit from the very medicine other Men were trying to steal. They should have been left to fend for themselves in the forest.

He shrugged the thought away, allowed the breeze to cool his anger.

Whatever the furry-faced one wanted with them was irrelevant. All Scar-

face wanted to do was rejoin his Tribe. And later view and honor the body of his nephew...

———

Romaine joined Carswell. The doctor spoke before he could.

'I wonder where they were heading?'

'You saw the Reaper?'

'Heard it. What could possibly be across those mountains that they'd be interested in?'

'Um, more Tigerclaw sites? Duh. Where are *you* heading, Carswell?'

The xenologist laced up his boots without hurry. 'Safe harbor. A little higher than this. It's about two hours' further hike. Even you can make it there.'

'And what then?'

He tied off the last lace with a flourish, sniffed the morning air and sighed. 'I love a new day. It bears the promise of a fresh discovery. And I predict that an important discovery awaits *you*, Mr. Investigator.'

'I'm not going any further up this mountain. I want to return to Columbus. Today.'

'But you can't.'

'I can't?' Romaine's voice broke with exasperation. 'I don't need to walk back through the forest. I'll get their attention here, wait for retrieval. Even I can figure out how to make a signal fire. I have my Plazer. That'll work.'

Carswell pursed his lips, cocked his head like a Jarinyi. 'And if they don't see your signal fire?'

'*Then* I'll walk it.'

The sliver of a smile appeared on Carswell's lips. 'Like I said yesterday, I'm not stopping you. But it'll be your funeral.'

'If it's dangerous ...' Romaine began. Carswell raised an eyebrow. 'Ok, no *if*. It's dangerous. So send a Jarinyi with us.'

Carswell laughed. 'I don't send them anywhere. I'm not their CO. And even if I could, I wouldn't. They're not here for your convenience. They have their own matters to attend to.'

'Matters to attend to? What? Walking around the jungle? Climbing mountains. Killing things. Lighting fires with stones. Yeah. These are matters of monumental significance.'

'You culturally stunted buffoon. Make your own choice. But if you turn back, they're not going with you.' Carswell stomped to the rock face and began climbing.

Romaine stared after him, seriously considering scooping up a stone and flinging it at him.

Fisher cleared her throat. 'Sir. If you need to get back, I'll walk with you.'

He breathed deeply, frowning at her mildly. 'You will?'

'It's a two day walk at most. Even if we don't have food, there's water everywhere. We could find a way to purify it. We'd survive.'

'And if one of those leopard things turns up?'

'We both have weapons. You also have your Plazer. We can make do.'

He regarded her for a few moments. Her expression was professionally neutral. 'Ok, Marine, that's your dutiful statement out of the way. Now what do you really think?'

She wet her lips and replied, 'I think, sir, that walking back is a bad idea.'

'Why? I mean, apart from the leopards and stray Jarinyi patrols who might mistake us for blackcaps.'

Her eyes lost focus for a moment as she remembered something. Around them, the Jarinyi gathered up nuts into skin-pouches and made quiet conversation between themselves, prepping to climb.

Fisher said, 'Back home, outside our town and our farms, it was just forest. Like this. City people and offworlders came to go hiking and got lost all the time. The ones we actually found – alive – swore black and blue that they were in *Place A*, but they were actually in *Place B*. Without satnav, or at least a compass, I don't think we should try for Columbus by ourselves.'

The Jarinyi began following Carswell up the mountain. A female came to Fisher and pressed dry Tigerclaw and a hunk of tree bark into her hand. The woman touched her palm to Fisher's forehead tenderly then bounded up the slope after her Tribe members.

Romaine looked around at the scattered copses of shrubs and wiry weeds jackstrawed by wind and shallow soil, looked toward where he'd seen the Reaper, looked back at Fisher and set his jaw determinedly.

'Time to make a fire.'

20

'When the only tool you own is a hammer, every problem begins to resemble a nail.'

- Abraham Maslow

BENEATH THE REAPER, the mountains gave way to the golden grasses of the savannah beyond. Donaldson eventually indicated she'd found a collection of life signs west that looked like Nguwuu and Todd told her to fly that way.

He triggered the augments which would increase blood flow to his muscles and heighten his senses. This would be a dangerous meeting. But a necessary one.

It was time to have a serious chat with the enemy of his enemy.

WHEN A SENTRY BEGAN TO HOOT AND WAVE, THE KILL-LORD NOTICED THE dot in the sky growing steadily larger as it sped toward his tribe.

The Skywarriors were here? Briefly he felt concern — many of his warriors were scouting in the mountains and the Jarinyi forest beyond. But the unease was quickly replaced by a thrill of wonder. The morning air had lied to him: this day showed true promise. The Spirits had chosen it for important matters.

On their last meeting, the Skywarriors had stopped him from achieving a great glory, the death of a Jarinyi, albeit a young and inexperienced one. However, he had received a weapon instead, one that no Kill-lord before him could have conceived of. He picked up the hard, cold object from the grass by his feet. There was still time in his life to slay a Jarinyi. And he now owned something powerful, almost magical. He was the greatest of Kill-lords.

He faced the flying thing as it approached, awaiting whatever events the Spirits had decreed. His tribe gathered behind him, making agitated noises until he waved them to silence. He would show no fear in the face of these Outsiders. If only he could find a way to truly understand what it was they wanted and why they had made a gift of their magical weapons.

CHUA STAYED WHERE THE AIRCRAFT DROPPED THEM, SETTLING INTO THE grass like a lion watching prey. Donaldson took the flier twenty meters up in the air and angled the nose-cannons toward the large group of aliens on the plain below. McGrath flanked Todd, '90 angled at the ground, finger on the trigger guard. The Nguwuu chieftain — as Todd thought of him — sallied out from among his people, an almost jaunty air about him. The other Nguwuu kept their distance. Those with primitive weapons fanned out. Others gathered in cliques behind the line of warriors. None made any noise at all.

Walking toward the chieftain, Todd checked himself. Reassuringly, he felt none of the fear that had gripped him during the battle with the Jarinyi. He was back in control. He was calling the shots.

The tactical part of his mind mused that maybe there were Nguwuu camouflaged like their Jarinyi cousins in the long grass nearby waiting to pick him off. *Nah.* He was reasonably sure the Nguwuu couldn't do that chameleon trick or they'd have done it the first time he met them.

Apart from the rifle slung snugly across the chieftain's back, he couldn't see any of the other AR90s. Even so, he stopped a good fifty meters from the main group and waited for the chieftain to approach. Maybe the '90s were offsite, carried by tribe members on a hunt, maybe they were buried somewhere.

Maybe they're trained on me now.

As the Nguwuu strongman loomed closer, Todd turned up his lip at the creature's appearance. *Ugly, ugly bastards.* Its flat eyes carried none of the spark of the Jarinyi's and the larger mouth looked more sinister. The Nguwuu boss wore about his body a collection of teeth, claws, bones and what could have been dried viscera or tendons.

'They certainly don't grow on you, do they?' he muttered to McGrath. She chuckled her agreement.

This was his second meeting with the chieftain. The creature had separated from his group then and he did so now, drawing near Todd with utter fearlessness.

How to get through to this *thing*? That was the problem Todd still faced. He'd thought his message had been clear that first time. He was still proud of the idea that had come to him on the plateau when he'd noticed the bound and squirming Jarinyi there. God only knew what the chieftain and his crew had planned for it, but it obviously wasn't a birthday party.

The chieftain now squatted on the rich soil and peered up at him. He'd done this the first time too. Todd crouched, mimicking him.

'Let's cut to the chase,' he said and fished inside the bag he'd brought along, fingers quickly finding Romaine's *chweechee*.

The moment the throwing stick landed beside the chieftain, the strongman shot to his feet, huffing and making frantic signs with his hands. Todd had no idea what the signals meant – he hoped they weren't battle orders to the line of alien warriors. It'd be a shame to eradicate a host of potential allies. In any case, he wasn't actually interested in anything his opposite number had to *say*. He simply wanted these creatures to know that he'd given them three rifles for one reason and one reason only.

Calmly he rose and took a step closer to the Nguwuu. The chieftain stopped gesticulating and watched him, wary for the first time. Todd stooped and snatched up the *chweechee*. He showed it to the chieftain again, then stepped away and held it up for the rest of the tribe to see. 'Jarinyi,' he said in a loud voice. 'Jarinyi!'

Then he reached for McGrath's shotgun. As she passed it over, a ripple passed through the Nguwuu ranks, but the chieftain didn't flinch.

Todd tossed the *chweechee* underhand, high into the air, raised the gun and blew it to pieces.

The crowd of aliens jumped and backpedaled, making excited noises that reminded Todd of farm animals. While they milled restlessly, their leader deftly snatched a chip of falling *chweechee* from the air, and raised it toward Todd.

Slowly and clearly, the Nguwuu boss said '*Cher ... in ... yee.*' He bent one arm behind his back and nudged the AR90.

'Jarinyi,' Todd said in return.

Something Todd hoped was realization blossomed in the Nguwuu's eyes and it began to strut and huff and gesticulate wildly toward his people. '*Cher ... in ... yee,*' he snarled. '*Cher ... in ... yee!*'

'I think he gets it now,' McGrath muttered.

Relieved, Todd headed for the flier. He gave the chieftain a backwards glance. 'Have at 'em, tiger.'

Jarinyi were created and sent by the Night-Spirits to test Nguwuu, to strengthen us.

This thought was so clear and sudden and profound that it had to be inspired. The Kill-lord dropped the splinter of chweechee and tapped his index fingers together in delight: he had solved the riddle. The Spirits had seen that he was powerful enough to be entrusted with this revelation. They had sent this red-furred sky-man to wake him up to the truth. The purpose of the Jarinyi was to grow the Nguwuu to their greatest strength.

Jarinyi were not a barrier to conquest, but the means toward it.

He rubbed the weapon at his back again, made excited signs with his hands and face, declaring his emerging plans to the sun and to the mountains, and to his clan who watched on with mounting fascination.

'And now that we have been given a new power, and now that I alone have come to understand this, our clan will not only rule all clans and tribes of all Nguwuu. We will conquer the Jarinyi! Mine will be the conquering clan, thus mine will be the spoils of victory: the land itself, its medicines and pleasures!'

The sun and the mountains did not reply. But they did not need to. The Kill-lord knew what to do.

He would eat and then he would ready his warriors.

TODD STAYED TO WATCH WHAT WOULD HAPPEN FOR A GOOD HOUR, leaning against the Reaper's tail flukes while his team members kept a watchful eye on the grass around them. He was confident this time that he'd gotten his point across. Somehow the Nguwuu would find the Jarinyi wherever they were hiding in the rain forest and either wipe them out, or distract them. He hoped it would be the former.

The Nguwuu assembled a large posse of warriors and even brought in three trilophants upon which to ride. The massive beasts had made Donaldson even more edgy, worried they would stray too close to the flier and damage it. Eventually Todd caught the chieftain's attention and showed him how to use the mini-missile launcher beneath the barrel of one of the rifles. He handed him a clip of three missiles then, on a whim, gave him his own Marine issue knife.

After that, Todd happily ordered everyone on board the Reaper. The last thing he saw before he climbed in himself, was the Nguwuu strongman placing the steel dagger carefully through his loin cloth.

'Let's get some brunch,' Todd told Donaldson, patting his stomach. 'I'm hungry.'

THE SMALL FIRE ROMAINE STARTED MADE A LITTLE SMOKE, BUT NOT

enough to satisfy either of them. Fisher suggested they put bed-branches on it. Still damp from the night's rain, the branches created curls of thick pungent smoke, a pleasing dark grey in color. Taking his cue from Fisher's logic, Romaine dropped other branches in nearby puddles for later use.

They waited the better part of an hour before hearing the sound of the Reaper returning across the mountains. Romaine jumped up, threw some more dry wood on the fire and followed it with another damp branch.

'Here we go,' he said brightly and began waving his arms in the air, moving to the edge of the small plateau.

———

SITTING UP FRONT WITH DONALDSON, TODD FIDGETED WITH THE BUCKLE of his harness and stared out of the side window, musing about how long it might take the Nguwuu to find the Jarinyi. He noticed the thin spiral of dark smoke a kilometer away at the same time as Donaldson exclaimed, 'Holy shit!'

She pointed to a life signs monitor which registered two human-spectrum readings on the hill near the fire.

'Slow down, but don't turn yet,' he said, curious. He leaned across to the belly camera controls, ignoring her questioning stare, turned the screen to face him and toggled the camera to zoom in on the patch of mountainside where the smoke was coming from. There on the shaky viewscreen were the unmistakable forms of Romaine and Fisher, waving and jumping about like sugar-hyped children.

'I don't believe it,' he said. How had they managed to survive the jeep crash *and* a forest crawling with Jarinyi gunning for human beings? Why were they all the way up there?

As Donaldson reached for the screen to look, he flicked the toggle and the image slewed away to take in nothing but the tops of trees.

'What are you doing?' she asked.

'Nothing to see here. Let's go.'

'What is it?' she demanded, holding her hand above his while his palm remained resting on the toggle.

He met her hard gaze calmly. 'Just Carswell.'

'Carswell?'

'Yep. Carswell.'

'And you don't wanna go after him?'

'What, you think I want to shoot him or something?' He shrugged. 'Let him live off the land with his weird little friends if he wants. He won't last long.'

'He's lasted this long living with them.'

Todd sighed. 'Maybe I'm becoming forgiving in my old age. Let's just go.'

She resisted. 'Just Carswell? Not the cop? Or the MP?'

He returned her gaze again. 'Just Carswell. Let's go back to Camp.'

With his hand still preventing her from seeing for herself, he knew she knew he was lying. She could have turned and flown in the direction of the life signs. She could have disobeyed him, given the circumstances. But she didn't. Her face hard with anger, Donaldson tilted the flier forward and ignored the questions coming over the rear compartment's intercom.

'No, nothing,' Todd responded. 'All clear.' After a while he said out of the corner of his mouth, 'And I'll be taking the memory cell from that camera when we get back.'

'Bloody hell,' the pilot said angrily. 'If that was the cop back there...'

'If it was, you're in this too deep anyway, *mate*.' He made the Australian term of endearment sound like an expletive. 'Besides, did you *see* Commander Romaine back there? No. You didn't. You're getting all flustered for nothing.'

It occurred to him then that the disappearance of Romaine and Fisher might effectively make them martyrs – and martyrs who would potentially gain a lot more sympathy with Separatists and working-class colonials than recons would. Even the loss of Carswell in the ambush could be useful to leverage public opinion against the aliens if this ever came out.

See how these so-called sentient beings treated someone who was living amongst them and cared deeply for them? Disgusting, aren't they? Just animals, in the final analysis. Not worthy of our respect.

So quietly that he almost didn't hear her above the hum of the aircraft, Donaldson called him a word he hadn't been called in years. Todd just smiled. That was a compliment where he came from.

AFTER THE *REAPER* HAD VANISHED INTO THE DISTANCE, ROMAINE SPOKE softly.

'Fisher?'

'Yes, sir?'

'Permission granted.'

'For what, sir?'

'To call me an idiot.'

ONCE THEY'D DISCUSSED IT, THEY REALIZED THEY HAD THREE CHOICES.

Climb after Carswell and the Jarinyi.

Stay here and hope to be miraculously rescued.

Hike back through hostile forest to Columbus, hoping some predator didn't take a fancy to them or that they didn't simply become as lost as the survey team's Rowland Devlin.

And so they came back to the only real choice they had.

'We climb,' Romaine said with more than a touch of glum.

'Okay,' Fisher responded, gathering herself. While unenthusiastic, she seemed resigned to the decision.

The Jarinyi now had over an hour's head start. They discussed how they might stay on their trail. The stream, they agreed, would probably lead them to the next camp or settlement.

This part of the mountain seemed arranged in rolling steps. Climbing then walking, climbing then walking, their feet usually found solid rock, but occasionally slipped or skidded on loose dirt. Arduously, they followed the stream up and across, up and across, until they found themselves staring despairingly at the point where the stream no longer flowed down the mountain, but emerged from it. There was no longer a stream to follow.

After he'd finished swearing, Romaine wondered aloud, 'Could it reappear higher up?'

'Or does this mean this stream *starts* here from a spring and the next Jarinyi camp is by a different water source?'

Romaine's shoulders drooped. 'And how can we know for sure?'

'Maybe we could shout for help or fire our weapons.'

'And possibly attract some of those Nguwuu people or a leopard thing? We have to keep climbing and hope ...' He let the thought trail off, feeling the importance of being positive, staying strong. 'We'll find 'em Fisher. Or they'll find us. It'll work out.'

'Yessir,' she said brightly and he wondered just who was bolstering who.

He consulted his seiko, horrified to discover they'd been climbing for less than an hour; it felt like a day. His muscles were already complaining and he felt as if gravity were sucking his life force out through his feet and into the mountainside. Nevertheless, he lifted a foot to a new ledge and stepped up.

'It is no measure of health to be well adjusted to a profoundly sick society.'

- Krishnamurti

'HOW ARE YOUR FEET?' he asked.

Fisher made a growly noise. She'd been trying not to think about that. Because her left foot ached under the arch. And both feet felt slippery and clammy within their leather prisons. 'Not real good. I slept in my boots. Probably should have let my feet air.'

'Me too. But I passed out; what was your excuse?'

He had paused, waiting for her. She caught up to him and shrugged. 'Didn't want creepy crawlies in them when I went to put them on again.' He looked at her. 'We had to think about that back home. Most of the wildlife on Centauri is tame but out where we lived there were these poisonous critters – frigs we called them...'

'*Frigs?*'

'Dumb name, huh? Anyway. They liked to hide in shoes. Bit my uncle. Two times. He nearly died the second time.'

'You'd think he'd learn to check his boots.'

'Oh, yeah. You'd think. When he got better, my aunt gave him hell over that.'

He nodded over his shoulder toward fresh rain clouds scudding their way. If they'd hoped to keep the rest of their bodies dry, they were going to be disappointed and soon. She could only hope they made it to the new Jarinyi camp and shelter before it rained.

'Bright side, sir? If we catch a cold, Tigerclaw should fix it pretty quick.'

He started climbing. 'I can see why CUSET's so keen to get that stuff out to the general populace. Even if there was no PBT out there,' he gestured at the sky, 'the pharmaceutical corporations within CUSET would make billions off it. That's why I'm here. That's why you're here.' He fell silent, concentrating on the way above him.

'Sir, you said everyone here is either earthborn or from Castor. How important *is* that?'

He grunted, navigating a slippery patch with care. 'It's either a coincidence or it means CUSET simply didn't want people who'd personally identify with the Jarinyi.'

'Because colonials feel hard done by?'

He grunted assent.

Does that include me? I'm no whining Separatist. 'So they – we, CUSET – came here intending to take the Jarinyi resources whether or not they would trade for them.'

'We're all following that time-honored tradition of screwing powerless people.' He shook his head, his voice turning as gravelly as the soil. 'As ticked at the Jarinyi as I am, I feel sorry for the little buggers. They never stood a chance.'

These ideas left her miserable. *Conflicted* was a better word for it. On one hand, she was raised to respect authorities, particularly to be loyal to her employer. On the other hand, she felt a great deal of sympathy toward the Jarinyi and her faith had a long tradition of siding with the underdog. To think of the locals as victims of wealthy, powerful people, it made her mad. She'd become a policeperson to stop people from hurting each other, to keep order. Now the very people who paid her wage might be the ones doing the hurting, destroying the order of another culture.

But then, she told herself, she'd known that CUSET weren't perfect, since her time in the Pan-Asteroid Communities. She'd seen their callous treatment of protestors firsthand. She knew that many people with Separatist leanings had been incarcerated awaiting trial without charge for months at a time; many had been deported from CUSET territory, either back to Earth or to the small collection of free holdings on Xerxes and Theseus who needed cheap labor. These deportees numbered two hundred or more, from Centauri and from the PAC. And they'd been sent packing with only the clothes on their backs, their belongings confiscated to 'recoup the administrative costs' of their relocation.

Yes, though she denied it, ever since that time in the PAC she'd felt a niggling doubt. Was she serving on the wrong side, working for an unjust and dehumanized regime?

Dehumanized regime. Gosh. It must have been a phrase she'd heard Carswell use. Was she starting to think like him? And if she was, was that so wrong? Despite his lack of social skills – manners, more like it – perhaps he really was on the side of good and right. On God's side.

And here was another question she'd been trying to ignore for the past two days: what was God's will in this situation? Specifically, what was his will for her? Did he want her to resign? To speak out against this injustice to the media? To complain to the fabled United Nations back on Earth? To keep quiet and go back home to work quietly on a farm? Or to become an Investigator like Romaine with more power to resolve things and correct things?

She heard herself growl out loud in frustration, ignoring Romaine's quizzical look as they climbed together. The question of God's will had always confused her. Utterly. She had never felt completely settled about a single major decision she'd ever made. She had once gone to her pastor about it. As they'd strolled along a stream outside of town, children laughing and splashing in the cool waters, he had simply said, 'You tell me how to discern God's will and we'll both know.'

She knew she looked shocked, because he laughed good-naturedly at her, waved a hand apologetically and asked forgiveness if he sounded cynical. 'It's just that, for thousands of years, people have used the notion of *God's will* to commit acts of malice, acts of greed, acts of self-ishness, abuse, abuse of power ... even acts of insane terrorism. All are in opposition to what we read of the character of God in our scripture. Yet they convinced others that it was God's will. Or at least, they convinced themselves.' He smiled his occasionally impish smile, twisted a berry from the tree he'd stopped to lean against, tossed and caught it. 'Me personally, Jennifer, I believe in faith.'

He tossed the berry between his teeth and chewed. After a moment, it became obvious he wanted her to ask him a question. Always wanting questions before volunteering more, always making her and her friends think. They all agreed he was really irritating at times.

'So what do you mean, you believe in faith?' she asked him.

'Oh, that,' he responded vaguely as if he'd forgotten their conversation. 'All I can do, dear girl, is trust my life and its conditions into God's hand. I trust him to redeem whatever messes I make and somehow guide the muddled thoughts in my head so I have some idea about improving myself and the universe. If astounding and inspired thoughts don't come, then I don't blame God and I don't blame myself. I simply do whatever seems best to me. And have *faith* that God will either change me so I act rightly or change my situation so my actions don't hurt others.'

'So is that what it's about? Working out how best *not* to hurt others? Is that God's will for us?' It didn't sound a particularly inspiring way to live, especially to a teenager.

'No, no, no. That's just me speaking out of regret. Life should be an adventure, especially for the young like you, Jennifer!' He had seemed so old to her then with his sun-dried skin and prematurely grey hair, though she now knew he had been about the same age Romaine was now. But despite his age and role, he had often behaved with childlike energy, even mischief. At that very moment of the conversation, he suddenly swung himself up into the fruit tree and regarded her with a challenging glint in his eye. 'Will you live an adventure, young Jennifer?'

Despite herself, despite feeling cheated out of a neat answer to the question that had bothered her, despite wanting to settle the question of what she should do with her life *now* so that she could get on with living it — and despite his silliness — she smiled at his antics. And at his question.

'How can I live an adventure around here?' she answered, pointing with both hands at the farmlands around them, the most boring location in the universe.

At that he had cried 'Aha! Who said you had to live it around here?' He picked another berry but his eyes never left hers.

'What? Leave here? And go ... where? Gracetown? Kuyata Island?'

'Mm. Maybe.'

'You mean ... *space*? Is *that* God's will for me?' She remembered her voice trilling upward girlishly as her spirit soared.

Just as quickly his next words brought her back to earth. 'No, dear girl, I'm not telling you to go into space; I'm just getting you to think big, to not set limits on the possibilities. I don't know if space is God's will for you.' His look became mock-stern. 'And if that's what this is about – you trying to figure out what God wants you to do for the next eighty years – then I'm afraid to tell you that you're—' He looked around him, rattled the foliage and laughed. '—barking up the wrong tree. He isn't going to tell you. Unless you're Joan of Arc.' He swung down from the tree and peered closely at her. 'You're not Joan of Arc, are you?'

'Who?'

'What do you mean, *who*? What do they teach you in school?'

She shrugged, impatient to return to the main topic. 'Stuff. So how will I know if I'm doing what he wants me to do? How do I make the right decision?'

The pastor became serious. 'Jennifer. Whether you call it *living right* or *cooperating with God's will*, here's my advice. Learn as much as you can about *him*, learn as much about the universe as you can, act in accordance with that knowledge to the best of your ability. Then when you have to make a decision, you do whatever seems best at the time. At the very least, your heart will be pointed in the right direction. The *faith* part is about trusting that he's big enough to take charge from there.'

SOMETHING PLINKED AGAINST HER EYE, SNAPPING HER OUT OF THE memory. She'd covered a lot of ground while she'd been remembering and was surprised to find they'd reached a narrow defile that cut through a ridge in the mountain.

And then she realized it was raining, the first few tentative drops striking them on face and shoulders as they hurried inside the slender pass, an instant before the rain became a deluge. Windborne dust and soil had lodged in the floor and in cracks along the walls so that sickly weeds sprouted up, vainly seeking sunlight. Their boots crunched on them, releasing spores and a scent like banana. They squeezed quickly up the narrow passage, Romaine ahead. At first, they remarked happily about the shelter provided by the rock walls on either side. Then runoff came pouring from the tops of the walls, turning them into mini-water-falls. The ground became slippery with it.

A few moments later they emerged from the defile onto the top of a long spur running toward the next slope two hundred meters away. The rain was bruising, punishing, merciless. Fisher wiped it from her eyes and squinted. The next slope appeared to have a series of solid rock steps they would be able to climb even with the water flowing down the mountain. Had someone cut those in? She led Romaine across the spur as quickly as was safe. Fisher felt confidence returning. They were on the right path now: the steps must be the track the Jarinyi had taken to their new camp. *Nearly there*, she told herself, calves complaining from running on the unstable surface. She shouted encouragement to Romaine behind her and he waved irritably then stumbled. She thought he might slip and go over the edge. But he regained his balance quickly and kept pressing forward.

Pressing forward. That's all today seems to be about.

The mood at Camp Columbus was subdued.

The ferry had taken some of the scientific staff with it and deposited more. 'Freshmen' McGrath called them as the Reaper flew over some of them: despite the pounding rain, the gaggle of newcomers wandered the camp perimeter like tourists, fascinated by the foreignness of the forest beyond the fence.

Via radio, Todd and the team had been told that no blackcaps had been assigned. And only three Marine regulars had arrived as reinforcements.

'Three!' Glass complained as Todd hopped down from the Reaper.

Donaldson abandoned her usual post-flight checklist and stormed off toward the Mess. Chua followed Donaldson's lead. Todd had a moment of anxious thought, wondering if they would end up talking about him, sharing suspicions. He forced himself to let it go, to pay attention to the CO. McGrath lingered nearby to watch her two commanding officers talk.

'What good are three more regulars?' Glass hawked and spat. 'A goddamn frontier situation surrounded by hostiles and they send me three pinheads. Hell, I've lost *four* in the last week! And no surveillance satellite, no AIDs.'

AIDs. Ironic name under the circumstances. Glass meant the Artificial Intelligence Drones that would scout and monitor the forest, but Todd remembered hearing about a killer 20th Century virus by that name. Glass continued, 'That's what I get for joining *corporate* armed forces. Shoulda stayed with...' His voice trailed off into a quiet growl. Two wide-eyed civilians sauntered near, holding Mess trays over their heads as makeshift umbrellas. They wished Glass a hearty good morning. He greeted the salutation with a *hack-off* stare. Their friendly expressions melting to humiliation, they picked up their pace and steered away.

'I thought they were sending another recon team, sir?' Todd asked when the hapless civilians passed out of earshot.

'That's what the messagepack said yesterday but there's a memo from Management that came with the ship. Simply said they'll send another ship in three days with personnel and supplies to set up a camp on *another continent entirely*. Maybe they're tired of me failing to deliver. Maybe I'm being sidelined.'

Todd shook his head placatingly. 'I'm sure that's not the case, sir. Just seems weird they'd drag their heels sending them when they're so desperate for Tigerclaw. With AIDs and more men, we could ensure the indigs don't get within a kilometer of the Pumpkin Patch.'

Glass wiped at his eyes tiredly, blew out a breath and pointed to the pair of freshmen as they approached the perimeter fence, said, 'Look at these morons. For all they know, there's a dozen alien bowmen out there drawing a bead on them.'

Todd caught himself staring out across the fence at the terrain beyond. Had that swelling at the base of that tree always been there? Was that small raised patch of ground in front of it there yesterday? No, there was no way they could be this close to base without setting off a sensor and he told Glass as much. If he wasn't careful, he'd be seeing indigs everywhere.

To his surprise, Glass chuckled. 'Sure. We have the finest military hardware available. *Available* being the operative word here. Did you know one of the sensors keeps recalibrating itself, switching off and running a self-diagnostic we can't interrupt or stop. That's a fairly weak link in the chain, huh?'

'We don't have backups?' Todd asked. Glass shook his head. 'Well, I'll get McGrath onto it, she's good with tech.'

'Yeah, you do that. But I suspect we have faulty goods.' He switched back to the topic of undersupply. 'Well, I guess they're worried about uprisings. Or the Proocs invading. Putting their assets in strategic locations. PBT is beginning to cause the kind of chaos that never ends well. I asked the three new grunts where the rest of their Company were. They told me Red Star. *Red Star.* CUSET's afraid the PRC will take the continent they "gave" us.' Glass scratched at his scalp beneath his cap. 'See, it could be worse for us, Sean. We could be back there waiting for an invasion that might never come. Or guarding a power station from Xerxian terrorists. Or babysitting some Centauran Mayor.'

'I guess waiting's the part of being a soldier you never get used to.'

Glass grunted affirmation. 'Or good at. Putting most of our best people and resources in strategic spots to keep the peace seems kinda stupid and short-sighted from where you and I stand. But Management are never at where you and I stand, they don't see it. Without Tigerclaw there might not be anything left to guard soon. Or anyone to fight.' He made a sour face and turned toward his office with a flick of his head. 'Walk with me.'

Todd gestured discreetly at McGrath not to follow. She seemed disappointed.

'Sean, despite the undersupply, they want us to get back out to that Patch asap.' Glass glanced up at the rain and let it strike him full in the face for a moment, before wiping it away. It was dwindling to a light shower, but in the heat, Todd found it less than refreshing. 'The sun's supposed to come out later today, but even so it'll be tomorrow afternoon or the following morning before the plants regain their high yield again. Any ideas about how we can harvest in safety?'

Todd nodded. 'I have an operation underway to undermine the Jarinyi, distract them. Let's hope that works.' Glass didn't ask for him to elaborate. 'When we decide to go back, I also recommend we keep two fliers in the air at all times. The Jarinyi may disappear from sensors when they go into their camouflage mode, but they have to move into the area before they morph and that's when we could get them.'

Glass entered the foyer to his office ahead of Todd, wiped his boots on the mat, brushed rain from his shoulders. He gestured for his Aide to take a break and applied hand sanitizer, facing Todd as the assistant left. 'Two Reapers is all we'll have. The other one's heading south in an hour. To stay. I'm sending a party to set up a small base hopefully far away from these damn indigs.' When Todd looked askance at him, he explained, 'The southern tip of this forest is four hundred clicks away. The coastline curves back around down there so the forest is close to ocean. Just like here. I'm hoping it's a similar enough ecology that there's more Tigerclaw growing there somewhere. But without the indigs.'

'How big a party, sir?'

'One pilot, three field researchers. Three Marines including one of yours, if you'll let me.'

As much as he wanted to say Chua, he shook his head instead. 'I'd feel a lot safer with the last remaining members of team watching my back than some pinhead. But, you're the Boss, sir.'

The CO lifted his cap, shook water from it, ran a hand over his buzz cut. 'Nice to know you still think that way, Lieutenant.'

Todd looked at him warily. He had never undermined Glass. All he'd done was make tactical decisions that fit his role. He let the silence hang in the air until Glass returned to business.

'You're right, you need your team here. I'll send someone else. So, what do we do if they're already there? The indigs at our Patch, I mean. What if they've hidden sentries around the place in anticipation?'

'I thought of that. Sir, let me ask *you*, if I may. What would you do if this was Bolivia and the Paraguayans and Chileans had hidden troops around Cochabamba?'

Glass pursed his lips knowingly. 'Microwaves? You think the Jarinyi will be affected by the same wavelength as humans are?'

'They have enough of a similar physiology. And really, any animal lifeform should at least be made very sick by that wavelength.'

'Ok, the Quartermaster has one emitter. I forgot about it, being a pretty old unit. We brought it in case the Proocs were already here. You can use that. I wish we'd been given sonics for the fliers; much more effective.'

'Mind if I head out and try it now, sir?' It would also give him an excuse to check up on what Donaldson and the others were talking about in the Mess.

'Be my guest. Hope you bag a few Jarinyi for your trouble. But you know, Sean, eventually we may have to make peace with these overgrown monkeys.' The Colonel leaned against the wall which bowed with his weight. 'This can be written off as a teething-trouble incident so far, a flash in the pan. Long-term, CUSET is gonna want to create wonderfully warm and cozy race relations on Eventide.'

Todd smiled wryly. 'I understand that sir. But I'm probably the wrong man for that job.'

22

'Such as we are made of, such we be.'

- William Shakespeare

THREE MINUTES AGO, the stone stairway had made a turn into a crevice. Runoff splattered their new path from high above, but it was far drier out of direct rain. Fisher was glad when Romaine paused beneath a wide overhang.

'Rest?' he asked.

She nodded with enthusiasm.

'You take a nap,' he said. 'I'll keep watch first. Twenty minutes each.'

'Ok.'

He moved a little further up, eased himself down until he sat sideways where he could watch in both directions. He placed his handgun on the ground before him, put his head against the rock wall.

She sat cross-legged, lay her head back in the same way, fidgeted to get comfortable and gave it up for a lost cause. Moist clothing chaffed her wherever it tightened or rubbed.

A moment later, Romaine started snoring.

So much for taking first watch.

She fidgeted again, needing to pee. *Really* bad. An entire day and night was one heck of a long time to hold on, but there simply hadn't been a private spot where she could go. She could go back and out of the crevice. Romaine might wake and come find her if she did. And that would mean climbing back up again.

The stone stairway they were on seemed to level out fifty meters further up. Maybe there'd be somewhere up there. And scouting ahead a little wouldn't hurt.

She stood and squeezed past Romaine. He didn't stir, his snores light and even. She took the wet, uneven risers carefully, still unable to tell in the gloom whether they were man-made or entirely natural.

Man-made, she scoffed at herself. *How about woman-made? Or Jarinyi-made?*

At the top of the rise, the way leveled out, though the cleft in the mountain continued another three hundred meters to where a sliver of brightness hinted at an exit. She *could* head out there to pee, she thought. Problem was she was already close to bursting. Besides, she'd hear Romaine coming long before he could stumble across her. Fisher reached for her belt buckle.

A minute later, much relieved, she buckled up and reconsidered that sliver of light ahead. She really should get back to the Commander. But it might be worth the extra minutes to scout ahead while he dozed. She might see something that would bring them hope, renew their strength. So Fisher set off toward the light, deftly avoiding the spreading slick of urine she'd created.

Emerging from the fracture in the mountain, she came into what may have originally been a crater, a football-field-sized arena. Immediately she flopped down against a fallen boulder and reached for her left boot. A sneaky little stone had wormed its way in there at some point during the day and had would drive her seriously crazy if she left it much longer. As her boot came off, the smell that hit her made her wish she'd left it on. In counterpoint, freeing her foot from its leather prison brought such sweet relief, she almost cried out with joy. She shook out the stone, flexed the foot and considered the clearing clouds above. Even more to be grateful for.

Fisher murmured another prayer of thanks for continued safety and was about to jostle the boot back on when she heard something. A foot scuffing against gravel. The sound did not come from behind her. She poked her head above the boulder. Her renewed optimism instantly snuffed out and her heart thumped hard against her ribs. Crouched on the far side of the narrow gorge ahead of her were a trio of indigenous folk, grey-skinned, tall and heavily muscled, with only the one set of gill-flaps.

These were not Jarinyi.

They had to be Nguwuu.

John Romaine dreamed. He sat in the front pew of a vast cathedral, full of colors which ran the spectrum between bland stone and gaudy stained glass. Alcoves were as deep as mountain crevasses. Icons cast shadows long as trains. Organ pipes towered like skyscrapers overhead. The thousands of seats were empty. But for him and for Fisher who sat beside him The MP offered her trademark mild smile in reassurance.

By the altar stood an unnaturally tall priest – tall as two men, golden-skinned and greasy-haired. In contrast to the expanse around them, the altar and its occupant were close to the front pews. The priest loomed over them, holding the elements of Holy Communion, his fierce black eyes aimed directly and accusingly at Romaine. Attending the man was Harshini, half the priest's height, dressed absurdly in altar boy garb.

The priest motioned for Romaine to come to the rail and take Communion. He looked to Fisher – he hadn't done this since he was a child. She encouraged him to go forward with a wave of her hand. Without having moved, he was suddenly kneeling at the altar rail. The priest stood before him, shorter now but no less fierce in aspect. Those eyes burned into Romaine's and in a booming voice, the holy man demanded Romaine confess his sins.

'I have no sins,' Romaine replied.

'Then confess your desires.'

Romaine found himself saying, 'I desire peace and quiet. I want to do my job and go home.'

'Good,' said the priest. 'What else?'

'I want to be happy.'

'Better. What else?'

Romaine noticed with a jolt that Admiral Dreyfuss now stood on the other side of the priest from Harshini. Dreyfuss had a smug look fixed on her face. She smiled at Harshini. The younger woman in altar boy garb scowled back at her, turned on her heel and marched away through a door on the far side of the altar.

'I want her back,' said Romaine to the priest, eyes locked on the door.

'What else?'

'Will you bring her back, Father?'

'No. What else do you desire?'

Romaine's knees should have hurt from kneeling on the cold, uneven, gritty stone of the cathedral floor but he couldn't feel them. 'Nothing else. Can I take the wafer now?'

'No. What else do you desire?' the priest repeated.

He felt at a loss. What was the priest getting at? In the way of dreams, Dreyfuss swam into and out of his view without him taking his eyes off the priest. He knew she was looking at Fisher and for some reason this scared him.

'What I want,' he heard himself say clearly, as if it were someone else speaking, 'is for people like her to stop getting rich off the suffering of others!'

The priest's mouth smiled; his eyes did not. 'Now you may take the cup.'

Cup? He'd never been offered that as a boy.

He looked back toward Fisher, expecting to see his mother — a good Catholic — and ask her advice. But it was still Fisher, only Fisher in this immense open space, now smiling widely and warmly. His hands reached for the cup ...

ROMAINE AWOKE WITH A START, THE IMAGE OF A SILVER GOBLET SEARED into his mind and a dull ache in the pit of his stomach as if he were pining. The lingering impression from the dream troubled him. The chalice *felt* important, but he could recall neither the context nor content of what he'd dreamt.

Shaking it off, he turned his head toward Fisher, embarrassed that he'd been the one to snooze.

She wasn't there. Romaine stood and craned his neck both ways, peering along the crevasse.

Sonuvabitch!

Where had she gone? Had someone taken her? No, that was stupid. They would have taken him too.

She might have scouted ahead.

He took a few steps down toward the crevasse entrance, back into the spurting splattering runoff from above.

'Fisher?' he hissed. Then repeated it louder. No reply. 'Sonuvabitch.'

His head felt woolly from dozing, but heart was thumping hard. He could shout for her, but there might be spiky leopard-things about – or Jarinyi strangers who didn't know which human he was. Aloneness pressed in on him with a weight like being buried. He could die here, isolated, alone in a bleak rock prison. Jarinyi might not find his body for days or weeks. Or years.

Move. Do something.

He sucked in a long deep breath, held it, let it out slow. His heart rate eased a little. But tremors raced up and down the muscles of his ribs, his legs. He should get going, head up to the top of the rise up there, see what was there, if she was there. But he couldn't find it within himself to comply with the idea.

Fisher will be back.

And if she's not?

Goddamnit.

The rocks around him above were painted the same grey as his thoughts. How in hell had he gotten here? How? Admiral Amanda Dreyfuss – CO of the MIO, Wicked Witch of the West, that was how. She had dropped him onto this toilet of a planet. She had dropped him into the middle of war between stone age savages and corporate Marines.

Hack it, if this wasn't a moment to take a drink, what was? He dug the small flask from his pockets and held it to his lips with shaky hands. A sip. Just one. He took two. Then forced himself to put the flask away as the alcohol burned its way down his trachea, warmed his stomach, lightly and reassuringly stroked his brain.

At the top of a mountain and the bottom of the rabbit hole.

He ground his teeth in anger. It wasn't fair, any of it. He – and Fisher – would die up here. And for what? It didn't matter who'd killed Gutierrez. It really didn't.

Except to his family, his fiancé.

Well, purge them. Right here, right now, Romaine couldn't bring himself to care about a bunch of people he'd never met. They would never thank him for risking his life to find their boy's killer. Any more than anyone thanked Harshini for giving *her* life in the course of duty. He would never have to look into their grief-stricken eyes. He'd never have to give an account to them, even if he did live to solve the crime. Screw the damn case. Screw Gutierrez. Screw the Jarinyi and Carswell and Glass and Fisher and every other sucking person in the galaxy.

He sat up. 'Yeah, screw you all.' He wasn't going to die here for any of them. He was going to make it. Survive, like he always had. Somehow, *somehow*, he'd do it.

His stomach rumbled, hunger and tension combining to irritate his bowel. And Romaine found himself laughing. All of his self-importance, his longwinded raving at the universe and in the end, he was just a human who needed to take a dump.

My kingdom for a bathroom.

Yes, that had to be it: Fisher had gone for a piss. She'd be back any minute now. Definitely, she would.

FISHER HELD HERSELF COMPLETELY MOTIONLESS. BREATHING FELT LIKE sucking sand through a straw into lungs no bigger than her shirt pocket.

The trio of Nguwuu crouched on the far side of the gorge, distracted for the moment, communicating via hand signs.

She forced herself to duck down until she squatted in a tight ball behind the boulder. Terror urged her to get up, get away, run fast, but running would draw attention. And although she had cover for the moment, if they headed for the passage behind her, she was a goner. Her smell – strange and alien to them – would certainly give her away even if they didn't see her.

She unclipped her sidearm, drew it, thumbed the safety. If it came to shooting her way out of this, would it work? Since basic training years before, she had barely fired a weapon, not including the incident with the spiky leopard. She got twenty minutes target practice three times a year. *I'm not going to hit a thing.*

One calf twitched in sudden cramp and she grabbed the muscle, kneaded it roughly, trying to fix the spasm before it locked on tight. The pain increased. The leg was not only tired, she was no doubt low on salt because of perspiration. She put the handgun down, dropped onto her butt and stretched the leg out in front of her, flexing her foot, working her ankle to work the calf. She stifled a gasp as the pain peaked. She wanted to leave the foot alone, lie on her back and ride it out but she knew she had to deal with it quickly before the –

Some intuition, either primal instinct or divine intervention, saved her life. Without knowing why, she twisted to her left, reaching for her weapon. A wooden club smashed into the boulder where her head had rested.

23

'Live every day as if it were your last
and then some day, you'll be right.'

- H.H. 'Breaker' Morant

ROMAINE PEERED out from beneath the overhang, studied the slice of sky visible far above him. He estimated that another day was already half over. He had the other half to find sanctuary and food. His stomach rumbled again and his bowel replied in kind. He hoped he could hang on until he made it back to a real toilet, but doubted it, had to accept that it would be at least another night and full day before he'd be back there. At least.

If I survive that long.

He reached into one of the tiny waterfalls nearby, rubbed his palms together, turned his hands over, studied the raised veins and the spots of soil that hadn't washed off. Four minutes now since waking and no sign of Fisher. He should go look for her.

Maybe a wee drink first.

You've had one, Johnny. One's enough.
Another wouldn't hurt, though. Take the ol' edge off.
It won't work though. Will it?

Lately – especially so soon after what had happened on Drop-in-the-Ocean – no matter what and how much he drank, that knot in his stomach just wouldn't go away. Nor would the dreams. Nor the black cloud of cynicism and depression – or whatever the hell was wrong with him.

And yet, he wanted it. Really wanted it. Booze: pain relief, salve for the soul, magnificent poison. He could almost picture the cartoon devil on his shoulder urging him on.

'But there's not even enough in the bottle to get drunk,' he told it, 'so what would be the point?'

In his imagination, the devil rubbed its chin, rethinking its strategy.

He'd been dry for a month after Harshini died. Trying to handle the grief and shock in healthier ways. There *were* healthier ways. Then a little bit here, a little bit there, he'd abandoned the wagon. He was drinking regularly and routinely by the end of the year, happy for that devil to camp on his shoulder, the demon that helped him drink enough to keep *other* demons from settling there.

Besides, other cops drank. It was expected. Cliché, even. Some in the Office seemed relieved when Romaine finally decided to join them in this traditional policeperson's pursuit. Orc209 – the same tekkie contact who had installed the anti-surveillance apps in his SCRoLL – had been the only one to voice concern about Romaine's change in behavior. Romaine had told him to shut his damned mouth.

And here he was, ten years later and light years away from the rest of the human race, fondling a metal bottle, and realizing he was at a crossroads. As a young man, he'd remonstrated that only fools and halfwits allowed themselves to become controlled by a substance. The flask in his palm said he'd become one of those fools. Continuing his passive-aggressive alcoholism was only one of the clichés he could embrace: what about *Carpe diem*, taking the window of opportunity, turning over a new leaf? Much better clichés.

Throw the damned flask away.

He'd started smoking and stopped within a few years, and they said cigarettes were still the most addictive habit there was. If he'd had the will power for that, surely he had it for this.

Might even help me survive here.

The shoulder devil whispered, *You're a junkie, Romaine. A weak, crybaby asshole. Dreyfuss's bitch. You'll die out here. Drain the damn flask and die with a buzz on, at least.*

'Admiral Dreyfuss's bitch,' he muttered. 'Yeah, ya got me there.'

Years ago, during an argument he couldn't even remember now, the boss had told him point blank, 'You, John, are a janitor. You clean up messes. You tie things up neatly. You keep the wheels turning with a minimum of fuss. That is your job. That is who you are. If you want to play real cop, if you think you have the skills, you're working in the wrong *context*. CUSET is a business environment. Maybe you'd consider a career in one of the Metropolitan police forces back on Earth?'

Since then, she'd done worse than veiled threats of firing his ass. She'd hamstrung the investigation into Harshini's murder. She'd ignored his remonstrations during the Drop-in-the-Ocean case when his investigation had been confounded and prolonged by bureaucratic interference. And he'd let it go.

'Come to goddamn think of it,' he said to the flask in his hand, 'she's the one sent me the case of malt to celebrate the end of the case.' It was her whisky he was drinking here.

Janitor. Clean-up man. Puppet. Souse. Sucker. He could no longer stand being that person. The wheel had turned in his heart.

Romaine stood, took the biggest windup he could and launched the flask down the stone staircase, watching it and Dreyfuss's whisky bounce and clatter.

He was fantasizing about it hitting the Admiral square in the forehead when he heard the gunshots.

FISHER FIRED BLINDLY OVER HER SHOULDER — ONCE, TWICE, THREE TIMES.

At least one round had caught her attacker in the abdomen. The Nguwuu crumpled, falling out of sight.

They had known she was there.

She'd taken her eyes off them and they'd taken advantage of it.

Stupid girl stupid girl stupid –

She tried to whip her legs up into a crouch but her calf wouldn't let her and she fell back. The second Nguwuu came scrambling over the fallen body of his companion. The third hurdled the boulder and landed before her, its eyes ablaze with bloodlust and its spear already in motion.

Fisher fired in reflex.

Dark pink blood sprayed from the alien's forehead. Its neck snapped back, body falling with a thud like a sack of flour. Fisher flipped onto her stomach to take aim at the other one but it – *he!* – eluded her, dodging and bounding then, strangely, sprinting around her rather than attacking. She fired four times, missed completely. Was it fleeing? Struggling upright, she leaned her forearms on the boulder and tracked him as he ran down the incline, fired twice more. Missed. Her hands shook. Moving inhumanly fast now, the Nguwuu tore across open ground and into another cleft in the rock. In seconds, it was gone.

Ignoring the sack-of-flour assailant with the pulverized brain, she limped past the boulder to stare down at the first attacker. He had rolled down the crater and lay snorting quietly through his twin breathing flaps, tapping his stomach wounds agitatedly with both hands.

Her heart beat as fast as the thoughts flying through her mind: *Oh, man, that was close that was close that was close!*

What now? Put the creature out of his misery or save her bullets? Moments later, the decision was taken out of her hands. A Jarinyi carrying a short branch sauntered into her line of vision, ignored her when she reacted by pointing her gun at him, then moved to the Nguwuu's side. He plunged the broken end of the branch into the Nguwuu's throat, twisted and ripped it out, discarded it.

Fisher grimaced: in contrast her own frantic self-defense, this killing had been dispassionate, cold. But as her rational mind wrested control of her thoughts back from her amygdala, she realized that the warrior's surprise appearance was her chance at surviving this ordeal.

And where the heck had he come from?

Must've been camouflaged here.

She lowered her pistol as the Jarinyi turned to stare her down. 'Thank you,' she started.

'Fisher!' The call came from inside the crevasse, Romaine chasing her. From the sound of it, he'd get here within the minute.

The Jarinyi took two steps toward her, cocked his head, narrowed those large eyes. He fluted and chirred at her, pointed left with all of his fingers, then started off in that direction.

'Wait,' she said.

The Jarinyi stopped, turned back to her, head cocked.

'Fisher!' Romaine's voice was closer now.

She called back, 'I'm fine! It's safe! There's a Jarinyi here, so don't shoot him.'

The Jarinyi hissed through its gills – maybe it was a sigh, she thought – then he dropped into an easy squat. Moments later, Romaine emerged, panting. His eyes widened at the Nguwuu bodies, and at the Jarinyi.

His chest heaved. He put his hands on his knees. 'What...what...?'

'Three of them. I only got two.' She pointed to the gouge in the Nguwuu's throat. 'Our friend helped with that one.'

Romaine approached the Jarinyi who stared up at him, apparently unconcerned. But it seemed the Commander could think of nothing to say. Or else, he didn't have the breath to say it.

'He wants us to go with him,' she said.

'Best offer ... I've had all day,' he wheezed.

THE WARRIOR LED THEM THROUGH ANOTHER OPENING IN THE mountainside, a tight squeeze for both of them. Perhaps, Fisher mused, he'd been blocking the opening while camouflaged, hiding it from the Nguwuu. Now she and Romaine emerged with the warrior halfway down the rim of an ancient caldera, fifty times larger than the crater she'd just been in.

She could understand why the warrior wanted to protect its entrance from the Nguwuu. It was probably a kind of home for the Jarinyi. And the woodlands below her looked beautiful.

'Oh, wow,' was all Romaine said.

Their guide didn't allow them any rest. With a snort, he moved on down the slope toward the woods and she and Romaine forced themselves to follow. He raised his chin and emitted a loud series of notes which was answered some seconds later from somewhere a kilometer or more away in the woods below.

'Friend or foe?' Romaine murmured. 'Are they having us for dinner? Or having *us* for dinner?'

Fisher wished he hadn't said that.

IT TOOK ROMAINE A FEW MINUTES TO REALIZE THIS CIRCULAR VALLEY must have been either the caldera of an extinct volcano or the impact crater from an ancient meteorite. The rockface became sheer where it rose above their entrance through the crater wall, an uninviting obstacle for the would-be climber who didn't know the tunnels in and out.

Below them, the trees of the valley floor were entirely different to those of the rain forest, shorter and thicker, some reminiscent of orange and lemon trees, others of pines and firs. They had entered just above their highest branches of the tallest tree he could see.

He could hear running water but couldn't see it, while the trees chirruped and chattered with an abundance of wildlife. Green grass carpeted the ground beneath the trees. The air was cooler and far less humid than back at Columbus.

A hundred meters inside the tree line, they met another Jarinyi relaxing in a pile of leaves by a brook. The new one wore Carswell's translator around his neck; he chatter-fluted something which translated as 'Come you tut-tut-tut-tut-tut-tut-tut-tut.'

Romaine exchanged a shrug with Fisher. 'Sure. Why not?'

As he traipsed behind them on level ground a short while later, Romaine inhaled a scent reminiscent of strawberries. This wood was so different from the rain forest of the lowlands. In a pededrama or nanobook, he would have called it enchanting. Soft sunlight poured through the leaves in golden streams that shifted around as if technicians were experimenting with stage lights.

Soon enough, he heard the sounds of community and Fisher let out a relieved sigh. A little taller than their indigenous companions, the two humans had to peel back underbrush to enter the clearing. The gleam of a slender creek winked at them from the center of the glade, running from north to south. The Jarinyi had constructed a lean-to village around it, just as they had in the rainforest clearing. He echoed Fisher's sigh: after a day and a night in the true wild, even this humble version of civilization seemed both attractive and secure

In contrast to his very first meeting with the Tribe, his reception this time was less than cordial. The children still stared until chased off by mature Tribe members, but few older Jarinyi even glanced his way. Most studiously ignored him.

'Perhaps if I wore blue?' he asked the ones who had been leading them. By way of response, one made a sign Romaine couldn't read then jogged away, his buddy with him. 'I think I just got flipped off,' he told Fisher.

For a time, they stood amidst the eddies of activity in the clearing and watched.

Finally, Romaine cleared his throat. 'So. Here we are, then.'

'Looks that way,' she agreed.

'You know the two of us have nearly died three times *each* in the last twenty-four hours – pardon, twenty-five hours. Four times for you, if you include Turk's attempted assault. That must be some kind of record.'

She turned away to watch the quicksilver ribbon of the stream, her normally impassive expression tinged with consternation. It finally occurred to Romaine that while shooting two attackers might be a common experience for some Marines, this may have been Fisher's first time.

Gently he asked her, 'Do you feel bad about shooting them?'

'No. I feel nothing. That's the problem. Shouldn't I feel guilty? Or relieved? *Something*?'

In that moment, Romaine felt he'd met the real Jennifer Fisher, the one without the title Corporal in front of her name. He saw a depth of character he hadn't met since, well, since Harshini. He saw a conflicted spirit, one that didn't want to hurt a fly but knew that flies had to be hurt sometimes. And strangely, even in her angst, he saw someone clear and childlike, honest and empathetic.

'The way I figure it, Fisher, you save your remorse for hurting good people, not the bad ones.'

'But ...'

'You did good.'

'But—'

'Corporal Fisher, we're in a bad situation here. We'll have time for second-guessing the moral and philosophical implications of our actions later. Right now, we do what we need to. That's an order.'

She made a wry face, perhaps relieved that he'd made it simple for her again. 'Yes. Sir. What do we do now, then?'

He regarded the clearing. Sylvan flowers broke up the greens and browns. Female Jarinyi lined the creek, busying themselves with a variety of simple tasks, like washing roots and vegetables and nuts. The males had clustered together at the northern end of the clearing and across the creek from them, engaged in conversation. He watched them for a few moments, recognizing the Elder and the tall warrior who'd demonstrated his archery skills by shooting the animal out of the tree two days earlier.

Was that really two days ago?

Perhaps they were discussing their next attack on the human invaders. For everyone's sake, Romaine hoped that wasn't the case.

'Find Carswell?' he suggested.

'We should be able to hear him if he's about. I don't see Scarface either. Perhaps they're hunting.'

Romaine jerked his chin at a pile of Jarinyi weapons nearby. 'Or maybe the Jarinyi are cutting Carswell's throat and burying him somewhere away from the kids.'

'You still don't trust them, sir?'

'What's to trust?' He rubbed at his eyes with a clean patch he found on one hand. 'Apart from giving me a *chweechee* as a gift and not killing us so far, what have they really done for us? And technically they're our enemy now.'

'Then technically we're POWs.'

They exchanged looks and shuddered at the thought. 'Let's hope our hosts don't see it that way,' Romaine said grimly. He moved his rubbing hand to the back of his head and neck. 'God, I'm tired.'

Fisher made a musing sound. 'Maybe we could take this opportunity to do what we said yesterday. Soak our feet.'

'Oh, yeah. That's the best idea I've heard in years.'

They decided to head to the south end of the clearing, downstream from the women prepping their dinner. With groans of pleasure, they removed boots and socks, rolled up trouser legs and plunged white and wrinkled feet into cold water.

Sweet relief lasted only a few minutes before Jarinyi women gathered to stare at them. Scarface appeared soon after, making loud noises, with reds and oranges rippling along his shoulders. He waved his fists at their feet. They got the message, gathered up their boots and scampered away, amused rather than frightened by his tantrum. When they looked back, Scarface let out a noise that sounded for all the world like an angry pig before he stormed away. That broke them up; they dropped on the ground laughing.

Must be hysterical, he thought, and laughed harder.

When the giggling exhausted itself, they lay with faces toward the sky and the caress of the breeze cooling their skin. The companionable silence stretched out for an hour, or more perhaps since Romaine lost track of time, dropping in and out of a light doze. There were no dreams this time.

As the day grew older, the sun painted the clearing in ever more golden hues. A change in wind direction stirred up a new scent like lilies and Romaine stirred with it. 'Fisher, while we're out here in the wilderness, do you think you could drop your professional demeanor for a while.'

'Sir, my what?'

'I want you to lighten up.'

She blinked. 'I'll try, sir.'

'Good. While we're smack in the middle of the worst time of our lives, how about we get rid of the Corporal-Commander-Yessir-Nossir crap. Out here, we're people trying to survive.'

'And trying not to pollute village water sources.'

'That too. Call me Romaine, alright?'

'... I don't think I could do that, sir. Commander.'

'How about John then?'

'Okay, John. I'm Jennifer.' She reached a hand across and he gripped it lightly.

'Nice to meet you. Jennifer.'

After a time, he glanced at her and found her despondent again. 'What?'

'I'm trying but I can't get the image out of my head. I caused the death of two intelligent life forms today. They were people.'

'The googoo-noowoos, whatever? Jennifer, they were trying to kill *you*.'

She let out a shuddering sigh. 'But the picture won't go away.' Before he could interrupt, she went on, raising her voice, 'And not just them. I keep wondering, if I hadn't upset Sgt Attikula, would he have been calmer? Would he have not killed those young Jarinyi? I should have defused the situation with words, not physically blocked him. It must have been like a red rag to a bull. Maybe this whole thing is my fault.'

Turk's irrational outbursts, his elevated energy levels, irrationality and dilated pupils, and his attempted assaults on Carswell, him, Fisher – the guy was on something. Was CUSET handing weapons to a bunch of brain-fried junkies and unleashing them on a newly discovered sentient species? He saw in his mind's eye Turk's shotgun firing, alien bodies on the ground amid the very plants that had restored his own health last night.

'The Jarinyi standing up to him was a red rag too. And it would have been that way whether you'd gone hand-to-hand with him or not. Listen to me. There were two deleted reports in Turk's personnel file – at least the one I received. He ain't here for his character; he's here for his skills. He's previously committed two criminal acts they don't want to deal with publicly because of those valuable skills of his. And something already had him grumpy before you stepped in. Whether it was a latent dislike of "eggheads" or a drug-hangover or withdrawal symptoms, I don't know, but whatever Attikula's background, when an armed sociopath with anger management issues gets dropped into a volatile situation, he's going to hurt someone. Besides,' he added, 'if I'd stepped in to protect you from Turk, or if I'd shot those Nguwuu and saved your life, would you be angry at me?'

'Of course not.'

'You're sure? Because you know I'm about to turn this back on you – I'm setting you up here.'

A smile crept onto her face as she saw what was coming. 'I wouldn't be angry at you, John.'

'So, why are you angry at yourself? You seem pretty gracious with other people. Cut yourself some slack.'

'Thanks. That helps.'

'Of course it helps. I'm a genius.'

He sat up and tossed a stone into the water, thinking. Attikula was involved in two tussles in one day. Two. Saying the man had anger management issues was one of the greatest understatements Romaine had ever made.

'You know, I don't believe that was an accidental shooting. That's what they'll try to pass the death of the young Jarinyi off as.'

'So... he meant to kill them?'

'Although it may be irrelevant now in the broader scheme of things, that's a question I'd love to have an answer for.'

Turk had been trying to say *something* to Todd immediately after he'd shot those indig kids.

Todd yelling, 'WHAT DID YOU DO?!'
Turk responding with confusion, not remorse: 'But...'
Todd's red face growing even redder. 'Shutup!'
Turk even more stupefied. 'I thought... Aren't we -?'
Todd shouting, lunging at him. 'SHUT YOUR MOUTH!'
What exactly *did* Turk think?
'I'd really love to answer that question,' he added.

CARSWELL RETURNED MUCH LATER, ACCOMPANIED BY TUTTUT. MAKING effusive noises over their arrival, he provided them with several plump and sour fruits before ushering Fisher away to help the women with their duties. Romaine felt offended on her behalf, but she took it with good grace. Perhaps it was her patent curiosity toward Eventide's indigenous. Perhaps she was happy to keep occupied.

When Carswell returned, humming tunelessly to himself, Romaine tossed his fruit cores away and regarded him with disgust. Carswell carried himself with the arrogant air of the lord of a realm in which Romaine was merely a guest. Power games always *always* irritated Romaine.

'So when are we going home?'

Carswell squatted by the stream and dipped his fingers in the water. 'You're calling Camp Columbus home? My how our spacer has evolved in only two days.'

'You know what I mean. When are we going back there?'

'Tomorrow morning. There's something I want to show you first thing, then I promise you I'll take you back.'

Romaine's rumbling stomach drew a raised eyebrow from Carswell and he realized it was time for what he'd been trying to avoid for the last couple of hours. 'Listen, O Great and Mighty King, I hate to bring this up, but I need to ... drop the kids off at the pool.'

'Do what?'

'Take a dump.'

Carswell pointed. 'Head *down* the stream until you see a rock with red moss growing in the rough shape of a triangle. Veer right about twenty paces past the rock and find some clean ground to dig a hole and do your business there.'

'Why there?'

'That's where I go. Plenty of nice soft leaves and grass. Away from the water supply.'

Romaine tried to smile, tried to bring things back to a lighter note. 'So you're letting me use your toilet?'

'Indeed.' Carswell gave one of his unnatural smiles in response, tacitly accepting the truce. 'And no one will trouble you around there.'

Romaine made a happy clicking noise with his mouth. 'Alright, I'm off to see the wizard. Back soon.'

After a moment, Carswell called after him, 'Oh, Romaine!'

'Yes?' he asked, turning.

'Careful where you dig.'

THE JARINYI WERE LIGHTING FIRES IN FRONT OF THEIR HOMES AS ROMAINE returned to the glade. He touched his Plazer: the small tool would be far more efficient than the old *flint-and-kindling trick*, if they'd let him butt in. After watching Scarface's burdensome efforts to produce nothing but smoke and blackened twigs, he decided to try. He squatted beside him, weary quad muscles complaining, and flicked the beam of the laser across the pile of sticks and leaves. Fire leapt into existence. The warrior huffed and squirmed. Romaine offered the Plazer to him, half-hoping he wouldn't take it. Still, it would be good to earn some brownie points with the guy. In response, Scarface turned his back, shuffling around on his haunches to face his hut.

Romaine stood. 'You know, just because it's new, doesn't mean it's bad. The universe is all about development, change. Change happens. Accept it, adapt to it, or ... or ...'

Or what, John?

He knew his words had not really been for Scarface. His goddamn subconscious was attempting to teach him something.

'Or perish,' he finished.

Well, I am adapting, I'm accepting new things. I even learned to wipe my ass with leaves. I just hope what I can learn enough to survive this.

He tossed the Plazer into the air and caught it. Scarface glanced around at the sound. Romaine held the shiny object in front of him.

'Whether you want it or not, I'm giving you this. Maybe Carswell can get you to use it later.' If only the Jarinyi would accept *something* from the hands of human beings they might realize that there was a potential to trade for the medicines humans craved.

He caught himself: what was he, a diplomat or a cop? Speaking to himself, he said, 'John Romaine, solver of the Universe's greatest problems. A lighter is going to change the course of both human and Jarinyi history, melding the two races together as best buddies for ever and ever. Sure. And I'll be growing wings and flying to Columbus any minute now.'

Nevertheless, he chucked the Plazer at Scarface's feet. Scarface gave him no response. The lighter lay partly buried in the spiky grass. He shrugged, decided to leave it there. Surely the Jarinyi's curiosity would bring him back to it later.

Romaine's stomach gurgled then, and this time he spoke directly to Scarface. 'It turns out I'm extremely hungry.'

The warrior took a breath as if he would speak, then stood and walked away.

'What's for dinner?' Romaine called after him.

He hoped it wasn't bugs.

24

'When a man desires a woman and a woman desires that man, each must test their own motives. If they desire the enriching of the other, if they long to empower rather than to possess, if they look upon the object of their affection as a reflection of God's own glory – only then should union be pursued, not as the gaining of an asset, but as the laying down of entitlements in service to the one they love.'

- Article 19: *The Articles of Life*
Published by The Society of Andros, 2101

SHADOWS LENGTHENED across the clearing as the sun dipped below the trees. Dinner wasn't bugs. But it wasn't much better. The Jarinyi skewered crudely butchered morsels some animal on sticks and held them over the fire. The meat came away blackened on the outside and almost raw on the inside. Stretched out on the grass before the humpy he'd been assigned, Romaine stiffened with revulsion when Tuttut handed him a stick. Wandering closer with a skewer of her own, Fisher wore a similar expression.

'Only hope I can keep this down,' she said. She had nibbled around the burned edge of the meat.

'Is it woo-woo?' he asked hopefully. At least he knew what that tasted like.

She shook her head, releasing a sprig of her hair from its tie.

Romaine sniffed it, felt his bile rise in response then handed it back to Tuttut and ducked his head apologetically. Tuttut blinked, ears pressed back like a dog relaxing. His small mouth nipped at the meat with relish and while he studied the two humans. Fisher took another small bite then she too handed it to Tuttut, washing the meat down with river water from her canteen.

A coarse and sticky object was pressed into Romaine's palm, more provisions from Carswell. He regarded the waxy disc dubiously while the xenologist beamed down at him. 'It's good, Romaine. Won't make you sick. It's like panela on Earth.'

'Panela? What's that?'

'My, we are uneducated, aren't we?' Carswell snapped off a piece from another disc before handing the larger piece to Fisher. 'The Jarinyi take the honey-coated wax from inside a local insect's hive, compress it into a patty and ... Bob's your uncle.'

'Wax?' Romaine stared down at his patty, noticing that the little black and brown flecks trapped in the honey were bugs. 'This is safe to eat?'

Carswell tossed his mall piece into his mouth and chomped down on it. 'Mmm,' he said as if encouraging a child to eat. 'Yum yum.'

Sharing a shrug, Romaine and Fisher followed his lead. The 'panela' was almost tasteless, eating it was like chewing soft cardboard, but after a couple of bites, Romaine knew it would fill him up. Carswell dropped one more disc onto the grass between them before he too stretched out on the ground. Romaine and Fisher discussed it and agreed to save it for breakfast.

As they ate, Tuttut scrutinized their wounds by the light of the fire Romaine had built himself. Their feet remained bare, their socks washed and drying by the fire, boots airing on sticks away from the two huts allocated to them. The children of the Tribe were fascinated by these objects; a procession of them were continuously dragged away by older Jarinyi who cast suspicious glances at the footwear.

Carswell laughed quietly as two more kids were sent packing and regarded Fisher with new interest. 'I hear you waged a little war of your own this afternoon.'

She nodded but said nothing, chewing her panela slowly and looking away.

'Fighting off a trio of Nguwuu is nothing to be humble about, Corporal. The Jarinyi have a sudden respect for you. They had thought you were a girl, but now you're a proven warrior, they're not so sure.'

My God, man, you sure know to smooth-talk the ladies, Romaine thought.

He changed the subject, more to spare Fisher further disrespect than out of genuine interest. 'What's the deal with these Nguwuu? Are they same species, mutation, different tribe, what?'

'Let's ask our hosts.' He flicked on his translator and asked Tuttut to explain where the Nguwuu had originated.

Romaine felt like he was immersed in a faux documentary about 19th Century Central Africa. He imagined soundtrack music swelling and a narrator's voice saying, *By night, the villagers tell stories around the fire.* 'It was a simple question, doc, I don't need a lecture.'

Carswell ignored him and encouraged Tuttut to speak.

And Tuttut did speak. Carswell had to ask him several times to repeat sections of the story using different words, but the tale emerged clearly enough ...

Tuttut told them that the Tigerclaw once grew from the sea to the Great River and up into the mountains. *Sweet Word* – the name of a ruler or elder – brought some people to the region from the other side of the river and began feeding them huge amounts of Tigerclaw. His apparent aim was to create a bigger stronger race of warriors to conquer the other tribes. *Sweet Word*'s people also longed for immortality, believing the Tigerclaw would give it to them. This was despite the Jarinyi belief that immortality already awaits them after death as a reward for serving the Creator through their life.

Sure enough, *Sweet Word*'s people began mutating in the ways he had hoped, and they bred like wildfire. But as that initial generation began bearing children, these children were very different. They were all born deformed, lacking the number of gills necessary to speak properly. In order to repair their ability to make perfect children, the people ate even more of the Tigerclaw. The defects got worse: now although the babies were bigger and stronger than previous generations of children, they were grey in color and they could not *blend*. At this point, the first generation of adults began to get sick, their bodies breaking out in a rash, their strength and speed waning, tumors developing on them and in them, vomiting blood. Eventually this crazy tribe who had threatened to dominate the world were easily conquered by the ancestors of today's Great River Tribe. Their deformed children called Nguwuu – a name that had no translation apparently – were banished to the far side of the mountains.

The River Tribe discovered that over many seasons, the crazy tribe had denuded much of the Tigerclaw from the area, apart from a small patch of ten plants in one confined rocky area where the soil was too thin for the larger trees of the forest to take root. The Jarinyi felt that the remaining patch was one that Creator had preserved for them. Other vegetation was beginning to regain a foothold in the region. It occurred to their Elder *Rainchild* that the Tribe's role in life was to protect the Tigerclaw from the forest but also to protect the forest from the Tigerclaw, to keep it in balance, and to ensure that the medicinal properties of the plant were no longer abused. They came to understand that the Tigerclaw's aggressive nature would lead it to take over the forest if it was allowed – in a similar way to the way it had taken control of the crazy tribe through their pride.

Over the next two seasons, other trees began to grow around the Tigerclaw patch and the River Tribe left custodians in the region who uprooted it wherever found outside the main patch. These wayward plants were always stored for their own medicinal use, shared with the main River Tribe and other Jarinyi Tribes ...

When Tuttut finished his tale, the group sat hushed in the gathering twilight, faces underlit by the campfire's glow.

The Jarinyi created the Nguwuu, Romaine thought. *Helluva legend.*

Carswell lay back and closed his eyes. Fisher stared into the fire, occasionally glancing at Tuttut as if she wanted to ask him a question. Tuttut stared at Romaine, who avoided his gaze – the background buzz of anxiety and irritation he'd been feeling for days was beginning to reassert itself. When Fisher finally spoke, it startled him.

'Dr Carswell, do the Jarinyi believe in one God or many?'

Carswell frowned to show he was taking the question seriously, giving it his professorial best. 'If I understand them properly, they believe in a supreme being who created everything. Everything, including another powerful spirit who ended up deciding to forge his own path a lot like *Sweet Word* in the legend we just heard. In a case of classic dualism, this lesser spirit brought evil into existence as a consequence.'

'Lucifer.'

Carswell's frown became less scholarly and more quizzical. He turned onto his side toward her.

She said, 'God made Lucifer wise and majestic and gave him the job of writing music and leading all worship in heaven.'

Romaine's mom had taught him that story when he was still young enough to believe anything. He joined in. 'And Lucifer decided he didn't want to share the attention. He wanted it for himself. He rebelled, turned into Satan and the rest is ... history.'

Carswell coughed. 'The rest is *mythology*, more like.'

'Not a believer, Carswell?'

'Are you?'

'No, but I don't go around insulting other people's beliefs either.'

Carswell drew a deep breath and said, 'I simply find it amazing that humans still believe stories and ideas that should have died out with Darwin. It's fascinating in the Jarinyi, but it's irrational in someone like Fisher who should know better. Presumably, she believes in a god of love and kindness and infinite perfection.' He waited for her to respond. She simply nodded for him to continue. 'Then why does he demand worship in the first place? Why fashion Lucifer and force the poor bugger to spend his whole existence and energy worshipping God? To me, that's self-centered, unkind and it smacks of insecurity.'

Romaine knew he'd have gotten deeply angry at Carswell if it were his beliefs in the crosshairs. This was just baiting, not *de*bating. He was pleasantly surprised when Fisher responded rationally and without hesitation to Carswell's goading.

'Well, I've thought about that long and hard and I figure the reason God wanted Lucifer and the rest of us to worship him is to train us to be focused on others and not on ourselves.'

Romaine's curiosity was poked, despite himself. Since telling his mother he no longer wanted to go to church, this was the fourth real conversation he'd been part of on the subject of religion. The other three, without exception, had consisted of him being bailed up each time by a single rabid fundamentalist – one Christian, one Muslim and one do-it-yourself Robbinsarian. After each encounter, Romaine had found it easy to brush off their bad behavior along with any interest in their perspectives.

Fisher however seemed far removed from those arrogant lunatics. Remembering his idea of a devil on his own shoulder earlier that day, he asked, 'So if the devil was the *best* that God created, and even he couldn't live unselfishly, how are we supposed to?'

Fisher looked thoughtful for a moment. 'Lucifer made one particular mistake that messed him up for good. He tried to do it himself. Alone. I think we can only become focused on others with the *help* of others. In our faith, we're taught we can only worship God with God's help. And I think the same is true in family, in marriage, in friendship, in professional life – maybe even with other lifeforms like Jarinyi – we can only live for others, by opening ourselves up to them and letting them help us know them and care for them.'

Romaine's curiosity began to ebb as a knot of unease developed in his gut. Fisher was outlining the exact opposite of his philosophy of life. He was glad when she changed topics to something far more mundane, with an embarrassed look on her face.

'Er, Doctor, I need to pee. Sometime before bedtime that is,' she added, avoiding eye contact with Romaine now.

Carswell relayed her need to Tuttut using the translator. The little

Jarinyi jumped up, indicating he would show her where she could go. Fisher followed him away.

'Just how safe are the woods in this valley?' Romaine asked after she'd left.

'Very. Only a couple of passes in and out which the Jarinyi disguise and guard. Nguwuu have never infiltrated here. Nor have any of the more dangerous predators of the lowlands. You and Fisher can wander around in perfect safety.' He stood and stretched. 'I'm going to get myself some of that delightful meat. Sure you wouldn't care for some? Nothing like a full belly to give you a great night's sleep.'

'Smartass,' Romaine replied and watched him leave.

In his mind he replayed Fisher's words and wondered bitterly why his own handful of attempts at 'opening up' to people had all ended so disastrously. Fisher was nice, but like all religious people, she lived in a cotton-coated reality where *everything will turn out fine* and ultimately *everyone can get along if they really really try*. The Universe just didn't work that way. Neither did human beings.

He brushed the thoughts away when Carswell returned with steaming meat on a leaf. He asked the xenologist, 'Whose beds did we steal for the night?'

'These two huts are vacant because their owners were killed yesterday. Just so you know, several warriors died in the battle plus two females who'd stayed at the lowlands camp the Marines destroyed from the air. One was the Elder's wife.'

'Ah, crap. I'm sorry to hear that.'

'Are you?'

'Of course I am,' he said, frowning. 'I wouldn't wish that on anyone.'

'But you don't particularly like the Jarinyi.'

Romaine fidgeted. 'Look, let's drop it. That kind of conversation gets us nowhere. What do Fisher and I do for bedding tonight?'

Carswell stooped and peered into the hut. 'That's pretty much it.'

'What? Sand from the river?'

'Mm-hm.' Carswell resumed his seat by the fire. 'It's more comfortable than branches.'

'Geez, Louise.' Romaine started a series of stretches. He asked,

'Tomorrow, we're heading back, yes?'

'You are, yes.'

He raised an eyebrow. 'You're not coming with?'

'I'll come till we're near enough to Columbus to point you in the right direction.'

'But you have research to write up. Friends and family offworld. When are you planning on heading back?'

Carswell nursed his leaf-plate on his lap, broke a twig apart and idly tossed pieces into the flames. 'I'm not.'

Romaine paused mid-quad-stretch. '*What*?'

'This is my home now, for as long as these people will have me. And whether they realize it or not, the Jarinyi need me for the time being, at least until CUSET either leave them alone or come to some acceptable arrangement.'

'Geez Louise,' Romaine said again, genuinely astounded. Carswell's tone was completely serious. They were quiet a time, each man considering matters mysterious to the other. Romaine spoke up suddenly, jolting the xenologist from his thoughts.

'What's a watcher?'

Carswell frowned at him. 'Pardon?'

'When we first met the Elder and you described my ... job to him. He asked if I was a watcher or a judge?'

'Oh.' Carswell paused, scratching absently at one forearm. 'The Jarinyi have a tradition – or a legend, I'm not sure which. I've heard them repeat this a few times around campfires. In every generation in every tribe, someone takes on the mantle of Watcher, watching over the tribe, protecting their interests.'

'So what? They're police? Priests?'

'More like a keeper of culture and values.'

'Isn't that the Elder's job?'

'No. He runs the Tribe on a day to day.'

'Doesn't make sense.'

'You're an alien. Their paradigms, their frame of reference is different to yours. Think of it this way... We've had legends and – later – pop media around the idea of the secret guardian of justice and honor and security, someone with a secret identity – mild-mannered member of society by day, something else by night. In their world, it's someone who makes subtle changes to their group dynamics without giving himself or herself away, maybe spreading a rumor, maybe making suggestions to the Elder, maybe even developing a new weapon ... and there *is* a story about a Watcher long ago who first invented the bow and arrow.'

'But how did they know he was a Watcher if his identity was secret?'

'Oral traditions like these don't have to hold water by your Twenty-Second Century human frame-of-reference.'

But Fisher's beliefs have to suit yours, he felt like saying.

'So do these Watchers ever kill people? To protect the tribe, maintain status quo.'

Carswell pursed his lips thoughtfully. 'There is a story about a mysterious death by poisoning three generations back. The Judge who investigated decided in the end that the dead woman, in this case, was a bad seed and a Watcher must've dispatched her. Case was closed. And so,' he added, 'is dinner! I'm off to do the rounds before bed.'

He slapped his thighs, stood and discarded the fatty portion of his meat into the fire then walked off into the night, leaving Romaine to listen to the gristle's angry sizzling.

Tuttut appeared a moment later and placed two peeled chunks of a new and sticky fruit on his hand.

'Don't know what you see in that smartass, Little Fella. If it were me, I'd have shot him dead months ago.'

As twilight turned to full darkness, stars filled the heavens above the encampment. Numerous campfires threw occasional wobbling shadows around the clearing, providing treacherous lighting for the careless wanderer.

The bitter fruit had made Romaine thirsty enough to seek the stream and refill his canteen. On the way back, treading carefully in the gloom, he began to regret tossing the booze. A headache was setting in.

Anxiety was prodding the barriers he'd erected in his mind, looking for a way to overwhelm him. He tried a breathing exercise. The white-tinge building at the corners of his vision abated a little, but the headache persisted. Maybe he needed more Tigerclaw.

Need? There's the junkie speaking again.

He stared into the dark of the hut they'd provided for him, willing himself to bunk down for the night. He didn't know whether it was the whirlwind of thoughts assaulting his mind or just the thought of sleeping where alien people had slept and left their personal parasites to lay eggs in the sandy floor, but laying down on that sand-mattress wasn't at all attractive.

Though his legs begged for rest, Romaine walked on, his mind continuing to run at a million kilometers an hour. *Why is this happening to me I can't believe I'm stuck here I don't know if I'm among friends or if I'll be tomorrow's breakfast and I can't get out of here and DAMN my head hurts!* He kicked a rock and instantly regretted it as his toe told him *you're an idiot* in the language of pain.

Keep it together Romaine keep it together it's gonna be okay...

Though the cool breeze trickling through the trees was a relief, with nothing but a torn fatigue shirt covering his torso, he knew he'd be shivering before long. He longed for the familiar sting of liquor on his tongue, for its friendly warmth to hit his stomach and spread like the touch of summer sunshine.

Don't go there, he told his embattled psyche.

He would settle for the warmth of burning wood instead and moved toward one of the campfires punctuating the night around the clearing. Was it coincidence that Fisher already sat there? The MP was intently watching something a dozen meters away, so engrossed that she seemed not to notice him sit. Romaine settled on one hip, stared up at the sky as the fire warmed his skin. Stars like a dusting of sugar crystals on pastry twinkled back at him. He liked the stars. They reminded him of the view from his window on Bona Vista.

Stones shifted underneath his legs as he changed positions and he tossed one into the fire. Sparks erupted in a shower that startled Fisher and she looked at him sharply.

'Sorry,' he said.

'Oh. No worries.' She returned her attention to a small gathering of Jarinyi by a neighboring – and larger - campfire.

After a few seconds, he broke her reverie by asking, 'What's up?'

'Wedding ceremony, I think. It's just started.'

'They ... marry?' An ember danced by his nose, carried on the slight breeze. He pulled back from it, felt a shooting pain as the sudden movement pushed one buttock onto a sharp stone, and cursed under his breath.

'Apparently. At least, that's what it looks like to me. But I'm no Dr Carswell.'

'Thank God for that.' Romaine shifted his weight and fished out the offending stone. He cast it into the shadows – into outer darkness – and tried to get comfortable. For a minute or two, he watched the ceremony at the neighboring fire with her. It all looked very solemn and deliberate. Practiced even.

The shorter Jarinyi – the 'bride' – laid a wreath of dried flowers at the feet of a taller male and stood back. The 'groom' squatted and slowly moved his hand around the circle of flowers, touching each gently in turn. Then he repeated the circle, this time plucking one petal from each flower. He stood and closed his fist around them, crushing them into powder, before grinding the residue into his chest. Then he pulled a stone knife from his pouch, pricked his palm, held it up to his bride who contemplated the dripping blood seriously before taking his palm and pressing it to her chest, leaving a dark stain there.

Surprised at the bloodletting, Romaine turned to Fisher ready to let fly with some witticism. It dissolved on his lips as he noticed the expression on her face. While the ceremony held a mild novelty for him, it held her in total enthrall. Her cheeks were flushed, her eyes wet. Although he'd really only known her for a couple of days, he was struck by the depth of her emotion. Normally pragmatic and professional, apparently when it came to weddings, she came over all sappy.

Oh, Christ. Next she'll be asking me if I think it's great.

'What do you think of this ceremony, John?' she asked him quietly.

'It's ... great.'

'It is,' she agreed in the same quiet tone.

Feeling he had to add something, he said, 'Without subtitles, it's a little hard to follow.'

Not that I really want to follow it. Damn, this soil's cold.

'Oh, not at all.' She sat up straighter. 'This is so similar to the marriage ceremony in my home town. I can't believe I'm seeing it *here*.'

'Oh ... kay.'

'The bride' – she pointed. '–brought a symbol of her life, the flowers. Maybe it's about her delicacy as a woman, or fertility. I think for her, it meant that her old life has been cut off or that her beauty is sacrificed for him. Something like that. In any case, he takes something of hers and makes it a part of him. He then offers his own blood, his lifeforce. Because he's a warrior, the blade probably represents something of his strength. She wears the mark of his life-force. He wears the mark of hers. It's pretty powerful imagery.'

Powerful imagery. The words sounded odd coming out of her mouth. Another ember sailed toward him. The breeze blew smoke in his eyes. Blinking the grit away, he shifted sideways around the fire away from her and away from the smoke.

The Jarinyi couple faced each other, pressed their left hands together, while another – it looked like the Elder – made sweeping gestures with his arms and spoke at length to them, occasionally glancing at the sky, the earth, to his right, to his left.

Jesus. Didn't this guy just lose his wife? And they've got him conducting weddings!

The couple huffed three times as the Elder turned in slow circles, humming a single note and touching his own eyes and ears. His tiny mouth worked as if chewing.

Romaine shook his head again. He was never going to understand *that*. 'This *home town* you come from? They swap blood and flowers at the wedding?'

'Not exactly. The woman brings a favorite childhood toy or keepsake. She burns it in front of him. That's her way of saying both that childhood is over for her and that he is worth any sacrifice. The man puts some of the ashes in a locket which he wears inside his shirt against his heart. That's his way of saying he accepts her love, will remember her sacrifices and will keep the things she treasures close to his heart where they'll become his treasures too. Then he gives her a gift of his own choosing – something that signifies his strength, to commit to always using his strength to serve and protect her, not to control or mistreat her. He's never allowed to take it back from her, no matter what. My brother gave his wife his favorite hammer. He's a builder.'

Romaine thought it better not to joke about the hammer. 'Where are you actually from on Centauri? I never heard of a wedding ceremony like that.'

'Well, you've heard of the Society of Andros?'

'Androsites. Aren't they a European cult?' Then his brain caught up with his mouth. 'Whoops. You're an Androsite. And I just called you a cult member. Way to build rapport, Romaine.'

'It's not a problem,' she chuckled. 'I grew up in a village about a thousand klicks from Gracetown. My folks were among a group of Androsites who migrated and founded it. They all decided they wanted the teachings, the *faith*, but not the trappings. No chapels, no clergy in fancy clothes. So we kind of just lived our lives as a township, and faith was a part of it. Taught in our school, taught in our homes, mentioned in normal conversation and highlighted at special times like Easter and Christmas. But our wedding ceremonies were very Androsite. And I kinda liked that. Still do,' she added.

To shift the conversation away from the topic of religion, Romaine asked, 'So you plan to marry like that? Or will you add some Jarinyi flavor to it, maybe give your man a big honking stone knife?'

She chuckled again and leaned back on her hands. 'I guess I'll see. Not that I'm likely to find a man I want in the Marines.' She cleared her throat and sat forward again with a jolt. 'Sorry, I'm rambling. How about you? Are you married? Did you have a nice wedding?'

Romaine squirmed where he sat. She didn't mean anything by it. 'I was married a long time ago. Didn't take.'

A pause. 'I'm sorry to hear that.'

'Don't be.' He threw a twig into the fire and stood, brushing dirt from his pants. 'I'm going to bed.'

'Okay.' He felt her eyes on him as he disappeared into the shadows.

Spoiling her moment with your cynical crap. Good move, cheesehead, he scolded himself as he angrily pushed past the branches that clutched at him out of the dark.

FISHER KNEW THE VENOM WASN'T AIMED AT HER, BUT IT HAD STILL STUNG. She tried to refocus on the ceremony but the emotional aftertaste of the conversation with Romaine stifled her curiosity like a wet blanket on a grass fire.

And his bitter outburst had made her realize that, for all his earlier talk of dispensing with formalities here, they weren't friends and couldn't be. For the first time, she began to feel truly alone. She'd been trying not to think of her family, to allow the fear of never seeing them again to invade her thoughts. But it pressed in now, and hard, bringing with it worries for their wellbeing. They'd be poorer without her, if she perished out here. A small stipend would arrive in their bank account a month after she was officially listed as KIA. The one-off payment wouldn't be enough. She had to make it back to Columbus. She had to continue to send money back to them. It was –

It was her purpose, she realized with a shock of clarity.

This is my life? To make money? To prop up my family?

No, I'm an MP.

Oh, ok. To put drunks and aliens in their place? That's my function?

The questions stung. Questions like this – questions of life's purpose and destiny and meaning – had plagued her since her teens and she'd worked hard to put them aside. There was no peace in pondering them – they were and always would be unanswerable. She squeezed her eyes shut, attempted a prayer for peace, the one invented and recorded by an ancient saint named Francis. It was about accepting the things that couldn't be controlled, flowing with the current of life. She repeated it over and over in her head, but peace eluded her.

Underneath all of her compliance, as Romaine had called it, rooted deep in who she was there was a single thought. *I want my life to mean something.*

She'd always thought of that as pride. But what if it was *God-given*? After all, here she was, one of the first humans to eat and speak and travel with an alien species, to notice how many of their beliefs mirrored hers. She was in a very special position.

She returned her attention to the next stage of the marriage ceremony. There was something here in the Jarinyi world she was meant to see, something that would shape her toward whatever destiny Heaven wanted for her life. She just had to open her eyes.

'Sonuvabitch!' The branch scratched him right across his thigh, leaving another small tear in the fabric.

At this rate, I'll be naked by the time I get back to Columbus.

Weaving through the shadows toward his hut, he estimated the time at 2200. Time to sleep, to rejuvenate enough to contend with tomorrow's downhill climb and jungle walk. The light from his own fire fluttered as he passed and then an alien face rose from the gloom to confront him at his door, the ravaged ear and cheek orange-tinged by firelight, as if Scarface wanted to check Romaine's ticket before entry.

The two stared at each for some time before Scarface strode off into the night. He had made no sound, no effort at communication.

What the hell was he doing here?

Had his least-biggest fan decided to leave a trap of some sort, a nest of flesh-eating insects under the sand bed, spiders in the thatched ceiling? Heart pounding, Romaine snatched up a firebrand, released his handgun from its holster and inspected his hut, nudging the floor with the pistol, waving the flames over the ceiling and walls inside and out. Nothing unpleasant appeared.

Not entirely appeased, he lay down in the river sand floor of the lean-to.

What was he up to? he wondered again. What thoughts went on in that weird triangular alien head?

He rolled to one side, folded his arm beneath his ear as a pillow. There was little camp noise now but sleep would not come. Before long, bugs real or imagined crawled over him. He scratched and slapped at them, making contact with nothing but his own body. He darted outside, took up the firebrand again, searched the hut, saw nothing, returned to attempted sleep.

Minutes later, he thought he heard Fisher's feet scuff the grass between their huts and he offered up a *Good night*, to which there was no response. Was she peeved? Could Fisher *get* mad? Perhaps it was someone else walking past. Still, the harsh way he'd spoken to her irked him; he hoped he hadn't burst her bubble of fascination with the Jarinyi ceremony.

He had to admit, from the way she'd described it, the ceremony had a profoundness that surprised him. In his mind's eye he saw the bride and groom standing somberly before the Elder, then flashbacked to the moment where he at thirty-four stood before his own bride. The moment had been a forward-looking one, the anticipation of completion, of something exciting.

He growled in the dark. Eight years later, it was gone. *She* was gone.

He had to change thought-tracks, but couldn't. The wave of grief broadsided him before he could. He shifted, cleared the lump from his throat by coughing. But when he turned onto his other side, she was still there, right there before his face, like a portrait.

'Harshini,' he whispered.

He hadn't been able to picture her for years. Why was she suddenly so perfectly formed in his mind, so crystal clear?

For once, for a moment, he gave her memory his full attention, imagined his hand reaching to cup her cheek.

Ah, babe. I never cried for you but it didn't mean I didn't care.

And we nearly made it. If we hadn't gone into the alley, those –

He squashed the memory back into its hidey-hole.

He let out a grunt of disgust in himself and in the whole hacking Universe, flipped onto his stomach and willed himself to concentrate on the night noises about him.

Hours later, he fell into a troubled sleep.

PART IV

SEVENDAY

'A single death is a tragedy, a million deaths is a statistic.'

- Joseph Stalin

25

'It's every person's business to see justice done.'

- Sir Arthur Conan Doyle

ONE MOMENT, Romaine was in a warm bath in his room on BV, sipping a cold one; the next, fetid breath was puffing in his face. Carswell hissed at him to get up, his shaggy mane silhouetted against the faint light of the doorway.

Romaine waved him away along with the invisible noxious cloud of his breath. He sat up. 'And that reminds me. I didn't get to brush my teeth last night. Did you?'

Carswell backed outside and clung to the logs that formed the hut's opening. 'Funny. Are you awake?'

'No. I'm talking in my sleep. Or wish I was.'

'Come on. You'll want to see this.'

Groaning, Romaine crawled from the lean-to, legs aching. Arms aching. Shoulders, hips, back ... Right then, he would have given anything for the hot bath of his dream.

The light outside was a pinky grey, barely dawn. His mouth tasted like dirty socks and he hawked and spat as quietly as he could.

'What is it now? A Jarinyi giving birth? A Bar Mitzvah? A Jarinyi of the Year ceremony? These indigenous folk are so *quaint.*'

Carswell was a fuzzy blur beside him. 'Fisher told me you enjoyed the marriage ceremony last night. Said you proposed to her on the spot.'

Romaine imagined how good it would feel to shove Carswell onto his ass. 'Stand-up comedy at dawn? What's got you so chipper, Professor?'

'Come for a walk and you'll see.' He led Romaine away through the woods, following the run of the stream. Carswell carried a thick stick for pushing back foliage.

Their way soon became an uphill one, further testing Romaine's tired limbs. His hips seemed to creaked stiffly for the first few minutes of walking. His tongue felt swollen and scratchy. 'I better not be the morning sacrifice, Carswell, or so help me.'

Carswell chuckled.

After a half hour, the way grew steeper and then the stream angled away into a hole in the caldera right where the wall began to separate from the valley floor. The hole was tall and wide as a space station double doorway.

Within that dark cavity, Romaine could make out a natural ramp descending, following the bank of the stream. 'In there? You're kidding me?'

'No bats on Eventide.' With his stick over his shoulder, Carswell started down without bothering to see if Romaine followed. But he called back, 'Not much further, pal.'

'Yuh. That's what you kept saying the other day too.'

With little choice, Romaine entered the cave.

The path eventually converged with the stream and for the final few meters of tunnel, they splashed cautiously through shallow water. Shady daylight appeared ahead, bright enough to dazzle after his time in the damp grotto. After a moment, Romaine realized that the sudden-ness of the light's appearance was due to a Jarinyi warrior who'd been blocking the manhole-sized exit. The sentry stepped aside. Romaine noted as he crawled past that the Jarinyi's skin was still mottled with the colors of the mountain rock.

He peered gingerly over the lip of a small waterfall, finding himself in a narrow crevasse open to the air far above them. The stream dropped two meters beneath him, disappearing into another hole in the rock beyond. Muscles burning, he followed Carswell down the stone wall outside, as water from the falls spattered near him. At the base, he pointed back up to the sentry's face above. 'Camouflaged the opening with his body?'

Carswell waggled his eyebrows. 'Clever, huh? Come on, almost there.'

'Stop saying that.'

The crevice was just wide enough for a man to walk unhindered, walls and floor slick with slime and condensation, forcing care. After a few minutes, the xenologist further spoiled Romaine's mood by saying, 'You're doing well keeping up there, my friend. Becoming quite the outdoorsman.'

Romaine muttered 'Thanks' with all the sarcasm he could muster, though he was quite proud of keeping pace with the more agile Carswell.

Minutes later, they squeezed through the end of the crevasse and out into direct sunlight. It took Romaine a few moments to adjust, taking in the enormity of the open sky and a far-off horizon. They had stepped onto a stone outcrop large enough to land two Reapers, ringed with stunted bushes and littered with fallen rocks. The view beyond the far end was of the forest lowlands, shades of brown and green as far as the eyes could see. He wasn't expecting to be so close to the edge of the mountain, and was further surprised to find Scarface, Tuttut and the Elder already here, immobile, impassive and focused on a spot midway along the outcrop.

He followed their gaze. And stiffened at the sight of two dead bodies.

Carswell indicated each of the corpses in turn. 'Jarinyi. Nguwuu. Welcome to another crime scene, Commander.'

'What in the good goddamn?' he whispered.

Even twenty meters away, Romaine could pick the Nguwuu without Carswell's help. He'd seen one yesterday. And with time to compare, it was a different color and size to the Jarinyi near it.

Carswell had brought him all this way to see this.

This!

And despite this indignity, this idiocy, Romaine was instantly captivated, abruptly comfortable now that he was looking at corpses, at a mystery. Death was the familiar in a world of the unfamiliar.

'Crime scene?' he said to Carswell. The xenologist shrugged his brows.

Romaine felt the old need assert itself, an addiction far stronger than alcoholism: the lure of solving the unsolved, of completing the puzzle. The bodies beckoned him. He moved to the first, the Jarinyi, and bent over it. Something had disfigured the side of its head, scoring a furrow through the edge of the brain. The cause seemed obvious to him, but he ran a scan with his CHAD to be thorough.

He heard himself speaking to Carswell as he straightened, feeling oddly detached. 'AR-90. Close range.'

Todd was here. That rat bastard.

Worse than the pulse rifle wounds were the ligature marks on wrists and ankles. A jagged gash had been cut along the side of the neck – the open wound remained a dark pink, but no blood lay beneath or around the body. He went over the visible wounds again, taking his time, until he heard the living Jarinyi shifting their feet near him. Nothing was clear about their demeanor: were they impatient, murderous or merely bored?

The corpse lay face down, but from the lividity marks on its back, he could tell it hadn't fallen this way. 'This body has been moved and turned over.'

Carswell grunted, surprised.

Romaine indicated the purple discoloration. 'Post mortem hypostasis. He either died on his back or lay on his back for some time after death. Most of the blood in his body settled there once the heart stopped pumping.'

'The warrior who first came upon the body a few days ago might have done it before raising the alarm.' He looked back toward the crevasse as a thought occurred to him. 'I believe this poor fella was on sentry duty, guarding the tunnel we came through. I think they rotate year-round.'

'If that's the case, then he found him a few hours after death.' Romaine scratched at his stubble again. 'Why would he turn him face down?'

'A measure of respect for the dead perhaps.' When Romaine asked him why, he merely shrugged. His eyes glittered with an energy Romaine found unnerving, inappropriate to the situation.

A finger of breeze tickled Romaine's nose, carried a mild odor of death from the other body. He stepped past the Jarinyi to squat by the Nguwuu.

It lay face up, limbs twisted in death. Though it wore a similar hide breechclout, it did appear to be a different species to Jarinyi, rather than a different tribe. With a more pronounced musculature and taller stature, this warrior would have made a tough opponent in battle. Even a few days dead, it appeared stronger than all of the Jarinyi he had seen. It too had a pulse rifle wound, a hole punched through its chest, reminding Romaine of the woo-woo outside Columbus. No bugs though. At this altitude and amidst the barrenness of the rocky terrain there seemed to be fewer of them, and fewer carrion-eaters. Both corpses were reasonably intact. Their skin had taken on a marble-like appearance as it dehydrated, losing elasticity and puffiness, clinging to the veins and bones and tendons beneath. Both abdomens were bloated. The processes of decomposition seemed to be universal.

He stood and allowed his eyes to slide across and around the scene. Eventually, they caught on something the way a razor blade catches on a mole. He moved to the rock wall, to an unnatural break in the stone, a round mark wide and deep as his fist, ran his fingers around it. The rock felt smooth, fused. A few steps to the left, he found two more pulse fissures.

He turned his search to the ground where eventually he found another tear in the stone. Blood and bone matter fused there with the soil and granite, staining the ground around it, filling small nicks and cracks in the surface. He fished a baggy from its belt pouch and used a pebble to scrape samples into it. The Jarinyi had died right here, shot at point blank range. What looked to be scuffmarks from the landing skids of a Reaper were visible over by the edge where the ledge jutted from the mountain.

Romaine could see it now: the Jarinyi had been thrown to the ground, or held on the ground, and executed. The shooter or a second shooter had fired at the upright Nguwuu over by the rock wall.

But why?

He blinked away the images, not ready to fully enter into them. 'Carswell, you knew these bodies were here when you dragged me through the jungle and up a mountain?'

'I did,' he replied.

The ambush, the trip here, the chatter about keeping him safe …

'When were they found?'

'The Jarinyi only told me that these two were freshly dead when they discovered them five days ago.'

Five days. That sounded about right from what he'd seen. 'And they told you when?'

'A day or so later.'

'And you didn't think this worth reporting to Glass? To me?'

Carswell just looked at him.

'Give me the translator.' Romaine snatched it from him as he moved toward the Elder. Scarface stepped between them and Romaine halted with a jerk, speaking slowly and deliberately: 'This Jarinyi.' He gestured at the body, mimicking the four-fingered point he'd seen them use. 'He is from your Tribe?'

The translator seemed to interpret the words flawlessly.

Scarface wheedled a note. 'No.'

'You know him.' It wasn't a question. There was something in the alien's body language that bridged the communication gap. He was sad.

After a pause, Scarface said, 'My sister's son.' Another pause. 'She *tut tut* Great River tribe.'

'Your sister's son lived with the Great River tribe?'

'Yes. River's son. Warm breath.'

Whatever that means.

'How do you suppose he ended up here?' The translator just *tuttut*-ed.

Romaine sighed in exasperation and Carswell took over: 'How could he die here?'

'*Nguwuu.*' Scarface grew agitated, bobbing his head up and down. 'Nguwuu take for *tuttuttuttut*. Killing for bad spirit.' His two companions made simultaneous and unreadable twitches of their ears.

Romaine took over again. 'But a Nguwuu is dead too. Why would Nguwuu kill Nguwuu?'

The frantic bobbing motion spread to Scarface's shoulders. 'Two killing for bad spirit! Nguwuu bad! I want kill all.' The Elder reached out and touched his arm almost tenderly.

Romaine turned to Carswell, paused the translation. 'Two killing for bad spirit? What is that?'

Carswell considered the bodies as he answered. 'You remember you were worried about the Jarinyi sacrificing you? Well, from what I hear the Nguwuu do practice sacrifice to their deity.' He jerked his chin at Scarface. 'He's saying they must have kidnapped his nephew from the River Tribe and decided this was a good place to sacrifice him.'

'And sacrificed one of their own for extra points? Sounds like Scarface is as disgusted by that practice as I am.' He breathed deeply and slowly. 'Nguwuu. Nguwuu,' he said, experimenting with the word, compressing his palate and flattening the vowels in a fair imitation of the Jarinyi pronunciation. 'What I don't get here is how alien Neanderthals got their hands on AR90s.'

'What makes you think they did?'

Carswell was blatantly hoping Romaine would conclude the Marines were behind this.

But it was still a good question.

He moved back to the bodies and began to scan them with his CHAD. The back of the Jarinyi's loincloth was coated with fecal matter after its bowels had relaxed in death. The excrement had run down one thigh, though most had washed away with the rain. Stuck to the side of the Jarinyi's thigh, glued there by dried feces, Romaine found two short hairs. Since the Jarinyi were hairless, these were either from an animal or they were human. He was sure that the latter was true. He would check that in a minute or two, once he was done with his examination. He picked the hairs off, avoiding contact with the feces, and slid them into a fresh baggy.

What else can you tell me?

He reached under the body to turn it over, caught the movement of the others from the corner of his eye. All three had taken a few steps toward him, raising their hands in what looked like warning, their expressions fierce.

'Carswell?'

'Don't turn it over. You're disrespecting the dead.'

He slowly moved his hands out from under the body and stood up. The group of Jarinyi settled down.

More. I need more info.

Romaine let his gaze slip around the scene again and, spying a flash of white on the far side of the ledge, he walked toward a patch of dried mud. There was no mistaking what he found there. The rains of the past week might have washed away hairs, skin, sweat but they had not washed away the cigarette butt. He was pretty sure the Nguwuu didn't smoke and if they did, it wouldn't be this brand of cigarette. He scanned it with his CHAD, compared the DNA found on it with the files he'd copied from Columbus, felt a thrill of excitement when the results appeared with a synthetic ping. He took the opportunity to do the same with the hairs – *Wind blowing hard, you scratch your scalp at the wrong time, you leave your trace, asshole* – and smiled without humor. He pulled another baggy, flicked the butt inside, sealed it and stuffed it away.

He turned to find Carswell right there behind him, anger beginning to show through the cracks in his smug visage.

'For all I know, you planted this,' Romaine said.

'DNA will tell.'

DNA did tell, but Romaine refused to disclose that to Carswell yet. He stalked carefully around the area, brandishing his CHAD. Over by the very edge of the outcrop, he found another butt beneath a ridge of dried mud kicked up by the Reaper's landing skids. Once again, the DNA scan was conclusive. The butt went into the same baggy as its twin.

He now had two smokers from Columbus placed at the scene. Rat-faced Sgt Maglic. And deceased Private Gutierrez. In addition, he had two hairs from the scalp of Lieutenant Sean Todd.

You devious little bastard.

He continued walking the scene but after ten minutes, he surrendered to an unprofessional impatience. Against his normal adherence to procedure and thoroughness, he told himself there was nothing else to be found. He didn't need it anyway. He already had some pretty strong evidence. And besides that, he could see in his mind's eye what had likely happened here...

THE NGUWUU STANDING IN A GROUP AFTER CLIMBING ONTO THE OUTCROP for whatever reason, ready to flee as the Reaper lands, terrifying them. Marines drop from the Bird. Todd strides forward, enjoying the moment. Brawny Sgt Chua follows, rifle trained on new contacts. Maglic is already reaching for a smoke as he slips out the door. A couple of other recons or grunts follow him. Certainly Gutierrez is there, frightened and keeping close by the flier; the young regular frowns and fidgets as he watches the scene play out. Perhaps Turk emerges from the Reaper now, carrying the bound Jarinyi over his shoulder and dumping him on the rocks. Todd fondles an AR90, his other men carrying the missing case of rifles from Menabu's stores.

Now a single Nguwuu approaches, attempting to communicate with Todd. Gutierrez lights up with shaking hands as he watches on from the shadow of the flier. Todd demonstrates the weapon by shooting at the squirming Jarinyi, the pulse skimming along the side of its thrashing head, rendering it unconscious but not dead. Not yet. Blood rushing to fill the impact crater left by the rifle, to soak into and spread into the thin layer of soil and dust beside it. A Nguwuu or blackcap leaning down to slash its neck, help it bleed out. Todd regards this coolly, hand moving in a smoothing motion along his scalp, dislodging the hairs that drift away, two settling onto the legs of his victim. Todd tosses the weapon to the Nguwuu and points to the Jarinyi as if to say 'Knock yourself out.'

And here the scene splinters into several possibilities. Perhaps the Nguwuu raises the rifle at Todd and gets itself shot dead by one of the other Marines. Perhaps it kills one of its own in mimicry of Todd. Perhaps Todd just leaves the rifle on top of the case and returns to the aircraft, the Nguwuu fighting over the weapons after he leaves. Perhaps, he teaches them to fire by aiming out over the lowlands, shooting at the clouds, until one begins to shoot at the rock wall, and a dim-witted comrade gets in the way...

The strands of the visualization converge on one final image: the case left open on the ground, the gaunt face of Maglic sneering as he tosses his butt out the Reaper's open door as the Marines lift off, a human rifle clutched in the grey-brown fist of a Nguwuu...

He knew he had the gist of it.

More questions arose. Some were easily answered, others not so much.

Were Marines giving modern weapons to Nguwuu to spark internecine warfare that would move the Jarinyi out of CUSET's way with CUSET able to claim the stealthy Nguwuu had filched the rifles themselves?

Why was Gutierrez killed? A message the Private had sent his sweetheart from Columbus had been deleted from his file. He was a witness to the murder of a Jarinyi and the illegal arming of the Nguwuu. Had he been silenced, and the Jarinyi framed as a result of his murder painting them as unreasonable and violent? Two birds with one stone?

Romaine's gut was convinced, but knowing it with his heart and knowing it with his head were two different things. His heart had only ever gotten him into trouble. His head never had. He had to *prove* this, play it carefully and safely. Now that he knew where to look and what for, he could investigate this even more thoroughly once he returned to Columbus. His first move would be to request Dreyfuss send two more investigators plus a retinue of MPs. If he phrased it right, she might even agree.

And making trouble for her would be a helluva lot of fun.

He looked over at Carswell who now squatted by the bodies. 'I have questions. A lot of questions.'

'Because you're not satisfied with the answers you already have?'

'What's that supposed to mean?'

'Romaine, do you find it difficult to make decisions?'

After a beat, Romaine replied evenly, 'I'm making a decision now, not to kick you in the ass as hard as I can.'

Carswell shifted to keep that target out of Romaine's reach. 'Tell me what you know.'

'Two dead individuals. Both killed with a Marine weapon. Cigarette butts found at scene –'

'And I seem to remember one of the Marines smoking at the sacred field. Oh. That's right. He blew smoke rings in my face.'

'Made me wish I smoked. That was the scrawny one named Maglic.'

'Yes, he's probably dead by now. That's karma for you.'

'There's other smokers among the personnel.'

'It was Maglic, though, wasn't it? I bet your little scanner told you that. Polluting a pristine world with cigarette butts.' He made a disgusted noise.

Carswell didn't ask if there was a second smoker and Romaine felt no compulsion to tell him about Gutierrez. Mimicking Carswell's professorial tone, he asked, 'What makes you think Maglic wasn't up here *after* the Jarinyi was killed? Perhaps he was just as cut up about an indigenous corpse as you are.'

Carswell actually laughed at that. 'Maglic was here, amongst others, and *during* the murder of River's Son. Are you going to debate that?' When Romaine didn't reply, Carswell continued, 'So you've made at least one decision. What else have you decided you know?'

What do I know for sure?

'That's about it. Apart from Gutierrez being killed with a Jarinyi weapon.' He shook his head in annoyance when Carswell glowered at him. Once again, he was being pushed onto the defensive. 'People wandering all over my crime scenes. Rushed from place to place without time to interview witnesses. Rain washing everything away. I was lucky to find the cigarette butts.'

Carswell chose to pick up on one of the things Romaine had said, talking over the top of him. 'I seem to remember you having time to interview the Jarinyi. I wonder who kept you from doing the same with the CUSET personnel.'

Romaine had to admit that made sense. Instead of spending Wednesday – Fourday, he corrected himself – taking witness statements, or digging deeper into the crime scenes, or finding out more about the mysterious Rowland Devlin, he'd been bundled off to the Pumpkin Patch. 'Then you better get me back there to interview them, huh? Especially now I finally have some momentum.'

Carswell ducked that and said, 'Interview *who*? Maglic? I told you, the Jarinyi will have killed him during the ambush. Him and all the others. And even if they didn't, surely the time for witness statements and interviews is over. You really don't have enough to make your report already?'

'I have *bits* of the truth. Not the whole thing.'

'Truth? Romaine, you don't deal in truth. Just in evidence.'

Some kind of creature shrieked in the distance, its voice carrying up from the lowland forest. Romaine wondered if it was the cry of the hunter, the hunted or the just plain relieved-to-be-alive.

'Get off my back. What do you want me to say? That the Marines snuffed a Jarinyi, the Jarinyi snuffed a Marine and called it even? Like that's going to stop further retribution. Especially after what happened two days ago.'

'You know damn well that's not what happened.' Carswell stomped about in a tight circle until he stood on the other side of the Jarinyi body pointing down. 'Someone tied his hands and feet. Even I can see that. Then they shot him with a human weapon. Who would do something like that?'

'I'll call in more investigators. Do it properly. I don't have the whole picture yet.'

'You really are a piece of work.'

'*I'm* a piece of work?'

'You sit on the fence, thinking life can be reasoned out. Have you ever taken a position in your life, gone out on a limb?'

'More than you'll ever know!'

'Like when?'

'None of your damn business.'

'I'd hoped for more from you. I'd hoped you had a conscience, some backbone.'

Romaine found Carswell's shirt bunched in his fists, their faces centimeters away from each other. 'You want backbone, you –!'

Abruptly the Elder and Tuttut were pulling him away, prying his fingers from Carswell's shirt. While none too gentle, they didn't seem angry with him, just casually protective of Carswell, their manner that of friends separating two drunk acquaintances without particularly taking sides. Scarface however hadn't moved.

'Ok. It's ok, fellas.' Romaine paced around to boil off some of his rage. His mouth was dry and craving rum and cola.

The last thing he expected was Carswell to continue his harassment. A sound made him turn and the man was right there, face still flushed with emotion. 'Romaine, are you free to make an unbiased decision?'

Face now carefully blank, he responded, 'A moment ago, you accused me of not taking a position. Now you want me to be unbiased? Well, which is it?'

Carswell faltered but only for a nanosecond. 'I mean unbiased by CUSET's agenda.'

'Ah. But biased toward the Jarinyi's agenda. Or at least yours. *That's* why I pursue evidence. So I can arrive at the correct decision.'

Carswell took a few steps backward, gathering his thoughts before adopting a different tack. 'You're a cliché. The emotionally isolated policeman. You think you remain uncontaminated by life if you can stand apart from it, analyze it, pass judgment on it. So how do you arrive at the objective truth of this?' The older man waved his hand at the corpses.

'What have I been saying to you, meathead? Evidence, deduction, reason. Facts.'

'Facts?'

'Yes, facts!'

'So, who killed the Nguwuu?'

'I don't know for sure. But I have my suspicions.'

'And they are?'

'Right now, I'll keep them to myself.'

'Ok. You do that. But they're *suspicions*, aren't they? I thought you said you deal in facts.'

Romaine groaned in frustration. 'Fine. You've out-debated me. I often resort to working theories and suspicions to make sense of the evidence.'

'You make assumptions and test them. And eventually you can tell the story of what happened with a minimum chance of error.'

'That's the plan,' Romaine sighed.

'But from whose perspective are you telling the story?'

'What? What the hell does that mean?'

'Every story is told from a perspective. I'd say the Nguwuu have their own perspective that makes sense of this evidence. The Jarinyi would too. And with a big pile of facts to build play with, there would be truth in both accounts. And truth is always more important than facts. Larger even than the sum of the facts.'

Romaine wet his mouth and throat with water from his canteen. Swallowing, he shook his head. 'So, the truth is found by looking at it from all sides. Is that what you're saying?'

'No, I'm saying that our perspective, our position, gives the events *meaning*. The evidence you've found here will help you form truth. But truth isn't just found in the evidence. Truth is found in *meaning*. It stems from our biases and beliefs and values. You will interpret this evidence by the laws you uphold. Or by the agenda of your superiors. Those are your biases. What I'm asking you to do is take a step outside your comfort zone to interpret the event happening here, not by the law, but by its meaning as a thing of history.'

'History. Sheesh.' Romaine stared up at the mountain above him, wishing he could be anywhere but here having this conversation. 'I'm not interested in history.'

Carswell changed tack. 'Look. You experienced an ambush. Jarinyi warriors killed Marines. Was this right or was this wrong?'

'It was stupid.'

'Fence-sitting –'

'Alright, it was *wrong*. Very wrong.'

'Finally. You take a side. You support a Marine's right to life above that of a Jarinyi.'

'I support the right of all sentient beings to live without someone else shooting them dead, whether that be with a pulse rifle or a bow and arrow! What the Jarinyi did was stupid. They are inviting further retaliation. It'll escalate.'

'But did they have the right to protect their land?'

'I guess so.'

'Then in truth what they did was acceptable. Because they acted on their right.'

'But CUSET also has the right to find a cure to avoid a pandemic. And that's where the ethics get muddy. It can't be black and white.'

Romaine swallowed more water from his canteen. Arguing semantics with Carswell was not the way he wanted to spend the day. 'Your ranting is making me crazy, Carswell. The only grey area here is whether you're a smart man masquerading as an idiot or vice versa. Let's go.'

He started back toward the narrow passageway out of the outcrop.

THE THREE JARINYI PASSED THEM DURING THE WALK BACK. ROMAINE wondered what they'd done with the bodies, but didn't ask. Before they could race ahead, Carswell entreated them at length, trying to make them understand that the Nguwuu must have Man-weapons ready to attack them. Romaine had kept this suspicion to himself, and the xenologist had deduced it for himself. Carswell added that while the Jarinyi were reasonably safe from Nguwuu here in the valley, the

Men might find them in their fliers. They should all go to the River Tribe and seek strength in numbers along with the shelter of even denser forest. Eventually the two leaders of the Tribe jogged away without reply, Tuttut in their wake. Romaine wondered if they'd understood, if they'd agreed or if they were just as eager for breakfast as he was.

———————

HE FOUND FISHER STANDING BY THE EMBERS OF A CAMPFIRE. HER HAIR was down and she fidgeted, winding her fingers around each other. The moment she saw them, the energy dissipated and she slumped. By the time they drew near, she had sunk onto her haunches to stir the embers with a long stick, not looking at them.

'You won't believe what I found,' Romaine started.

'*What I showed him*, he means,' Carswell interjected.

'Where did you go?' she asked quietly.

'Doctor Pain-in-the-ass here took me out through the valley wall. To another crime scene. Two more dead bodies.' He waited for her to respond, to ask him whose bodies. Carswell continued to hang around, a solid representation of the cloud of his own body odor.

When Fisher didn't respond at once, still poking about in the coals with her stick, Romaine frowned and dipped his head to peer under her hair. She moved so that her hair continued to obscure her eyes.

'Jennifer? What's wrong?'

'Nothing,' she responded, too calmly.

Oh dear.

'I'll ... go talk to the Elder ... make plans for our hike back.' Carswell said it lightly, giving Romaine a *you're-on-your-own* look. Romaine gave him a *thanks-for-nothing* glare in response.

'What is it?' he said gently. He crouched too, ankle and hip smarting as he did.

She shook her head as if to brush away his question, but he could see a puffiness around her eyes now that made him balk at pursuing the subject.

He tried another tack. 'Anyway, we'll be getting out of here now. Back to base.'

'That's good.'

What did I do? he wondered. Probably better to get it out in the open. 'Jennifer, something's bugging you.'

She brushed her hair away from her ears, her jaw grinding, continuing to avoid eye contact. Finally, she spoke, words emerging in a rush. 'I woke up this morning. You weren't here. He wasn't here. I thought – I thought you'd left me.'

'We didn't leave you,' he said. Something in him wanted to tell her that he wouldn't do that, would never do that. He pushed the thought away: it felt like a line from a romance streamie.

She was suddenly businesslike again, getting to her feet, gathering her hair into its normal bun and pinning it there. 'It's fine, sir, really. I'll just refill my canteen and I'll be ready to leave.'

Sir?

He watched her go, wishing her hair was still loose.

You jerk. You asshole.

He'd taken off and not even thought to inform her. How long had she been awake, alone in the camp without even the translator to help her? He'd been gone for almost three hours.

Carswell returned with a handful of the nuts Romaine had eaten the night after the jeep crash. 'I'll get some more for Fisher,' he said. 'She alright?'

'How do you think she is? We left her here alone without letting her know where we were going or when we'd be back.'

'Extra breakfast for her. Then we leave.'

Romaine followed him toward the trees, keen to keep things moving. 'Are any of them accompanying us?'

'Just my friend. Tuttut as you call him.'

Carswell took him through the first layer of trees to a line of short bushes loaded with the nuts. Romaine filled a shirt pocket with the ones he already had and helped Carswell pick more.

'Good of Tuttut to come,' Romaine said eventually. 'But isn't that a little dangerous for him? Heading closer to Columbus again? I mean, it's his land and all. But we get found and he's not exactly going to be welcomed with open arms, is he?'

'Nice to know you care, Commander.' Carswell stripped a whole branch of its nuts in one swift stroke, scooping them into his trouser pocket. 'You're becoming positively Jarinyi-friendly.'

Romaine growled and copied his action. 'I had to go and engage in conversation.' He filled his own pocket with food and turned toward the clearing, shelling another nut with his thumbnails and placing it on his tongue. The flavor was beginning to grow on him.

Carswell fell into step beside him. 'That dead Marine, Gutierrez, was a symptom of the problem. I know he's the reason you're here, but those bodies out on the mountain side, they're a bigger crime. Gutierrez is a side note. And,' he added, his voice lowering in volume but rising in intensity, 'he was not killed by a Jarinyi. Of that, I'm sure.'

'A Nguwuu?' Now there was a new thought.

But Carswell shook his head impatiently. 'No, no. There are no Nguwuu near Columbus.'

'You're suggesting it was another Marine.' Romaine started shelling another nut and hoped Fisher hadn't drifted too far. He wanted to offer her the meager breakfast as a peace offering.

'You said yourself you haven't had time to interview everyone at Columbus. Perhaps it wasn't even about Tigerclaw.' He scratched at his beard. 'I've watched crime fiction. A jilted lover perhaps? That immense Chinese woman could certainly pull that bowstring taut. Maybe a gambling debt. Maybe the dead man owed *Turk* a couple of thousand. Or –'

'Or Professor Carswell should leave the investigating to the investigators, and stick to getting us back to base as safely and quickly as possible.'

Carswell nibbled at a nut and stopped talking.

Fisher had reappeared from another part of the forest and was treading wearily in their direction, lips set in a tight line, still evading eye contact. Romaine figured it would take her a while to get over this. If she ever did.

Loud birdsong filled the air, a Jarinyi alert of some kind. Carswell took his arm and steered him toward the stream. People all over the camp dropped what they were doing or emerged from among the trees and assembled there. By the time a full forty of all ages were there, Fisher had caught up and Romaine had given her most of the nuts from his pocket. He'd started shelling the ones he had left.

Silence had fallen, and Romaine noticed belatedly that all Jarinyi eyes had turned to him. Carswell cleared his throat and stepped into the space between Romaine and the Tribe. He spoke loudly in the modulated voice he used around the Jarinyi, although they couldn't understand him with his translator off.

'Before we leave,' he said, 'I wanted you to take one last look at these people. Remember them for who and what they are. Look at their nobility, their intelligence, their generosity. Your people murdered their people. Your aircraft destroyed a settlement of theirs. But. They cared for you when you were injured. They've cared for Fisher's hand and their beliefs have much in common with hers. I saw you watching them marry. You've seen they are complex people, not two-dimensional savages. You've seen they have amazing gifts – their speed, their sense of smell and hearing, their ability to blend with the land. They are part of this world in a way we can never be.

'You've seen that they will rise up and defend their people, their land, their resources. But I don't think you've understood that they defend and care for these – not because they own them, not because they want them for their own wealth or power – but because they believe they are custodians of this land and ecosystem. They believe wholeheartedly that their god placed them here to both enjoy it *and* care for it.' Carswell moved closer to the Jarinyi, held his hand out for a child to sniff and rub its ear against.

He smiled. '*Look* at them Romaine. Yes, they are different from us. But they're still *people*. They are men, women, children, youths. And they do not deserve to be plundered and murdered.'

Romaine hated being played, resenting the emotional game Carswell was playing. But – though he still distrusted them, as any good cynic would – the things that Carswell said about the Jarinyi resonated with him.

Just as they obviously did for Fisher, he noticed. Something had shifted, something had occurred in her internal world. She wore a look of astonished clarity on her face. Anxious, angry and wounded mere moments ago, she looked abruptly peaceful. Not for the first time, he wondered what she was thinking.

'Do you see them?' Carswell asked. 'Do you really see them, Romaine?'

'Yes, meathead! I see them.' He sighed and adjusted his belt, not looking forward to the long slog back, but ready to get the hell out of here.

When several of the females approached with more handfuls of sour fruit for him and Fisher, he shifted his gaze toward the stoic form of Scarface who watched with a spear clutched tightly in one hand. Romaine added, 'I'm just not sure they all see me.'

26

'The web of our life is of a mingled yarn, good and ill together.'

- William Shakespeare

As HE PUSHED AHEAD of the three humans on the narrow game trail, Tuttut let out a warning note that reminded Romaine of a parrot. Carefully the little warrior took hold of a thorny branch blocking the path, cut it off with his bone knife and held it before Carswell's face, before he threw it into the underbrush far from the path.

'Poison, probably,' Carswell explained.

Romaine had already guessed that. He tried to cement the image of the thorns in his memory.

The ground ahead was dappled with sunlight trickling through the thick canopy of leaves far overhead. Gloomier than the open spaces of the mountains, the forest held a renewed sense of menace for him even without the close encounter with poisonous thorns.

Carswell had told them the first leg of the journey would take them to the destroyed campsite where Romaine and Fisher had originally met the local tribe. This was partly because the best trails passed that way and partly because Carswell wanted to see the damage from the Reaper attack. Probably they would spend the night there and set out for Columbus at dawn. Carswell assured them they'd be eating tomorrow night's dinner in a CUSETMA Mess.

The forest trail dipped downward again, following the undulations where forest met foothills. Fisher and Romaine both faltered as they navigated a deeply rutted slope, slippery with recent runoff. When the ground leveled out, Fisher hurried ahead to squeeze past Carswell and join Tuttut taking point. She had been like that all morning: detached, evasive, preoccupied.

Carswell waited for him then fell into step behind him, jabbing him in the ribs with a bony finger. Romaine batted at it and missed.

'Romaine, you're a strange man.'

Romaine lacked the energy to respond out loud. In a day's time he would never have to talk to this clown again, unless it was in a formal police interview.

'You know why?' Carswell asked, oiling the wheels of conversation himself. 'You've got your head stuck so hard somewhere unpleasant that you miss the good things around you.'

'Good things, huh? The sky, the fresh air, the cuisine?'

'Fisher.'

'*Fisher?*'

'Why not?' Carswell said in a voice of reason. 'It's rather elemental out here, you know.'

'If you had half a brain, you'd know there's regulations against military personnel fraternizing on active duty.'

Carswell made a loud scoffing noise. 'And I'm sure that's stopped you in the past.'

Romaine shook his head in tired disgust.

'Guilty silence, huh?' Carswell teased after a few moments and chuckled. 'Alright, alright, so you're a pillar of professional integrity. But come on now, pal, out here what do regulations matter? There's no office politics or policies out here. There's no office.'

Romaine deliberately reached up to a low-hanging branch and scraped at the bark with his palm so that it fell behind him in a shower onto Carswell's hair. 'Out here is exactly where you need those things most, to keep some civilized structure to our lives.'

'Civilized, huh?' He could hear Carswell brushing at his hair, trying to pick out the bits of bark. It was Romaine's turn to chuckle. 'So you're not the least bit attracted to her?'

Romaine hoped that the young woman couldn't pick out Carswell's words from the background buzz of the forest. 'Enough of this, moron,' he said through clenched teeth. 'The last thing she deserves is a couple of old guys thinking lecherous thoughts about her.'

'I'm not old! I'm only fifty-one. I'll be around for at least another fifty years.'

'With your personality, I very much doubt that.'

For some reason, Carswell liked that and laughed out loud. 'So, how about it? She's an attractive girl, if you look past the military haircut and the mountain dirt. And, Romaine,' he added, voice trailing off to a conspiratorial stage whisper, 'she likes you.'

Romaine stopped dead and Carswell bounced off his shoulder as he whirled around. He leaned in menacingly. 'She doesn't. I'm not interested. Now, stow it.'

'You applying for Pope, now? You're no saint, pal.'

'Neither are you, you puke. But ... she is.' Strangely, he found his own words a revelation, discovering in a flash why he'd felt bereft without her companionship these last few hours. Fisher was one of the few truly good people he'd met in his life. With most people, he was used to scratching the paint and finding rust. But each time he scratched the dull grey paint of Fisher's military persona, gold shone through.

He poked Carswell in the chest. 'She deserves better than this, so you'll shut up now or I *will* resort to violence. Bodyguard or no bodyguard,' he added when Carswell's eyes flickered past him searching for Tuttut.

Carswell raised his hands. 'Ok, ok. Just trying to make friendly conversation.'

Romaine left it at that and returned to the labors of the game trail.

Soon Carswell went on ahead and sent Fisher back to take up the rear. As she waited for Romaine to pass, he asked how she felt. Upon receiving another one-word answer, he decided not to press it.

'We're just one big happy family,' he muttered to himself.

———————

THE JOURNEY DOWN THE MOUNTAINSIDE HAD FILLED THE MORNING AND overflowed into the afternoon. At 1600 hours, they stopped beside the trickle of a stream, refilled canteens and ate the last few fruits and nuts brought from the Jarinyi's hidden valley. Tuttut and Carswell supplemented their own meals with grubs scrounged from under a log. Romaine and Fisher still preferred hunger to a full Jarinyi diet.

Too soon for Romaine's liking, it was time to move on. He felt like he was pushing through a curtain of heavy air, conscious of his breathing; the mountain breezes which took the edge off the heat were missing here.

At one stage, a mass of beetle-analogs filled the path. It was as if someone were shuffling the pieces of a mosaic to form a new picture without ever deciding on what that picture would be. The closest thing Romaine had seen to it was coolant fluid bubbling up from a ruptured pipe aboard a frigate. As they made their way around the beetles, Tuttut drew his head back into his shoulders as if cold. Romaine wondered if the Jarinyi flinched because he was scared or because he was missing the opportunity for a feast.

Romaine brushed a flower-laden plant and a cloud of pollen spread around him. The scent was sharp like orchids, and instantly the back of his throat and inside of his nose itched as if someone had sprayed chili sauce there. He hated orchids. They'd been his mother's favorite and each time she'd brought some into the house, he'd complained with typically obtuse adolescent fervor. Knowing now how miserable her life had been, he wished that he could have allowed her that one small pleasure without sullying it with his own smartassness.

As the kilometers brought him closer to Columbus, he began

admitting to himself he was going to need Fisher's help. Having this heavy silence between them would not aid his cause. Ahead he could see that Carswell and Tuttut were shifting course from the intersecting game trails they'd been following toward a damp stream bed and he leaned tiredly against a decaying stump.

Fisher caught up, idly digging dirt from beneath her fingernails with a slightly cleaner thumbnail, eyes watchful.

'Jennifer.' He spoke her name with as much meekness as he could muster. 'I want to apologize for disappearing on you this morning. It was thoughtless and wrong.'

Some of the tension in her shoulders bled away. 'It's ok, sir. No worries.' They crossed into the stream bed and fell into step. She tilted her head at him. 'I'm sorry too. For being so feral, I mean. *And* calling you "sir" again.'

'You had every right. Must have scared the puke outa you, waking up to find your only two human friends had disappeared.'

She waved his comments away and sucked in a weary breath. 'I hope I didn't look like I was mad at you all day; I wasn't really. I've been thinking about other things.' She flinched at a nearby animal noise, hand on holster, relaxed again when no danger was forthcoming. 'And I was a little freaked this morning, but inside I knew the Jarinyi wouldn't hurt you. Or me. They're ... not like that.'

He screwed up his face, considering that. 'Well, I'm happy to be heading away from them, that's for sure. And I agree with you: even though their motives are alien, they're probably not the bad guys here.' He pointed his chin at Carswell a good twenty meters ahead of them. 'What I *am* starting to wonder about again is our other friend here. That ambush was pretty opportune for him. As a way of getting us up there, I mean,' he added, jerking a thumb at the mountains behind them.

'How could he know about the ambush before it happened? Even if the Jarinyi had planned it before the two young ones got shot, he was caught up in it too. He nearly died like we did.'

They stepped over deadwood on the stream bed.

'You have a point, but I remain cynical,' he said. 'My cynicism has served me pretty well in life.'

That little trademark furrow creased her brow. 'If he'd known about the ambush beforehand, it seems crazy for him to sit in one of the jeeps, especially the lead jeep.'

'Maybe he saw an opportunity when Turk killed those kids. Maybe he knew what might happen as a result, but he had to stick by you and me in the hope he could spirit us away. Like he did.'

'He wasn't even going to leave the Patch until we pressed him into joining us.'

'Stop making sense, Fisher,' he smiled. 'But something about him is still messing with my gut.'

She asked him then about what he'd found at dawn, what had made him so excited. He explained in detail about the bodies. She blew a bug from her arm and said, 'Maybe Doctor Carswell was sitting on the information about those two bodies up there, trying to find a way to suggest you come see without a Marine escort ... and the ambush presented an opportunity.'

Romaine sucked air between his teeth. The professor *felt* like a criminal, but there was nothing criminal about him. He was just annoying. 'Maybe you're right. He's good at thinking on his feet. Look how many approaches he's used to get us up here: appealing to reason, leveraging our fear and vulnerability, playing the best friend, even flattery. The sonof – Sorry. The *gentleman* changes tack according to the prevailing wind. Primarily, he wants our sympathy for the Jarinyi.'

'He wants yours, not mine, John.' She smiled wryly.

He acknowledged the truth of the statement with a shrug. 'Mr Misogynist. But that's dumb in itself. Because you seem a lot more endeared to them than I am.'

'You don't think we should do something to help them?'

He made a *don't-bust-my-ass* sound and kicked a hunk of rotted wood out of his way. 'Once again, I'm here to present a finding on a CUSET matter, to find a murderer. The best I can offer the locals is stating for the record that *they didn't* do it.'

'You believe that?' He heard the hope in her voice.

'Yes. I do. But, I'm not here to help them specifically. I'm not their "Judge". And I'm not their advocate.'

She ventured to the edge of the creek bed they were walking in, picked a large stiff leaf from a bush there, fanned her face with it and asked, 'So who did it? Who killed Private Gutierrez?'

He pretended to consider her question when really he was considering her. She wanted him to do something for the Jarinyi. To help them somehow. She was disappointed that he wouldn't consider it. But what really could he do? There wasn't anything else, apart from going public as Carswell had suggested, shoot off a message pack to a couple of pedecasters or something.

Yeah, sure, and get myself kicked out of CUSET, blow my career, lose my livelihood, wind up in a gutter somewhere planetside without a job or a home. Been there done that, never going back, Jack.

Should he tell her who he suspected? Of course he should, he rebuked himself.

You're going to ask for more MIs and MPs. Well, you've got one MP here already and you need her onside.

'Todd did it,' he said, low enough to keep Carswell from hearing.

Fisher gasped and stumbled.

'Or at least, someone with his sanction or approval,' Romaine finished. He patted the SCRoLL and CHAD in their pouches. 'I have evidence right here. But I'm gonna need more.'

Over the next few steps, he watched the expression on her face shift from bewilderment to consideration. 'He wanted to frame the Jarinyi. He wanted an excuse to remove them, to make people hate them. But ... *how* could he do that?'

'See it from his perspective: if he's been ordered to get Tigerclaw out there to save hundreds of thousands of lives from PBT, he'll do whatever it takes. And he'll see that as a *duty*, rather than a crime. His brother's one of those lives, by the way.'

'It's no excuse for murder. It's not. It's – it's despicable.'

Drawing her out, Romaine asked, 'You don't think he has an obligation to put the needs of his species over the needs of one individual? Or over another species?'

There was steel in her words and her tone. 'I think murder is always wrong. And I think that the Jarinyi have a sacred duty to watch over that amazing patch of Tigerclaw, and human beings shouldn't just stomp all over it. Treading on their traditions and taking their plants as if we're more important than them, that's wrong too.'

'But PBT. What if we have to ignore their traditions to save our species?'

She took a deep breath as if willing the more professional and even-tempered Corporal Fisher to return. 'We had a pastor in our town when I was growing up. Whenever I get confused about right and wrong, I come back to two things he made us remember. First, it's never right to use someone else. Second, God is in control of the Big Picture; we're in control of the small ones. Personally, I don't believe our species will die.'

Romaine scratched at his stubble. 'God'll protect us? That sounds a lot like the climate denialists of the Twentieth and Twenty-first. We almost wiped ourselves out there.'

'But we didn't.'

He waited until the loud squawking of some excited or amorous forest-dweller had died down before he said, 'That's not proof of God, Fisher. That's dumb luck.'

'Okay, then. I look at it this way: there's always an excuse to take what belongs to others. But it's never right.'

'That, I can agree with. But Todd and thousands of others won't. The rich people, who always have the most to lose.'

She hummed a little. 'There's probably enough Tigerclaw for all of us on this world. If we looked properly. We don't have to steal it from the Pumpkin Patch. The Corporate Union's hardly sent any staff here for such a big emergency situation. If they *had* sent more, maybe we could have had it in time to prevent PBT from spreading as quick as Todd said it is.'

Fisher had started calling CUSET 'they'. That was an interesting development.

'Kinda makes you wonder where they're investing the rest of their resources,' Romaine said by way of agreement. He nudged her toward a fallen log on the stream bank, then lowered himself onto it. 'The fatheads in Management should have pulled researchers out of their cosmetics labs and sent them all over Eventide, and away from the Jarinyi.' He caught himself, realizing with a start that he'd obviously arrived at an opinion himself, he'd begun to take sides.

It actually felt good.

27

'A compass is narrow-minded; it always points north.'

- Billy Graham

AT 1900, Carswell signaled another rest break. Romaine sank grate-fully on to some warm rocks by the edge of the streambed where the ground was driest.

The xenologist reached into a cluster of dry-looking bushes and picked some small berries. 'Another hour and we'll be at whatever's left of the Jarinyi camp,' he said, handing over a few of the tiny fruits.

Romaine bit into one tentatively, enjoying the squirt of warm juice on his tongue and the unexpectedly sweet taste. As Tuttut and Carswell darted off between trees ahead to scout around, he began tossing pieces of bark and dirt into the center of the streambed where the pebbles were glued together by the mush of damp mud and leaf litter.

'I wonder what it's like being a Jarinyi child,' Fisher wondered aloud. 'Eating straight off the tree. Growing up in the wild.'

'No streamies, no pedevision. No sugar.'

'No drugs. No gangs.'

'Nguwuu and spikey leopard monsters out to get you.'

'No pedophiles out to get you.'

'You're assuming that.'

'Sure.' She shrugged.

'I don't envy them their life.'

'Me neither, I guess,' she sighed. 'But it's an amazing one. Even in the middle of all this upheaval, they seemed pretty happy. You can always tell by the kids. And their kids seemed at peace.'

He snorted. 'Well, lucky them, then.'

'Permission to speak freely, John?'

'Sure.'

'It's the sarcasm. The way you react to ... nice things. Things like the wedding we saw. You said something about your marriage, I think. Did...did your wife hurt you that bad?'

'Not the way you'd think.' He cringed, but he'd done it now, he'd opened the lid. Maybe he was just tired of keeping it screwed on tight. 'Harshini was a partner in both senses of the word: a cop as well as my wife. CUSET lets you do things like that. Dumb things like that. But, no, the marriage wasn't bad. It was ... the opposite. And then ... Then she went and got murdered. On a case, on the job,' he added as if a death-in-the-line-of-duty softened the fact of her death, and somehow canonized her, qualifying her for special mention in the pantheon of the dead. He wondered whether cops across the ages had always seen their fallen this way.

'What happened?' Fisher asked gently.

Romaine sighed: no going back now. 'Eleven years ago, we were Lieutenants, trying to break a Bliss trafficking ring at the Edge-of-Nowhere Asteroid Mines. CUSET of course were concerned that the member-company who managed the mines would embarrass all the other corporations if news media found out that Bliss use was rife throughout the miners and admin staff.'

If there was one thing that CUSET feared almost as much as losing ground to the Chinese it was the sullying of its reputation.

'We figured out pretty quickly,' he continued, 'that the mines' CEO was a key player in the trafficking. His seven-figure-salary obviously wasn't enough; he had to make a tidy profit on the side by feeding people's addictions. But knowing it was one thing. Proving it became the problem – weeks of hard work and frustration. When we finally got our breakthrough, the bribes appeared. Then when the bribes didn't work, the threat came.'

He scowled, remembering the slip of paper pushed under the door of their hotel room. *Leave on tomorrow's transport or you won't live to regret it.* He'd told her that he wanted to go, they could close the case from a distance. She had refused to capitulate.

'We stayed just twenty-six hours longer than the deadline the bad guys gave us. We didn't even make it to the New Year.'

Meaning *she* didn't make it...

He told Fisher how they'd been taking advantage of New Year's Eve celebrations, reveling in the Mine's shopping and restaurant mall, enjoying a rare break from their work. Over fajitas and sundaes, martinis, and strawberry daiquiris, they'd chatted about watching each other's backs, about the evidence they had and the evidence they still needed. They'd talked about buying an apartment on BV in the new year.

They had also discussed the timing of Commander Dreyfuss's arrival at the mines, purportedly pursuing some unrelated case of her own. Harshini and Romaine were divided over their opinion of the MIA's most senior investigator on staff at the time. Harshini disliked and distrusted her. Romaine had always found her helpful to him professionally, and clear in her communication style...

Interrupting him, Carswell let out a low whistle and motioned them to get up. They rose to their feet with effort and began trudging again, while Romaine found his place in his narrative.

'Harshini's comm rang forty minutes before the calendar clicked over.' He took a moment to recall the smile that had spread across her face. He'd loved that smile, the predatory one, the one that meant she was about to pounce on some poor perp and ruin their life forever. 'One of the manager's personal staff wanted a meeting, a guy we'd already interviewed three times. One of those guys who knows more than he's telling. He said that while everyone was distracted by the celebrations, it was a great time to meet privately. He wanted to hand over invoices and messagepackets, and we were keen to take them. I hoped it would be the final piece that meant we could get the hell out of there and convict the guy's boss from a safe distance.' Fisher hung on every word, eyes wide and round. 'We were so excited ... so *stupid*. The meet was in an alley between cargo hangars and a fuel depot. An alley at night, for God's sake. Why did we do that?'

Of course, the meet had been a set-up. An ambush as sure and deadly as the Jarinyi's. The three thugs attacked from the shadows. Harshini had shot one dead, Romaine had winged another, before the third pistol-whipped Romaine and blew a hole in Harshini's chest. He clearly remembered the man with cold eyes standing over him, pointing a barrel in his face, about to finish him off when his colleague with the injured arm told him, 'Leave him. This will do.' The man did 'leave him', but not until kicking him hard in the ribs and the head. And they'd taken both his gun and hers, preventing Romaine from firing down the alley after them as they'd jogged away.

'The results of this excursion for John Romaine? A concussion. Two broken ribs. And a dead wife. Three strikes. You're out!'

Carswell, a long way ahead, turned and waved him quiet while Tuttut sniffed the air nervously.

As he and Fisher closed the distance to the other pair, Romaine dropped his voice, wanting to finish the story, to race to the end. 'And now for the epilog. The two heavies who hit us both turned up dead the next day. The one with the injured arm suffered a massive coronary – while hanging from a rope around his neck. A damn good job that, tying the rope with only one good arm.'

'And the other guy?' Her voice was almost a whisper.

Romaine forced a chuckle. 'The other fell into a trash crusher. Strange place to be wandering beside, huh?'

'Did you find out who they were working for?'

They came up on Tuttut just as the little Jarinyi forgot whatever had spooked him and carried on.

'The manager. Who else? And before you ask what happened to

him – well – I knew what I *wanted* to happen to him. And I wanted to be the one to do it. But I never got the chance.' Synapses fired in Romaine's head, the habit of years asserting itself: the best way to maintain emotional distance was with a drink in his hand. His arm actually twitched as if it would reach for a glass. He shoved his hand in his pocket. 'Before I could pull myself out of my infirmary bed, stagger into his office and shoot him in the face, he was killed in an accident. "What kind of fool would enter a zero-atmosphere sector without checking his suit integrity?" people muttered.'

What kind of fool, indeed?

Amanda Dreyfuss had visited him in his infirmary bed the day after his beating – the only person from CUSETMA or Management to bother. She offered flowers, a pat on the hand, and condolences. 'We all lost a great friend and teammate, last night, Lieutenant.' The day after that she'd visited again, to announce she would be the one to tie up the case. 'Management handed it to me while you recover. Believe me, John, the trafficking will stop and will not reoccur. I'll make sure of that.'

Two months' paid leave followed his return to his rental on Bona Vista, then a promotion and a pay rise. Six months later, Romaine had bought that Bona Vista apartment he and Harshini had discussed. But he'd done it alone.

'I'm so sorry, John. Harshini sounds like she was amazing.'

He licked his dry lips, tasting the residue of the berries from earlier. 'She was the rarest of people, Fisher: a company cop with high ideals.'

And it's not the job that kills you, it's ideals.

THEY KNEW THEY WERE COMING CLOSE TO THE JARINYI CAMP WHEN A wall of debris appeared ahead, dumped across the creek bed. A stench hung in the air, the smell of smoker's breath and death and change. Jagged pieces of trees blown outward from the Reaper bombardment littered the forest floor and had caught in the underbrush.

The forest was growing dark beneath its high and heavy ceiling of foliage. Some time ago, Fisher had dropped behind, allowing Romaine to slip into introspection. Nostrils flaring at the acrid bite in the air, he slowed to let her catch him, offered her a weary smile to say *almost there*. She pressed her palms together in a gesture of thankful prayer.

His spirits lifting slightly at the prospect of rest – albeit the prospect of a night spent in the open air – Romaine forced his mind away from the past and toward the future. 'What are you going to do when your tenure is finally up, Corporal Fisher? When she didn't respond, he added, 'I seriously think you should consider a role with the MIO. We need people like you.'

'Strangely, sir, the time out here in the wild, with you, with the Jarinyi, it *has* helped me come to a decision. When my tenure's up, I'm going to be a pastor.'

He stopped dead and turned on her. '*What?*' He could not have been more surprised if she'd announced she was becoming a belly-dancer.

She shrugged, overdoing the nonchalance. 'I think it's what I'm meant to do: help other people find their way.'

Romaine squeegeed sweat from his brow with his index finger and flicked it away. 'You're going to give up the opportunity to stop crime, to use that brain of yours, all so you can counsel girls against looking twice at cute guys and preach long sermons about whether or not it constitutes stealing to taste grapes in the fruit co-op before buying them?'

She scratched an eyebrow, bit her lip. He'd irritated her by making light of this.

'You came to this decision just before we left the hidden valley, didn't you?' he asked. 'When Carswell assembled his audience for his final soliloquy.'

'Yes. It all made sense. Right then. I could suddenly see why I was led up there.'

He must have looked skeptical or disgusted or something because her brows lowered and she continued in a quiet, insistent tone. 'I know you want to work with someone you can trust again, John. But this is what I've been trying to get straight for my whole life. Ever since I was a girl, I've wondered what my life was *for*.'

You still are *a girl*. He managed to keep that thought from falling out of his mouth: it was idiotic. 'People have been wondering that for thousands of years.'

'And I'm one of them. I've never been able to shake the feeling that there's more to life than doing a job, being a good person. I feel like all of us get to ... make our *mark* somehow.' She looked away to the left, remembering something. 'I was told by a lot of people this is pride, and I should remember I'm nothing special.' She met his eyes again. 'And I'm not saying I am. I'm just me. But I do believe there's something we're all meant to do ... or be ... Does this make sense?'

He couldn't think of anything to say and she seemed to take his silence as affirmation, relaxing a notch or two.

'When I looked at the Tribe, that one last time, I saw something. Our communities, our human ones, they fracture. The Jarinyi don't. They have a single purpose. We don't. But if I look after the needs of a community, the way my pastor did for my hometown, then I free them up from the burden of looking after themselves to look after others, instead of trying to take, or hide, or bully.' In her excitement, her pace had picked up, forcing Romaine to skip a little to keep up. She said, 'One of the Articles of Andros says, "My life exists to improve the lives of others". This is the point of my faith: everyone can have what they need if we'll only care for one another. I finally believe that. I finally *get* it.'

They were close now to the wall of wreckage strewn across the creek. Romaine opened his mouth to respond, but the conversation was cut short by an explosion of sorts, the sound startling, alien, *polluting*. The booming report fell like an exclamation point, sucking all other noise from the air as surely as vacuum pulls atmosphere from an airlock.

For one brief moment Romaine worried he was having a stroke.

It was then he noticed that Tuttut no longer had a head.

28

'The proud have hidden a snare for me, and cords;
They have spread a net by the wayside;
They have set traps for me.'

- Psalm 140:5

THE CONTINGENT of *Nguwuu* had taken one of the gentler paths through the mountains. It was proving longer than their normal routes, but the three trilophants they'd brought could never have made it through those narrower passes. Though they made occasional noises of irritation at being pushed so hard, the three cows obeyed the careful goading of the *Nguwuu*, recognizing the small creatures as their masters. The Kill-lord had used trilophants before in inter-clan warfare, but never had a *Nguwuu* thought to bring the creatures through the mountains to use in an attack on *Jarinyi*.

Because he was traveling up with the trilophants at the leading edge of his phalanx, he was among the first to hear the signal.

T'k t'k!

The sound was so low, that none in the Nguwuu war party would have heard it if they hadn't been practicing absolute silence.

The lead rider held up a hand and the Kill-lord repeated it. The riders tapped at the cows' left ears, signaling them to stop. All three beasts let out a grateful sigh, their three-fingered trunks feeling about them for water and grasses.

T'k t'k!

The warriors closest to the Kill-lord in the caravan passed back the gesture and slowly the caravan began to halt. The Kill-lord strode forward between the shoulders of two trilophant and approached his scout as the warrior climbed out from the rocks ahead, wondering where the other two who'd accompanied this one were. He demanded a report with a jerk of his chin. Using sign-language only, the scout explained that he had seen one of the Skywarriors higher up the mountain. It had killed his two companions.

A swell of shock rippled through those in the throng close enough to read the gestures. The Kill-lord glanced around to see several signals pass between riders.

One asked, 'Are they safe-to-us?'

The other, 'Weren't they sent by the Spirits to help us?'

The Kill-lord turned his back to them, concentrated while the scout continued his report. Before he had left the area where he had fought the Skywarrior, he had seen it meet with a Jarinyi. Together they had vanished through a hole in the rock, one hitherto unnoticed by any Nguwuu. The scout pointed up and east, concluding that the Jarinyi must have a settlement hidden amongst the unexplored peaks there.

Excitement rippled through the war party as this news carried from the front to the rear. Again, the Kill-lord shut it out and concentrated on this news. Whoever that Skywarrior was, their inexplicable behavior was a problem. His warriors might decide he had allowed the creatures to deceive him, to allow them to fall into a trap. In that case, not even his superior fighting prowess would save the Kill-lord when the entire party turned on him. He shifted his thoughts inward, sought the Spirits' presence, that tingle in his chest.

And then the answer came, emerging with startling clarity like the sun from behind thick clouds. The Skywarriors were not agents of the Spirits.

They were merely creatures of the world! They must be creatures who could make their homes in the clouds, split there into tribes the same way the Nguwuu and the Jarinyi were. Yes. One of those tribes had made their allegiance with the Jarinyi and another with him. He conveyed this to his closest warriors, who relaxed visibly at the idea before passing it along the line.

This solved one immediate problem, but it raised another. Not only were the Jarinyi more powerful than the Nguwuu, but so were the Skywarriors. One of them had killed two of his scouts. They possessed weapons of great power.

To conquer the Jarinyi, and to protect his people from the Skywarriors, he would require not just the weapons of the Skypeople. He would require their essence too.

The tingling returned and he grunted in acknowledgement: now he truly understood the Spirits' intentions. They had bestowed the greatest gift upon him. And their greatest opportunity.

———

SOMEHOW EVEN BEFORE TURK ROSE FROM HIS HIDE AMONG THE RUBBLE, Romaine knew he was in there.

But the knowledge didn't prompt him to take out his handgun and fire. As completely stunned as Fisher and Carswell, he merely stared while the huge man got to his feet, towering over them.

Tuttut lay curled on his side and would have appeared sleeping, if it weren't for the ragged flaps of skin that hung from the top of his neck, framing a spreading patch of gore on the soil beneath.

Carswell's jaw worked, but no words came out. He stood with arms spread wide, unable to tear his eyes away from his friend's mutilation. Blood, bone and brain had speckled his beard, face, hair and one sleeve.

'I never get sick of doin' that!' Turk roared in triumph. The blackcap had fired from three meters away, the shotgun pellets in tight enough formation to rip through the Jarinyi without strays hitting Carswell. He himself was caked with mud. Small twigs and curls of bark adorned his camouflage clothing like badges of honor. The eyes inside the dark dirt-mask blazed with barbarous delight. He waggled the shotgun toward the three of them, reminding them he had them covered, then he pushed off both feet to leap from his hidey-hole onto a clearer patch of creek bank. He landed a pace or two from Tuttut's body, on the opposite side of it from Carswell.

Romaine stood some way back but his ears still rang from the blast of the shotgun and the roar of his own pulse. Still, when Turk stretched, he thought he could hear the loud pop of disused joints unlocking.

Carswell made a wretched sound, a strangled cry. One of his boots was fixed close to where Tuttut's blood leaked in a dwindling stream toward the center of the creek bed. The thought flashed through Romaine's brain that with all his manipulation, Carswell hadn't seen this one coming.

Fisher, wide-eyed and white-faced, was the first to move. Displaying remarkable control of her emotions, she raised her empty hands to a halfway position, avoiding eye contact and addressing her words to Turk's chest. 'Sergeant, you've finished your mission. Well done. It's over now. Let's go back to Camp. Do you have a radio?'

Turk stared at her for a long while, while Romaine's gaze swung between them and back. What the hell was Fisher saying? Evidently, Turk was wondering the same thing, though it was difficult to read his expression through the muck on his face. Eventually, the blackcap mocked Fisher loudly, the flat line of his mouth and protruding lower lip moving rapidly up and down as if he were some monstrous hand-puppet: '"Do you have a radio?"'

Fisher's shoulders slumped. Romaine caught on then: she'd tried to play him. And he wasn't buying it.

Holy hell, Romaine thought. *Holy shit.*

Suddenly Turk's expression was clear. It was one of hunger. They were at the mercy of a man who could kill them all, knowing he might never be found out. And probably, Romaine thought as he noticed the artificial sheen in the man's eyes, right now this junkie asshole couldn't even think in terms of consequences.

'Ok, Sergeant,' Fisher said quietly, still avoiding eye contact. 'Ok.'

Turk's gaze lingered on her for a moment then swung to Romaine. The shotgun followed. Romaine jerked involuntarily.

Fisher had the right idea, he thought. *Take control of the situation. Steer it somewhere safer. Get him talking.*

'That was very clever, ambushing the ambushers like that,' he said and gestured at Tuttut's body. 'You saved us from this creature. Thankyou.'

For a moment, uncertainty flickered across the face beneath the mud-mask. Then Turk smiled a yellow-toothed smile and took his hand from the shotgun. He waggled his trigger finger at Romaine as if to say *Nice try*. The finger pointed to Romaine's sidearm. 'No way they took you prisoner an' you kept that,' he rumbled.

Carswell began to move, taking backwards steps, distancing himself from the horror of Tuttut's body. One glance told Romaine that the man was far from dazed, however. Though he feigned it well, a calculating anger and fear revealed itself in the set of Carswell's jaw and shoulders, the lines around his eyes. Turk seemed too stupid to notice or care. Or perhaps he was too insane, or too high. Carswell's backwards stagger took him up the mild incline of the creek's far bank until the trunk of a large tree blocked his way, a tree untouched by the damage to the nearby campsite. He settled his back against it, hands reaching down and back to draw solidarity from its realness, its firmness.

Turk hawked and spat in the xenologist's direction. The sputum fell well short. To all of them, he barked, 'Hands on the back o' ya heads!'

Romaine complied. Fisher too, though she kept her fingers from entwining, he noticed. He carefully disentangled his own, hoping for some advantage. A millisecond could make all the difference. Carswell just stood there, staring at his fallen friend.

Turk took six large strides across the creek, lifted his leg and smashed his boot against Carswell's chest, clamping him to the tree. The shotgun hovered above Carswell's head as if Turk would smash it with the stock. 'I said put your hands 'hind your head, dog!'

Carswell complied, struggling for breath.

Turk kept his boot where it was, turning his head. 'You. Romaine.

Left hand down. Right hand still on ya head. Take out ya handgun and hold it by the barrel. Good. Put it there.' He indicated a meter-thick, meter-long chunk of tree near his hidey-hole. 'Tha's it. And your canteen now. Hand behind your head. Right, stand *there*.' He pointed with the shotgun butt to a spot in the center of the streambed, not far away from himself. 'Yo. Princess. Same deal. Hurry *up*! Ok. Now next to ya boyfriend.'

Fisher trudged to a stop near Romaine, closer to Carswell than him, placed her hands behind her head again.

Turk put more weight behind the leg pressing against the xenologist. The shorter man gasped. 'How 'bout you, slick? Any weapons I should know about? Maybe an indig knife? No?' He pushed off from Carswell's chest, whirled on the other two, made a face like snarling dog. Then he laughed and marched to where they'd left canteens and sidearms.

He has lost his mind, Romaine thought.

'Hack, I'm thirsty,' Turk muttered and drained Romaine's canteen in several loud gulps, his adam's apple bobbling madly. He wiped his mouth with the back of the hand holding the canteen before throwing it at Romaine; Romaine thanked Fisher's God that it missed. 'You humps can put your hands down now. You can't do nothin' to me.' He lapsed for the moment into unknowable thoughts; the slow nodding motions of his head reminded Romaine of the lap of tiny waves.

The man's brain was swiss cheese from using whatever the hell he was using. Romaine thought, *What in hell can we do? Except keep trying to talk him round.*

'So, Sergeant, if you'll just use your radio, you can return to Columbus a hero and we can all get some chow and some rest –'

'You shut ya hole! Because a' you, an' *you*, an' *you* –' He motioned toward Fisher and Carswell. '– this whole thing's screwed ...' The words trailed off as his eyes glassed over and some line of thought blocked the physical world from view.

With poor timing, an itch began along Romaine's hairline, persisting as the seconds ticked by and the world seemed to hold its breath. Even scratching might be enough to set Turk off, forcing him to ignore it as best he could. He focused instead on tactics, mind racing. Turk had just told them there was something he was pissed off about, something he held them responsible for. That gave Romaine an angle. Maybe.

'Ok, Sergeant. Tell us. How can we help you? How can we make this better?'

'Better? Better? Maybe if he gets down on the ground and begs me not to blow his head *off*!' He aimed at Carswell. 'I *mean* it, dog!'

Carswell looked to Romaine for help, but all Romaine could do was encourage him to comply, play for time, keep Turk happy. The xenologist lowered himself onto his knees. 'Please, don't kill me.'

'Please what? Please WHAT!' Turk took a step closer, knuckles straining against skin as his hands tightened around the gun.

'Please don't kill me, sir!' All the blood had drained from Carswell's face and tremors as they raced along his arms. He was feigning nothing this time. One of his legs shifted forward as if he would get up, but moved no further.

Turk exploded into laughter and staggered toward the log that held their weapons. 'Sir! That's great. That's funny. *Sir*,' he mimicked Carswell's shaking voice. 'Ya don't call sergeants *sir*, slick!' Still chuckling, he lay the shotgun on the log and unscrewed the lid of Fisher's canteen and raised the water to his lips.

Romaine felt her eyes on him, questioning the opportunity to rush the blackcap now while he'd dropped the weapon. Romaine shook his head once without looking her way. There was no way they'd make it. Turk was too seasoned, too hyped up. They had to close the distance somehow if they wanted a chance at taking him down. While Turk wiped water from his mouth and stared off into the trees, Romaine met Fisher's gaze then made a subtle motion suggesting they get Turk to move toward them. She blinked her acknowledgement.

'Hey!' Turk was suddenly animated again. 'This is your bottle, princess, ain't it?' He pointed with it, dark eyes fixing her like spotlights made of antimatter. 'What else would make it "better"? Maybe if you and I had some alone time, princess.'

Romaine's breath caught in his throat. He'd been hoping Turk wouldn't go there.

As quickly as it had come, however, that thought fizzled out while another took its place, twisting his features. 'Maybe you could admit you tricked me. You didn't fight fair, did you? You got augments too. Huh? Admit it. Huh?'

Fisher looked genuinely mystified. 'N-no,' she stammered.

'Shutup!' he roared. 'You do! You do have augments! I don't know how you got 'em. Maybe your daddy's rich and bought 'em for ya birthday. But you got 'em, I *know* you do. Ain't no way you coulda beat me without 'em.'

For a moment, Romaine felt a glimmer of hope: if Fisher *had* been augmented like some of the recons, she might get them out of this after all — augments *would* make sense of how she had bested a hulk like Attikula in unarmed combat and killed a couple of Nguwuu. But in the same moment, his hope evaporated as Fisher's puzzlement dissolved it back into fear.

Shit. Back to Plan A. So, what do we do? How do we draw him in? Maybe I could make him angry enough to want to hit me. He found that funny, had to force himself not to laugh. *Yeah, I can take a punch all right. But Fisher can give 'em too. Let's do it, Johnny. Turn on the charm now, son.*

'So what are you on anyway, Turk? A little Hammer? Some Zeus? Harpy Dust? Or maybe it's *U*?' he finished, using the street name of the synth-amphetamine *Utopia*. It certainly wasn't Bliss, that much was obvious.

Turk's eyes narrowed at that final guess. 'Why not? Costs me nuthin'. Good when your boss is your supplier.' At this revelation, his grin took on a maniac sheen as if he'd outsmarted the universe.

'Your ... boss?'

'Hah! The smart cop ain't so smart. Ain't figured it out. Who's fundin' this operation here? Huh?'

'CUSET,' Romaine returned lamely, sure he was missing something.

'But what *part* of CUSET? Huh? Ever heard of Yaghuchi Pharmaceutical and Genetics? Huh? Them's the boss of this particular op. So far, they's the owners here.'

It made sense to Romaine. The discovery of a species of plant that could spawn an entire line of wonder drugs and designer balms. Yaghuchi would be the most interested in such a discovery and the most expert at exploiting it on behalf of all the members of the Corporate Union.

So, they were also supplying *U* to their pet soldiers? He'd always suspected Yaghuchi delved in designer drugs too. Whether Turk arrived at CUSETMA with his addiction in place or it had been cultivated by Yaghuchi, he couldn't be sure. Probably a little from Column A, a little from Column B. Anything that made a tough Marine even tougher, stronger, faster, was sure to be in CUSET's best interests. At least until that Marine was found dead of a heart-attack or aneurism. *Or* until he went out in a blaze of psychotic glory — when such an incident happened, Yaghuchi execs would be at the front of the line of people shaking their heads sadly and denouncing the evils of 'this day and age', evils which they claimed they were working hard to diminish.

He pursed his lips and considered Turk with fresh eyes as the recon bobbed up and down like an excited kid about to get his first pony ride. So there was more incentive for the blackcaps to expedite this job than the mere fate of the human race. 'You're on *two* payrolls. CUSETMA and Yaghuchi.'

Turk clicked his fingers, gave Romaine a wink and a thumbs up. 'You got it, chief. You worked it out. I's prouda you! We're all on their payroll. All on their payroll. Magic, Fester, Vgrevski, Chua, even that dog Lieutenant. Recons for hire!' he shouted to the trees. He paused to sip from Fisher's canteen. 'Recons for hire. Recons for hire.' He rolled the words around in his mouth several times more, savoring the feel of them.

Carswell murmured something like 'I knew it'.

Turk giggled around the mouth of Fisher's canteen, dribbling water down his neck and coughing slightly as he added, 'And it's your indigs who's holdin' back my bonus, Carswell.' He cursed in Turkish, suddenly flipping from manic good humor to severely pissed-off.

Carswell only just ducked in time to avoid being hit in the head by Fisher's canteen. The last dregs of water splashed onto the tree trunk behind him.

'Ok, ok,' Romaine said soothingly. 'Maybe we can still help you get those bonuses.'

Turk snorted another curse in his native tongue and ran a hand over his face. Romaine could see the pilot light of the man's rage had stayed lit for days, but something about what Romaine had said had abruptly turned the gas to full. 'Too late, dog. 'S too late. We hadda have that plant harvested two days ago to get the bonus. *His indigs screwed it up!*'

Turk had raised the shotgun as he bawled this last sentence. Chest constricting, Romaine knew the time for talk was over; there would be no further stalling. He saw Turk's finger moving to the trigger, then Fisher moving fast, sprinting to intervene...

Fisher reeled backwards, falling, rendered starkly against a halo of red spray. Carswell spun around the tree and crashed through underbrush, obscured by the bulk of the tree, now jinking from side to side with Turk lunging after him, Turk firing once twice three times – some obscure part of Romaine's mind counting the shots that had been fired.

That's four shots now – he has six left at the most!

And Romaine was stumbling toward her, toward Fisher, walking through treacle, pushing through a riptide of time. Turk was back, striding around the tree, striding toward *him* now, Romaine out of time, out of luck ...

Something flew from the trees behind Romaine and lanced through the Marine's left thigh above the knee. Turk pitched sideways, firing past Romaine and into the bush. Romaine reached Fisher –

Her mouth worked, blood bubbling up in it like the living pile of beetles they'd passed that morning, her throat convulsing.

Romaine's own mouth worked, but no words emerged.

Not her! God not her!

Funny how fast the mind worked, *how* the mind worked; in the space between another two shotgun blasts, he thought of Harshini, felt the steel bands he'd wound around those memories completely relaxing, finally allowed the guilt to wash over him, the shame of not touching her while she died, the shame of keeping himself clean and unsullied by her blood her fear her agony, found motivation in remorse, motivation in Fisher's perplexed childlike expression, reached out to touch her, to try to keep her from leaving him, to throw a lifeline that might stop her sinking into the abyss.

Not her, not her.

The shotgun boomed one last time.

He grabbed her hand. *No! She might not feel it! Her head, her head.*

He plunged his fingers into her hair, lifting her head, felt the almost comforting warmth of her body fluids touching his knee where it pressed into the hard stones in the creek bed, vaguely registered the smell, the result of bowels and bladder loosening.

He stared into her face, her eyes flicking around with great intensity as if taking in the world one last time. They settled on him. Something indefinable, rose from them, something mystical, passing through his own eyes and into his heart, settling there like a bird in a nest. Romaine startled with the touch of it.

And then, he was in another reality, where he was not looking at Jennifer Fisher any longer but at the glazed and waxy eyes of a corpse.

'No ...'

Clack!

The shotgun was empty, the hammer closing on an empty chamber. His enemy, her murderer, was down on one hip, injured leg stretched awkwardly in front of him. Turk removed one hand from the gun and snapped one side of the arrow in his thigh by squeezing his massive fist around it.

Then Romaine had launched himself from the ground with an energy he didn't know he possessed, crashing into the distracted Marine before he could react, plunging his fingers into the leg wound.

Turk roared. The shotgun clattered away but the big man clubbed Romaine across the ear with his forearm, stunning him, knocking him aside.

Time passed. A second? A year?

Flat on his back, Romaine watched a missile sail by overhead. He craned his neck to see Scarface bowl into Turk, twisted onto hands and knees to see better though spots blotted his vision. Marine and Jarinyi rolled across the ground, piling against the mess of debris across the stream. In no time, Scarface lost the upper hand, with Turk on top of him, the Marine's forearm across the Jarinyi's throat. Scarface's bone knife had wedged in the webbing hanging from the back of Turk's armor, and his wiry arms were pinned.

Woozy, Romaine got up and staggered past them to the pile of confiscated weapons and equipment. He leveled his handgun at Turk, surprised when his hand didn't shake. Turk and Scarface were only two steps away from him — his finger curled on the trigger — but firing carelessly could hit the Jarinyi.

'Hey!' he shouted.

Turk's face whipped around and Scarface took advantage of the distraction, headbutting the Marine in the ear and wrenching a hand free. Almost too fast for Romaine to register, the free hand whipped out and latched onto a splintered torn end of a branch lying nearby, pulling it close. As Turk's face came around and his right eye met the stick coming across and up. The blackcap spasmed, and slumped.

Kicking and clawing, the Jarinyi dragged himself from under the deadweight of his adversary. He swiped at the goo of blood and water and brain matter coating his face while Romaine's gun-hand drooped and they traded gazes for a long moment. Insect-analogs began to chir again, ferns *shoosh*ed in a fresh and lazy breeze, a bird-analog squawked – the noises of the forest reasserting themselves where moments before had been the sounds of violence.

DUSK CAME SUDDENLY TO THE FOREST FLOOR. IN THE PREMATURE GLOOM, two beings from different worlds and different species stared down at the remains of one of their own, someone they had counted a friend.

Scarface stood above the decapitated body of Tuttut, humming quietly.

Romaine rested again in the twigs and pebbles by Fisher's side, staring at her lifeless eyes. Eyes that should still be drinking in their surrounds, or turned attentively to the needs of another being, or clouded in thought. Those were the things that the real Jennifer Fisher's eyes would do. *Should do. Again. And again. For decades to come.*

But they wouldn't.

She was gone.

Romaine hadn't cried since he was eight years old. Hadn't cried all through late childhood and adolescence while his parents dragged him from Santa Fe, from Christchurch, from Vancouver, from Tokyo, from Dublin – up-rooting his life over and again. Hadn't cried when his father's crimes caught up with him. Hadn't cried on any of the three terrifying nights he'd sheltered behind a dumpster in back of Seattle's Westlake Center until taken in by a kind cop and his family. Hadn't cried when his mother hanged herself in her psych ward three months after that.

And he hadn't even cried over Harshini.

But a wisp of Corporal Jennifer Fisher's auburn hair wafting gracefully in the breeze broke the dam. Romaine felt himself sucked into a singularity of desolation.

Scarface looked up at the noise. No, not danger. Just something strange. The Man-Judge, convulsed as if vomiting. Yet nothing came from his mouth but the kind of strangled gasps of an ensnared animal. Water poured across the Man's cheeks as if waterfalls were hiding behind his eyes.

Scarface huffed in sudden comprehension. The Judge was in agony over the loss of his friend. Sadness twisted the warrior's chest and he groaned deeply in sympathy.

He squatted. Gently, he turned Warm Heart from his side onto his stomach, settling the skinny arms by his sides. The earth would ultimately claim this body, after the forest creatures had taken what they needed from it. These would be Warm Heart's final gifts to the world. Then his soul would fly to the stars to be one with the Creator, as it should be.

He stood again and turned toward the Judge. Now he believed. The Men who were evil like Nguwuu wore shells on their back. The others like the Judge and the Furface and the newly dead female-warrior – they had souls and feelings, just as Jarinyi did. The Judge had lost his friend and he mourned.

Just as I do.

Perhaps this Man served the Creator. Perhaps Furface did too. Perhaps Furface was the Cssoool after all.

Scarface wished he knew how to join the Man-Judge in mourning, how they could combine their grief. But pragmatism – survival instinct – took over. Where there was one of the Man-warriors, there might be more. This dead one, he had found a way to blend without actually blending, a clever act. Perhaps others could do it, perhaps more were around.

Also there was a strong odor of death upon the air now: it might draw other dangers besides Men. Scarface needed to check the area while the Judge mourned. He bounded to the tree beneath which the Judge mourned the female-warrior and began to climb.

IT FELT LIKE COMING BACK TO LIFE, ROMAINE'S MIND CLAMBERING ITS WAY out of the pit of despair and dragging him into the real world.

His throat stung, his knees and palms ached, his face was cool but tight with tears. Within him a vault had opened up and freed some psychic space he hadn't known he owned. Blinking his eyes into focus, he raised himself into an ungainly squat and pulled the dog tags from Fisher's neck before they could become glued there by congealing blood around the devastation of her chest. He wiped the tags clean on his pants. The blast hadn't hit her shirt pocket; Romaine knew she kept a battered paper journal there. He retrieved it, checked to confirm it was a diary as he suspected, and shoved her belongings into a pocket of his own. It belonged to her family now.

Above him, Scarface perched on a branch like a hawk. Romaine wasn't sure what had prompted the warrior to intervene but it probably hadn't been affection for him.

Nearby the body of Tuttut lay on his stomach now. Scarface must have turned him over. Alien or not, Romaine felt a pang of sorrow for the little guy. Two of the kindest beings he could imagine, both dead. Senselessly, needlessly dead.

Their murderer lay dead himself, unable to answer for his crimes with the kind of lingering punishment Romaine would sorely have loved to inflict upon him.

But Turk was not the primary cause of the deaths, not really. He'd merely been a loose cannon set here by rich and greedy people who wanted to be richer and more powerful. So much of what was wrong with the universe was due to these people, time and time again. The faceless nameless ones who sat high and dry in strong towers while peons murdered and raped and pillaged on their behalf. Anger roiled, white-hot hatred ballooning within him. He hated them purely and simply, these pukes who'd willingly spread the cancer of their selfishness into his life, destroying everything beautiful that ever came his way.

Fisher was dead. Turk was responsible, Todd was responsible, as were Glass and the people in charge all the way to Yaghuchi and maybe beyond.

On the tree branch above, Scarface made a sound. The meaning was unclear. Romaine shook his head. Where had this guy come from when he'd attacked Turk? He must have been tracking them, shadowing them. He'd saved Romaine's life but he hadn't been fast enough to save Fisher's.

If you'd been a little quicker, you –

He bit down on the thought. The Jarinyi didn't deserve that. And, he realized, he might yet need Scarface to survive.

Or maybe he wouldn't need him at all.

Rummaging around Turk's armor he quickly found what he was looking for. Turk's long-range commlink.

'No more tears now; I will think about revenge.'

— Mary Stuart, Queen of Scots

SATISFIED *the area was as safe as he could gauge it to be, Scarface climbed from the tree and joined the Judge where the Man stood studying a new object, turning it over and over in his hands. Another weapon? It didn't look like one. But that meant nothing. The Men's weapons were mysterious. Mysterious and powerful. He had seen the remains of his Tribe's summer camp. What hope did his people have of protecting the sacred patch of Leaf against creatures who could tear trees from the ground? The Men would bring more weapons, more flying things, more warriors. Eventually they would overpower his people. What could he do in the face of this?*

The sound of approaching feet cut across his thoughts. He had started blending in reflex before he recognized the footfall. The Furface approached.

Distracted and fuzzy, Romaine had assumed the person standing over near Fisher to be Scarface. But Scarface was beside him, he realized, studying the commlink. A whiff of very human body odor snapped Romaine's head around in recognition.

'You,' he said. He hoped his tone conveyed all the words he wanted to say but couldn't find the energy for.

'I ... I'm sorry, Romaine.' Gaping at Fisher's ravaged corpse, Carswell sounded genuine, looked pensive, miserable, stricken.

Romaine shifted attention to Scarface. 'You didn't need to do that, buddy.' Scarface reached out a hand and gripped Romaine's shoulder briefly before letting it rest on his bony hip. Something grew between them, the connection forged only in battle perhaps. Maybe there were things this warrior could understand, even without the translator. 'Get out of here. I'll give you twenty minutes before I call for evac.'

Scarface cocked his head, didn't move.

Romaine sighed and said louder, 'Go on, *get*.'

'What are you doing?' Carswell asked.

Romaine shifted hostile eyes toward him without turning his head. 'Tell your friend to get out of here or the flier'll pick up his life signs.'

Carswell – who'd spent the last few days staying a step ahead in whatever chess game he was playing in his head – now seemed lost. 'What flier?'

Romaine lifted the commlink.

Carswell gasped. 'You *didn't*?'

'Not yet. I'll give him twenty minutes. Tell him.'

Carswell took a step toward him and away from Fisher. 'Romaine, let's talk about this. Twenty minutes won't give him enough time. And if they see ... Tuttut's ... body, they'll go looking for more Jarinyi. They'll find him.' He pointed at Scarface, Romaine noted, in the Jarinyi fashion, using all four fingers, thumb tucked into his palm. 'They'll find him,' he hissed more desperately.

'You, I don't owe anything. You're filth. You ran while she –' He choked, but forced his throat to open, to emit words. 'While she threw herself in the way and took the blast you should have taken.'

Carswell had the sense to look ashamed, remorseful, shoulders hunching. 'If I could change that... I would. Romaine, he killed my friend too.'

'Forty minutes, then. But that's it. Tell him.'

Carswell frowned at Romaine through the gathering gloom. 'Listen. He won't stand a chance. Let's finish what we started; I'll take you near Columbus before letting you walk the rest of the way yourself. He can leave us now and have a hope of reaching shelter before they send a flier out to recover these bodies in the morning.'

'You want to take me the rest of the way? Over*night*?'

Carswell gestured toward the line of debris that marked the edge of the ruined Jarinyi campsite. His voice was equal parts desperation and wrath. 'That is what CUSET thinks of the Jarinyi. *That* is what CUSET thinks of the Jarinyi,' he repeated pointing at Tuttut without looking at him. 'It'll happen to him too – what do you call him? – Scarface. You want him dead too?'

Romaine shook his head and pretended to study his seiko, ran a finger around it. Fifteen years old, it had now received its first set of scratches. 'Thirty-nine minutes.'

Carswell growled with frustration.

Romaine fished in Turk's pockets until he found a set of night-vision lenses he could clip on the bridge of his nose. He slipped them into his own shirt pocket for later, patting at the bulge. Carswell wandered about, muttering to himself. Scarface watched them both in silence.

Thirty-nine minutes.

As tough as he was, as gifted and talented as he was, Scarface was no match for the storm of CUSET force that would descend on this forest in the weeks ahead, sweeping away the finely balanced ecology, the Jarinyi culture, perhaps the very existence of the indigenous inhabitants of this region. Romaine might not owe Carswell anything, but he owed his life to this warrior. He owed him more than a forty-minute head start. But there was a bigger problem to solve here than how both he and Scarface could survive the night. Far bigger than the murder he had originally been sent to investigate. The cause of all the ills that had befallen this world in the last two weeks boiled down to Tigerclaw.

He dropped the commlink to his side, frowning at Scarface. 'So what do we do about it?'

Carswell wheeled and stomped closer. 'What? What?'

He smelled more than Carswell's rancid funk now, realizing that he'd knelt in Fisher's piss and blood as she'd died. One knee was stained with it, still damp.

How did I not smell that before now?

Fisher. Dear Fisher.

There's enough Tigerclaw for all of us on this world if we looked properly, she had said. *We don't have to steal it from the Pumpkin Patch.* A noble sentiment, just like her other noble sentiments, ones that had gotten her killed like *My life exists to improve the lives of others*

He stiffened as a thought hit him.

We don't have to steal it from the Pumpkin Patch.

The Pumpkin Patch!

'Carswell! The legend that Tuttut told us, the one about where Tigerclaw came from. He said it grows aggressively when left to itself and destroys other plant life.'

'What of it?'

'While we were chatting yesterday, Fisher mentioned she'd seen a tree dying at the edge of the Pumpkin Patch with Tigerclaw seedlings all around its base.'

'Hm. The Jarinyi mustn't have seen it happening. Usually they remove the plants before they encroach upon the forest.'

'Carswell. Where there's a little bit of Tigerclaw, might there be more?'

The xenologist made an impatient sound. 'What? What are you talking about?'

'How much Tigerclaw is in this forest would you say?'

'In total? How would I know? There's at least one kind of bird that eats the fruit and spreads the seeds. You see a few plants here and there. But you certainly don't see big patches of it.'

'But it does grow out here? You and Tuttut said the Jarinyi's sacred task is to uproot it wherever they find it.'

'Sure. They pull it up, dry it and use it later. What are you getting at, man?'

'They stockpile it! Get your translator out. Get it out!'

Carswell fumbled to comply. When it was on, Romaine snatched it away and faced Scarface. As he started talking, he saw the slow dawn of comprehension and hope upon Carswell's face.

The translator interpreted his first words with no error noises. 'Tigerclaw. Men want it. Jarinyi want it. Jarinyi protect it. Jarinyi protect the forest. This is true?'

Scarface cocked his head one way then the other. 'Yes.'

'It grows under the trees. You don't want it to grow there. It will kill the trees if Jarinyi do not take it away. This is true?'

'Yes.'

'When you take it away, *where* do you take it?'

Scarface rolled his shoulders one way then the other, presumably considering whether or not to answer. He jabbed four fingers at the mountains and then through the trees to the east.

Romaine heard the pitch change in his own voice as he asked, 'You store it up?'

When the Jarinyi didn't respond, Carswell took over, the excitement plain in his own voice. 'You put the Tigerclaw in the mountains?'

'In holes there. Also we leave it with the River Tribe. They have many dry holes also.'

The two humans regarded each other with optimism, their enmity momentarily forgotten. The Jarinyi had more Tigerclaw than they could ever use and they stockpiled it.

'I'm thinking–' Romaine started.

'We might just be able to salvage this situation,' Carswell finished.

'And protect the Jarinyi. *If* there's enough of it. And if it's still useful to our eggheads after it's been sitting in a cave for years. Got another idea though.' He raised the translator toward Scarface. 'Friend. Men need Tigerclaw to stop a great sickness. It is killing Men. Up there. In the stars.'

Scarface looked toward the dim sky above and said, 'Cssoool told me.'

'Ok. You know it. Good. I think Creator -' He waited until the translator caught up, the name for the Jarinyi deity cementing Scarface's attention and interest. 'Creator sent us here. To your world, your *forest*. He wants you to help us.'

'The *tuttuttut* is sacred. Men must not take Tigerclaw from there.'

'The Pumpkin Patch, he means,' Carswell said.

'Yah, I got that. What if...' He faltered, the translator *tutt*ing at him. Perhaps the Jarinyi didn't think in hypotheticals. Better to keep it concrete and simple. 'I can talk to the Men. Stop the killing. The Men could help you, not kill you.'

Scarface made a *fwwth* sound. 'You, Judge, can help us. You are good. Bad Warrior Men not help us.'

Romaine winced. Scarface hated and distrusted the Marines. And with good reason. This was perhaps his one chance to make a pitch that could simultaneously solve the interspecies tensions and mutually exclusive goals of both races. And Romaine was no diplomat, just a cop. No training for diplomacy; no real understanding of the nuances of Jarinyi culture and values. No -

'Just say it, Romaine, for Christ's sake,' Carswell hissed. 'He's a warrior, a cop. Like you.'

Romaine cleared his throat. 'Friend. Men can stop going ... to the sacred ... place. Men can take Tigerclaw from the forest. Men can stop Tigerclaw from killing trees. Men can help Jarinyi; Jarinyi can help Men.'

Scarface was quiet an unnervingly long time, before a tremor rippled across his shoulders and down his torso. He put a hand on Romaine's shoulder, gills flaring. Romaine grimaced at the horse-smell of the Jarinyi's breath but didn't pull back. Gingerly, he put his own hand on Scarface's shoulder in imitation.

'You are Judge,' said Scarface. 'I will speak to my Elder and to River Tribe's Elder. We will talk much. I cannot *tuttuttututtut*.'

'I think he means he can't promise anything,' Carswell said. He reached for Romaine's other shoulder. 'But this is the beginning of a solution. As long as you can keep CUSET from trampling this forest into the dust while they're about it.'

Romaine pulled away. 'I can't promise anything either. We'll just have to see where this idea takes us.' He turned back to Scarface and asked him about the stockpiled Tigerclaw.

Scarface assured him he'd discuss that with the Elders too. But first Romaine had to convince the 'Warrior Men' to stop hurting Jarinyi. 'You are our Judge with the Men,' he said in closing.

'I'm guessing that means I just accepted a temporary post as ambassador.'

Carswell sobered. 'You really think that, Romaine? That stuff about God's will?'

'No. Maybe. How the hell should I know? It sounded good when I said it.' *And maybe, just maybe it is true*, he thought with a sad glance toward the dark mound of Fisher's body.

USING ROMAINE'S PLAZER, CARSWELL AND SCARFACE MADE A LARGE FIRE in the creek bed where Romaine could sit by the bodies of Tuttut and Fisher while he waited. He had promised them a two-hour head start before he commed Columbus. Carswell assured him there was a hidey hole they could reach by then where they could sit out the night before they returned to their hidden valley.

'Anyway,' continued, 'I have my radio up there in the hills. The Elder took it up there for me. Let me know when it's safe to meet on the plateau where the two dead bodies are. Use the codeword *Tuttut* to signal it's safe.'

Romaine told him to stay away from the rock ledge tomorrow because he'd be taking Glass there after sending his case files offworld. He submitted to a handshake, a brief one. He hadn't forgotten Carswell's manipulation and treachery - nor would he ever find it in his heart to forgive it - but at least they shared a common goal now. Scarface mimicked the handshake, making Romaine smile.

As the two figures faded into the shadows, his smile faded with them. He gathered the available weapons and kit, settling by the fire.

Marking the time with his SCRoLL, he began to arrange his data so as to present a tight case against Todd and Turk.

From time to time, the fickle flickers of firelight would play curiously upon the wall of trees around him, and Romaine would look up expecting God-only-knew-what to come leaping out, growling and hissing at him. But there were only trees. Occasionally those same flickers of light would play across the body of Fisher in such a way as to pull at his peripheral vision, making it seem as if she'd moved. In those moments he would cast his eyes her way, would remember her in life, refusing any longer to be the guy who never looked back, who ignored his ghosts and demons.

Ah, Fisher.

He wondered: if there was a heaven, did it reserve a special place for cops who'd paid the ultimate sacrifice? He hoped that wherever she was, Jennifer Fisher was proud of the choice she'd made. For his part, he would make sure that it meant something. That her life's dream, to make a mark upon the universe, would be fulfilled.

Even in death.

My life exists to improve the lives of others, she'd said.

Fisher, Fisher, Fisher. Let's see if we can do something for the Jarinyi then.

His SCRoLL chimed gently when the two hours were up. He nodded and continued working on his files for another twenty minutes before reaching for the comm.

THE KNOT OF PEOPLE PARTED AROUND THE REAPER'S LANDING PAD, allowing it to settle. When the rear door slid open and Romaine stepped wearily onto the ground of Camp Columbus, many of the civs recoiled, muttering at his appearance. With Chua and McGrath shepherding him toward the Medcentre, Romaine felt the stares keenly. A hot flush crept up his cheeks, touched the back of his neck. They were staring at him as if he were a leper. Or a PBT carrier.

Or a Jarinyi.

He twisted, snatching his elbow out of reach as McGrath tried to grab it.

'We need to get you to Sickbay,' she said in the unfriendliest show of concern he'd ever heard.

He was pleased to see an honor guard of four regulars carrying Fisher's body bag along in his wake. Ignoring McGrath, he turned to Chua.

'Where are they taking her?'

'The meat locker, back of the sickbay. Where Gutierrez is.'

'Make sure they take care of her, Sergeant? No autopsies. No mishaps. She's been through enough. You get me?'

An odd expression crossed her face, like a breeze brushing still water. It might have been respect. She nodded. 'Yes, *sir*.'

McGrath looked displeased as Chua marched back to the group holding Fisher's bag. She muttered something to the regulars then gently took Fisher's body in her own arms, carrying her like a child. A child sealed inside a body bag. She passed Romaine and McGrath, her mouth set in a sympathetic line. 'Let's go, sir. You need the Doc to take a good look at you. I'll take care of Corporal Fisher.'

'Where's the Colonel?' he asked, when McGrath ushered him through the door. Chua disappeared into the back of the building with the body bag. The knot of people following at a distance broke up behind them, the murmured conversation dissolving as they moved off.

McGrath's expression was wary. 'Doing Colonel stuff. He said to welcome you back and he'll debrief you after you've been examined. And had a shower.'

Romaine wondered if he now smelt like Carswell. Ranarith sat him on a bed, fussing over him. As the small physician cut away his torn and filthy shirt, McGrath turned her back disinterestedly, staring out the open doorway. Chua returned and slumped onto another bed, studying Romaine's bare torso. She winked when he caught her looking.

'Sir,' she added.

Romaine actually felt himself chuckle at that.

The camp physician placed a thermometer in Romaine's ear then made him drink something that tasted like sea water.

'What's this?' Romaine spluttered. The bottle was awfully big. He was thirsty, but not that thirsty. And it was nasty stuff.

'Oral rehydration salts. Drink it.' Ranarith shifted a packet from the bench beside the bed to Romaine's lap. 'Then take this in four hours, dissolved in one liter of drinking water.' He pushed the bottle to Romaine's lips again.

Romaine pulled away. 'Can't I drink this later?'

'It's this or an IV. Up to you.'

My, we are snippy tonight.

He took the bottle from Ranarith and sipped while the physician pulled out the thermometer and squinted at it. He tossed it aside, attached a heart monitor and took a blood sample. Upon removing the needle, Ranarith pressed a small gauze pad to Romaine's arm and told him to hold it there for thirty seconds. Then he peeled off his gloves and dropped them in a tiny incinerator unit. 'And don't touch anything. Or anyone,' he snapped as he stomped off into the lab section of the building with the syringe.

'Nice bedside manner.'

'Dunno how you did it, sir,' Chua said.

Romaine took another sip, grimaced and placed the water bottle carefully on the bedside table. The packet of salts, he transferred to his trouser pocket. 'With a little help from Fisher. A lot actually.' For the time being, he'd leave the Jarinyi and Carswell out of it. That was information to be handled carefully.

'Where did you *go*?'

'Around. It's a big wilderness out there.'

She dropped her head as she seemed to struggle with a thought, then she asked, 'And Turk. He just ... found you? And killed her?'

McGrath made a scoffing noise from the door. 'And that indig that was dead there too? Maybe Turk was saving their asses from it?'

'Turk murdered him. In cold blood.' The words came out in a rush before he could stop them. He detected sympathy in Chua. But in

McGrath, there was a hardness that said *You mean less to me than a gram of spit*. It reminded him of Todd, of Glass. Of Dreyfuss.

'You needn't concern yourself about it,' he said to her. 'I'll tell the rest to the CO, when he can break away from his Coloneling business long enough to see me. I'd like you to wait outside.'

McGrath stiffened. 'You what?'

'That's "You what, *sir*". Wait outside.' She hesitated, face clouding. He told her, 'See, what you do is you go through the door, to a place where there's no roof. That's called outside. Then you close the door behind you.'

McGrath chewed her cheek for a while. 'My orders are to stay with you.'

Chua intervened before Romaine could respond, surprising him. 'We got those orders from the Looey. The Commander here outranks him. Out you go.'

Now anger contorted McGrath's face, her fists clenching. 'I didn't just hear that.'

'It's called chain-of-command, girl. You want I should go out too, sir?'

He pretended to consider that for a moment. 'Nah, I need someone to update me on what's happening with PBT et cetera. Can you do that?'

'Certainly can, sir.'

McGrath took the three steps necessary to place her directly outside the door, then she whirled again to present the most childishly smartass expression on an adult face that Romaine had ever seen. It was not endearing.

'Shut the door please, Sergeant,' he told Chua and lay his head back on the pillow. He didn't need to see the venomous look he knew would pass between the women as she complied.

When Chua pulled a chair over to his bed, he began to apologize for any trouble he may have caused her, but she shrugged it off. 'Just following orders, sir, being professional.'

She flipped the chair backwards and straddled it.

'Professional, huh?' he asked.

She shrugged and smiled again.

'So tell me what you can.'

She tapped a short rhythm on the chair back. 'First, I have to ask you something.'

She caught herself as Ranarith returned. The medico was clearly unhappy that Romaine seemed fine. He unhooked the heart monitor and began swabbing Romaine's cuts and bruises, none too gently. After a minute of this, he registered that he'd interrupted something. Still swabbing, he turned his gaze from Romaine to Chua who gave him a long cold stare. The meaning was obvious. At first the physician looked incredulous: she was ordering a Captain out of the room. But then, considering her size as well as the fact that she had Romaine's support, he made a *pfff* noise, threw the swabs on the floor and trudged outside, slamming the door behind him.

'He'll be straight over to the Colonel's office,' Romaine said.

'McGrath probably beat him to it. Sir, I been talking to Donaldson.' When he looked askance at her, she said, 'She's the pilot who brought you in. She told me something I don't wanna believe. But I don't know why she'd lie.'

'What'd she say?'

She shook her head. 'Just gotta ask *you* one question. I need to know the truth about this and you can trust me to keep my mouth shut. I'm better at that than Donaldson is.'

'What's the question?'

'Were you and Fisher up on that mountain?' When he blinked but didn't answer, she added, 'Yesterday morning.'

Romaine nodded. He held her gaze until she broke contact, her face tightening in anger.

After a moment, Romaine got it. 'The flier. They *saw* us?'

Chua tapped the chair again. And mimicked Romaine's nod.

He rolled toward her and lowered his voice, more for her sake than his. If the room was bugged, his SCRoLL would take care of it. But she didn't know that. 'Who exactly saw us and left us there?'

It took a while, but eventually she raised two fingers and lay them on her shoulder.

Lieutenant's bars.

The anger that had warmed Romaine's chest for hours now metamorphosed into a cold knot, a slab of marble laid against the inside of his ribs. Todd had seen them and left them there to die. Todd was the center of gravity for all that had gone wrong here.

'And the rest of your team who I haven't seen tonight?' Romaine asked quietly, keeping his anger from his voice, his tone gentle, sympathetic. He needed information now, and a way to ensure Chua was onside. 'Todd made it, right? But they didn't?'

It was apparent she understood his inference. She made a fist as if to punch her own thigh but shook it out then folded her thick arms.

When she spoke again, it was so softly Romaine had to strain to understand her. 'You know, you do your job. You don't know anything else. Just your job. You get on the bird, land somewhere, do what the situation requires. You do what they tell you. But sometimes you wonder if you should.'

Romaine let the silence settle for a long time. She obviously had more to tell – about Turk, about Todd, about Yaghuchi bonuses, about things he couldn't imagine – but it would take finesse and a more secure venue to get it out of her. If she and Donaldson would return to BV with him and testify, then finally he could see some genuine justice done. And the man whose actions had ultimately led to Fisher's death could rot in a penal colony for the rest of his natural life. A life that Romaine hoped would be cruelly and mercilessly long.

Romaine sighed, struggled off the bed and onto his feet. Every damned part of him hurt. *Guess a nice quiet coma is out of the question.*

'C'mon,' he said. 'I was ordered to take a shower. You can brief me on PBT on the way over there.'

McGrath was not waiting outside.

"... the only real tragedy in life is being used by personally-minded men for purposes which you recognize to be base."

- *Of Man and Superman*, George Bernard Shaw

IT COULD HAVE BEEN the single greatest shower of Romaine's life but he couldn't stay under it for nearly as long as he wanted, and he couldn't just stand there enjoying it.

Not with what he needed to get done.

Not after what he'd just heard from Chua.

The past two days' messagepackets told of a catastrophe in the making. Twenty-four hours after its Orbital Platform had been infected, PBT had broken out at Theseus's south pole. Yun Dao looked to be going the way of Fu Xing. A bunch of Chinese stations had been locked down. No one knew any more about Chinese space than that, because the PRC had cut communications with CUSET out here in space. On earth, various sides were making noises about war. Some CUSET ships had gone missing; for all anyone knew, they were fleeing for earth and carrying the virus. *Waypoint2* was off-limits, nonresponsive to communications.

So far Oceana, Centauri, the Dioscurin Moons and the research community on the Anachromite world Anticus and the Chinese planet Pride of Mao seemed unscathed. But people on Centauri had found out about PBT via a pedecaster leak. New riots broke out. Martial law had been declared.

Chua had simply shrugged when he'd asked about Bona Vista. And he'd left her outside the male amenities block while he'd showered and his own thoughts spiraled into despair.

For the last few days, the gritty demands of sheer survival – and the horrors of losing people – had diminished the more distant threat of pandemic *out there*. As much as he owed justice to Fisher and Gutierrez and Tuttut, there was a more immediate issue to deal with first. He had to bring Glass the news that the Jarinyi might yet share their resources.

Regretfully he turned off the water jets, and lingered a few moments more in the steam with his head against the wall, savoring the moment of feeling utterly clean. Then he came out to find his MI uniform and undies, laundered and pressed and waiting on the bench seats. Someone had left them without him knowing. The crispness of clean clothes was almost as intoxicating as the shower. At the scrape of boots, he looked up to see Chua entering the room. He was glad he was almost dressed, with only his boots to pull on.

'Time to see the boss?' he asked.

The tall Sergeant stood at ease, hands behind her back. 'When you're ready, sir.'

'Fisher?' he asked lightly as he started lacing his right boot.

'In the ... meat locker. Where I left her.'

'As soon as I can be ferried up to my ship, I'll take her with me. If I can send a message tonight, to get authorization for her body to remain completely under my jurisdiction, that'll make things easier. To see her safely home, I mean.'

Something like a stress fracture rippled across Chua's face for a moment before the dam wall settled into place over her emotions. 'I'll take watch once I escort you to the CO. Make sure she's not disturbed.'

She shifted her feet. 'You must be tired, sir. Sure you don't want a nap before you see the Colonel?'

'There's a strong chance the Jarinyi will provide us with a large supply of Tigerclaw tomorrow. If I can set it up safely with the Colonel.'

She blinked at that and hummed a little.

Legs complaining, Romaine stood, rolled his sleeves. 'Take me to your leader.'

THE MESS WAS EMPTY AT THAT TIME OF NIGHT, THE CEILING AT HALF lighting, bain-maries dark and cold. A lone coffee pot gurgled happily at one end of the service counter. Bob Glass lifted it and poured himself a mug when Romaine entered, giving the newcomer a tight smile.

'Romaine! Coffee?' The Colonel poured cream into his cup and grabbed four sachets of sugar. 'Good to see you alive, by the way.'

Romaine shook his head no for the coffee. He slipped a hand into a pile of stale danishes and confiscated two, stuck a banana from the fruit bowl in his breast pocket for later and followed Glass to a table across the aisle from where Todd already sat. The recon officer regarded him coolly.

'Lieutenant.'

'Glad to see you, Commander.'

Glass let out a *I just remembered something* noise. 'Where are my manners?' From the seat beside him, he produced a bottle: brown liquid with a red label. 'Get the Commander a cup, Sean.'

Romaine waved a *no* at that offer too. Todd hadn't budged anyway. 'Thought you ran a dry camp,' he said.

'I do,' Glass replied. 'But I also believe in the tradition of rank having its privileges. A belt might do you good. From the look of you.'

Romaine's eyes felt like they were sliding out of their sockets. His head ached. His muscles ached. His soul ached. *Sure I want it*, he thought and shook his head. 'All yours.'

Glass moved the bottle aside. 'Holy Hannah, you must have a story to tell!' Holding the sugar packets in a cluster, he tore the tops off them in one practiced movement and poured them into his coffee. The swishing sound of the sugar reminded Romaine of the breeze whispering through the trees in the forest. The clink of the spoon as the CO stirred was the sound Jarinyi fire-rocks made when struck together.

He tried to eat while the colonel went through his ritual. The danish tasted like filtered air, flavorless and dry. Romaine regarded it reprovingly for a moment then dropped it onto the table, chewing without enthusiasm.

'Bad luck about Fisher,' Glass said and blew on his coffee. Todd dropped his eyes and nodded with just the right amount of gloominess.

'Sure is,' Romaine replied. Swallowing the lump of pastry in his mouth was like swallowing the false goodwill in the room.

Glass sipped loudly. 'You know what I'll miss when it all goes pear-shaped, when this virus unravels our mighty civilization? Coffee.' He blew over the rim again. 'Shee-it, man, I'm able to travel between stars. I've seen things my granddaddy couldn't imagine. I've cuddled a baby Anachromite. I've looked through a viewport into the heart of a star. I sleep every night in a bed that shapes itself to my body and folds into a briefcase when I pick up and move. I enjoy all the trappings, the results of twenty thousand years of human progress.' He sipped again, smacked his lips and swished his mug. 'But coffee, my friends? Coffee is the single greatest thing in the galaxy. And I'm gonna miss it, terribly.'

Before Romaine could decide whether or not to interrupt, Glass squared his shoulders and gave Romaine a candid look.

'And it will unravel you know,' the colonel continued. 'The way things are now, it's obvious we've done too little too late. Like the bean-counting imbeciles they are, Management haven't sent me anywhere near enough troops or eggheads. If they'd sent more with us a week ago, it might have made all the difference. But by the time we leave this planet, there won't be much out there to return to. Populations deci-mated, a few survivors descending into lawlessness, facing outbreaks of other diseases as the bodies start rotting. I mean, the good thing for *us* is we can take some Tigerclaw with us, find a way to use it. We can keep a small number of people safe, hang secure in orbit somewhere for a year and maybe resettle some small colony. We could create a safe haven here, even – find a nice quiet island, farm, create some law and order. But most of those poor buggers out there?' He slurped coffee then shook his head sadly.

'Maybe we can raid a coffee warehouse and bring it all back here,' Todd suggested, his eyes on Romaine.

'Great idea, Lieutenant. Good to stay positive.' His next slurp was a loud one and he smacked his lips in pleasure as he put the mug aside. 'So. Commander Romaine. Where are we with your side of things?'

Romaine steepled his hands in front of him. 'I'm hoping we can avert the kind of apocalypse you were just describing.'

Glass dropped his hands to his sides, slapping the seat loudly. 'Cops! God, I love the way they think. These little cryptic statements designed to bait you. Ok, I'll bite: what's this about averting catastrophe?'

The only hope of putting an end to the killing – both on Eventide and out in the rest of colonized space – was to get Glass onside, get him to consider the plan. Romaine dived in, explaining how Scarface had protected him from Turk, and outlining the ideas he and Scarface had discussed.

As he spoke, Glass's face did nothing but blink. Todd stared as if Romaine were crazy and once asked how he had communicated with the Jarinyi. Romaine could only tell the truth, that Carswell and his translator had helped him with that. Todd lapsed into silence again, jaw working.

After Romaine outlined the deal he'd brokered with Scarface, he fell silent too. The buzz of refrigerators and the coffee pot's gurgle seemed to grow louder and louder. Glass reached for his mug, turning it around and around in his hands. Abruptly, Todd lurched up and away for a coffee of his own.

'Well,' Glass finally said as Todd returned to his table. 'Well, well, well. It's a promising idea, that's for sure. The idea of accessing stock-piles of the plant is worth further thought, but I'm not sure it'll do us much good now. Also, your idea is pretty labor-intensive and as I said, we don't have a large labor force, especially not to scour a forest this size for pockets of weaker Tigerclaw. Then there's the issue of trust. Not sure my people would feel entirely safe associating with the Jarinyi after what's happened, and in *their* territory.'

Romaine straightened in his seat. 'I realize there's a difficulty there, Colonel, but–'

'Maybe if your Jarinyi friends could de-boobytrap the Pumpkin Patch, as a gesture of goodwill?'

'I've just explained to you that the Patch is their sacred space.'

'Starting to sound like Carswell,' Todd groaned.

'Now, now,' Glass scolded. He drained the rest of his coffee and rubbed his cheek with the empty mug. 'Romaine, I'll think about it. But we need what's in the Patch and we need it now.'

'Colonel–'

'It's better yield, it's there for the taking, it might save some lives.'

'Colonel, what they've stockpiled is potentially a lot more than what's in the Pumpkin Patch.'

In his impatience, Romaine had started talking over the top of Glass. Color rose suddenly in the older man's cheeks. He slapped the table top. 'I'm not going crawling on my belly, begging a bunch of monkeys for second-rate medicine when we have the real stuff growing under our noses. For all we know, they'll feed us poison. You don't know this but we took a small team to the Patch this morning and two of our field workers died. The Jarinyi threaded some kind of poison thorn around the base of some of the plants. God knows what else is in there; we've been waiting for some EP suits on the next transport, which is still two days away.' The Colonel put down the empty mug with a clunk. 'And do you know how many Marines they killed that day you disappeared?'

'As many people as he's killed here?' Romaine said, stabbing a finger at Todd.

Glass flinched, his head pivoting between Todd and Romaine. 'Don't tell me you're accusing Sean of Gutierrez's murder? Is that what you're saying?'

'Colonel, I'd like Lieutenant Todd to leave while I discuss this with you.'

'He's not going anywhere.'

'So, all these people I killed, who are they?' Todd asked.

Romaine forced some calm into his voice. 'Let's start at the beginning. There's a case of AR90s missing from supply. All the evidence I've collected says you armed the traditional enemies of the Jarinyi *and* you murdered a Jarinyi, hoping to provoke hostilities. You did this to distract the Jarinyi so you could move in and harvest Tigerclaw unhindered.'

'I don't believe this guy!'

Glass interjected, '*Provoke hostilities*? You're saying Sean killed an indig and they replied in kind? So, you do believe the Jarinyi killed Gutierrez then?'

'Hostilities between Jarinyi and Nguwuu, I meant. I honestly can't yet prove who killed Gutierrez ... but I know it was you, Todd, you or someone you put up to it.'

'Mother of God, you're insane.' Glass thumped the table with his fist making the mug jump and the danishes skitter sideways.

Todd appeared on the verge of violence.

'You give me a chance to make my case, and I think you'll see it, Colonel.'

Glass handed his mug across the aisle to Todd. 'Make me a fresh one.'

Scowling, Todd shot to his feet and obeyed. He slammed the mug down so hard beside the dispenser, Romaine was surprised it didn't shatter.

Glass waved a finger in the air then tapped his ear. 'Have you been listening to me, Romaine. Unless there's a miracle, civilization will crumble somewhere in the next few weeks. Apocalypse, to use your word. It doesn't matter who killed some pissant grunt on some pissant planet nobody ever heard of. It doesn't even matter whether someone took those rifles or if there were any goddamn rifles in the first place. We did everything we could to play it by the book as far as the Jarinyi were concerned. At first, I thought Gutierrez handed us a gift by dying the way he did: a way to paint the Jarinyi as the bad guys; we'd be able to sway public opinion against them when news about them eventually leaked. Right now, public opinion doesn't mean juicy squat. Soon there'll be no public opinion to worry about.'

Romaine scratched at the back of his head, trying to generate his next idea.

Glass leaned in. 'Let me make this as clear as humanly possible. The Gutierrez case is redundant. It was never about him anyway. The man's a statistic.'

'You know what Stalin said about statistics?'

'No, I don't and I'm not interested.'

'People are still gonna want to know what happened to that young man.'

'What people? His *family*? Assuming the Colonies recover from PBT, someone somewhere in CUSET can dream up a cover-story. They'll spin some horseshit about a weapons malfunction *et cetera et cetera*. Pay the family damages. And it'll go away.'

'So, for all your rhetoric about me handing down a sensible verdict and getting my job done, the law can go purge itself?'

Glass shifted on the bench, adjusted his trousers. 'Romaine. Under these circumstances and out here, my mission is the law. And here, I'm the Judge, Jury ... and if need be, I'm the executioner.'

An icicle pierced Romaine's heart. What the hell did that mean?

Glass settled back. 'See, the Jarinyi were not the point of our coming here. They're a curiosity, not a resource. Once we knew what we had in Tigerclaw, that's all that really mattered. And now, it's *definitely* all that matters. As soon as it's safe to do so, we'll send in workers under safe conditions and we'll take everything we can out of that Patch. Like I said, it may be up to us to salvage what we can of civilization out there.'

While he talked, Romaine rubbed at his sternum as if to melt that icicle behind it. 'And if you manage to somehow save something for us to go back to when we leave? What then?'

'Maybe we'll find that warehouse Sean mentioned and I won't have to give up coffee.'

Todd laughed and placed the fresh mug in front of him, leaned on his own table instead of sitting.

Romaine pressed on. 'It'll all come out. It always does.'

Glass exhaled in a weary sigh. 'We're not stupid, Todd and I. Hell, I've always practiced the great military tradition of CYOA and I always will.' It took Romaine a beat to decipher the acronym. *Cover Your Own Ass.* Glass picked up a document from the seat beside him and dropped in on the table. Romaine wondered what it was; the CUSET letterhead was a concern. 'I *will* take your verdict on this case, but it'll be the one that suits our needs. Now, don't get me wrong. I believe in law and order. I have a great respect for your profession. If CUSET gets a future, it needs men like you.' He reached forward and gripped Romaine's forearm in manly fashion. 'Buddy, I respect your – what's the word? *Tenacity*. Your commitment to your mission. You know, deep down, you and I are so very alike.'

Grimly, pulling his forearm free, Romaine said, 'I don't think we are.'

'Yeah we are! We're both career men. Not like these other upstarts here. Gutierrez, that dumbass Quartermaster. Hell, even Sean here.' Todd bristled at this. Glass ignored him. 'They'll put in their five, ten, fifteen years, pocket the money and move on to some other career.'

Glass lifted the document and scratched his nose with the edge. 'You and I, on the other hand, we're lifers, creatures of the system. We do our jobs. We don't get emotionally caught up in peripheral issues. Outcomes are what's important, and the most important and constant outcome we're always seeking is *holding things together*.' He let go of the paper and it drifted across the table to land perfectly before Romaine.

As he skim-read it, he wasn't sure what frightened him more, the false content of the document or the truth in Glass's words. Perhaps Glass had been talking to Dreyfuss. Or perhaps he was just good at reading between the lines in a man's file and the lines on a man's face. Whatever the case, the Colonel had described exactly the man Romaine was determined he would no longer be.

Glass held out a pen. 'So, sign it. Then let's get on with saving the human race.'

Romaine tapped the paper with his finger, ignoring the pen. 'Did you sanction the bombing of the Jarinyi encampment?'

Glass sighed again. 'Retrospectively, yes. So what?'

'Did you order Lieutenant Todd to arm the Nguwuu and inflame interracial tensions here on Eventide?'

'No,' Glass replied with an amused glance at Todd. 'I'm still not seeing what these Nguwuu have to do with anything?'

'Did you know about Yaghuchi paying recons financial incentives to harvest Tigerclaw by a certain date?'

'Sure. They're paying me that too.' He chuckled. 'Win-win as I see it.'

'Did you have Private Gutierrez killed?'

Glass roared with laughter and Romaine could plainly see the man's surprise was authentic. 'You're hilarious, Commander. Damn, I needed a good laugh.' Glass offered the pen one last time then shrugged and pocketed it, and held out a hand. 'I'll have Fisher's dog tags, and anything else you took off her body.'

Romaine cursed silently. Why hadn't he put it someplace safe? 'I'll take care of them, if it's all the same.'

Glass's face darkened. 'It's *not* the same.' He hollered for Chua and a second later, the Sergeant stepped into the Mess. 'Have Commander Romaine locked in his room until the next ferry. He's permitted a trip to the restroom and the Mess at 0700 each day, but he is not permitted to speak with any personnel. And confiscate all of his belongings.'

'Sir,' Chua responded. If she was unhappy with the order, she didn't show it.

'Might wanna stock up on bananas.' Todd pointed to the one in his pocket as Romaine stood.

'My commiserations on the loss of your team,' Romaine replied. 'Thank God you made it back alive.'

They regarded each other evenly until Chua cleared her throat and Romaine followed her out.

TODD WISHED HE COULD SHOVE THAT BANANA SO HARD DOWN ROMAINE'S throat, the bastard choked on it.

As the door closed behind Chua, Glass said, 'Sean, what's this Nguwuu business?'

Here we go.

'Sir, your orders were to either negotiate with the Jarinyi or distract them. Until Gutierrez got himself killed and complicated matters, that's exactly what I was doing.'

'Answer my question.'

'In politics they call it *plausible deniability*. It's my gift to you, sir.'

'Are we on the same team here, Lieutenant?'

'We most definitely are, Colonel.'

'Ok, then.' Glass picked up his coffee and drank deeply. 'Damn, I hope we beat this bug. I really don't wanna give up coffee.'

PART V

EIGHTDAY

In a boat at sea, one of the men began boring a hole in the bottom of the boat. When the other men protested, he answered, "I am only boring under my own seat."
"Yes," said his companions, "but when the sea rushes in, we shall all be drowned with you."

- The Talmud

31

'During times of universal deceit, telling the truth becomes a
revolutionary act.'

- George Orwell

THE TIME on Romaine's seiko flicked over to 00:00.

Eightday, he thought.

Midnight, and all ain't well.

Could it be possible he was cursed? He'd allowed himself to get
close to three women in his life. Those same three women were dead.
Did he have to avoid friendship, romance, familial love – not just for
the sake of his own reclusive ways, but for the safety of others?

It was absurd, his logical side said. It was neither coincidence nor
curse. His mother had been a victim of her own mental illnesses and of
her husband's life of crime. Fisher and Harshini had died because they
worked in perilous situations and fell victim to evil people: police work
was the frontline of a war that had existed since humanity decided to

organize into societies. In each case, the Universe would have been better off had it been him to die, not them. He was a compromised, self-deceiving yes-man. He pushed against the system only when it suited him and when he knew the system wouldn't push back.

And you're a mediocre detective, self-absorbed and immature just like Carswell had said you are.

He rubbed one palm against his brow as shame prickled across his soul.

Fisher. Fisher Fisher Fisher.

Why didn't I say something to her, something to ease her passing? I just stared like a fool. I could have told her 'You'll be okay' or 'We're gonna get them' or ... anything!

He leapt up from the bed and kicked the wall. Fisher's death had been senseless, pointless, meaningless, a tragedy. *Stalin was right.*

His reverie was interrupted by the hut's outer door slamming and the thump of boots along down the hall. He braced himself for Todd to come crashing through the door and beat him senseless. But the footsteps passed before the next door along opened and banged shut. A pause then reggae music started up, a soulful tune, almost a lament.

Menabu.

Maybe there was something he could do after all.

He slammed his hand three times on the wall that separated them. 'Tristan!' he hissed. There was no response. He hit the wall again and raised his voice. 'Tristan! Come here!' The music got louder. He cursed and banged repeatedly on the wall, deliberately out of time with the music.

You're not getting any sleep tonight pal until you talk to me.

'Menabu!' he shouted, hoping there was no guard posted outside the building.

Finally, the music stopped. After a pause, Menabu spat a single word his way, from close against the wall: '*What*?'

'Get in here. I need to talk to you.'

'Tell me through the wall.'

'It'll take too long.'

'No way, mon. They'll crucify me if they catch me in there.'

'Come here or I'll keep talking loud. If they hear *that*, they'll crucify you.' No movement. No comment. Romaine slammed his hand into the wall. 'I know what happened to your missing rifles. You want your pay docked for the next ten years? Because that's what they'll do; you were right about that. Three AR90s. That's a lot of money, Tristan, that's–'

A rustling sound in the hall outside stopped him. His door opened a crack and Menabu entered in stages, one foot slipping through first, then head, shoulder and finally the rest of him shooting through the door and closing it quietly behind him. He stayed against it, bobbing around as if standing on a boat.

Romaine leaned against the opposite wall, giving him as much space as he could in the small room. It was ironic how ridiculously cramped it felt after days in the open air. Less than a week ago, its womblike compactness would have been comforting.

'Why do you think it's dangerous to be in here, Tristan?'

'It's called common sense. You're in trouble with the boss, then you're trouble for me.' Much of Menabu's former caricature of an accent had disappeared, dried up by the anxiety of the situation.

'Tristan, they keep spare AR90s, so they can reequip fast if one's damaged. Right? And you had some of them on the manifest but missing from the box.'

'That's old news. Whatchu want from me?'

'I know where they are. I need you to go back and get me a copy of that manifest and your inventory–'

'No way.'

'–and I need my SCRoLL, the rollup notebook I brought with me, and in the inside pocket of my kitbag you'll find a small transmitter–'

'No *way*.' His bobbing and weaving started to resemble a nervous boxer awaiting his next bout.

'You heard about Fisher, right?' Menabu ceased bobbing. 'You heard one of them killed her. Not an indig. A psychopathic sono-fabitch blackcap who thought nothing of killing her. It was sport for him. You like being on first name bases, Tristan? Her name was Jennifer. She wanted to be a church pastor. She had a family back on Centauri...'

'Alright, alright, ALRIGHT!' Menabu made a chopping motion and glared back, the difference in rank totally forgotten. 'Stop it.'

When Menabu reached for the door behind him, Romaine came off the wall and stopped a half meter from him. 'The Jarinyi didn't kill Gutierrez, Tristan.'

Menabu's eyes grew round. 'You ... have proof?'

'The manifest is the last bit I need. If you get it to me, and my SCRoLL, I can get a message offworld. I can make this right. For Fisher. For Emmanuel.'

Menabu dropped his gaze to the floor, struggling within himself. Seconds ticked by with painful slowness.

'Do it for them.' Romaine felt not one iota of guilt over playing the young man. 'Hell, do it for yourself. You're better than these bastards. Don't become like them.'

'Manny.'

Romaine frowned. 'Say again?'

Tristan's shoulders slumped. 'Gutierrez. He liked to be called Manny.'

ROMAINE FLICKED THE SCRoLL OPEN, POPPED OUT THE STYLUS AND clipped the tiny transmitter to the port on the top edge of the SCRoLL. His deftness did nothing to impress an increasingly nervous Menabu, watching him.

'Hurry up,' the Quartermaster hissed.

Romaine had edited and compiled a list of files while waiting by Fisher's body. Now he dragged the folder, opening a new memo for attachment.

'Going as fast as I can.' He nodded at the slim in Menabu's left hand. 'Beam me your manifest.'

'Send *your* message. You got thirty seconds then I'm leaving with that SCRoLL.' He played a hand over the butt of his sidearm. Romaine stared him down until he shoved the would-be gun hand into his pocket and threw the slim onto the bed with a snort of irritation.

Romaine snatched it up and beamed the relevant page to his SCRoLL, then tossed Menabu's device back to him.

Romaine drag-dropped the manifest file into the folder, then – ready to send the packet offworld – began scribbling into the memo.

To: Admiral Nagaya, CUSETMA Chief of Staff.

Attached is evidence that Lt Sean Todd stole (or ordered the theft of) CUSETMA property consisting of several assault rifles. These rifles were passed on to traditional rivals of local indigenous tribe of Jarinyi upon whose land Tigerclaw grows. (Rivals' name: Nguwuu).

I charge Lt Todd with inciting factional warfare, a clear breach of the UN Bill of Non-Terrestrial Species Rights to which CUSET companies are signatories.

My finding on the Camp Columbus murder is that Pt Emmanuel Gutierrez was killed by human agents. Lt Sean Todd is responsible for the killing of an unarmed indigenous individual (Jarinyi) killed with an AR90 for reasons unknown, on or around February 1st. Gutierrez can be placed at the scene of this killing and may have objected to it, giving Todd reason to believe he would go public with his knowledge of the event.

It is my opinion that Todd acquired a Jarinyi bow perhaps from the dead individual and either killed Gutierrez himself or had him killed by a subordinate, making it look like an aggressive action on the part of the Jarinyi. This would serve his ends of getting the Tigerclaw harvested quickly (without a treaty with the Jarinyi) and making it look as if all diplomatic protocols had been observed, only to have the Jarinyi attack a Marine without provocation.

Sergeant Umit Attikula (deceased) attempted to murder Doctor Edward Carswell and was prevented from doing so by Corporal Jennifer Fisher. Corp Fisher was instead murdered by Sgt Attikula. Attikula was in the act of turning his weapon on me before a local Jarinyi intervened and saved my life by terminating the Sergeant (in hand-to-hand combat; no arrows).

There was indication that Attikula was operating under the influence of the synth-amphetamine known as Utopia. He stated to me that this was being supplied to him by Yaghuchi Corp, but without an autopsy on Attikula's body (yet) I am unable to forward that evidence.

The Jarinyi have also personally indicated to me that they are considering an arrangement under which CUSET would have access to large quantities of Tigerclaw with no cost to CUSET except that of gathering/processing/shipping. Col Glass refused to consider this offer.

Please investigate this matter fully. Please ensure that Corp Fisher is buried with full honors and her family receives the appropriate compensation. Please also note that Col Robert Glass and Lt Todd have placed me under house arrest because of this evidence and because of my assertions, and I am unable to complete my own investigation of this matter.

Regards,

Cdr John Romaine, MIO

Nagaya was Dreyfuss's superior, a career naval officer now in his eighties, a major shareholder in several CUSET corporations, an executive on the CUSET board and the only stakeholder Romaine believed had any shred of integrity left.

Perhaps that shred would be enough.

And perhaps it wouldn't.

Romaine considered adding one more address to the message packet, a blind one, cloaked to keep it secret from Nagaya's office. A year ago, Romaine had accidentally discovered the identity and whereabouts of the most popular anti-establishment pedecaster operating in space. Her alternative angle on reporting events had been a major thorn in CUSET's side for over a decade. As a secret fan, Romaine had tucked away her identity and contact details in the back of his mind.

This time, if CUSET decided to bury this information, her 'casts certainly would not.

Romaine added her address.

His stylus froze above the screen.

Well, this is it.

All he had to do was tap 'send'. It should have been a reflex action, a no-brainer.

'What the hell are you *doing*, mon? Writing your biography?' Menabu stuck his head out the door to check around.

'More like my resignation letter.'

Would anyone do anything with the information when it got through? Would history hail him as a champion of the repressed, or vilify him as the man siding against humanity and with recalcitrant hoarders of Tigerclaw? Would he lose his commission, his job, his CUSET citizenship? Would he be happy with this decision or regret it for the rest of his life? Would he finish his days sleeping in a stinking dumpster, at the back of a mall, a drunken bum found dead one morning in a Seattle gutter, swept up with the rest of the trash?

For a moment, he sagged under the weight of the decision. And then as if a cloud had passed from before the sun, a question – just one – flashed through his mind. What would Fisher have done?

The stylus stabbed down on the *send* icon.

———

Bob Glass had a holobook going when the bedside intercom beeped.

The watch commander Yario's voice was apologetic. 'Sir, I thought you'd want to know. Commander Romaine's ship is still in orbit and someone just sent a transmission to it. From the base here.'

Glass's neck grew tight with increased blood pressure. How in hell had Romaine had managed it?

'Locate Lieutenant Todd,' he told Yario. 'Have him meet me at Romaine's cabin.'

He rose to don his boots and jacket.

———

The small hut shook and swayed with the weight of heavy bodies storming into the narrow corridor. *News travels fast*, thought Romaine, rolling off his bed and onto the floor away from the in-swing of the door.

The door flew open.

Glass took a step inside with Todd blocking the doorway at his shoulder. Outside, McGrath took up a position against the corridor wall.

Romaine raised his upper torso from the floor, as if caught part way through a set of crunches. 'One hundred thirty-one,' he grunted out, then gripped his knees, regarding them with a quizzical smile. Todd attempted to slide past Glass before the CO placed one arm firmly in his way.

The colonel levelled his coldest glare at Romaine. 'You always do exercises in the middle of the night?'

'I do when I'm stressed out and can't sleep.'

Glass sniffed. 'Search the room.'

Todd rushed forward to comply, kicking Romaine's feet aside.

Romaine slid his legs and ass against the wall. 'If you're looking for smokes, I'm all out, sorry.'

Todd snarled, 'I'll kill you, Romaine.'

'Keep searching, Sean,' Glass interjected, then pointed a finger at Romaine. 'You speak when spoken to and keep it civil, or I'll let him at you.'

There was little to search in the tiny room. Todd spat a curse. 'There's nothing here.'

Finger still levelled at Romaine, Glass said, 'How'd you send that transmission?'

Romaine frowned. 'Transmission?'

'Don't play games!' Todd shouted. He was very close to Romaine, leaning over him. He gave Glass a sidelong look – *Wants permission to beat the hell out of me*, Romaine figured

But Glass tapped a finger on the wall, deep in thought. 'Who's next door?'

'I think it's Menabu,' said McGrath from the narrow hallway.

'Go get him.'

They waited, as McGrath knocked on Menabu's door then opened it. Romaine held Glass's gaze and avoiding Todd's.

She returned after a few seconds. 'No one home.'

Glass said, 'Sergeant McGrath, get to Supply and check the box with Romaine's gear inside. The list will be on the lid. See if it's been tampered with or anything's missing.'

The small hut rocked as McGrath jogged outside.

For a full minute there was no sound in the room but the three men breathing. Then Glass sat himself on the bed near Romaine. Todd leaned against the side wall behind Romaine's back.

Glass pressed the heels of his hands into his eyes. 'Commander, you seem to live under a misassumption. I tried to explain this *delicately*. When you first arrived. And then again, the next day. Didn't wanna hurt your feelings. I wanted you to feel – important.' He glanced at Todd with a wry half-grin. 'I'm a sensitive guy.'

Todd laughed harshly. His proximity continued to make Romaine extremely nervous.

If that message doesn't fall on friendly ears soon ...

Glass continued, 'This time I'll be blunt. You still think you were sent here to investigate. But that wasn't your job. Your job was tick boxes, sign your name with a flourish, and leave.' He raised three fingers. 'Three simple tasks. Pretty much anyone could do them.'

'Those boxes I should be ticking – would they be the ones entitled *The Jarinyi did it* and *We're the good guys here*?'

Glass tapped his nose. 'And here I was thinking you were an idiot. The shame of it is, Romaine, you didn't tick the boxes. You didn't sign the form. And now you've made even more trouble. For all of us. See, we waited as long as we could before harvesting. In the end, we've had to drive the Jarinyi away so we can utilize that field. The trouble wasn't Sean here, whatever he did or didn't do. It was the damn Jarinyi's unwillingness to help us. When we asked for it nicely,' he added hurriedly when Romaine tried to interrupt. 'And you understand that people's lives depend upon Tigerclaw, don't you?'

'Of course I do.'

'It's a good deed we do. Wouldn't you agree?'

'If only the universe were that simple, Colonel. The Jarinyi won't think the killing of one of their people – unarmed – was a good deed. Nor the theft of what amounts to their property.'

Todd banged the wall with his fist. 'It's the survival of our species that's at stake. Don't you care about that?'

Romaine shuffled away from Todd then stood, sliding his back up the wall, saying nothing.

Glass shook his head angrily. 'Now you've gone and sent God-knows-what information offworld and God-knows-who will see it. This is supposed to be a *classified* operation. There are Separatist elements right throughout our colonies. You may have fueled further insurrection at the very time we need to hold our civilization together!'

'What the hell did you transmit, anyway?' Todd asked.

He sighed. There was no point playing the game any longer. 'Everything.'

'What's everything?'

'My working theories, my summations, the evidence I've collected … the fact that you're holding me here.'

'Yeah, well don't count on that to save you.'

Something in Todd's voice made Romaine's scalp tighten. 'Colonel?'

Glass nodded and stood. 'There are bigger issues here than your opinions … or your survival.'

For a time, no one spoke, then Romaine let out a sardonic cough of a laugh. 'Gotcha. You can discredit me, since I "ran off with" the Jarinyi. And I die in an accident. Or an *incident*. Just like Gutierrez.'

Todd's face wore the expression of the teenager with the brilliant smartass comeback. 'We didn't kill Gutierrez. Marines don't kill Marines. *But you aren't a Marine, are you?*'

Romaine swallowed heavily. This was a good time to pad, to stretch things out, to keep them talking while he thought of something. But his thoughts gummed up, just as they had when Turk splattered Tuttut's head into a thousand pieces.

'See, here's the story as I see it,' Todd continued, warming to the task. 'Corporal Fisher has been resisting your advances over the past few days. When Ranarith autopsies her, it'll be obvious she's been raped before being murdered. By you. You'll escape custody tonight. You'll be discovered missing in the morning, having disappeared into the forest never to be seen again. And now our only decision is whether to shoot you or drop you out the open door of a Reaper.'

Romaine glanced at Glass, incredulous. The CO wouldn't meet his eyes, distancing himself. A conscience still survived somewhere in the man, but his resolve was clear.

Romaine addressed his next comment to him. 'How the hell are you going to sell that? No matter how much you desecrate Fisher's body, the evidence just won't be there.'

Glass responded evenly, 'There's plenty of bent cops Admiral Dreyfuss can send me. It's just too bad you couldn't be one of 'em.'

The hut rocked and McGrath returned to the doorway.

'Sir, no sign of tampering. But Menabu was in there, sweeping. Looked kinda jazzed up, nervous. He coulda put something back in the box.'

'What was it, Romaine?' asked Glass. 'Your notebook? Got a customized transmitter?'

'What did you tell Menabu?' said Todd.

Romaine knew he had to give in. They might torture Menabu if they felt he knew something.

'He knows nothing. He just gave me the SCRoLL and put it back again. All I told him was I could fix the mess with the missing rifles for him and save him some money.'

'And that makes his treachery okay, does it?' Glass stood. 'You're very bad luck to your friends, Romaine.' He turned to McGrath. 'Sergeant, warm up one of the birds and grab Menabu quietly. This time of night, that shouldn't be hard. Stun him if you have to. He and Romaine are going skydiving.'

McGrath bolted from the building. Todd just smiled cruelly.

Better think quick, Johnny. Two more lives in your hands. And yours is one of them.

As he tried to come up with his hail Mary, Romaine's thoughts *and* his fate were interrupted by a sharp crack outside and a shout.

Hell was breaking loose in Camp Columbus.

McGRATH HAD JUST EXITED THE HUT WHEN AN EXPLOSION LIT UP THE FAR side of camp. She ducked and rolled instinctively, lay quietly for a ten-count, her eyes and ears scouring the night for danger. Someone began shouting from the north-west perimeter and, as suddenly, their voice fell silent.

McGrath's first thought was that some grunt had gotten spooked by another woo-woo bird and tossed a grenade at it. Then from beyond the fence on her side of the camp – uncomfortably close to the accommodation huts where she lay – came a sound she had never heard before. The bellow of some animal — some *large* animal. Her skin crawled as the sound trailed away into the night.

'What the hell?'

It came again. Closer. And then came an electric crackle and flash of blue light meaning that something had contacted with the fence. The next bellow was a roar of pain.

The air beyond the huts that way came alive with weapons fire.

McGrath launched herself off the ground, sprinting along the line of huts to the one closest to the action. She took a knee at the corner, took a peek around it. The perimeter fence had been breached. A lighting tower lay fallen, smashed and dark. The circle of a flashlight played in the direction of the breach until it caught on the creature responsible: a gargantuan trilophant from across the mountains.

What the hell?

The behemoth was double the size of an elephant. The flashlight wavered as someone presumably spasmed in shock at the sight. But McGrath had already seen what she needed to: the beast had lost a front leg, sliced and torn presumably by the wire, while blood ran from puncture wounds along its ribs. Lying on its side, it labored to breathe, trying to lever itself up on one good front leg.

Two regulars approached it carefully now, she saw, their weapons high, a male and female, the man prattling into his collar comm. The woman began firing a shotgun rounds into the trilophant's head.

These things don't live in the jungle! thought McGrath, still on the ground. *What is it doing—*

The male sentry's head collapsed as if staved in by an invisible fist.

Pulse rifle!

In the instant before his body dropped, McGrath put it all together. She knew what had happened, knew what was about to happen, knew exactly what it meant.

We screwed up, Looey. We screwed up bad.

The unseen sniper in the forest opened up again with the AR90 and the fleeing female sentry fell.

32

'The enemy of my enemy is also my enemy'

- Various

BOB GLASS GAVE Romaine a final murderous look before relocking his door from the outside. He'd be back for the investigator when he resolved whatever the hell was happening outside. Todd had already run from the building and Glass couldn't see him when he stepped outside. He raised his sidearm above his head, crashed the butt against the prefab's outside light, then folded into the shadows, listening.

A shotgun had been blasting away not so far from here, but it was silent now. AR90s opened up from the other side of the camp, the night having fallen quiet enough to distinguish the deep *thump-thump* of their EM pulses. Over that way, a thin tendril of smoke rose through the perimeter light from whatever had exploded. Glass headed that way: his camp was under attack but he hadn't the slightest idea who was attacking or why. They were questions he could ask after he'd won this.

He pressed a small handcomm to his ear and said, 'CO for Todd. What have you got?'

Todd's voice was steady despite him moving: 'Can't see yet, sir. Get back to you.'

A missile exploded somewhere near the LZ, unmistakably a small *Zheng* fired from the loaders rigged beneath the barrels of some '90s. Dirt and dust blossomed upward from the impact. The dirt was a good sign; the *Zheng* had probably missed anything manmade.

Glass took cover by a generator, gaze catching on the round hut a dozen meters away, the one with the biotoxins inside. An icy fist clamped over his heart.

Thirty samples of PBT. God help us if someone hits that.

It struck him that this might be a good spot to stay for the moment. If he had to personally defend any piece of this camp, this was the piece that most needed defending. Still, he couldn't stay here forever without intel. And maybe a generator wasn't the smartest thing to kneel beside. He sprinted across to the shadows by the Supply hut, almost the center-camp. From here, he could cover all the labs clustered nearby. Within the Supply hut, someone turned out the light then, but remained inside, keeping quiet. Probably Menabu.

Civilians emerged from the largest group of accom huts behind him, milling in the pools of light by their front doors. Chatting excitedly.

Dumber than house bricks.

Someone sprayed ballistic rounds from the direction of the LZ. The civs *ooo*-ed and *ahh*-ed. And Bob Glass needed to see what was happening, needed to *command*. He needed to get up in the air. He was about to call the signals hut when the handcomm buzzed with an incoming call tone.

'Glass!'

'Watch Commander, sir.' Yario's voice was scratchy and breathless, something rustling against his mic. He might have been crawling. 'We have a sentry down between the motor pool and the ferry pad, and a sniper or snipers in the trees outside that location.'

'Which is it, son? Singular or plural?'

Yario paused for breath and Glass heard the muted curse of another soldier with him. 'Sir, so far only Private Felicitas here has seen anything and she was unable to get a clear fix on numbers. Two Mi-Mi's fired from that location.' *Mi-Mi's* meant mini-missiles. The *Zhengs* he'd heard. 'One missed everything; one destroyed a jeep. And EM rounds that took out the sentry. Sir, what do we do?'

'Stay low and protect that perimeter. We'll get the Reapers up and take care of it.'

'Thank you, s–'.

Glass cut him off and stalked off toward the LZ, thumbing his communicator one more time. 'Signals? Comm the pilots, son. Wake 'em up. Get Norris up and scouting, but tell Donaldson to meet me by her bird.'

---

*T*HE *K*ILL-*lord rocked on his heels, eyes shut, picturing the chaos his ears could hear. He congratulated himself on his tactics: two groups converging on the enemy from either side, crushing them in between, and a hunter with one of the sky-weapons on either side of the camp to pick off any Skypeople stupid enough not to hide.*

The two hunters with sky-weapons had been told to destroy any of the strange stones that the Skypeople had left around their camp. Scouts who had watched the creatures for the past few days had reported the objects when he'd met up with them just after sunset. He had shot one of them himself, delighted by the strange eruption of sparks from within. What else could they be but traps?

He snorted derisively. Traps. Jarinyi leave traps. Traps are for the weak.

With a sigh, he considered one regret before returning to thoughts of battle. He had given one hunter the sky-weapon with the arrow-caster beneath it, the thing that struck with the force of lighting, throwing thick and stubby arrows that fragmented whatever they touched. He had wanted to use that weapon himself and dearly, but knew it would attract more attention than he wanted to face in the early stages of this battle while he was still watching and learning. They had three of the lightning-arrows, and he had instructed the warrior to fire two of them anywhere he chose to. But the final one was only to be used to destroy a flying thing if one rose into the sky.

He congratulated himself on his wisdom there.

The third sky-weapon, the thing that spat death, he had kept that for himself.

He sat quietly now, awaiting the moment that he would enter the fray. He was not interested in wading into battle and indiscreetly killing for its own sake. Let his warriors enjoy that glory, since in all likelihood many would be killed in the process.

The Kill-lord's glory would be that of destroying the greater warriors of the Sky-tribe. Those ones would not shelter in their camp; they would bring the battle out into the forest. Of this he was sure. He tapped the shiny new knife at his side, feeling pleasure at its weight and lethality. When they came, he would be waiting.

ALL THOUGHT FLED YARIO'S MIND AS HE AND FELICITAS WATCHED TWO OF Eventide's native mammoths smash through the fence. The first trilophant demolished that section of fence but paid a heavy price for it, losing the lower halves of its two front legs, before being trampled underfoot by the second who used it as a bridge.

The survival instinct in Yario's brain told him to run or he too would be trampled, but he was too fascinated to move. The intact beast shook itself, turned right and stampeded toward the LZ corner of the Camp. He glimpsed two riders on it —

Riders?

— and went to say something to Felicitas. But she'd gone!

Someone got to their feet near the collapsed and dying trilophant. In the dark, it was hard to see exactly who it was. It couldn't be Felicitas. Before Yario could make them out, they bolted away in the wake of the living trilophant, moving at inhumanly fast speed.

Holy...

More movement caught his attention. A mass of shapes appearing outside the wire flowing across the body of the trilophant and into Columbus.

Jarinyi!

Or were they? They seemed bigger than the ones he'd seen.

Yario fired his '90 as the aliens scattered. Some ran upright, some on all fours. His shooting dropped three of them. Two more saw him, racing directly at him on hands and feet, fast as greyhounds.

He adjusted aim, fired at one and shattered its arm. It stumbled and rolled. The other tacked sideways, dodging his next shot, then leaping with unnatural strength and grace. Sailing through the air toward him, it slipped a weapon from its loin cloth. His rifle forgotten, he gaped at oncoming certain death.

Someone knocked him sideways against the wall of the hut. The crack of a handgun by his head dulled his hearing, making his vision blur. A strong hand stabilized him then Lt Todd pressed his face close.

'Thank me later,' Todd said.

The attacker lay dead, leaking brains, so close Yario could prod it with his boot. Todd fired again and again, dispatching others who'd decided to venture their way.

Yario had to shake himself. It was happening surreally fast.

Todd let go of his sleeve to tap an earpiece. Yario heard him live *and* via his own wrist comm. 'Nyst, record this. Signal all personnel. Message from Todd. Attackers are Nguwuu, not Jarinyi. Repeat, Nguwuu. AIRTARs are authorized.' He paused to fire over Yario's shoulder. Yario recoiled and stepped away, looked around to see what he was shooting at. Todd continued, 'Nguwuu cannot chameleon. Switch to single-fire and watch for–' He fired again '–friendly fire. Message ends. Then, Nyst, get on the cabin intercoms and tell the civs to stay the hell in their huts on the floor.'

Cacophonous noise erupted from the LZ. Todd let go of his earpiece and grabbed Yario again. 'Labs and biodomes,' he barked. 'Guard them. Go!'

He shoved Yario away and disappeared into the dark.

Yario cradled his rifle and headed back to the center of the camp at full speed.

As Glass rounded the Medcentre, the two pilots caught up with him – they running, he walking. All three stiffened, wishing what they saw wasn't real. One of the massive grasslands herbivores was lumbering toward the parked Reapers.

'No!' Donaldson cried.

The trilophant barreled into a flier, head down, and barely broke stride before continuing through to the fence. In the uneven light, Glass saw two bodies jump lithely from its back and thought them Jarinyi before he recalled Romaine's accusation against Todd. These bastards were bigger.

Nguwuu?

The busted Reaper skidded around on its axis, tail scraping its sister craft, one side crushed and ruptured. The trilophant met the fence head on, losing part of its face and suffering a deep slice into its shoulder as it fell forwards, dragging the fence with it.

'Sir?' the pilot named Norris asked in a strangled voice.

'Get to Supply, get a rifle and protect the labs.' He took Donaldson's arm and dragged her with him. 'We need to get in the air.' One of the figures who'd ridden the trilophant was edging around a small generator by the LZ. It saw them and drew itself up, brandishing a spear.

Glass shot it through the abdomen twice without missing a step.

He and Donaldson ducked under the tail flukes of the damaged aircraft and the pilot climbed clumsily into the cockpit of the other, while Glass stood watch by the door. Once the repulsors started up, he climbed in and pulled hard on the door.

'Up! Up!' he yelled.

'Where else am I gonna go?' Donaldson muttered back through the headset. 'Sir.'

Nancy Chua was running when she came around the corner of the southernmost accom hut and collided with someone as big and hard-muscled as she was. She spun around and pitched sideways into the dirt. Whoever had hit her lay nearby, stunned — almost as stunned as Chua was when she realized it was a Nguwuu. As it tried to shrug off its shock, she lashed out and punched it hard in the throat. Its hands wrapped around its own neck as it started choking, and Chua mounted its torso, slipping her knife from its sheath and stabbing repeatedly until the bastard lay still.

She pushed herself upright, wiping the dagger on her pants, spitting in case the foul taste in her mouth was the thing's blood, then rubbing at the sore spot on her ribs. 'Shoulda put armor on.'

In the collision, her handgun had bounced away into the shadows and it took her a few moments to find it. She moved to the next corner with a little more caution than previously. Two aliens were hacking at two Marine bodies by the fence. Chua fired. Two rounds, two head-shots. Near the bodies lay the huge corpse of a trilophant.

Energy pulses punched through the air from across the fence line, smashing into the hut to her right. She leaped left and a trio of energy pulses passed harmlessly overhead. She rolled over, scurried along the ground until she found refuge in the shadows. A number of other shots kicked up dirt nearby but the shooter seemed to have lost sight of her.

'Yeah, I really shoulda worn armor,' she muttered.

The shooter had not been using an AIRTAR. Had to be an alien firing that weapon.

A dozen more Nguwuu were emerging from the dark forest beyond the perimeter, aiming to use the dead trilophant as a passage across the wire. They made no noise but for the scuff of their hands and feet as they galloped along like monstrous chimpanzees.

What have we done? What have we done? The words played like an annoying childhood campfire song round and round inside her head.

It was time to get Romaine. She fired several times into the enemy swarming across their grisly bridge, scattering them, and got up to sprint for the shelter of the buildings.

Romaine's was the second last building in the next row and as she neared it, her eye caught the silhouette of a woman civ standing in the space between huts, frozen in terror. And there in the shadows slinking toward her from behind, *another* hacking Nguwuu.

Where did you come from?

She tried to aim while she changed direction, picking up the pace. 'Down!' she shouted.

The woman put a hand to her throat as if to say, *Oh, dear, you frightened me!* Chua's slug whizzed past her at waist height and hit the ground somewhere behind the Nguwuu. The warrior must have decided it was time to abandon stealth, putting on his own burst of speed. It leaped into the air as it passed the woman, driving something sharp and hard into her shoulder as it flew, continuing forward faster than Chua could believe. The woman let out a startled cry and crumpled. Chua's next bullet struck the Nguwuu in the shoulder from four meters away.

'Poetic *justice!*' Chua snarled at it as it spun and fell, spasming as it tried to get its feet under it. She skidded to a halt and fired three more rounds until it stopped moving. Kneeling by the woman, she grabbed her hand to stop her pulling the spike from her trapezius. 'You'll bleed more if you do that.' The woman shrieked in response. 'Shut *up*, you stupid cow. Listen to me and you'll survive. Stay here, stay quiet and I'll be back to get you in thirty seconds.'

'N-no,' the woman whimpered.

'Y-yes,' Chua said and stood, pointing to the woman's injured shoulder. 'And don't touch that.'

<hr>

THE REAPER LIFTED INTO THE AIR AND SAILED LOW ACROSS THE FENCE line, moving slow as Donaldson fumbled one-handed with her harness.

'Pilot, you have your missile scramblers on, right?' Glass snapped.

'Oh hack, sorry, sir.'

Her hand reached for the control, but never made it. Both Reaper occupants' heads jerked right at the launch flash of a *Zheng* from the trees. A second later the mini-missile smashed into Donaldson's side of the aircraft, shattering the starboard repulsor and batting the rear of the craft into a lateral spin. Donaldson screamed. Glass had the impression of blood and burns across her face as it turned his way. He barely had time to brace himself against the roof and the door as the flier slewed and crashed fifty meters inside the forest, wedging between two huge Eventide trees.

DREAD HUMMED IN ROMAINE'S CHEST LIKE A FAULTY NEON. THE CLAMOR outside meant the camp was under attack. Either the PRC had arrived or the Nguwuu were putting those missing AR90s to use. The chilling animal bellows he kept hearing led him to believe the latter hypothesis was the accurate one.

For several minutes after Glass had left, he rattled the door and hammered uselessly at the disabled control pad his side of it. Then he slumped on the floor and stayed there, trying to figure a way to break out.

A scream directly on the other side of the outside wall made him jump to his feet and face it. A handgun fired. Another scream. More shots made him hit the floor again, tucked into a ball. Moments later, the hut vibrated and swayed as someone pulled open the main door and tramped inside. They fumbled with the lock and he scrambled to the far end of the bed, heart thumping against his ribs.

Chua's flushed face appeared in the doorway. Her uniform was spotted and streaked with blood. 'Time to go, sir.'

'Where?' he demanded. Was this *rescue-the-cop* time or *bundle-the-cop-into-the-aircraft-while-everyone's-distracted-and-kill-him* time?

'I got a wounded lady out there. Let's get the *hack* outa here and bunker down in sickbay. I'll even find you a gun, if you want.'

He used the bed to get up, followed as fast as his shaky legs would carry him.

'I knew I liked you for a reason, Nancy.'

33

'Only the dead will see the end of war.'

- Plato

THIRTY METERS ABOVE THE GROUND, two sets of eyes watched havoc unfold with fascination. Carswell had convinced Scarface, as Romaine called him, to take advantage of their head start but run toward the camp rather than away from it, to take advantage of the hide he'd been building these last few weeks since the initial survey mission.

Something was going to break tonight; he had been sure of it.

But he hadn't expected *this*.

Their hide lay directly in line with the apex of the Camp's east-north and north-west diagonal boundaries. He and Scarface had arrived in the mesh of branches and vines just in time to see the flier return carrying Romaine. They had watched him limp tiredly away with a Marine escort along with one who carried a bag ahead of them.

The bag had probably held Fisher; it was certainly a lot lighter than the one that other Marines wrestled from the aircraft after the main group had left, the one that obviously held Turk's body.

Now as three giant trilophants lay dead or dying around the fenceline and Nguwuu rushed across the breaches they had made, Carswell felt a mix of terror and elation. While Camp Columbus were getting their just deserts — Todd had no doubt brought this disaster upon their heads — two things worried the xenologist: his own proximity to a large group of Nguwuu, and Romaine's survival long enough to get the story and the evidence out to whoever would listen.

Once the colonies knew what was happening here, CUSET would be forced to tread carefully and respect the rights of the true owners of Eventide and its resources.

An insistent tapping on his arm made him look to Scarface. The warrior was a blur as seen through Carswell's pince-nez night-lenses. He felt the Jarinyi's hand on the translator. They hadn't used it since arriving. He felt for the controls and turned the volume down low, turned it on, then whispered, 'What is it?'

Scarface fluted just as quietly, pressing his head close. 'I go.'

'Go? Go where?'

'I go. Smell *tuttut* Nguwuu *tuttuttutttut.*'

His attention split between the muddled words of the warrior and the sounds of an aircraft taking off, Carswell felt Scarface press a hand to his chest.

'*Cssoool*,' the warrior whispered and slipped from the hide.

With a giddy thrill, Carswell murmured, '*Cssoool* indeed.' *He's accepted me. That's incredible. That's wonderful.*

A moment later, yet another small missile streaked out of the bush to his left, this one pounding the Reaper from the sky. 'Wow,' he whispered. 'Best seat in the house.'

THE NOISE OF THE REAPER CRASH MADE TODD PAUSE WITH ONE HAND ON the door control of his room. He cursed quietly, listening to the echoes bounce around the long Columbus Valley, then pushed through the door. A rifle muzzle appeared and his handgun whipped up in response.

'It's you,' he said with relief and let the weapon drop.

'None other,' McGrath replied. 'What was that noise just then?'

'I think we've lost both our fliers.'

She made an angry sound, dropped the rifle on the unmade bed and picked up her Tensar vest where she'd left it in the corner earlier that day. She busied herself with the clasps on her body armor. 'That's Nguwuu out there,' she told him.

'I figured,' he replied.

She shrugged. 'We'll take 'em out. Coming in, I passed Ranarith sticking his head out the door like an imbecile. Told him to get to sickbay and wait for casualties.'

Watching her connect the final clasp in the room's mild emergency lighting, Todd felt uncharacteristically touched. There was something about her he was coming to appreciate, something more than the hard resolve in her eyes and grim set of her jaw that reminded him of himself. He found that he actually wanted to see how far this thing between them could go.

And then as he rechecked the clasps on his own armor, he found his thoughts turning to his brother on Oceana. This PBT thing was a disaster, bungled by CUSET from the beginning. If he and McGrath got out of here, somehow he'd find a way to get to his brother and –

And what, exactly? An image flashed into his head – his brother lying dead on the sands, blood pooling around his mouth, leaking from his eyes and nose. What if that was what he found when he finally got to Oceana?

Carswell and Romaine, they had complicated this and they had to pay. Them and their damn Jarinyi. Clenching his teeth and slapping the clasps together, he forced his focus onto the job at hand, onto matters that were in the present tense.

'I told everyone to –' he began but she cut him off.

'I know. I heard it, but I don't think many have their earpieces in. There's two dead grunts by the east-south boundary.' She checked her weapons pouches out of habit. 'That doesn't leave many of us.'

'Hopefully Nyst will keep the damn civs in their huts.'

A grenade exploded somewhere in the camp, the *crump* of detonation muffled by the walls of the hut. A man cried out in a staccato note of alarm and anger and pain. A moment later, a woman or maybe two women screamed, the sound quieter as if it were inside one of the buildings on the other side of camp.

I caused this.

No! I did what I could, the best I could, to make this situation right!

'Go get Romaine. We left him locked in his room. We can kill two birds with one stone here.'

'Romaine?'

'Totally. That humptard slowed things down instead of speeding them up. He knows about the rifles. If there's anything left of CUSET to go back to, it could be prison for you and me. Well, me anyway. I'd keep your name out of it ...'

She was already shaking her head, indicating she didn't need protecting, didn't want that, didn't want him going to prison any more than he wanted her to.

Good.

'I'll get him,' she said simply.

'Make it look like the Nguwuu–'

'I get it, Sean.'

She shook her hair, braced her rifle. He remembered how good she looked sleeping the hour before Glass had roused them. He thought about how weird it was that in the midst of all this crap, he had started to *care*, and about how badly he didn't want to lose her. Soon she might be all he had...

She touched his arm, as if reading his thoughts. 'Where *you* goin'?'

'They just used their last *Zheng*, but someone better find those snipers.' He closed the gap between them in the low light. 'May as well be me.'

'I should come with.'

'This is my mess. I'll clean it up.'

Lightly, they kissed. He could only wish it wouldn't be the last time.

The Kill-lord trembled with anticipation. If anyone was alive within the wounded flying thing, he could snatch some of the kill-glory from the hunter who had shot it down.

He sped through the forest, vaulting obstacles, swinging from low branches, proud of the way he balanced stealth and speed in the dark, proud of his craft. Soon he found himself looking at the wreck of the flying thing, savored the ticking noise it made as it died. With eyes suited perfectly to the Eventide night, he spotted the movement to the side where someone emerged from an opening there. He crouched, crept forward silently. His trembling stilled, overtaken by bloodlust when one of the sky-warriors fell from the pouch inside the flier.

The Kill-lord saw the grey fur of a senior warrior, smelled the mineral scent of the Skypeople's blood. He felt the invigorating weight of the alien weapon on his back, slid it forward into his arms. This would be a wonderful kill.

Groggy with shock, Glass knew he should feel pain right about now, but it wasn't immediately forthcoming. Donaldson had survived the missile strike, but she hadn't survived the crash. The thick branch that had plunged through the windshield and halted them had decapitated her; he'd seen that much before the cabin lights fluttered out. He shouldered the door open and fell onto the earth outside. His left arm flopped in an unnatural way and when he felt it in the dark, something sharp and sticky was poking up through the skin near the elbow.

That shouldn't be there. Badly broken.

Pains began registering in that arm, his back, his left knee, his chest, his neck, all registering like units calling in their locations. Clarity returned in a rush.

Gotta get back to camp.

Through the ringing in his head, the only thing he could hear was the creak and crackle of the Reaper's metal sagging and cooling. God only knew what was out there in the pitch darkness. He struggled to stand, pulling with his good arm at the wreckage of the Reaper, steadying himself so he could remain upright. Light. He needed light. Feeling around inside the cabin produced a clump of lightsticks held together by a thick rubber band. He positioned them on the chair he'd been in, pulled his belt knife with his good hand and managed to saw open the band. He sheathed the knife and took a lightstick, gripped it between his knees and twisted the top. Light flared immediately, dazzling him. He pitched it away to land four or five meters away.

His eyes began to adjust as he took hold of a second lightstick. Then he froze. Forgot about the lightstick. Forgot his pain. Someone was standing not three paces away from him and to his right. Slowly he turned his head, blinking focus into his eyes, unable to draw breath. Like a demonic apparition from his worst nightmare, a creature like and yet unlike a Jarinyi stood there, statuesque and silent, black eyes twinkling from the lightstick's glow.

A moment later Glass noticed it held an AR90, the business end angled his way.

'Well ain't that dandy,' he said, finding his breath again.

There was no hope he could release the lightstick from his right hand, draw his pistol and swivel in time to shoot this *thing* – not a snowflake's chance in hell.

And yet as it shifted its grip to target him squarely, something as unexpected as everything else in this situation and far more miraculous – to Glass at least – occurred. The creature's eyes widened in shock and it pitched forward, the rifle flying from its hands to land midway between them before it crashed on top of it. Reflexively he pulled his legs out of the way, his knee feeling like it was caught in a meatgrinder. The Nguwuu's arms shot forward as if reaching for him, then it shuddered and lay still.

Frowning, Glass looked up into the face of a Jarinyi – one with a long nasty scar on the side of his face lit up by the lightstick, and a piece of ear missing. Todd had told him about this one: a favorite of the Jarinyi tribe's Elder. The Jarinyi took three loping steps forward, pulled a blade of some kind from between the shoulders of the Nguwuu and leaned over the body toward Glass.

Glass stiffened, held out his hand as if warding off an evil spirit. Scarface leaned closer, studied him and ... sniffed at the palm. Then he straightened. Confused, Glass considered grabbing at his own knife when the Jarinyi put his hand in a small pouch on his loin cloth. He let the knife stay where it was when he saw what the Jarinyi was holding out to him.

There was no mistaking it, even in bad light. The Jarinyi was offering him a Tigerclaw leaf.

Glass reached out and took it, looked deep into the eyes of the Jarinyi.

And passed out.

———————

A HUDDLE OF STORAGE SHEDS LAY BETWEEN ROMAINE'S HUT AND THE Sickbay and beyond them a wide patch of open ground. With Chua taking point, Romaine steadied the injured woman, who whimpered with each step. They paused in the dark lane between two sheds and took their bearings.

All was chaos in Camp Columbus. A grenade exploded near the Gate and a man called out, his cry cut short. From their right, presumably near the labs, they could hear more shooting. A few screams and the crunch of a plastic window breaking came from the accommodation area they'd left behind.

'Shouldn't we go back and help them?'

'What are you gonna help them with?' Chua's voice hissed from the darkness beside him. 'You armed?'

He wasn't. She had yet to deliver on her promise of a weapon.

Chua took a big breath and shushed the injured civilian who was whimpering again. Romaine saw the Marine's profile set against the ambient light of the camp when she peeked around the corner. Then she withdrew her head fast. He was about to ask why when a Nguwuu dashed by, holding something long and floppy. Romaine hoped it wasn't what he thought it was. It had looked like an arm.

When the woman began to groan, Romaine felt and heard Chua grab her by the hair and bang her head lightly against the wall of the shed, then murmur to her.

'Shut. Up.' A few seconds later, she peeked around the corner again, then whispered, 'We're moving.'

With the woman leaning heavily on his arm, Romaine marched her forward, struggling to keep up with Chua's pace. Before them lay an informal courtyard formed by the sheds on three sides and two small office bungalows on the other. There was no choice but to pass directly through the broad pool of light beneath the two light-towers standing in the middle of it. One of the bungalows was Glass's office. Romaine wondered if there were guns in there. He really wanted a gun.

'Shouldn't we head to Supply?' he whispered, as they passed between the towers. She executed a complete three-sixty without slowing, casting her eyes all around them. 'If bimbo here hadn't been wandering around outside, we could do that. She needs a doctor.'

'Bimbo?' the woman snuffled.

'Suck it up,' Chua growled.

Romaine saw movement in his peripheral vision, snapped his head around. 'Nancy!'

She turned, swore and fired twice. Five meters away, the Nguwuu carrying the human arm dropped like a stone.

'Is that ... Is that ...? Oh!' The woman began to dry retch.

Exasperated, Chua slammed the warm handgun into Romaine's palm, pulled the woman out of his grip and picked her up in a fireman's carry. The shock of pain the woman must have felt put an abrupt end to her retching, replacing it with sharp intakes of breath.

'About six shots left, I think, maybe five,' Chua said, and set off at a lumbering half-jog. 'What you been eating, girl? Damn, you're heavy for a bimbo!'

Romaine curled his finger around the trigger and tried to keep pace with her.

Todd had done a lot of weird things in his life. But using the still warm corpse of the trilophant as a bridge felt like the weirdest. He kept his AIRTAR off and his augments on, preferring the technology in his head to the stuff on the rifle. His nightvision clip-ons showed him a terrain beyond the fence eerily green and grey. The sniper was up amongst the gently sloping woods to the north, but Todd cut across the open ground between the fence and the trees at an angle, rather than directly toward where he thought they were. The sniper must have been either distracted or on the move too, because the shots didn't come until Todd was a few meters from cover.

His augments warned him of an AIRTAR lock, gave him the impression of the shooter's location nanoseconds later then jammed the signal just as the shooter's finger closed on the trigger, throwing their aim off. Todd ducked and rolled as several rounds passing harmlessly above and behind him, then came to his feet in a fluid movement and sprayed fire into the forest even as he entered it. His opponent returned fire but again it was wide. Todd came to rest against the rough bark of a tree and fired a long burst from the hip again, certain this time he'd hit his target. He slid behind the tree and checked his clip – thirteen rounds left. There was no return fire.

Better make sure.

Duck-walking, he moved carefully up the slope toward his enemy.

The door to the Medcentre formed a bright rectangle against the dark of the camp. Romaine took the first tentative steps inside, pistol in both hands with Chua on his heels.

'Ah, squat!' he said.

Ranarith lay dead by the bed Romaine had earlier occupied. Though he lay chest-down, his head was turned almost completely around, like an earth owl's. His attacker had torn out his throat and either hacked or ripped off his left hand.

'What the –?' Chua said as she passed, dumping the woman as carefully as she could on to another bed. The woman had almost lost consciousness by now; she rallied for a moment, then saw Ranarith. Her head hit the thin hospital pillow with a soft *thunk*.

Chua turned, starting to suggest to Romaine to get a blanket to put over the dead doctor but gave a cry instead and pointed behind him.

He was already whirling around, feeling the impact of someone jumping onto the step outside. An unarmed Nguwuu, slick with sweat and blood, sprang forward and kicked Romaine hard in the arm before he could aim. He found himself spinning toward the bedside table above Ranarith, skidded along the floor in the man's blood and hit the plastic cabinet with his shoulder, then began scrambling for the hand gun that he'd dropped.

Before it regained its balance, Chua delivered the Nguwuu a spirited front kick that sent it flying backwards out of the door. She lunged sideways to grab a chair for a weapon just as Romaine's fingers found the gun. The Nguwuu seemed to bounce right off the ground and back in through the door as if made of rubber. It was already back in the room by the time Romaine got a grip on the pistol. He fired from the hip once, twice as it lunged for Chua, missing completely.

Chua met the oncoming attacker by swinging the chair from down to up like a baseballer. The Nguwuu tried to anticipate the trajectory, ducked as if to slide beneath it but one chair leg caught it beneath its ear. Romaine heard a sickening crack and then the alien was flopping onto the floor like a sack of wet laundry, where it shivered, as if cold. Muscle tremors. *Probably already dead.*

Chua brought the chair down on its head again to make sure, shouted in a Chinese dialect, '*Qu si!*' Then she was hopping gracefully over the body, slamming the door shut and beaming an adrenalized grin at Romaine.

'Me three, now,' she said. '*You* zero. Where'd you learn to shoot, guy?'

He shrugged, trying to catch a breath. 'Navy.'

'Figures.' She pulled open some drawers, found a vial of a clear liquid and a clean hypo, tore the paper cover from the latter. 'You ok?' she asked him.

'Better than her,' he replied, rubbing at the hot pain in his arm nevertheless.

'Know how to give her this?' Chua raised the vial and hypo and Romaine nodded. 'I'll go look for something to fight with.'

'What's wrong with the chair?'

'Too small for me.' She winked and vanished into the next compartment of the hut.

Romaine half-smiled and got busy. He placed the vial into the handle of the hypo, a movement which always reminded him of locking a new magazine into a pistol. He sedated the unconscious woman so she didn't become conscious again, took a quick look at her wound and winced. The object protruding from her shoulder was a piece of bone, a primitive dagger, and she'd lost a lot of blood. Pulling compresses, surgical tape and bandages from drawers, he packed and bound the wound as best he could. When finished, he straightened and grimaced. The blood was already soaking through. The only surgeon in town was dead, but surely someone else in a camp full of medical researchers could help her. If they got to her soon. And if any of them survived the night.

Chua reappeared holding a surgical laser-saw. 'Better than nothing.'

'What can we do for her?'

'Not much. Let me see.' She dumped her improvised weaponry by the woman's legs and leaned over her. 'I think you've done as much as we can.'

A chorus of aliens hoots and howls somewhere outside made Romaine look toward the door again. 'We need to get out there and do something. Our civilians—'

'No you don't. Maybe *I'll* go help some time. But you're staying put.'

'Nancy–'

'I said no. You ... you got a story to tell and you gotta stay alive to tell it. This is your chance, dammit. You're staying here and you can keep the gun.'

'Sergeant–' He froze at her expression.

'Don't try that one on me, navy-boy,' she growled.

Romaine exhaled hard in exasperation. He turned to regard the Nguwuu body, flashing back for a moment to another body up in the mountains.

'Your boss did all this. He caused it.'

'The Looey? Yeah, he did. I guess I did too,' she added softly.

'What the hell was he thinking?'

'He's not evil, Romaine. Just an asshole. Probably thought he was doing his job.'

'He did it wrong.'

She was nodding, tracing a finger around the bandages on the woman's shoulder. 'Yeah, I can't improve on that. Hope we can get another doc soon to fix her. What an idiot, running around outside when there's crap like this going on.'

'Nancy,' he said, getting her attention. 'I need you to tell me everything. If Todd's not evil, he's not a good guy either, you know.'

'No. No, he ain't. Guess I'm not either.'

'*You* didn't leave Fisher and me to die on the mountain. And you were following orders with whatever else you did do.'

'Yeah. Orders. You know, even though us Marines ain't paid to think, the last couple of years I keep wondering, if orders are a good reason?'

'Reason for what?'

'Reason to do the shit we been doing.'

'Like?'

'Getting nice girls like Fisher killed. Like giving these things guns!' She kicked the dead Nguwuu. 'Like ... other stuff.'

'Nancy. I know Todd armed these Nguwuu so they'd attack the Jarinyi, and I assume later he was gonna claim the Nguwuu snuck in and somehow stole the rifles. But I need you to tell me everything you know.'

'Later, when this is over.' She lifted a hand when he tried to object. 'Hey, Todd's done wrong. No doubt. He let Turk get away with stuff he shouldn't've. More than once. More than twice. And he left you guys on the mountain. And yeah, he gave these things rifles. Now they're killin' *us* with 'em. McGrath probably won't testify, too hackin' semper fi. But I will, if you need me to. Crap like this has to stop. We gotta make this right. All of it.' She stared through the wall for a moment. 'I gotta get back out there, see if I can help anyone. Sure you're ok?'

'You're going out there with surgical instruments? Sergeant, take the gun.'

She shook her head, picked up the laser-saw. 'It only has a few more rounds. This I can use over and over.' She winked. 'You watch yourself. Watch this door. And you shoot anyone you have to. Ok? We want you to survive this. *Ok?*'

'Like I'm going to argue with that.'

Chua eased open the door and ducked out into the dark.

TODD SENSED THE SHOT A NANOSECOND BEFORE IT HIT HIM. NO AIRTAR signal this time to warn him. His armor absorbed the impact and energy of the round. He pirouetted around toward the injured Nguwuu, saw the damaged leg, the chunk torn from its abdomen, couldn't believe it was still alive, couldn't believe he'd walked straight past it.

Through the green and grey filters over his eyes, it looked perturbed that a point-blank shot hadn't even injured the human. It was so surprised that it didn't fire again.

Todd did.

Something prickled then against the back of his mind and he whirled in the other direction.

What was that?

He wasn't sure if something in the forest had triggered his augmented senses or if he'd imagined it. He narrowed his eyes as he peered through the lenses, eyes panning the area. He couldn't see anything. Actually, that wasn't quite true; he could see *a lot*. He would eventually see it if something was there, but it could just be a woo-woo bird, an alien snake or...

Jarinyi?

Would they come here while the Nguwuu were around? Why would they come here at all? It was far too dangerous for them. But there it was again, that prickle in the back of his mind. An odd stump uphill from him caught his eye. He was sure he'd seen that shape before but elsewhere in the forest. Did the Jarinyi draw on the same repertoire of shapes when they chameleoned?

Aiming his rifle at it, he flicked the AIRTAR on and off, expecting it to wriggle about trying to acquire. Nothing happened. He fired a round into the stump anyway. Again, nothing.

Just a stump.

He turned his back on it and started down the slope toward the camp, carefully jogging around and over obstacles. There was one more sniper to track down and exterminate.

34

'Victory goes to the player who makes the next-to-last mistake.'

- Savielly Grigorievitch Tartakower, Chessmaster

SCARFACE RETURNED his skin follicles and pigmenting cells to a neutral state, untwisted himself from around the tree and ran a cautious hand over the scar the Man's weapon had left on the nearby stump.

Until this moment he had thought that the Men had no true craft. He had thought that their only strength was their ability to make things, things that gave them the powers and craft of other creatures and objects. Their thick sticks fired invisible stones mimicking slings and bows. Their flying trees mimicked flying animals. The shells they put on and took off mimicked the shells of burrowing and sea creatures. The flat thing the Man had worn over his eyes – like the thing that Cssoool also wore at night – obviously helped him see clearly in the dark. Neither Nguwuu or Jarinyi needed any such help.

But somehow the Man had not only avoided death at the hands of a Nguwuu, he had also sensed Scarface was nearby, despite his blending. Perhaps their wits were not quite as dull as he had thought.

He could see clearly now that Jarinyi would do well to make friends of the Men rather than keeping them as enemies. Hopefully the old one, the Man-Elder, had understood his gesture when he had saved him from the Kill-lord.

Scarface turned at a crack of twigs many paces away and was relieved to see Cssoool making his way carefully through the ground fog beginning to seep up from the soil. The fur-faced Man's craft had improved remarkably over the past thirty days and nights, but at times he was still clumsy. It was just as well the red-furred Man-warrior was gone. The noise would have cost Cssoool his life, or forced Scarface to intervene once more between two Men in battle.

What a strange life I live, *he thought.* What a strange story will be told around the fires when I am gone to the soil.

He walked to the Nguwuu body, prodding him with one foot to ensure the old enemy was in fact dead. Satisfied, he stooped and picked up the Man-weapon left by Red Fur, and at another crackle of dry twigs underfoot, he turned and handed it to Cssoool.

The Man who lived among his people broke a small part off the object and threw it deep into the brush. He then threw the rest of the weapon in another direction. Through the talking thing on his chest he said, 'We don't need Man weapons, friend. We are Jarinyi.'

ROMAINE SPENT A FEW MINUTES WRAPPING RANARITH'S DISFIGURED corpse in a blanket and dragging it along the floor into the meat locker where he left it against the far wall, rather than inside one of the drawers. Manhandling a body was no easy task unless you were as brawny as Chua. Romaine had enough to worry about without earning himself a prolapsed disc.

He returned to the ward area and threw another blanket over the bloody mess on the floor where the surgeon had died, then used his feet to shove the Nguwuu corpse against the wall. Finally, he allowed himself to rest, sitting on a bed, placing the handgun in his lap. He had to stay alert.

Romaine was half-dozing, dreaming about food, when the door

opened and McGrath and Yario came in. He snapped awake, the taste of fries and steak and eggs still eerily present in his mouth. He lifted the handgun and frowned even more deeply when McGrath ignored it, pushing Yario into the room ahead of her. The Canadian had a few blood spots seeping through his uniform shirt.

'Put it down, man,' she said to Romaine, letting her own rifle swing around on its strap to hang behind her as she closed the door.

Yario half-staggered past him to the bed two down with more than a little melodrama in his movements.

'What happened to you?' Romaine asked him, keeping his eyes on McGrath. Despite her nonchalance, he wasn't convinced she'd forgotten Glass's order to prepare the Reaper for his murder. He would shoot her if he had to.

'Got attacked. Lots of aliens. Something hit me in the chest.'

Romaine eased himself off the bed and looked over at him. 'Doesn't look too serious. You were lucky.' He pointed to the woman with a blade in her shoulder.

'Hurts like hell though, sir.'

Romaine watched McGrath go to the desk, keeping a good distance between them as she took some of the bandages and swabs Chua had left unused on the cabinet.

'Man's a hero, Romaine,' she said as she tore Yario's shirt and started disinfecting his wounds. It looked like he'd taken a couple of shrapnel fragments from a grenade maybe. The tiny wounds still oozed blood. 'Took out over a dozen hard-ass Nguwuus on his own. Probably saved us a lot more casualties than we've already taken. Think I'll buy you a beer, Yario, when this is all over.'

'What's happening out there now?' Romaine asked, coming over to watch her ministrations. Her rifle remained hanging around the back of her armor and he held a loaded pistol by his side; there'd be no chance of her winning a cowboy style quickdraw.

'Now?' she said. 'Not much. I think most of 'em are dead. But we won't know for an hour or so, till it becomes light. Hack it, I'm gon' have to stitch the hero. Hand me them sutures in the drawer, Romaine.' She gestured behind her with one hand while the other one held a gauze pad to Yario's wounds, keeping pressure on them.

Romaine walked over and looked into the drawer, his eyes off her for a split second. The next thing he knew, he was rebounding off a cabinet and falling to the ground, pain flaring in his hip. He caught himself with arms fully extended and managed to avoid falling all the way down, springing awkwardly upright. But he'd dropped the pistol and McGrath had kicked it deep into the sickbay area immediately after she'd kicked him in the backside.

'You're an idiot, Romaine. Hold this,' she told Yario, pushing his hand onto the gauze.

Before he could respond, the door opened behind him and he turned, stepping back from both it and McGrath. Chua came in and stopped short. She was short-of-breath and sweaty, regarding the tableau before her without curiosity. She tossed the laser-cutter on a nearby bed.

'A hacking nightmare out there.' Her voice was flat, hollow.

McGrath gestured at the dead Nguwuu, voice businesslike. 'We can use that thing. We'll make it seem like friendly fire, like I hit it and him at the same time.'

Chua frowned and took a couple more steps into the room, level with Romaine. 'Friendly fire what?'

'The CO wants him taken care of.' She inclined her head toward Romaine.

Him, Romaine thought with resurgent anger. Once people decided to kill someone, they often stopped using their name and used pronouns instead.

'Nobody's doin' nothin' to him,' Chua replied matter-of-factly. She took another step closer to McGrath, putting him behind her. 'Romaine's cut a deal with the indigs to supply us with Tigerclaw. He can do what the Looey couldn't.'

Romaine shifted uncomfortably, thoughts bitter and sarcastic despite the danger he was still in. Was this what it came down to in the end: people's value based solely on what they could accomplish? He'd been sure Chua saw him empathetically, as a person, or at least as a law enforcement officer she respected.

'And here I was thinking you only liked me for my body,' he muttered.

'There's that too.' She asked McGrath, 'You do want the human race to stop dyin' out there, don't you? Or are you really just a puppet? Coz sometimes you have all the emotion of one.'

McGrath began turning the color of Yario's blood gauze pad. 'Watch your mouth, Chink.'

'Name calling. Racism. Hm. Guess you can take the girl from the bayou, but you can't take the bayou–'

'*Shut up*! Lean that indig up against the wall and let's get this over with.' McGrath's righthand had moved to the trigger guard of the AR90 behind her. She slid the weapon back and forth on its shoulder strap as if hesitant.

'Don't you even think of pointing that thing this way,' Chua warned.

McGrath swore. 'The Looey did all he could to keep things *nice*. The Jarinyi didn't give him a chance. Romaine knows about Yaghuchi and about the Nguwuu. Glass wants him done so we can walk away from this okay.'

'We'. Everyone except me and Menabu, Romaine thought angrily. *And Yario now too?* He looked past them at the sweating scarecrow who watched the conversation with wide eyes.

'We'll get that leaf, one way or another,' McGrath finished.

'Did you hear or see any of what's been happening out there?' Chua responded. 'We just got a whole bunch of people killed, not to mention Gally and Fester and the others. And Fisher. We gotta stop this screwup. We got no idea what we're doing here. Romaine can get us the Tigerclaw without more people dying, so put the rifle on the table behind you and finish bandaging the little pipsqueak.'

'Hey,' Yario protested then blanched when both women looked his way.

Still staring at Yario, McGrath said, 'The cop didn't broker no deal with the indigs. He's makin' it up to save himself. He can't leave knowin' what he knows.' She must have seen Yario swallow because she added,

'And hero here can back us up that it was accidental friendly fire what killed him. In the middle of a mêlée.'

Yario said nothing but his eyes slid slowly toward Romaine, then dropped. *C'mon Yario, be a* mensch *not a* yutz.

Chua was talking again. 'He lives, Cath. Don't matter what happens to us. If he lives, maybe a few hundred thousand other people do too.'

'You dumbass, he'll crucify us! He'll crucify *Sean!*' Romaine could see her hand tightening around the grip of the rifle, but she didn't swing it forward.

'Sean?' She straightened. 'Sean. First name basis. Best buddies, now, huh?'

'Oh, just get out of the way...'

McGrath whipped up the AR90 but the shot went wild, punching a hole through the wall. Romaine would have been dead if it weren't for two things: McGrath slipping slightly as she stepped forward onto the blanket which covered Ranarith's blood, and Chua dropping into a low crouch to sweep McGrath's legs out from under her.

Any normal person would have landed flat on their back, but McGrath landed sideways on one hand and one foot then sprang upright and backwards, putting space between herself and Chua. She still held the rifle in her other hand, but before she could get her trigger finger fully back into position and target Chua, the larger woman had scooped up the chair she'd used earlier and cracked it hard across the barrel, fracturing the mount. She followed this up by bringing it around less surely on McGrath's left forearm.

McGrath screamed in rage and pain. The rifle clattered to the floor. She jumped back again, holding her left arm against her side, pulling her knife with her right hand. She now stood by the head of Yario's bed while Chua took a position near the foot. McGrath snarled. Chua stared back, still holding the chair in both hands. They faced off this way for several seconds.

Romaine slid along the wall, shifting positions and wondering what the hell to do. Yario, sat cowering in the middle of the bed, wounds forgotten, knees drawn to his chest.

To Romaine it was tough to tell which of them had the advantage.

McGrath was smaller and obviously less proficient at hand-to-hand than Chua, but she wore body armor that left only her limbs and head unprotected. She also held a knife and had her own handgun strapped to her left thigh.

He had to do something. If Chua went down ...

His eyes found the pistol under a desk. He couldn't get to it without jostling Chua and she couldn't get to it either, even if he told her where it was, not without getting stabbed or shot or both.

'Yario, use your knife,' he heard McGrath hiss. Yario just groaned in reply. '*Marine*! That's an order!'

'I wouldn't,' Chua mumbled his way.

Yario didn't move, except to draw his knees up tighter.

'Knife!' McGrath barked again and then stumbled sideways as Chua feinted with the chair.

Knife?

Romaine went to the bed closest to the door, where Chua had tossed the laser-saw. He snatched it up, tried to figure out the controls. A thumb-pad, a toggle – the meaning and use of both made no sense to him. He heard the scuff of feet as the two women continued to feint and avoid each other.

Maybe I can throw it at her.

He moved across the room again, so that he could see McGrath past Chua's shoulder. They'd moved enough that he might get to the handgun under the desk. He saw McGrath's eyes flick to him anxiously before Chua took advantage of the slight distraction to thrust forward with the chair and Romaine knew it would make contact this time.

McGrath surprised them both by raising her knife-arm high, angling her damaged left arm away and taking the impact on her chest armor, before sliding sideways so that the chair-legs glanced away, leaving Chua unbalanced. Moving right and forward, McGrath continued her turn a full one-eighty degrees slashing at her opponent. Somehow, Chua avoided the knife but had to let go of the chair and fall slightly to her right to do so, ending up with her body leaning against the edge of a partition between Yario's bed and the next.

Behind her, McGrath darted forward to drive the knife into her back, but Chua sensing her coming, launched off her left leg, and spun to land facing her. McGrath continued forward and almost succeeded. The blow was too low and Chua was able to block her knife-arm with both of hers, wrists crossed.

Her hands twisted around and seized McGrath's wrists, then she spun and tossed McGrath over her shoulder so that she crashed upside down into the edge of the next partition, bouncing off and landing on her head. Romaine's eyes squeezed shut reflexively and he wished he could have done the same with his ears. Even from a few meters away, the sickening crack of the woman's neck breaking was as clear as a gunshot in the confined space.

When he opened his eyes. Chua was half-smiling, half-growling with adrenaline. And possibly with shock since she had growing patch of blood on her shirt. She followed his gaze down to the tear in her shirt. She touched her belly and snorted. 'Damn. Thought I was better than that!'

He lurched forward to look at the injury, but she angled away. 'Lotta blood,' he said.

'I'm *alive*,' Chua replied. She slumped against a desk. Then she masked it with a broad grin, slapped her bloody palm back onto her belly, kicked him lightly in the shin when he came closer. 'You often have ladies fighting over you, Romaine?'

Firmly he pulled her hand away to look at the injury. A stab wound. Not too deep: but the blade had torn the flesh when Chua threw McGrath over her shoulder. 'Not as often as you might think.'

She laughed, but there wasn't much spirit in it. For a moment, Romaine considered the fact that protecting him had meant killing a colleague, a sister. Whether or not Chua had liked McGrath – and it was fairly obvious the two hadn't been friends – killing someone from her own team must have hurt her.

'I'll ... put her in back,' Romaine said. 'In a minute.'

Chua's hand dropped to her side and she allowed him to rifle through drawers looking around for the self-sealing bandages without further comment.

When he found them, she snatched them away. 'I've done this

before.' She shoved him away. Romaine considered forcing her to lie down and attending to the wound himself. But she probably was better at this anyway.

'There's sutures and a needle under that pile of crap there,' she added.

He passed them over, then rattled around a fridge at the rear of the room before he found a supply of blood. 'What type are you?'

'Oh, I'm definitely yours, baby.' She laughed, then grimaced and hissed as she worked. 'This is the life, huh, fellas? Join the Marines, see the galaxy, kill your buddies, operate on your own body without anesthesia. Who could ask for a more satisfying working life?' She pressed a hand over her wound, eyes jammed shut, giving herself a moment before she returned to her grim task.

'What blood type are you?' he repeated.

'There's *oBlood* in there somewhere. Artificial blood. I'll get it. You go look after McGrath, would ya?' She asked it quietly, without looking at him. Her eyes were still shut and she began cursing in Cantonese.

It took Romaine a moment before he could pick McGrath up. It wasn't just the prospect of a prolapsed disc or the way her head lolled unnaturally to the side. Were it not for Chua's presence he would have dragged the woman into the meat locker by the feet and dumped her, feeling no pity for someone who'd been about to murder him. Eventually, he crouched down, slipping one arm beneath her hips, the other around her shoulders, hand bent awkwardly to cradle her head like an infant's. She was heavier than he expected.

He levered open the door to the meat locker with one elbow, arms wrapped around a corpse, and wondered how things might have turned out differently, how he and others might have been spared the horrors and pains of the past few days had he not been so hell-bent on being a real cop, if he'd remained the compliant public servant CUSET preferred. Could he have changed these events if he'd given lip-service to an investigation the first day he was here, created an official report that blamed the Jarinyi for Gutierrez's death? Would Fisher still be alive? Would Turk? Would McGrath? How about Tuttut?

He lay McGrath down as carefully as his aching joints would allow him to, straightened her flopping head and closed her eyelids so that she looked asleep.

Look where following orders got you.

That thought put things in perspective for him. None of this was his fault. All these things would have happened anyway, no matter what Romaine had or hadn't done. He had to admit - and not happily - that he'd been a peripheral player in this situation. Nothing he'd done had affected events in any significant way. Perhaps if the message-packet he'd sent went on to create sympathy for the Jarinyi. Perhaps if he was able to bring Todd to justice ...

Then what, Johnny? You can be a hero? You can be famous? You can feel important? Get over yourself. This is not about you.

He knew Fisher was in here. Both times he'd entered, he'd seen her from the corner of his eye inside the transparent body drawer but he'd avoided looking at her. He didn't want to see her again, not this way, not dead and cold and in storage.

But he did, he pulled open her drawer, and he looked at her, feeling old and tired and sad and defeated all at once. Her pale face looked peaceful, almost noble. She had never tried to be a hero, but a hero she had been, a person focused on serving others. He reached in and touched her cold cold hand with his.

'Gotta go get some more testimony, Jennifer. Then get it off to Nagaya. A cop's work is never done, huh?' He let go of her hand and closed the drawer.

––––––––––––

ROMAINE LEFT THE MEAT LOCKER, WALKING WITH FRESH PURPOSE through the research compartment of the building and back into the sickbay proper. Chua and Yario looked up from where they sat on their respective beds. Chua had recovered her gun; it sat beside her while she finished applying her pressure bandages.

Romaine said, 'It's nearly dawn. Do you think most of the Nguwuu are dead now?' The scarecrow just shrugged and stared back.

'I took out ten,' Chua said.

And McGrath said the hero here took out at least a dozen more.

'Well, let's hope so. I'm going over to Supply to get my SCRoLL – the CO had all my gear confiscated tonight. Nancy, I want your statement recorded and sent off to Nagaya tonight, this morning – *now*. In case there are more attacks by these things ... or in case your Lieutenant somehow manages to murder us all.'

Hearing that, Yario turned the color of the sheet beneath him and put a hand down to brace himself. Romaine tried to take into account things that the man had presumably been through tonight: fighting off a horde of vicious alien warriors, seeing friends and colleagues die, coming close to death himself, sustaining a wound in battle. Compared to Fisher, Chua, even McGrath, the guy was still a wuss.

He told Chua, 'Management have to know it wasn't the Jarinyi that did this and they have to know exactly why it happened.'

She nodded tiredly. 'Take the gun,' she said, tapping it with a fingernail.

'Don't need it.' Romaine reached around to the back of his belt and lifted out another, McGrath's. He placed McGrath's spare clip beside Chua. From a desk he lifted a penlight flashlight – one of the ones Ranarith had probably used to see inside body cavities more clearly – and stuck it in his pants pocket. 'Stay safe.'

'You too,' she said seriously. 'And when you get back, we'll talk.'

COLUMBUS WAS UNCANNILY QUIET NOW AS ROMAINE SLIPPED THROUGH IT. For a moment, he thought he heard crying but the sound evaded him when he tried to focus on it. Given what had happened, he didn't blame anyone for hiding and weeping.

The combination of mild light and deep shadow on the ground between the Supply hut and Medcentre was worrisome, making it difficult to see details clearly. In one patch of black behind the Medcentre, he stumbled over a corpse but didn't linger to ascertain its species. Closer to Supply lay the bodies of a civilian and a Nguwuu both. He checked the man's pulse, but he was very much deceased.

The doors to the darkened Supply hut were wide open, the doorway littered with torn food packets, their contents strewn. He felt around inside the door frame and the wall beside it, but couldn't locate one of Columbus's antiquated light switches.

Goddamnit!

He pulled out the penlight, playing the narrow beam around the room, gasping when it reflected from dead eyes on top of the service counter. He finished sweeping the building from where he stood, saw nothing but trashed equipment and supplies, then returned the light to the body. He took a few steps inside. His bile rose when he recognized a twisted version of Tristan Menabu's face.

Oh man oh man oh man ...

He darted past the counter, searched along an aisle for the box with his belongings, frustration fast turning to panic. With several aisles of shelving to search in the dark, he might be here for hours. Something clattered against the wall, back by the door. He whirled, gun and flashlight clasped together. Nothing. He moved past the counter toward the front door, careful to avoid anything that would crunch or snap beneath his boots. He whisked the light around the entryway then, certain no one had gotten inside, turned it off to avoid detection by whoever was out there. He imagined a Nguwuu crouching beside the building outside, tending to its wounds, or chewing on a human arm –

Stop it!

He counted out a full minute, allowing his eyes to regain some night-sight while the rectangle of the door distinguished itself against the dark interior of the hut. He heard nothing but his own shallow breathing; it reminded him of the susurration of leaves out in the forest.

He wondered, *What's that smell?* —

— and recognized the cologne a moment before Todd kicked him in the side of his knee.

Romaine landed hard on the other knee. He knew Todd kicked the pistol from his hands. He knew he was getting grabbed by the shirt collar and dragged a few meters. But he felt none of it; for now, the pain spearing up from his leg was beyond anything he'd felt since the beating in that alley, a consuming agony drowning out all other sensation.

Vaguely, through the humming in his ears, he began to make out his own groans and growls and heard Todd mention something about damaging a ligament as the recon moved deeper into the darkness of the hut.

Light flared blindingly into existence. Romaine pressed a forearm over his eyes while trying to hold his knee in a position that wouldn't feel like someone was tearing it off.

He was lying on the floor close to the wall between the counter and the entry. Teeth clenched, he dragged himself back to sit against it, before a fresh stab of pain from his knee drove the air from his lungs and froze him in place. Todd made sure of his attention by cuffing him lightly across the face with something that might have hurt if he didn't already hurt so much. When it fell with a clatter to the floor nearby, Romaine saw it was a pair of clip-on night-vision lenses.

Abruptly, as if someone had finetuned a radio signal, he found he could hear and concentrate on what Todd was saying.

'... fitting finale to one hacked up day.' Todd squatted a few steps away, side-on to the doorway, face turned to Romaine. 'Actually, I've had a hacked-up week. And a lot of that hacking has come from you, you dumb puke.'

Todd paused as if waiting for Romaine to respond. Romaine could think of little but pain, pain and the urge to kill Todd. He blinked hard, trying to form words, to get a grip on his thoughts.

Todd smiled grimly. 'So. Let's pick up where we left off. Although, we can't really do that, since we were going to drop you out of a Reaper. Don't think that'll be happening now, you'll be glad to know. They're both pretty trashed. We *could* make Commander Romaine the unfortunate victim of friendly fire. No? Well, that's ok, I've got a better idea anyway.' Todd had shoved something inside his webbing and he fished it out now, a wooden artefact of some kind, holding it up for Romaine to squint at. Romaine had seen it before. The *chweechee*. 'I think we'll make Commander Romaine one of the unfortunate victims of this indig incursion.'

In a voice like sandpaper on wood, Romaine asked, 'And how are you going to explain away the Nguwuu?' Todd cocked his head, looking bizarrely like a Jarinyi. Sucking in a breath at a fresh stab of pain, Romaine continued, 'CUSET will have your head for this debacle. Killing me isn't going to make things better for you.'

'I disagree. It'll remove a witness, for one thing. And for another, it'll be ... cathartic.'

Seeing something bestial enter Todd's expression, Romaine recognized a thing he could work with, if he played it right. The clichéd villain monolog Romaine saw in streamies and books did not often happen in real life. The men who'd murdered Harshini for example had preferred action to words. But once in a while, life imitated art. His interrogation instructor had once told him, *You get someone worked up enough, they can't help talking.*

Under the circumstances, it was a straw worth clutching at.

'You've got one chance here, Todd. CUSET already know about you arming the Nguwuu. So do the pedecasters. Your only hope is to try to plead that you were following orders.'

Todd's didn't blink. 'Not gonna fly. Even if it were true, it's always the guy lowest on the food chain who takes the fall. Right now, you're the lowest on the food chain.' He picked a splinter from the makeshift club, rising to full height. 'Besides, you earned this.'

Despite his fear, or perhaps because of it, Romaine found himself shouting. 'You caused Fisher to die, you sonofabitch! You've killed all these people tonight! What makes you think I'm the bad guy here? What the hell have I done to you?'

Instead of advancing on him, Todd raised his face to the roof and let out a bloodcurdling scream of rage and frustration. 'What have you done? What have you *done*! You delayed us, you hacking *cabrón*! You took the side of those indigs. My career could be over because of those freaks. The whole goddamn human race could die because they got in our way. My brother is probably dead because of them!'

For a millisecond, Romaine entertained a fantasy that Chua would come striding through the door and put a round through Todd's head.

She didn't.

Todd stepped closer, hand tightening on his club. 'You wanted to take their side? Then you can suffer the same penalty they will!' Spittle flew from his mouth and Romaine knew that Todd was beyond being played now.

And just as surely that he was about to die.

Not for the first time this week, time slowed, skewed. He threw himself to his left as the club swung in, felt the wind of its passage and the crack of its contact with the wall at his back. He had intended to roll over completely but the agony in his leg prevented him, the injury an anchor holding him in place. He flailed an arm among the trash on the floor, grasping for a weapon or a shield, and found nothing but raw grain and precooked carrot sticks. He flung a fistful of it anyway. It bounced off Todd's legs like rain off a windshield and Todd braced again. Romaine snarled hatred at Todd, watching the Marine lift the club high, waiting for one final explosion of pain ...

Todd grunted and fell heavily on one hip, feet thrashing around in the contents of a torn bag of rice as he turned over onto his ass. The *chweechee* had fallen beside him. He pushed up onto both knees, staring blankly at the arrow poking out both sides of forearm.

Romaine jerked in shock as another arrow skewered Todd through the hip. Blood spurted. The young man howled again, in frustration and this time in pain. His eyes scoured the room for his attacker as his left hand fumbled at his holster. Romaine could see the moment the blackcap's augments kicked in, giving him the surge of strength to launch up onto his good leg. Fumbling the handgun and forgetting Romaine, Todd looked toward the doorway –

And froze, astounded.

A moment later, he pitched backwards, one final arrow through his throat. More blood squirted. His eyes rolled. Pink froth bubbled at his lips which curled as if in distaste at the flavor.

When finally Todd ceased to move and to breathe, Romaine tore his eyes away, sure that with Nguwuu at the entry, he would be next. What he saw there was the last thing he expected to see.

Just beyond the doors stood Carswell and Scarface.

But it was Carswell who held the bow.

PART VI

ONEDAY

'The flus of the early part of this 22nd Century were banished once and for all by advances in natural medicine and modern nanotics during the 2130s...

'Viruses have posed the greatest threat to our species for millennia... but with the perfecting of nano-technology in the past decade, it is believed that for the foreseeable future, viruses have ceased to exercise their dominance over the human race and its history.'

- from *Werber's Encyclopedia of Human Endeavor, January 2141*

35

'Every contact leaves a trace...'

- Dr Edmond Locard

'BREAKFAST?'

Romaine didn't turn right away, watching the forest. It seemed peaceful this morning, not at all the province of death and danger he knew it to be.

He had donned another Marine regular uniform, clean and pressed from the Supply hut. His MI uniform he'd tossed onto one of the burning piles of trash and Nguwuu bodies that had polluted the Eventide sky for most of the previous day. The uniform was his size according to the label, but shirt and pants both hung a little loose on him.

Note to CUSET dieticians, he thought: *forget controlled kilojoule diets; instead, make people eat nothing but alien nuts then force walk them across a jungle, up a mountain and back.*

Chua came around to his shoulder, clearing her throat. 'I said, *breakfast*, Commander?'

She held out a bottle. Liquid swished within the colored glass.

He flicked it with a fingernail, but didn't take it. 'What's this? The CO's sauce?'

'No. Mine,' she grinned.

'I didn't think you could bring it in. Menabu told me so.'

She tapped the Marine insignia on the front of her black sun cap. 'Menabu wasn't a blackcap. We can get away with ...' She faltered, then finished the sentence weakly. '... stuff.'

She unscrewed the lid, offered it again.

Romaine looked at the bottle, scratched at his nose. He was being asked a bigger question and he knew it. Not *Do you want a drink?*, but *Who do you want to be?* He shook his head ruefully and mimicked one of her eyebrow waggles, watched as she shrugged and took a long pull.

So who are you gonna be, Johnny? If not the guy who's numb, then who?

Purged if I know. Guess I'll find out when I get home.

Chua wiped a hand across her mouth. As if she'd read his thoughts, she asked, 'Back to BV now?'

He tasted anxiety in the back of his throat at the thought of his next meeting with Dreyfuss. Or Nagaya. 'Guess so. Got some music to face with Management.' He hitched up his trousers. 'If I still have a job in a week, I might go visit Centauri; pay my respects to Gutierrez's fiancé. And Fisher's family.'

'You'll need these, then.' Chua slid a set of dog tags and a tattered paper book out of a shoulder satchel she carried. She offered them instead of the bottle.

Romaine wrapped the dog tag chain around his fingers and slipped the book – a diary – into his thigh pocket. It was a tight fit.

'I kept 'em with me. When Looey told me to put 'em in Supply.' She shrugged and took another pull on the bottle.

They let their gazes stray toward the forest for a time, Romaine running his thumb across Fisher's name on the tags. Late morning sunlight burned through the humidity, burned into his face, making him feel like he was standing too close to a ship's drive. He glanced down at his hands, noticed the tan, knew the flesh beneath his sleeves would seem even more pale now by comparison.

'How's the gut?' he asked.

'I won't be doing any crunches for a while. How's the knee?'

'Not as bad as it could have been. Luckily the Nguwuu left a nanotics expert alive who can treat ligament and cartilage damage. I'll be running on a treadmill again by next week.' Romaine hadn't run on a treadmill for the past three years.

The knee still hurt of course, but nowhere near as bad as yesterday. *Thank God for nanotech.*

And for the big fat chunk of Tigerclaw Scarface had slipped between his lips while he sat slumped on the floor of the Supply hut. He had more folded in one pocket too — he'd probably lose it at the next customs counter he passed, but smuggling it out was worth a shot.

Chua cleared her throat again and fixed him with a perplexed expression. 'Gutierrez. Carswell killed him?'

Romaine nodded.

'*Carswell*?'

'Yep.'

'I can't believe that sack o' crap would do that.'

Up until recently, neither did I. How could I have been so dumb?

He pictured Carswell drawing Tuttut's bow when they'd been back at the Jarinyi camp, ineptly sending an arrow skittering along the dirt, then shutting Tuttut up before the Jarinyi could say 'What's wrong with you man? You can shoot better than that!'

It was all pretend. And Romaine had been more than happy to believe it, wanting the xenologist to be weak, wanting to feel better than him.

'And he killed the Looey too,' she added with obvious mixed emotions, shaking her head. She took another pull from the bottle.

'Weird, isn't it?' Romaine said quietly. 'Carswell committed the crime that brought me here. Put me in harm's way. Then saved my life.'

In his mind's eye he could still see the dark stain spreading across the Supply hut floor, could see Carswell striding in to make sure Todd was dead, could see Scarface looking as nonplussed as Romaine felt while giving him the scrap of Tigerclaw. Right then, he knew he'd been played, as facts tumbled together to form a rough truth that explained all that had happened here.

A barking voice brought him out of his reverie. Glass wandered from behind a building, harrying his adjutant and Nyst – two of the last three remaining regulars onsite – into completing some task. Yario followed meekly with a satchel under each arm and one eye on the wilderness beyond the fence. For an hour now, Romaine had stood out here, alternating between staring into the forest and watching the Columbus staff busy about the camp. Yesterday, once day had dawned on the embattled camp, he had helped them repair fences, dispose of Nguwuu corpses and bodybag the human ones. Some of them had hooked up cables between jeeps and dead trilophants, dragging them out into the open space beyond the fence when they'd been left for carrion eaters for the time being. Romaine could smell them whenever the wind changed.

Three civs inspected the contents of a case by the ferry pad. He studied their washed-out faces, slumped shoulders, red eyes. There had been little conversation in the camp since the battle ended, largely due to emotional exhaustion, though Romaine suspected a lot of it was survivor's guilt. He was familiar with that particular psychological scar. And no one ever fully recovered from picking up the body parts of colleagues.

'Better hide that bottle,' he said clearing his throat and nodding toward her CO.

'CO can go to hell, sir.' She smiled and took another pull, but put the cap back on and slipped it into her thigh pouch. It stuck out like a tumor.

'So. *Carswell*,' she said again. 'What's up with that?'

'Why'd he kill Gutierrez?' Romaine pursed his lips for a few seconds, then said, 'Okay, I'll give you my best summary, as far as I can figure it. Carswell goes native. Learns to live and think and hunt and fight like a Jarinyi. Amongst the skills he picks up is the use of a bow. He practices — a *lot*. I reread his file with new interest last night. He went on a similar jaunt with indigenous South Americans a while back and possibly learned to use bows then. Somehow, a few days back, he found out that Marines armed the Nguwuu and killed a Jarinyi warrior in the process.'

He glanced at her now. She chewed her lip, jaw working. 'Bad move,' she admitted. 'I wasn't there for it, but I still wish there was someone I could apologize to.'

'Todd's decision, not yours. Anyway, to Carswell, killing the Jarinyi is murder. In the Jarinyi culture, the way to deal with a murderer is shoot them through the neck with an arrow. He can't get at Todd, but then he probably doesn't *know* Todd ordered it. To him, all Marines are part of the military and corporate machine that's threatening this people and their livelihood. He crouches in the bushes waiting for a Marine sentry to come into range. Does he know it's Gutierrez? That he was one of the men who was at the rendezvous? Probably not. It doesn't really matter because it's not personal. As he prepares to shoot, the sentry's weapon detects him, fires, wounds a nearby woo-woo bird, maybe because the woo-woo confuses the AIRTAR. Cool as the proverbial cucumber, Carswell sights his bow and fires.'

Romaine slapped his neck loudly.

'Hack me,' Chua murmured.

'This is his blind self-righteous arrogance at work. He probably doesn't know that it'll bring in someone from offworld for an investigation. But I'm a godsend to him, and he's an opportunist. I'm his chance at getting the word out to the Colonies. I always wondered why he didn't simply refuse to liaise with us. All of his behavior from the time I first met him was designed to bias me against the Marines.' He sighed, wound the dog tag chain even tighter around the meat of his palm. 'I even believed it. The night the Nguwuu attacked, I'd already sent off my case against Todd to the Admiral. And to a pedecaster. But Carswell never pushed me into making that judgment; just lead me to information which would make me paint the picture myself.'

'Man's a very smart smartass.'

'Yep.' A shadow fell across them and he squinted into the bright sky. A trio of flying creatures swirled around a hundred meters into the air, local buzzards circling the dead trilophants, waiting for things to quiet down so they could come feed. 'So is all that neat enough for you, Nancy?'

'It's pretty tight, guy. And that's the way you'll write it up?'

Romaine paused. In his mind's eye he replayed the scene again: Carswell striding into the Supply hut, bow in hand, a skin quiver with a couple of arrows slung over a shoulder, swaggering right by him to stand over the body of Lieutenant Todd and nod with satisfaction.

Don't thank me, Romaine, he had said. *Just make sure the human race finds out what they're doing here.*

Then he'd turned and disappeared into the night, Scarface following behind mutely.

Romaine sighed. 'I really don't know what I'm going to say. But I *do* know I won't be blaming the Jarinyi for any of this.'

Out where the jeep bay used to be, a civilian responded tersely to Glass's haranguing. The two voices rose in pitch. Romaine and Chua smiled and chuckled at the exchange for several moments before Chua let out a mirthless snigger and turned to him.

'Better go do some work before he starts yelling at me. Coz then I'll get angry and then you'll be investigating me for kicking the man in the goolies. Although, I wouldn't mind you doing a bit of investigatin' round me, Romaine.'

Romaine blushed and tried to laugh.

'I'll be on the ferry after yours.' She pointed skyward. 'Transport ship that's come for us is a McDowell X228, I hear. Those babies have killer bars in 'em. Pre-dinner drinks?'

He laughed, then trying to be serious, said, 'You're good people, Sergeant Chua.' He straightened and saluted her.

She smiled, returned the salute then slapped him hard on the backside as she swaggered past. 'See you in the bar,' she said over her shoulder. 'Shall we say 1600 hours?' After her thick bulk had disappeared behind a building, she called out to him, 'And it's your buy!'

He rubbed his smarting butt-cheek.

'I have the weirdest luck with women.'

Romaine ventured inside the Mess which — in the wake of the Nguwuu attack — was living up to its name. Rummaging through piles of debris, he laid his hand on some bottled water. He drained one, then took another outside, slipping it into his kitbag. A high-pitched whine made him look toward the mountains. Finally. The ferry.

He watched it with such eagerness, lost in tired thoughts, that he jumped when another voice spoke in his ear.

'Well, I s'pose that puts an end to the work day.' Eyes fixed on the approaching craft, Colonel Glass held a slim in his good hand, a chunk of what looked like Tigerclaw wedged between his knuckles. One arm was plastered and hanging in a sling, while tight bandaging had been wound around one knee over the fabric of his trousers. A bruise the color of overripe plums stained his forehead. He continued, 'Second last ferry of the day. None of these civs are gonna hang around here longer than they have to.' Glass had a small canvas bag similar to Romaine's kitbag slung over his shoulder.

'You leaving on this or the final one?' Romaine asked, caught between wanting to ignore the man and wanting to slug him.

'Oh, I'm damned sure you don't want me on either of 'em. You probably don't want me on the same ship as you.' Dropping the bag between his feet, the Colonel raised the dark green Tigerclaw leaf to his nose and took a long sniff. 'Actually, I thought I'd hang around Eventide and see if that Jarinyi offer is still open. You sure don't wanna stay? Quite seriously, I could use your rapport with these *ind...*' Glass stopped himself. 'These people.'

The ferry was over the landing pad now, descending. A knot of eager passengers gathered near it, milling and shuffling like farm animals at feeding time. Like them, Romaine wanted nothing better than to get on board.

'I'm done here, Colonel.' *We're done.*

'Shame. Well. This came for you on this morning's packet.' He held out the slim, making Romaine wonder what had happened to his SCRoLL. The slim screen displayed a memo, but Romaine didn't take it. He didn't need to.

'Ordered back to Bona Vista?' he asked.

'That's the gist of it.' Glass pointed upwards with his chin. 'I believe that's where the transport's headed first.'

Romaine shrugged, followed the direction of Glass' gaze upwards and noticed the ferry had scared away the buzzards for the time being. He said, 'Anywhere's better than here.'

'I doubt that, Romaine. I very much doubt that.' Glass eyed the message himself and made a tutting noise that reminded Romaine of Carswell's translator. A half smile formed on his face. 'You really sent a copy of your case file to a blogger? What are you, some kind of a crusader?'

Romaine just stared at the cerulean blue skies above them.

'If civilization survives, you can kiss your career *adios*.' Glass pushed the slim inside his unbuckled chest armor. 'You know, if there's any of them left out there, I *could* tell 'em this memo was part of a corrupted file, and we couldn't open it, and you didn't get it. You could come with me, help me set things up with the locals. Go native like our killer xenologist.'

Romaine felt anger twist his gut. Thirty hours ago, Glass had wanted him to disappear for different reasons. And in a very different way.

I guess people change. One day you're my killer, the next day you're recruiting me. That's the CUSET way.

People were beginning to pile onto the ferry. He knew it wouldn't leave without him, but he still had to fight the irrational desire to rush after them.

'Go native, huh? I don't think that's going to work for me. I like showers too much. And steak.' He imagined the space beyond this sky, thought about the restaurants on BV, wished he was looking forward to a dinner there with a friend like Fisher rather than eating alone. For a second he thought about her family and what he might say if - *when* - he visited. He shifted his kitbag with his toe. 'Memo or no memo, I'm going.'

'Well, I hope you got something to go back to. The captain of that ship up there commed me this morning and told me communications with Earth system had blanked out.' Romaine's chest filled with ice.

'Now, it doesn't mean anything conclusive; there's been no report of PBT there. Might be part of some quarantine procedure there. But it makes you wonder what the hell will be left soon.' He took a deep breath of the Eventide air as if sucking on a fine cigar. 'This might just be a good place to wait it out.'

'Will you stay *here*? Fix up Columbus?'

'Not sure yet. We may keep it as our base. We may move to one of the beta sites when the last Reaper returns this afternoon from the islands.'

'We?'

'Yeah, my adjutant is staying. Nyst too. They're like me, thinking it's better off to face dangers at the end of a rifle than death at the hands of a virus. I'll need their extra hands, too.' He lifted his broken arm.

Romaine noticed he'd made no mention of Yario and was not surprised.

Probably be just him and Nancy on that last ferry.

'Handful of the braver researchers are staying, too,' Glass was saying. 'Someone's gotta process all this Tigerclaw your friends will be sending our way. Let's just hope someone else comes back to pick it all up.' He glanced toward the domed hut with the biohazard symbol. 'We'll microwave most of the PBT cultures we have here and just keep a tiny amount for quality control.'

A tiny amount, Romaine thought with a shake of his head. A tiny amount could kill this planet. 'And if sometime you get sick of waiting and want to come home yourself? What then?'

Glass frowned at him momentarily as if he were an imbecile. 'There's still *your* ship up there. You're not taking that with you, are you?'

Oh, yeah. Forgot about that. 'If you use it, make sure you try the orange juice,' he told him with a straight face. 'It's excellent.'

Romaine bent to pick up his kitbag and straightened to find Glass holding something out to him. The slip of Tigerclaw.

'They were all out of olive branches,' Glass said, 'so I thought I'd try this.'

Romaine took it and put it away, not mentioning the stuff he already had with him.

'This too,' Glass added, pulling a small plastic container from a shirt pocket. It was clear and held four small orange capsules. 'Vaccine. Four doses. Expensive stuff.'

'You're kidding me.'

'Let's say you earned it.' He reached over and shoved it into the slit of Romaine's breast pocket. 'Take one as soon as you can. Keep the other three for whoever you have that you care about out there.'

At the other man's touch, Romaine's temper flared. Trembling, he asked, 'This is how you say "Sorry I tried to kill you"?'

Glass pursed his lips for a long time then said, 'It's not often I truly regret something.' He turned face on to Romaine, stuck out his hand. When Romaine didn't take it immediately, he added, 'Not often I admit I'm wrong, either, Commander.'

A moment later, Romaine shook it. Fisher would have liked him to do that.

They stood there staring at the sky for some time, before Glass gave Romaine a final nod, turned and walked away, barking orders at Marines and civs alike.

Romaine took out the plastic container and studied the little pills for a moment. For all he knew, they were cyanide. With a sigh, he put one in his mouth and washed it down with the water bottle he'd brought from the Mess. When he hadn't died after twenty seconds, he unzipped his kitbag and dropped in the water bottle, the pill box and Fisher's dog tags.

He pulled at her diary inside his thigh pocket. It snagged against the seam then came free with a jerk. A couple of pages and a slip of plastic flipped out and fluttered around him. He caught the pages before they could blow away and slid them securely inside. Fisher's thoughts, her secrets, they belonged to her family, intact. The scrap of plastic film had landed by his feet. He was surprised to find it was a page from a nanobook. Someone had carefully separated it from its binding, leaving the thin strip of its power cell intact. Curious, he stroked it to life. A medieval scene unfroze and began to play. A middle-aged man with a shaved head prayed by the side of a muddy track. The footer told him enough to know it was a moment from the life of Francis of Assisi. He had heard this prayer somewhere before. Maybe his mother had read it to him as a child. Or perhaps she'd owned a plaque with the words embossed upon them.

He listened to the prayer and thought that nothing could be more like Fisher, nor more honoring to her memory. Romaine had been wishing for something to mark her passing, an invocation, a eulogy, a … benediction, if that's what they called it. Surely this was it. Words that must have deeply impacted Jennifer Fisher's soul, defining her character and her choices. Strong words that resonated with her so much she had torn them from a valuable nanobook and carted them around the galaxy with her from world to world.

He let them wash over him.

> *Lord, make me an instrument of your peace;*
> *Where there is hatred let me sow love;*
> *Where there is injury, pardon;*
> *Where there is doubt, faith;*
> *Where there is despair, hope;*
> *Where there is darkness, light;*
> *And where there is sadness, joy...*
> *For it is in giving that we receive,*
> *It is in pardoning that we are pardoned,*
> *It is in dying that we are born to eternal life.*

The tiny Italian man froze on the page.

Romaine rubbed at his eyes.

After he had prompted the scene and the prayer to start over, he placed the page face down on the ground, the way a Jarinyi might turn the body of a dead friend. The words continued to pour into the soil. Jennifer Fisher's remains might be coming up with Chua and Yario on the last ferry, but if there was such a thing as a soul, Fisher's soul would not be onboard. He could only hope she might find rest here on Eventide, that these familiar words sown into the soil might remind her of all the goodness she had sown during her too-short life.

With the prayer reciting behind him, John Romaine swung his kitbag over his shoulder, limped toward the ferry, and did not look back.

EPILOGUE

THE WATCHER STOOD *among the trees, doing what he did best, what he had been trained to do and had spent a career perfecting.*

Watching.

Observing.

He smiled. Watcher. *The word in Jarinyi was Cssoool. And Carswell loved the double meaning in both languages. Here he was watching the human intruders scurrying around in panic. But he was also Watcher in the truest sense of the Jarinyi title: one had taken on the mantle of protecting this tribe's interests. On this world, he had become all that he could be and it filled him with pride. He had become both student and guardian over the Jarinyi. The one who came to appreciate them from the outside and who watched over their welfare.*

Beyond the hastily-repaired fence, Romaine read from a scrap of paper. For a second, Carswell was curious as to what it was, then dismissed the thought as irrelevant. The only important written words were those on the message Romaine had told him he'd gotten out the night of the Nguwuu attack. Now Romaine would return to CUSET as an advocate for the Jarinyi.

And what if no one listened? He had to ask himself that question.

If Romaine's message didn't reach the general public, didn't turn public opinion against human incursions onto this planet, didn't force CUSET to back off—what then?

Well, perhaps enacting Jarinyi justice on that Marine and forcing an investigation had delayed the harvest of Tigerclaw enough that the pandemic would keep humans away from this world, from spoiling it further. As if responded to that thought, Romaine stooped and lay the paper on the ground, littering. Carswell allowed himself a quiet snort of disgust.

He knew that Glass would stay here; maybe some other brave souls. He knew that the Jarinyi would take Romaine's idea seriously and share whatever Tigerclaw they had stored up. Carswell just hoped that no one would return to get it.

He breathed a sigh that was part relief, part satisfaction in a job well done. It was finished. He'd done what he could. Romaine was mounting the ramp to the ferry.

It was time to rejoin the Tribe.

The bushes barely shifted when the watcher moved away.

GUIDE TO HUMAN-SETTLED SPACE, 2142 COMMON ERA

Anticus: CUSET name for the home world of the apparently-sentient race called Anachromites (or 'mound-builders'). Human scientists have not yet found reliable ways to communicate with Anachromites, and this is part of the reason that the Anachromites' status as sentient beings is still debated.

Bona Vista Station: large artificial habitat in space.

Castor and Pollux: two habitable planets of the Dioscurin system (not to be confused with the stars originally called Castor and Pollux in the constellation Gemini).

Centauri: agricultural world with two continents and three archipelago chains.

Chi: PRC refueling station and way stop near PRC asteroid fuel mines.

Drop-in-the-Ocean: remote starbase in interstellar space, refueling station

Eventide: CUSET black site. Home world for the sentient Stone Age race who call themselves Jarinyi. A sub-species of Jarinyi known as Nguwuu also inhabit an area of Eventide but remain hostile to humans.

Foucault's Moon: resource-rich CUSET world.

Golan Refueling Station: a rest and refuel stop between Red Star and Chi, or between Red Star and the Edge-of-Nowhere mines, as Romaine says, 'depending on which way you fly'.

Nakayama Station: A habitat orbiting one of Centauri's moons; primarily a multi-corporation server-base and storage facility.

Oceana: Predominantly water world whose largest land mass is a small archipelago chain.

Pride of Mao: a Chinese (PRC) world.

Red Star: disputed world and source of the PBT virus

Theseus: an earth-sized world, uninhabitable around its equatorial zone because of extreme daytime temperatures.

Xerxes: newly colonized world, first settlement and mining/farming commenced 2131. First urban center established in 2138. Three waves of settlement, predominantly Spanish, Filipino Central American, Mexican, Scottish, US and Irish settlers.

Yun Dao: PRC world.

SUBSCRIBE AND RECEIVE A FREE EBOOK

Never miss out on news of a new book. Sign up for email updates from Peter J Aldin and receive some bonus material free as a thank you gift. Go to https://petealdin.com/the-cuset-dchc-universe/ebook-gift-for-newsletter-subscribers/ and follow the prompts.

Email updates are roughly bi-monthly to begin with, becoming less frequent as time goes on. They're intended for entertainment and information, not to spam you: you can unsubscribe at any time.

SCRAPPER
PETER J ALDIN

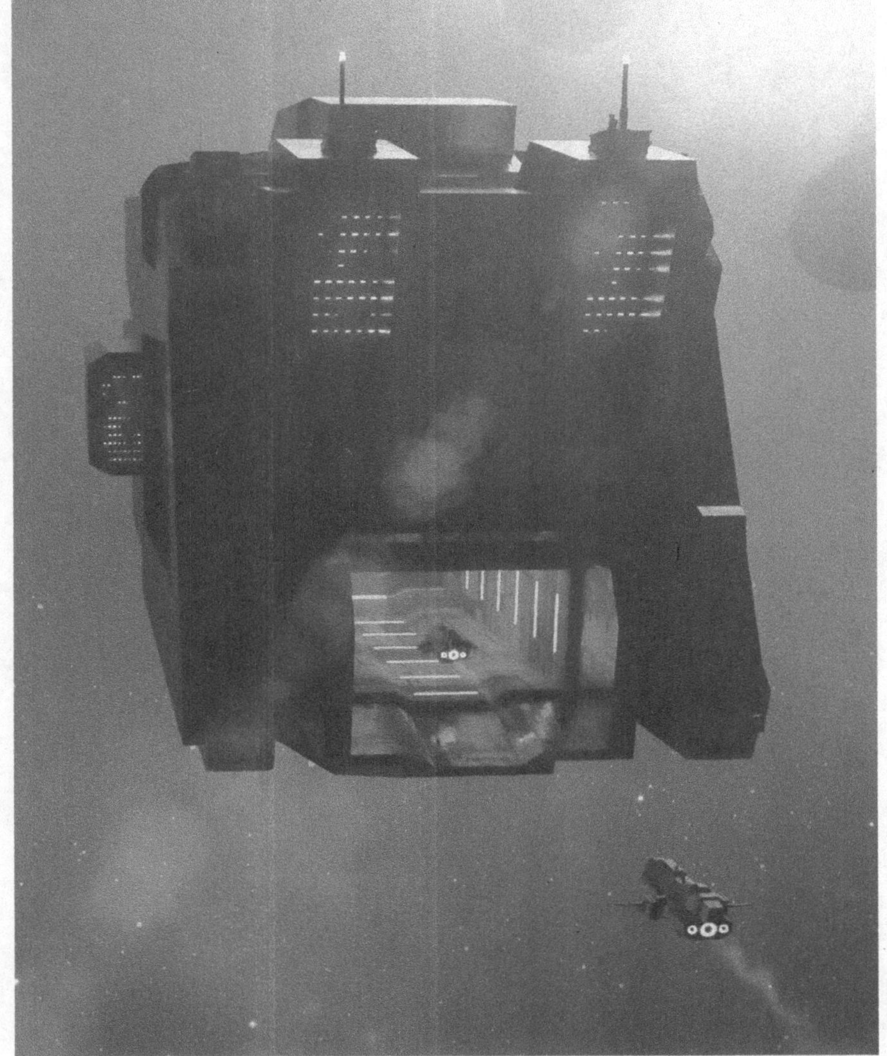

SCRAPPER

Four years back, she escaped them.

Now they've tracked her down.

Shelby Denayer is a scrapper, her days spent collecting and refining asteroid ores, her nights spent reading 19th Century science fiction, her name and hairstyle both radically changed to avoid discovery. All is well. Life is peaceful.

Until her father hides his little runaway.

Shelby went against the family code.

Now Dad's on his way.

And he's not happy ...

Available on Amazon or from the author.

* 9 780648 309277 *